The Windfell Family Secrets

Diane Allen was born in Leeds, but raised at her family's farm deep in the Yorkshire Dales. After working as a glass engraver, raising a family and looking after an ill father, she found her true niche in life, joining a large-print publishing firm in 1990. She now concentrates on her writing full-time and is an Honorary Vice President of the Romantic Novelists' Association. Diane and her husband Ronnie live in Long Preston, in the Yorkshire Dales, and have two children and four beautiful grandchildren.

By Diane Allen

For the Sake of Her Family
For a Mother's Sins
For a Father's Pride
Like Father, Like Son
The Mistress of Windfell Manor
The Windfell Family Secrets

DIANE ALLEN

The Windfell Family Secrets

PAN BOOKS

First published 2017 by Macmillan

This edition published in paperback 2017 by Pan Books
an imprint of Pan Macmillan
20 New Wharf Road, London N1 9RR
Associated companies throughout the world
www.panmacmillan.com

ISBN 978-1-4472-9514-3

1 3 5 7 9 8 6 4 2

A CIP catalogue record for this book is available from the British Library.

Typeset by Ellipsis Digital Limited, Glasgow
Printed and bound by CPI Group (UK) Ltd, Croydon, CR0 4YY

Visit www.panmacmillan.com to read more about all our books
and to buy them. You will also find features, author interviews and
news of any author events, and you can sign up for e-newsletters
so that you're always first to hear about our new releases.

The Windfell Family Secrets

1

Windfell Manor, 1882

A warm summer's breeze played gently with the copper-beech leaves as the carriages drew up beneath the spreading boughs of the mighty trees that lined the driveway to Windfell Manor. Soft music from the quartet that was playing inside the immaculate walled garden pleased the ears of the guests as they ascended the steps to the most prestigious house in the district of Ribblesdale, which lay in the furthest reaches of North Yorkshire. The day was one of celebration, especially for the Atkinson family, with Isabelle turning twenty-one.

Charlotte, her mother, leaned over the bannister that swept down into the marble-floored hallway of Windfell Manor. She had hesitated on her way down to the celebration, as her eyes filled with tears when she heard the laughter and love that were being shown to her most precious daughter. The manor, she knew, was filled with well-wishers and would-be suitors for one of the most eligible young ladies in the Dales; old friends and new, as well as those with influence within local society, mingled and enjoyed the luxury of the manor and its surroundings. All for her Isabelle, the birthday girl, who had grown into a beautiful young woman, with jet-black hair and eyes as blue as the forget-me-nots that flowered profusely in the gardens outside. Her hair was the only telltale sign of her true parentage – the only visible aspect of the long-dead cad who had been her true father, Joseph Dawson.

Charlotte fought back the tears as she remembered the year Isabelle came into the world; the horrendous murder that Isabelle's father had committed; and her own fight to save Ferndale Mill and, with it, the realization of how dependent married women were upon their husbands. It had meant that she had to grow up quickly and become independent in her own right, fighting to keep her position as mistress of Windfell and owner of Crummock Farm. Unlike her daughter, who up to the present had led a privileged life, not wanting for anything.

'Hey, what's this? Tears on our Isabelle's birthday – I'll not have that.' Archie closed their bedroom door and put his arm around the woman he loved. 'Listen to all that giggling and cavorting. There's no need for tears today, my love.'

'I'm sorry. I was just remembering when she was born, and how life was such a struggle back then I didn't know if I would last from one day to the next.'

Charlotte smiled weakly at Archie, her rock through all the years of despair.

'And then you married me, and you have never looked back since.' Archie squeezed her tightly to him and kissed her on the cheek.

'You mean I married you and got another worry.' Charlotte smiled as she wiped away the tears, for it had been the best thing she had done in her life, despite her teasing words. 'Where's Danny? Is he downstairs already?'

'Downstairs and out in the garden with that lass from over at Langcliffe. I watched them out of the bedroom window, holding hands and giggling as they ran to the seat under the beech tree. He takes after his father, does that one – knows how to catch a lady's eye.' Archie grinned.

'Which lass from up Langcliffe?' Charlotte sighed. It was true that Danny was a devil for the women; and he'd inherited Archie's mop of blond hair, and his wicked smile made all the young women titter and giggle at the slightest glance from him.

'Here, come and have a look at her, you'll know her name, once you see her. I can't think who she is, I think they farm up at High Winskill.' Archie opened their bedroom door and urged Charlotte to look out of the window to view the courting couple.

She pulled back the heavy drape of their bedroom curtains and sneaked a look at the pair sitting on the metal seat that encircled one of the beech trees in the immaculate gardens of the manor. 'It is the lass from High Winskill. The family are called Armstrong, aren't they? She is the youngest, Harriet; her older sister got married last year to one of the Warburtons over in Lancashire. I remember because it was a big wedding, and her mother was bragging all over Settle about how well her daughter had done to catch one of the Warburton lads, as everyone knows they aren't short of a bob or two. You don't think she's after Danny for his money? I wouldn't put it past her, if she takes after her mother.'

'Now, Charlotte, stop worrying. Besides, if she *is* after his money, she'll be in for a shock, for Danny hasn't got any – not yet anyway. He'll have to wait until after our day. And I'm not thinking of going any-where just yet, and you look fit enough to me.' Archie pulled her away from the window. 'Now, let's go down and join this party, and stop worrying about nothing. What will be will be, and you can't keep your eye on them all the time. Think on what your father said about me; he didn't have much faith in me, and I might not have had any money, but I knew how to make you happy. And that's the main thing.'

Charlotte looked back through the window as Archie urged her down the stairs and she caught just a fleeting glimpse of a stolen kiss between the lovers, who were lost in one another's eyes. She didn't care what Archie said; the Armstrong lass was a little too forward with her affections, for her liking.

Archie and Charlotte walked down the sweeping staircase into the hallway, smiling at the throng of elegant, well-to-do-people who were attending the prestigious event. The ladies were dressed in luxurious gowns in all the hues of the rainbow. Their hair was adorned with feathers, and glistening jewels were draped around their slim, elegant necks. Their husbands stood like pompous penguins in their black-and-white suits, hanging on every word that was uttered, and sipping their port genteelly as they discussed the topics of the day.

'Mother! Mother, look at what Robert has given me. Isn't it just adorable?' Isabelle pulled on Charlotte's arm, dragging her to where a kitten was being stroked by a group of her adoring friends. 'I'm going to call it Bobby – after Robert – and then I'll always remember this day.' She picked up the long-haired grey kitten and stroked its head as it mewed, distressed by all the noise and commotion around it.

'Just put it down, Isabelle, before it does something on you!' Charlotte's face revealed what she really thought of the gift; she was not keen on cats, which belonged outside, keeping down the mouse population, and she didn't have time for inside pets.

'Oh, Mother, you are such a bore. He's adorable – look at those eyes. How can you *not* fall in love with him?' Isabelle held the kitten tightly and flashed a smile at the young man from whom she had received it.

'Do you mean that cat or the man?' Charlotte quizzed, noticing the look that passed between them.

'Mother, I don't know what you mean!' Isabelle grinned.

'I think you do. Don't forget I was once as young as you.' Charlotte looked at her blushing daughter and recognized a great deal of herself in the flirtatious young woman.

'Yes, and look who you married: my lovely step-father. Whom I love dearly, apart from that dratted stepbrother of mine. Have you seen him with that awful Armstrong girl? She is so common, Mother, and she is simply throwing herself at Danny.' Isabelle petted her kitten. 'When I find my perfect man, he's going to be wealthy, with excellent manners and a brain – unlike that ninny.'

'Both your father and I have noticed her infatuation with your brother. We don't know much about her, but I'm going to make it my business to do so. And you, Isabelle, must make yourself known to the rest of the room, and not just Robert Knowles. There are some very eligible young men here. That is partially what your party is for: one day Windfell will be yours, and you need the right man by your side.' Charlotte looked sternly at her simpering daughter. If only Isabelle knew how much the grand manor of Windfell had cost her, and how much the future happiness of both children meant to both Archie and her.

Isabelle strutted away from her mother and went to stand next to the open bay window of the drawing room. She loved her mother dearly, but everything was always about business and eligibility – had she never been young? She knew she was privileged, living in such a beautiful manor house with its sweeping gardens and grand grounds, but for just one day she wanted to flirt and enjoy herself with whomever she chose, without any thought of their connections and eligibility. She looked around the room and spotted Luke Clark: now he was one she could have a laugh with and at the same time irritate her stepbrother, as Luke was one of Danny's close friends. She smiled to herself and walked over towards him, while the kitten was being handed to the person nearest to her.

'Are you alright, Father? You look a million miles away.' Danny spotted Archie gazing out of the window and knew that he'd rather be viewing the stock at Crummock than be in a room full of giggling youth and his stepmother's business associates.

'Aye, I'm fine, lad.' Archie looked at his son and smiled.

'Now then, Father: if you've got worries, heaven help the ordinary man in the street. Crummock will be alright for an odd day without you.' Danny tried to cheer up his downcast parent.

'Aye, I know, but these fancy dos are more your mother's thing than mine. I'd rather be turning them stirks into the top pasture, away from their mothers. Anyway, enough of me and my worries. Who's this bonny thing on your arm? You are no gentleman, Danny – you've not introduced us.' Archie turned to the quietly intent girl on his son's arm and watched as her face lit up at being introduced to her beau's father. She was a pretty thing, there was no doubt about that. Perhaps a little plain, compared to Isabelle, but she'd a sparkle in her eyes that would capture any young man's heart. She was dressed a little plainly, but the blue taffeta gown she wore flattered her petite figure.

'This is Miss Harriet Armstrong, Father. Her parents farm at High Winskill at Langcliffe. I've been wanting to introduce her to you and Mother for some time, but have not had the opportunity.' Danny held out Harriet's hand and passed it to his father to shake, while Harriet smiled at the man she had heard Danny talk about so much.

'Delighted to meet you, Miss Armstrong. I know High Winskill. Not that big a farm, and it'll be a bit wild in winter, but you'll have a good view of Pen-y-Ghent.' Archie looked at the girl that his son was obviously in love with.

'Delighted to meet you, Mr Atkinson. Danny talks about you a great deal, he's very proud of you. You have a beautiful home here. I don't think I've ever been in a place so fine.' Harriet looked around her and her cheeks filled with colour as she tried to impress Archie.

'Aye, it's alright. It's all my wife's doing – she's got a good eye for suchlike. I just let her organize it, and I concentrate on what I do on the farms, although she still keeps her hand in at the cotton mill; she's down at Ferndale every day, making sure it runs smoothly. Do

8

you work, Miss Armstrong, or do you help your parents at home?' Archie waited for a reply, while noticing over Harriet's shoulder that Charlotte was urging him to join her.

'Yes, I work in the jeweller's along Duke Street, Ezera Bloomenber's. I'm the shop assistant there. I don't think I've ever seen you or Mrs Atkinson in there?' Harriet watched as Archie failed to hide the shock on his face.

'No, no, I don't think we have ever given the Bloomenbers our business. Perhaps it is something we will have to think about.' Archie smiled politely, recovering himself quickly. 'I'm sorry to cut our meeting short, but if you'll excuse me, I think my wife needs me.' He made his excuses, patted Danny on the arm and walked over to Charlotte, to tell her his worrying news.

'Well, that was my father. Sorry he didn't stay longer, Harriet. My mother obviously needed him urgently.' Danny smiled. 'I think she wanted my father to join her as she talks to Hector and Lorenzo Christie. She secretly admires them both, as they are the biggest businessmen in Craven. They both dress so finely and have made themselves small fortunes. And with Lorenzo and his son Hector owning rival cotton mills to hers, Mother likes to keep them both close. So close that Hector is Isabelle's godfather. That was good planning on my mother's part.'

'I think the Christies were an excuse for your father

to leave us. Perhaps I shouldn't have mentioned where I worked, like you said.' Harriet sighed.

'They can take it or leave it – I love you, not where you work.' Danny squeezed her arm and passed her another drink. 'And I do love you, despite all our family secrets.'

2

Charlotte had tossed and turned all night, unable to sleep for thinking of all the things that could go wrong, if Danny and Harriet Armstrong were serious about one another, and of the consequences it could have on the family. Her worries had grown out of all proportion as the night had worn on. In the darkness everything had looked so bleak, with the mill being lost for having no rightful heir after Isabelle was rejected by polite society, and Danny running off with a penniless hussy, if her worst fears were realized.

'You've tossed and groaned all night. Even with a drink or two in me, you've kept me woken. I might as well get myself up and go and look at the stock at Crummock, and see what Arthur's got to say for himself.' Archie sat on the edge of the bed and pushed his shirt into his breeches, before pulling on his braces. He stood up and drew back the heavy drapes of their bedroom window and squinted in the morning's sharp light, before looking at the time on the clock. 'Six o'clock: you stop in bed for another hour, there's no need for you to be up this early.'

'Get back into bed, Archie, and I'll get up. Although to say you've not slept all night – you were snoring loud enough, at one time.' Charlotte yawned and rubbed her eyes. 'I couldn't sleep. I'm sorry, I'm just worried about things.' She sat up in bed and watched as Archie put on his jacket.

'I told you yesterday: stop fretting, the lass from Winskill seems grand. Now, I'm off. I'll tell Lily not to disturb you for another hour or so, if she's up. You put your head back down and stop worrying – all will work out fine.' He looked back at an anxious Charlotte and decided not to chance his luck with a parting kiss, as he usually did every morning, for fear of her trying to change his mind.

'What about your breakfast?' Charlotte asked, as Archie made for the door.

'I'll have it up at Crummock. Mary will not see me go hungry.' He closed the door quietly behind him and was glad that he had the excuse of Crummock to escape to.

'You are up early, sir.' The scullery maid stopped and tidied her mob cap and wiped her face, as she was caught unawares carrying a bucket of ashes across the hallway.

Archie picked up his riding crop from the hall stand and looked at the young lass in front of him. 'Aye, couldn't sleep. The mistress won't need Lily yet,

12

although she's wide awake. I've told her there's no need for both of us to be up and going. I've told her to lie in until her usual time; she'll happen get an hour's peace, if I'm gone and not snoring next to her.' He hesitated as he drew back the bolt on the front door. 'You'd better tell Cook there's one less for breakfast.'

'I will, sir. Enjoy your day.' Eve, the parlour maid, curtsied, before picking up the bucket of ashes and disappearing downstairs to tell Mrs Batty, the cook, and her helper Ruby Baxter that there would be one less for breakfast. Then she passed on the rest of the information to Lily.

Archie walked across the yard to the stables and opened the door. The smell of horse sweat and polished leather hit his nostrils, and his bay horse whinnied at the sight of its master.

Jethro, the groom and stablehand, watched motionless and unnoticed as his master patted and whispered sweet nothings to the horse he loved. His dark, swarthy looks blended into the darkness of the tack-room. Jethro had served the Atkinsons as man and boy and now, at the age of nearly forty, he was still as fit and handsome as ever, turning many a woman's head, but always keeping himself to himself, preferring his own company.

'By, she loves you – that is a fact, sir.' Jethro walked out of the shadows and made himself known to his master.

'I sometimes think she's the only woman who does, Jethro. As long as I live, I will never know how a woman's mind works.' Archie leaned on the stall gate and patted his horse.

'Why do you think I'm single, sir? Women baffle me too, never can figure them out. I'd rather have my women with four legs, too. I take it you need this one saddling?' Jethro unbolted the stable door and led Sheba, Archie's favourite mare, out of her stall, before reaching for her saddle and harness.

'Aye, let me go somewhere I know something about and get up to the farm. I'll be back later this afternoon. The mistress will need the gig later this morning; she'll be off to Ferndale. Can you make sure it's ready for her?' Archie waited until Jethro had prepared his horse and then he led it out and pulled himself up into the saddle.

'Will do, sir.' Jethro looked at the gentleman farmer and watched as he trotted out of the yard. You'd have to travel a good distance to get a better master than Archie Atkinson, and he was lucky to work for such a straight-talking man.

Charlotte lay in her bed and watched the clouds scuttling across the greyness of the early-morning sky. She couldn't get back to sleep, for her mind was too busy ticking over things. She'd dress herself, and not wait for Lily to help her with her toilet and dress. Throwing back the covers, she sighed as she looked at the stays that really needed two pairs of hands to lace them up. Reaching for her dressing gown, she decided to have a wash and to brush her hair, if nothing else, before

Lily's arrival; then stopped in her tracks as she realized there was no warm water in the empty jug and bowl on her washstand. How had she become so dependent on servants? She looked at the empty jug and thought fleetingly about investing in one of those newfangled bathrooms that all the best people were installing in their homes. That would save the constant running back and forth for endless hot water for the tin baths in which the household bathed, and for water in which to wash in the morning. Mrs Batty and the kitchen staff would appreciate having hot water on tap, instead of having to use the boiler in the outhouse every day, she was sure; she would have to discuss it with Archie later.

She sat in front of her dressing-table mirror and ran her hairbrush through her long blonde hair and looked at herself. The hair she had been so proud of was beginning to show traces of silver now, a telltale sign of how hard a life she had endured, while her once-clear forehead now showed faint worry lines across her brow. She sat and twisted her hair into the usual bun that kept it in place for her daily duties, then pinned it with hair clips. Looking at herself again in the mirror, Charlotte smiled at her reflection. She might have aged a little, but she was still not bad-looking, and her eyes had a twinkle in them that showed a lust for life that she would never lose.

Her thoughts were interrupted when a knock on the door brought her back to the present.

'Enter.' Charlotte turned on her stool and waited.

'Morning, ma'am.' Lily came into the room and smiled at her mistress. 'Eve said you were awake, but not to disturb you, but I knew you'd be wanting to wash and for me to do your hair. I knew you wouldn't be in bed, once you were awake. I see you've already won me with your hair. I'll take your jug and bring you some warm water from the kitchen to wash in.' She reached for the ornate jug and made her way out of the room.

Charlotte sat and looked at herself again in the mirror and placed her head in her hands. She didn't want to face the day, not if it meant falling out over Danny's choice of woman. It was just like Archie to hide away up at Crummock rather than face reality, damn him!

Isabelle and Danny sat around the long walnut table in the manor's dining room, discussing the previous day's celebrations, both taking pleasure in their choice of friends and lovers.

'What did you look like, with that Harriet Armstrong on your arm? She's a silly giggling ninny,' Isabelle teased her brother over the breakfast table while she helped herself to scrambled eggs, which Thomson, the butler, offered her while trying not to listen to the two young people. 'She's so common, Danny. But I did admire the dress she was in, although the material was cheap.'

'You can just keep your views to yourself. Who are you to say that Harriet is a giggling ninny? You weren't much better. As for flirting – I was embarrassed when you kept making eyes at Robert Knowles. He's only a farmer, you know; he's not William Christie, your precious college boy.' Danny stabbed his bacon. Isabelle could be so scathing sometimes and she didn't mince her words.

'William Christie! That's my mother's doing. He wouldn't look at me twice, no matter how much she plots and plans, nor I at him. He loves his books too much. I know Robert farms at Feizor, but I don't care; he makes me laugh, and his friend Luke is so charming.' Isabelle grinned and blushed.

'You were such a flirt, I don't know how you can criticize Harriet. At least she's only got eyes for me.' Danny leaned on the table and looked across at his stepsister, in whom he knew all his friends were beginning to show an interest. But he could not see the fascination; Isabelle could be so mouthy and rude, and at the moment she was intent on disliking Harriet, his true love. 'Now, Luke Clark, he's a good man, always lets me have a free biscuit out of that big glass bottle they have on the counter of their grocery store. Have you tried them? They are from Carr's biscuit factory in Carlisle. They are bloody good.'

'You are always thinking of your belly. I'm not bothered what either man does, as long as they treat me right. We should both look for that in a suitor. Remember the mistake my mother made.' Isabelle smiled at her brother; she loved Danny so much and never thought of him as a stepbrother. 'Anyway, where's Father this morning? I saw Mother in the morning room, but there's not a sign of Father.' She looked up quickly as Charlotte entered the room.

'He's gone up to Crummock. He couldn't sleep, and he left the house just after six o'clock. What mistake have I made then? I just caught the end of your conversation.' Charlotte walked across the dining room, pulled out her chair and sat down with her children, then sipped her tea as she waited for Isabelle to explain what she had been discussing.

'Sorry, Mother, I was just saying that you were mistaken in thinking Robert Knowles took my eye, as Danny has pointed out that he farms at Feizor – not that being a farmer is anything to be ashamed of. Look at Father, he's a true gentleman.' Isabelle covered her tracks quickly. She and Danny had known the truth about her father from the day they were able to sit in the manor's kitchen listening to the kitchen staff gossiping. Neither had ever let their parents know that they knew, although sometimes curiosity got the better of them both, before deciding such things were best forgotten; besides, both could not wish for better parents, and Charlotte's true father did not deserve a second thought.

'Robert Knowles – I think you are telling me lies, Isabelle. I saw the way you looked at him. Where is that dreadful kitten he gave you? I hope you are keeping an eye on it. What a silly birthday present to give you. I suppose one of the farm cats will have had kittens and they'll want homes for them – it'll have cost him nothing.' Charlotte smiled silently to herself while she buttered her toast. The Knowles were a good family who farmed a stone's throw away from Crummock. Isabelle could do worse, although Robert would know nothing about cotton, so he would be useless if Isabelle was ever to inherit Ferndale Mill, which gave the family its wealth.

'Bobby's in my bedroom. He's perfectly clean and has slept on my bed with me.' Isabelle was quick to defend her birthday present.

'Is that the kitten or Robert, little sister?' Danny couldn't stop himself.

'Danny, wash your mouth out! We will have none of that, not until you are both respectfully married. What did Miss Armstrong think of your home, Danny? I believe she works in the jeweller's, your father informs me.' Charlotte waited and watched for both children's response.

'She thought it was beautiful, Mother, but was disappointed that she did not get to meet you. Yes, she does work for Dora Bloomenber. I think old Ezera, before he died, treated Harriet more like his daughter, as he and his wife had not been blessed with family of their own.' Danny waited for his mother's response. He'd known that once Harriet said who she worked for, she would not be welcome in the family home, but she had decided to tell the truth, regardless of his mother's reaction.

'Mrs Bloomenber will be my aunt, won't she, Mother? I'm right in thinking that she was my father's sister? Not that you have ever told me, or that I have ever been introduced to her.' Isabelle caught her breath and felt inwardly sick, for this was the first time she had dared to mention Dora Bloomenber and her knowledge that Dora was her aunt. She'd always been secretly fascinated by her father and his family, but knew it hurt her mother too much even to mention his name. Harriet had unknowingly given her the chance to ask other questions that she had never dared to raise, and she wasn't going to waste the opportunity. She'd also decided that, despite Harriet being common, Danny was obviously in love with her, and Harriet working for her father's relations should not be held against the girl.

Charlotte was shocked. 'How do you know that? Dora Bloomenber is not someone I would want either of you to be associated with; or Harriet.' She threw down her napkin and looked at both of her children, who were obviously in cahoots. She had dreaded the day this woman entered into their lives, as Charlotte knew she surely would. And now her daughter was telling her that she had known about Dora, and about her real father. 'She is pure poison, Isabelle, which is why she has never been mentioned in this house, and I forbid you to have anything to do with her.' Charlotte's voice trembled as she looked across at Danny and Isabelle. She felt physically sick at the thought that for years Isabelle and Danny had been keeping the secret of Isabelle's parentage to themselves. She had fought so hard to protect Isabelle from the scandal

20

that her father had cursed the family with, and now it was out in the open.

Danny sighed, not quite knowing what to say and do. The tension between his mother and sister was unbelievable, and he felt guilty knowing that it was the introduction of Harriet into the family that had brought it about. 'Isabelle, tell Mother just how much we both know about the past. Perhaps it's for the best that she knows all. After all, it is a secret that is better out in the open. We've both been pretending for so long that we knew nothing.'

Isabelle left her seat and pulled up a chair next to her mother. She'd known all her life that Charlotte had been lying to her regarding her parentage, but was also aware it had only been done to protect her. 'Mother, I love you dearly – we both do – and that is why we never talk of my father and his sister. As Danny says, we know all about my father and what he did to you; we've heard people gossiping about him since we could barely walk, let alone talk.' Her eyes filled with tears, for she had wanted to tell her mother all this for so long, but hadn't wanted to hurt her. Isabelle reached for her mother's shaking hands and looked into her worried eyes. 'We know my father, Joseph Dawson, was a cad and a murderer, and that Dora Bloomenber is probably just as evil.'

Charlotte looked at both her children – the children she loved and would gladly lay down her life for. 'I've been thinking for so long that it would break your heart if you were ever to find out, Isabelle. And then

21

yesterday, on your birthday, the past came back to bite me, when Harriet said she worked for Dora Bloomenber. I knew that your father's terrible ways could no longer be hidden. You know that Archie has brought you up as his own and loves you dearly. He will always regard you as his.' Charlotte kissed her daughter's bent head. 'Danny, please be careful. Dora is a nasty piece of work. I wouldn't want you influenced by her.' She held out her free hand for Danny to take.

'Mother, I know that you and Father love us both equally. I'll make sure I keep Dora at a distance. After all, Harriet only works for her – Dora's not her mother.' Danny squeezed his stepmother's hand. 'Even my snotty stepsister has stood up for me this morning, which is quite a shock to the system.'

'Eh, less of the snotty. And I expect your support when I find the man of my dreams.' Isabelle lifted her head from her mother's chest.

'I'm just so glad it is all out in the open, as both your father and I have not slept a wink for worrying. If there's anything else you need to know, just ask me.'

'No, it's in the past, Mother. Archie is my father and Danny is my brother – it's as simple as that. I have hated hiding all that I have known about my parentage, and I know Danny has, too. Perhaps Harriet courting Danny has laid bare the past and all its secrets.' Isabelle kissed her mother's brow.

'From what I understand, Dora hated her brother, so Harriet says. He treated her as badly as he did everyone else. So I don't think she'll give us any trouble.' Danny leaned back in his chair.

'So Harriet knows about all the scandal, and Dora talks about it?' Charlotte was taken aback.

'Yes, but as I say, it's history now. What does it matter? You own the mill and employ half of Settle and the district, and my father is one of the leading farmers of Craven. Times have moved on.' Danny poured himself another tea and looked at his sister and mother, thinking of all the worry that had been caused by one selfish man. He could never be like that.

'Your father's gone to Crummock with the weight of the world on his shoulders. He knows I've worried about Harriet and her connections all night. Now it seems you've heard it all, over the years. I'll be honest, Danny. I told your father that I didn't want Harriet in the house, and that he had to try and stop the romance you are both entwined in. I'm still unsure about you courting her, but I suppose time will tell; as long as she doesn't come between us all – your father and I would never allow that. I do know what loving someone means, and I know love conquers all things, so from this day on you have my blessing.'

Charlotte pulled her chair back from the table. She had a busy day ahead, with a visit to the mill later in the morning, and a social meeting with Tom Beresford from the Craven Lime Company in the afternoon, but the confession around the breakfast table had taken her by surprise.

'Both your father and I have been so careful in

23

trying to protect you from any harm. We both have so many bad memories, and of course your father was broken-hearted when your mother died, Danny. I feel guilty about not discussing it with you both before now. There just never seemed a right time, and I thought there was nothing to be gained by unearthing the past.' Charlotte stood up, although her legs felt like jelly and her stomach was churning.

'Mother, all we have ever known is love and protection from you both, so we need no apologies. I was curious about my father when I was younger, but I simply had to ask any of the servants downstairs, if I needed to know anything about him. They were quite forthcoming with their thoughts, while I was helping them with the chores. Please believe me that nothing anybody says or does can hurt me. I'm glad Harriet has entered our lives, as it's made us talk about my father.' Isabelle smiled across at her mother and brother.

Charlotte shook her head. 'I don't know; those gossiping servants, they saw it all, but they were my rock when I needed them, along with your Great-aunt Lucy. Bless her soul, I would never have managed to buy the mill or afford to live here, without her.'

'Great-aunt Lucy, who was your father's cook and very close friend.' Danny laughed.

'Is there nothing you two don't know?' Charlotte glanced at Danny, and the impish look on his face told her that he knew the truth regarding her father's relationship with Lucy Cranston.

'Not a lot: we hear and see everything, don't we, Izzy?' Danny grinned.

'We certainly do.' Isabelle smiled, for twenty-one years of secrets had just been laid bare – the best birthday present she could have wished for.

3

Charlotte sat back in the gig. She'd never realized that both children had kept so many secrets to themselves, and the conversation had completely thrown her. She couldn't help but question herself for keeping so much from Isabelle – had she done the right thing? It seemed so, as Isabelle had shown no interest in her parentage and had always accepted Archie as her father, despite secretly knowing the truth.

'Lovely day, ma'am.' Jethro smiled at his mistress, who was obviously deep in thought, as she had not said a word to him since she had climbed into the gig at Windfell.

'It is indeed, Jethro.' Charlotte looked at the man she had employed since he was a young lad. Had *he* told Isabelle about her father? She couldn't help but wonder.

'Mister Atkinson was away in good time this morning, ma'am. Is everything alright up at Crummock?'

Jethro asked, making idle conversation as he urged the horse on towards the mill.

'Fine, thank you, Jethro. He just couldn't sleep, and they are in the middle of scything their main meadow, so he went up to help. You know what it's like: many hands make light work, especially when the weather's like this. Best to get the grass mown, dried and into the barn, ready for winter.'

'He likes to keep to his roots, doesn't he, Mister Atkinson? Many a person would just sit back and give the orders, but not him. He's a good man.' Jethro smiled.

'That he is, Jethro. I was a lucky woman the day he married me.' Charlotte looked around her, watching the sun play on the sycamore leaves as the horse and cart trotted down the lane towards the mill.

'Aye, but he knew he'd got a good catch with you, ma'am. You may have had your problems at the time, but he knew you were a determined woman.' Jethro had been thinking about the past, like everyone else, since Isabelle's birthday and couldn't believe where the time had gone.

'That's the trouble, Jethro. Nobody ever forgets, and my family is a little bit more public than most. Still, I'm not complaining, because we want for nothing and at least the mill is back making a profit and everything seems to be going well. You might be able to help me, Jethro! Do you know anything about the Armstrongs at High Winskill? I don't know much about them, apart from occasionally seeing the mother.' Charlotte

27

was aware that Jethro knew everything there was to know about all the local families in the Dales, and so she waited.

'Is this because Mister Danny was walking out with Miss Harriet yesterday? I noticed them when I was grooming Sheba.' Jethro turned around and looked at Charlotte quickly, before concentrating again on the path in front of him.

'You don't miss much, do you, Jethro? Yes, it is. You know me: I like to know what or who I'm dealing with, and Harriet is a slight worry. No matter how much I try to deny it.' Charlotte waited.

'They are a good enough family, ma'am. Harriet's father, Ted, will have inherited High Winskill up near Pen-y-Ghent from his father, and he's steady enough. Her mother thinks herself a bit better than she is, and I bet she leads old Ted a fair dance, wanting things just right for her and her daughters. Agnes, the oldest, married Roger Warburton last year; she was the flighty one, so be thankful Danny isn't walking out with her, and that it's Miss Harriet has taken his eye!' Jethro hesitated.

'Yes, go on. Tell me about Harriet.' Charlotte stared at Jethro.

'Well, I don't know her that well. I've only seen her around Settle when she's been going to and from work. She seems a nice enough lass. Perhaps a bit quiet for Mister Danny, but that's not for me to say. I'm sure she's got a sensible head on her shoulders.'

Jethro pulled on the reins as the horse trotted into the mill yard.

'As long as her family are decent, I'm going to have to grin and bear it. After all, if Danny decides to marry Harriet, she will be part of our family and will hopefully put Dora Bloomenber behind her.' Charlotte stood up and offered her hand to Jethro to hold as she climbed down out of the gig.

'I wish you well, ma'am. You must be going through hell worrying about the lass. Let's hope Dora Bloomenber does not influence her too much. Because, as they say, a leopard never changes its spots.'

'Don't say another word, Jethro. I keep thinking that and I just hope I'm looking on the black side, because the lad is smitten with her. Let's hope we are both wrong, for all the family's sake.'

'You take care, ma'am. Do you want me to wait for you, or are you walking back this morning?' Jethro asked, while holding onto the jingling reins of the eager horse.

'No, I'll walk back later, it will give me some time to think. Thank you.' Charlotte walked across the cobbled yard and up the steps into the mill. Nothing ever went smoothly, and she couldn't think of a time in her life when she had not had a worry, since her father died. She could see that things were not going to get better in the future.

Isabelle sat painting a picture of the bowl of roses that had caught her eye, when Mazy had brought them in

29

earlier and placed them on the sideboard in the parlour. She leaned back and looked at her handiwork, critically assessing her brushstrokes. She heard the doorbell of the manor ring, as she sighed with annoyance at her attempt to do nature justice.

Mazy re-entered the room and stood beside her mistress. 'That's just lovely, Miss.' She looked at the painting that the young woman had done, and admired both the picture and the woman she had seen grown up to become a well-rounded individual.

'No, it isn't, Mazy, it's absolute rubbish. I can't portray the softness of the petals, and just look at that bud. Nature would never form anything like that. I'm hopeless!' Isabelle moaned.

'Now, Miss, I think you are seeing all the faults, and none of the beauty that you've painted. I think you could be proud of that. I would be, if it was mine.' Mazy glanced at Isabelle, whose face looked as if she was chewing a wasp, and tried to build up her mistress's confidence.

'Yes, but you haven't had art lessons with Mr Jelly for the past twelve months. My mother will think she's completely wasted her money, if she sees this.' Isabelle tore the painting off the easel that it was resting on, screwed it up and threw it across the room. 'I'll start again, and this time I'll get it right. Who was at the door, Mazy – did you tell them nobody's in except me? And no one ever wants to see me.'

'It was the post boy from Settle, Miss. It was for you, as it happens; he brought you this small parcel. A

30

late birthday present, I expect.' Mazy handed over the brown-paper package and then went to pick up the discarded painting. 'May I keep this, Miss? You might not like it, but it would brighten up my room, if I can flatten it out.'

'Yes, do what you want with it, but believe me, it belongs on the back of the fire, not on your bedroom wall.' Isabelle looked at the small, square wrapped box with a Settle postmark upon it and put her paintbrush down upon the ledge on her easel.

'Thank you, Miss, I think it's beautiful.' Mazy smiled and tried to smooth out the painting as she walked from the room.

Isabelle untied the string around the parcel and unwrapped the brown paper, revealing a shagreen box. She opened the long, slim box to reveal an elegant pendant adorned with diamonds and rubies. She lifted it out of the box and held it to her neck, and then up to the morning light that filled the drawing room. The diamonds and rubies glittered and shone, and she gasped at how delicate the gold-work that bound them was. Who could have sent her such a beautiful necklace? It must be worth a small fortune. She picked up the small card that had been hidden between the wrapping paper and the box, and looked at the hand-writing upon it:

This belonged to your grandmother.
Your father would have wanted you to have it.

Isabelle dropped the necklace back into its box with shock. Who had this come from? There could only be one person responsible, and it must have been Dora Bloomenber, especially with the postmark being Settle. She recoiled in horror at the thought of the necklace once hanging around her grandmother's neck, and at the repercussions of telling her mother and family that she had received it. What was she to do? She didn't want to hurt her mother, for Harriet's involvement with the Bloomenbers had already brought upset to their normally smooth-running family. She closed the box quickly, screwed up the wrapping paper and placed it onto the parlour's fire, watching it burn in the flames. Keeping the handwritten card in her hand, she looked at it and wondered why it had been sent – perhaps her long-lost aunt simply wanted to know her. Dora had never done the family any harm, and perhaps her mother was wrong about her; after all, time did change people. She opened the box once more and looked at the beautiful jewels inside. It would be a shame to return them; she'd hide the necklace, not tell anyone, keep it to herself and see what came of it. After all, if it was her grandmother's pendant, there was no harm in keeping it.

She quickly made her way up the stairs and to her bedroom, hiding the necklace deep within the chest that held the spare bedding. No one would ever find it there, and it would give her time to make up her mind what to do with it. It would be her secret, until she had time to think.

*

The sun shone down relentlessly on one of the warmest days of the summer. The sky was bright azure-blue, with not a cloud in sight. Danny had dawdled on the five miles from Windfell to Crummock, thinking of the morning's upset and of the love that he had for Harriet, as he revelled in the beauty of summer in the Dales. The smell of meadowsweet and of hay drying in the roadside fields nearly made him feel light-headed, with their heavy summer fragrances. The track up to Crummock led him past the 'Norber Erratics', boulders left over from the Ice Age thousands of years ago, around which grew wild thyme that honey bees dined on, filling the air with their buzzing as he slowly climbed the winding track on his plodding horse. Danny tethered it outside the long, low farmhouse and opened the kitchen door, expecting to hear some response as he shouted his arrival into the usually busy kitchen, but none came. He untethered his horse and led it round to the stable, handing it over to the stable lad before making his way down to the hay meadows, where he knew all Crummock's inhabitants would be, along with his father.

'So this is where you are – you look jiggered.' Danny looked at his father, who was leaning against the drystone wall at the bottom of the largest hay meadow at Crummock, his scythe by his side. 'Leave it to the hired men to do. That's what you pay them for, and anyway I'm here now.'

'About bloody time and all. It's nearly dinner time, and half of the day's gone. What have you been doing?

Calling on that bit of lass from Winskill, before coming to help your old father, I bet.' Archie mopped his brow and watched as his son took off his jacket and rolled up his sleeves.

'No, I haven't. There's been a bit of a to-do over breakfast, and I waited until it had calmed down. Besides, the weather didn't look that promising this morning. It's only in the last hour that the sun's got out. Let's hope it keeps fine for the next day or two, until this lot's safe and dry in the barn.' Danny reached for the scythe and started to sharpen it with the whetstone that his father had placed on the wall behind him.

'Just stop your sharpening and tell me what this "bit of a to-do" was. Was your mother upset over your lass? I know she wasn't happy that she works for Dora Bloomenber.' Archie waited for his son's reply.

'She said you'd be worrying. It's alright, Father. A lot was said this morning – stuff that should have been said years ago. You know, Isabelle and me are not daft; we've known about her father and what he did for ages, it's just that we've never spoken of it because it opens old wounds and causes hurt. I can't help it that Harriet works for Dora Bloomenber. I love her, Father, and no matter what anyone says, I think she's the one for me.' Danny looked at his father; he loved him dearly, but if he had to make a choice, then he would make a new life with Harriet.

'Bloody hell! You mean you've always known about that bastard Joseph Dawson? Your mother's tried so hard over the years to keep him as the skeleton in the cupboard, never to be talked about; she just didn't want Isabelle to be hurt. Was my Lottie alright, lad? It will have really shaken her up.' Archie rubbed his head with his handkerchief and looked around him. 'She fought so hard to bring you up correctly, and with love. She's a good woman, is my Lottie – headstrong, but can easily be hurt. That's why, lad, you've to swear to me that you'll not let that lass of yours tear us apart, because she could do, if she lets that bitch of a woman, Dora, back into our lives.' Archie grabbed hold of Danny's arm and squeezed it tightly.

'Mother was upset, but I think it is better that things are now out in the open. As for Harriet, I swear I won't let her or Dora bloody Bloomenber hurt any of us.' Danny looked at his father. 'I've made it clear that Dora will not be welcome in our family home. I promise that nothing I do will bring any more hurt to the family.' He picked up the scythe and started mowing where his father had broken off, every cut of his aimed at the woman who seemed to be going to cause his family worry yet again.

'Aye, well, we will have to see how we go on with your Harriet. I'll ask your mother if she can come to Sunday tea this weekend, and we'll get to know her a bit better. See which way the wind blows with her. Does that sound alright with you, lad?'

Danny nodded his head, his arms swinging in rhythm with the scythe as the long grasses and meadow flowers dropped in submission to his actions.

Archie looked around him, to the high scars of Moughton with the white limestone pavement and screes dazzling in the sun, and then down to the valley bottom, with the rolling hills and meadows lying out before him, green and lush in full summer bloom. He'd grown to love the farm as much as Charlotte did; he'd put nearly twenty-one years of his life into it, and hoped that once Danny had a wife and family, he would move into the farmhouse and bring up his family there. That was the plan, and always had been, in the back of his mind. Whether the Armstrong lass was right for his lad was another matter – time would tell, no doubt. Right now he couldn't help but worry about the news Danny had brought with him. How would his Lottie have coped with the shock revelation that both children had known about Joseph Dawson all their lives? A secret that Charlotte had wanted to take with her to her grave.

'Are you away now, Mister Atkinson?' Arthur Newhouse walked towards his master as he noticed Archie's son take his place in the mowing.

'Aye, I'll be away; my lad's taken over from me, as he should do. The hired men seem to be doing a good job. Are they all toeing the line, Arthur, no misbehaving? Not like last year, when we found that paddy drunk under an empty beer barrel in the barn. That barrel shouldn't have been touched until after the harvest was in.' Archie grinned; he was cross at the time, but now he found it amusing. Needless to say, the Irish hired hand had been given his marching orders, and they had been a man down all summer.

'Aye, they are all behaving themselves, we've got a good lot this year. Mary says they are all polite when she gives them their meals; and, as I say, they are all workers.' Arthur leaned on his scythe and chewed the end of a stalk of grass as he watched the men under his control.

'You can't ask for much more then, Arthur. I'll get away. I'm just going to call in up at Butterfield Gap; since my mother died last year, my father's been a bit down. I worry about him up there on his own, and he'll be thinking he should be hay-timing, when he's not up to it. Once we've done here, I'll send one of your men to get it done with our Danny.'

'Yes, that will be fine. Your father must be getting a good age now – he does well to stop up there by himself,' Arthur replied. His interest in knowing how old Charlie Atkinson was keeping was for selfish reasons, for he fancied trying to buy Butterfield Gap after Charlie's day and becoming his own man, instead of being the farm man at Crummock.

'Aye, he'll be seventy-five in November. Charlotte and I have asked him to come and stop with us at Windfell, but he'll not be having any of it. Says to let him be with his few sheep, as it's them that keep him going.'

'Aye, well, give him my best, and I'll get back to the lads.' Arthur put his scythe over his shoulder and walked off to the meadow. Archie made his way back to the farmhouse and stables, where he mounted Sheba and trotted down the stony lane into the village of Austwick and across the valley to Eldroth, enjoying the warmth of the summer sun upon his back.

'How was your day?' Charlotte sat on the edge of the bed, pulling her long cotton nightdress over her legs, before propping herself up on the pillows and bolster and pulling the bedcovers over her. It was the first chance she'd had to talk to Archie all day, as he'd been late back from his visit to his father.

'Never mind about my day. I understand from our Danny that both children came forth with a revelation or two. Were you alright, my love?' Archie waited, as he knew Lottie would have been upset.

'I didn't know what to say to them both. I had no idea they knew so much. It's a relief, but a shock at the same time, and I don't know if it makes Danny's love for Harriet any easier.' Charlotte breathed in deeply and sighed. 'Isabelle was so matter-of-fact about it all. I think she realized I only withheld the truth from her to save her heartache. How can you tell your child that her father was a crook from the back streets of Accrington, as well as a murderer and a bankrupt? I still stand by what I've done, even though it caused upset this morning and neither of our children will look at me in quite the same light ever again.'

'Come here. I know what you did was for the best, but even I am slightly relieved that the past is now out in the open.' Archie opened his arms to Charlotte and held her tightly. 'I spoke to Danny up at Crummock and I've suggested that he brings Harriet to tea on Sunday. Let's not condemn her before we know her, if you are in agreement.' Archie looked down at a worried Charlotte.

'I suppose we could invite her. No matter what we do, your Danny's that stubborn he'd court her behind our backs. Best to get to know her, and then we're sure what we are dealing with and can try to find out just how much influence Dora has over her life.' Charlotte squeezed Archie's hand. 'Anyway, enough of the children – we can't undo what's been done. How's your father, is he coping?'

'He's a bit low in spirits and he's nearly bent double with arthritis. He's such a stubborn old devil. I told him that he's more than welcome to come and live with us. But no, he won't have any of it. He doesn't think it would make life any easier for all of us, if we didn't have him and Butterfield to worry about. He thinks he's farming it, but he'd be lost without our Danny and me. I spent all my day doing work around the farm and making sure he was alright, then he insisted I stop with him for something to eat. I'd rather have had Ruby's braised beef than that fatty lump of bacon he fried over the fire, with an egg that he wondered was fresh or not.' Archie leaned back in bed and reached for Charlotte's hand above the covers.

'You'll be just as stubborn when you are his age. You are getting that way already.' Charlotte grinned at the disdain on Archie's face. 'Talking of Ruby, she's asked me if there is anything we can do for Mrs Batty, as her sight's beginning to fail and she's struggling with her work; she's nearly seventy, but still insists on helping in the kitchen. She really does get in the way, but there's nowhere else for her to go. I've been thinking about what we could do for her, and I wondered if she would like one of the cottages down at the locks that's just come empty. She'd be better down there, in her own home, instead of being in her room in the servants' quarters. They all look after one another, down at the locks; besides, she deserves a place of her own.'

'And the rent? Let me guess: you'll charge her a pittance? You are too soft, Lottie, it's a wonder you make any money.' Archie chastised her, but he knew her kindness towards others less fortunate than herself was his wife's strongest point.

'She's old and she deserves some comforts in her last few years, and the young ones have no patience with her. Besides, it will give Ruby her own rule in the kitchen. Too many cooks, and all that! I think things get a little strained down there.' Charlotte smiled.

'Whatever you think, my love. I'm sure you'll do it without my consent anyway. You usually do. As long as we all pull together, we will be alright as a family – that I promise.' Archie turned and kissed Charlotte on her cheek. How he wished he believed his own words, but only time would tell.

4

'I don't know, I've always been used to a life in service. I'll be lost without all you lot giving me grief every day. And what if I can't manage on my own? I've nobody down there to look after me.' Mrs Batty sat, rocking herself gently, in her usual chair next to the fire in the kitchen at Windfell. 'I know it's kind of the mistress to give me my own cottage, and some folk would bite her hand off for such, even if it is the cottage that Betsy Foster lived in, but it's a big decision, at my stage of life.'

'Well, I think it's the perfect move for you. Besides, you'll not be on your own; you know old Gertie Potts, she'd be next door to you. She'll never be out of your house, because she must be lonely since her husband died. And I and Jim are only over at Stackhouse. I'll be walking past your door on the way up to Windfell every day.' Ruby rolled out her pastry on the pine table, and then decided to stop and talk to the doubting old cook. 'You'll not have all those stairs that you hate to climb up and down every day in the manor. I know how you hate them, and there's a lot to be said for having your own independence.'

'You see, that's where I went wrong. I never got remarried after I lost my Harry, so now I'm in this pickle, with no one to care for me. You'll be alright when you are old; that Jim Pratt you married is a good man, and he will always be there to look after you. I'm not daft, you know – I know you want me out from under your feet. I'm neither use nor ornament, with my failing sight, so you needn't say no more.' Peggy Batty sniffed and then wiped her tear-filled eyes.

'What's all this about?' Mazy entered the kitchen and went over to kneel by the side of Mrs Batty, whom she had grown to love in her years of service with her. She held her hand tightly as the old woman sobbed.

'Mistress Atkinson has offered Mrs Batty her own cottage, down at the locks, and I've been trying to convince her that it would be ideal for her to take up the offer.' Ruby shook her head as Mazy smiled at the stubborn old woman and pulled up a stool to sit next to her.

'So, what's all the tears for? A cottage – I'd die for one, instead of living in that cramped room of mine up in the rafters. I'd be able to have my own furniture and have my friends around. Go shopping in Settle when I wanted, and come back when I wanted.' Mazy squeezed Mrs Batty's hand.

'Aye, but you are still young, and I'm an old woman

and my eyesight is getting worse with each day. I know my way around here. I know every nook and cranny, and I know you lot will look after me.' Peggy sniffed.

'You know, Mrs Batty, you've seen me grow up from being a brash, foul-mouthed scullery maid up to being nanny for Miss Isabelle and Master Danny, and then up to housekeeper. But I would do anything to have a home of my own, like Ruby and her old man has, and like you are being offered. You can make it your home, and you'll not be on your own, for we will call in nearly every day.' Mazy knew that more time was being spent on looking after Mrs Batty than the kitchen could afford, and she also knew it would only be a matter of time before the old cook would miss a step and fall the full length of the servants' stairs.

'It doesn't seem five minutes since you came into this kitchen, Mazy. Aye, you were a handful, and now look at you: a fine young woman with nearly as many airs and graces as the mistress herself. It's a pity you can't find yourself a man. I suppose it's getting too late for you now.' Mrs Batty smiled, wiping away her tears. 'You are both right, and I'm an ungrateful old woman. You've got young Nancy to help out in the kitchen, and she'll peel the veg and help wash the pots when I've gone.' She sighed deeply.

Mazy leaned back and looked at the crestfallen cook, who had slightly upset her with her talk of Mazy still being a single woman. It was true that she hadn't been lucky enough to find herself a man, but she wasn't worried, for she preferred her own company. 'Nancy, put the kettle on and make us all a cup of tea. I think we are all in need of refreshment.' Mazy looked over to the young lass, who was sniggering to herself as she washed the breakfast pots in the sink.

'Yes, Miss.' Nancy bobbed and filled the kettle, before putting it on the range to boil.

'Now, I've a bit of news for us all. Something that the mistress will be worrying about, I'm sure.' Mazy waited.

'Well, go on, tell us what it is!' Ruby quickly finished putting the lid on her apple pie and brushed it with egg-wash, before placing it in the range's oven and sitting down on the chair on the other side of the table from Mazy and Mrs Batty.

'We are to entertain Harriet Armstrong on Sunday – she's coming to tea. It would seem that Master Daniel is quite serious about her. It must be causing his father and mother some worry, with her working for Dora Bloomenber.' Mazy watched as Mrs Batty's mouth widened as she took in the news.

'Oh, the poor mistress, she'll not want anyone linked with that family courting young Daniel. It will bring memories of the past rushing back,' Mrs Batty gasped.

'All Settle was agog when Ezera Bloomenber married Dora Dodgson, and then it turned out she was the late Mr Dawson's sister. I remember her walking around the market once and everyone was whispering about her behind her back.' Ruby took her cup of tea and sipped deeply.

'Well, let's hope she doesn't bring any troubles to the family. They don't deserve any more worries.' Mazy sighed.

'We'll not have to judge the lass until we get to know her. After all, Dora is not Harriet's parent; it's just that Harriet works at the shop, and old Ezera was a good man. It would be him that employed her, before he died the other year. But if that woman manages to worm her way back into this house, through young Harriet, then I'm glad I'm leaving it,' Peggy Batty exclaimed.

'So you've made your mind up then?' Ruby quizzed.

'Aye, you are all right. I'd need my head examining, if I turn down my own little cottage and it's already furnished, even though I know it was the one Betsy Foster lived in. But I'm not afeared of any ghosts that might haunt the place. Gertie Potts will keep an eye on me, she's a good woman. And I'll get out from under all of your feet. I'm not daft, I know I'm a nuisance sometimes.'

The kitchen went quiet; old Mrs Batty might be nearly blind, but she definitely wasn't daft, and nothing went over her head. She'd be missed.

'Well, Harriet, it's a pleasure to have you join us for tea this afternoon.' Charlotte looked across at the young girl who had stolen Danny's heart and smiled. She watched Harriet as she glanced quickly at Danny before replying.

'The pleasure's all mine. I couldn't believe it when Danny said I had to join him for tea this afternoon.' Harriet smiled shyly, aware that all eyes were upon her.

'*Had* to join him – I do hope he didn't make you come here.' Charlotte sipped her tea from the delicate bone china and looked across at the nervous young woman, trying to forget who Harriet worked for. She'd still have preferred any other girl to be on Danny's arm, and she was hoping that if she was cool towards Harriet, then she would be put off from courting her stepson.

'Sorry, it's my clumsiness with words. He didn't say I had to, just would I wish to join him, and of course I was delighted to accept. You have such a beautiful home, and I wanted so much to meet you all. Danny is always talking about you.' Harriet blushed.

'You are never clumsy with words, my dear. It's Mother being pernickety. Did you know, Mother, that Harriet made the beautiful dress she's come in today? Do you not think it is a lovely creation?' Danny beamed at his love by his side.

'Did you really, Harriet? I think it's beautiful. I love the delicate lace around the sleeves. I wish I could sew.' Isabelle latched onto the conversation, trying to defuse the frosty looks between her brother and her mother. The dress was pretty and could have fooled anyone into thinking it was sewn by an experienced seamstress. However, Isabelle thought she herself would have added a lot more detail to the bodice.

'Really, Isabelle, you could sew, if you put your mind to it. After all, you are very adept at art, and designing a dress is second nature to you. I've seen those endless sketches that litter your room. Harriet's dress *is* beautiful – a simple dress made different with a few lace accessories that make it look a little special.' Charlotte rattled her cup down onto her saucer.

'Well, I think tha looks right bonny in it, lass. You are to be congratulated on it. You should start your own tailoring shop – give Ralph's on Chapel Street a run for their money. God knows, they've had enough money from the women of this house in their time,' Archie blustered, before being kicked under the table by Charlotte for stepping out of line.

'I've always wanted to have my own shop. I'd love to be able to design and sew dresses all day, but unfortunately my parents think it a frivolity and something I could not make any money from. Besides, I work for Dora Bloomenber and I am happy there. I shouldn't complain.' Harriet quickly took a delicate mouthful of cake, stopping herself from mentioning the name of her employer again, a subject that Danny had told her not to approach.

It was too late, for Charlotte saw an opportunity to quiz Harriet further about the family that employed her.

'Do you have a lot to do with Dora Bloomenber? I've heard people say that she treats you like a daughter.' Charlotte could not stop herself; it was best she got everything out in the open.

'I see her perhaps once a week. I miss Ezera, he was such a kind man. He treated me like his daughter, only because they have no family of their own. Mrs Bloomenber can be a little cool sometimes, and not as open as Ezera used to be. But can I say that I know your concerns, if I am not speaking out of turn. Danny has told me not to speak of them today, but I feel I must. To put your minds at ease, more than anything. I am here under no false pretence – my love for Danny is true. It is not because of Mrs Bloomenber's scheming and her past links with your family. Indeed, she did not know who Danny was, until he picked me up from the shop on the day of Isabelle's party. I had never mentioned him until that afternoon. She was interested in Isabelle reaching twenty-one, and I believe she has sent you a gift, Isabelle, which she thought rightly belonged to you. I took it to the post office myself, on her behalf.'

Harriet breathed in, after giving a quick glance at Isabelle, who looked as black as thunder. It was up to the family now; they all could either like her and make her welcome or ask her to leave straight away. Either way, Danny would stick by her, of that she was sure.

'Well, you certainly say it as it is, Miss Armstrong. You hold nothing back, which is to be commended. I've got to say that there is bad blood between our families and, as you are no doubt aware, Mrs Bloomenber is – unfortunately – Isabelle's aunt.' Charlotte was taken aback by the straight-talking girl, for up to that moment she had thought there was not much to the

48

milksop on Danny's arm. 'Isabelle, did you receive a gift from Dora Bloomenber and, if you did, why didn't you tell me?'

All eyes turned on Isabelle as she lowered her head and fiddled with her napkin.

'Yes, I did; it came in the post the other afternoon, like Harriet said.' Isabelle looked across at her brother in hope of support, but he didn't acknowledge the pleading look in her eyes.

'And where is it now?' Charlotte asked.

'It's hidden in the bedding box in my bedroom. I didn't tell you, Mother, because I knew it would upset you.' Isabelle looked straight at her mother.

'No more secrets! I am sick of this family holding back secrets. Now tomorrow, Isabelle, you and I will return in person whatever Dora has given you, for we do not want anything from that family. Harriet, I am grateful for your frankness, but if you go out of your way ever to hurt a member of my family, you will live to regret the day you came across me and mine. Now have I made myself clear to everyone?'

The table went quiet as everyone realized just how protective Charlotte was.

The silence was broken by Archie. 'Bloody hell, lass, poor Harriet will never want to see any of us ever again, if you lose your temper like that. I'd run for it now, lass, while you can – make a break for the door.' He winked at the newcomer to the family and noticed Danny squeezing her hand tightly.

'I've no intention of running, Mr Atkinson. I love

49

Danny, and he me. I know I'm your worst nightmare and, believe me, if I can find another job I will, just to ease your minds and distance myself from Dora Bloomenber. I'd do anything to keep my Danny.' Harriet smiled at her beau.

Charlotte put her napkin down. 'I'm sorry, let us continue with our tea, now that we know exactly where we stand with one another. Harriet, my apologies. I'm not usually so rude to our guests, but your association with Dora Bloomenber has caused me some worries. And, Isabelle, I thought you'd know better; but not to worry – least said, soonest mended. We will visit your aunt in the morning and satisfy any curiosity you may feel about her. Now, another slice of cake, anyone? Let us now welcome Harriet to the family properly and show her that we don't always argue.' Charlotte pushed the cake in front of her and sighed. Isabelle had let her down; she could be as secretive as her father, and that was a bad trait to have.

Charlotte and Isabelle stood on the immaculately scrubbed steps of Ingfield House, waiting for the bell that they had rung to be answered. The house stood along the roadside into Settle, square and solid, with pillars on either side of the doorway. The garden around it was tended to within an inch of its life, and the curtains at the windows told of the wealth within, leaving passers-by in no doubt that the owners were well-to-do people.

'Nobody's in, Mother, let us go. It will save Jethro

waiting for us.' Isabelle's stomach was churning, for she was about to face the aunt whose shadow she now knew had cursed her family all her life.

'Nonsense, give the maid time. Harriet said Dora was always at home on a Monday. It's no good getting cold feet now; it's time to face your beloved aunt. I must admit I'm curious to talk to her. I haven't spoken to Dora since your father walked out. Although I have seen her around Settle, I ignore her and walk across to the other side of the street when I can. Besides, she keeps herself to herself, from what I hear. It's best that she does so, for people have long memories in this part of the world.' Charlotte whispered the last few words, as she heard the faint patter of feet from behind the door with its highly polished brassware.

'Good morning, ma'am. May I help you?' the pretty maid enquired with a curtsey.

'Yes, we would like to see Mrs Bloomenber. Here is my calling card. We will wait in the hallway.' Charlotte pushed past the young maid, with Isabelle hard behind her.

'Very well, ma'am. I'll tell her you are waiting.' The maid opened the doorway into the Bloomenbers' drawing room and left the guests standing in the hall.

Isabelle gazed around the hall; it was not as large as Windfell's, but it was grand, with elegant ornaments and rich paintings. Her aunty was obviously a woman of wealth. Charlotte patted her daughter's hand as she watched Isabelle's complexion drain when the maid returned.

'Mrs Bloomenber says to please join her in the drawing room.' The maid left the door open as they passed her and, once they were within the room, she closed the doors.

'So, Charlotte, you've decided to give me a visit, after all these years.' A voice with a slight Lancashire accent came from behind a high-backed chair that was turned towards the fireplace, the centrepiece of the high-ceilinged room.

'I have, Dora, and I've also brought Isabelle to see you and to return the gift that you sent her. You can understand why I wish her not to accept it. Your brother did not actually leave my life, or Isabelle's, on good terms.' Charlotte moved forward and ushered Isabelle with her, until they both stood in front of the woman that Charlotte had once hated. Twenty-one years ago she had been afraid of Dora, frightened of the hold she had over her husband and of the way Dora had always made her feel small. Now the woman had no such hold, and Charlotte was looking at a frail, grey-haired old lady. However, looks could be deceiving and, as Jethro had reminded her, a leopard never changes its spots.

'I thought you'd have something to say about it. But it was the girl's birthday, and her father would have wanted her to have something. Come here, girl, let me have a look at you.' Dora beckoned Isabelle to stand in front of her and grinned when she saw her. 'Aye, you are your father's alright – look at that black mop. Got your mother's eyes, though, those soft, come-to-bed eyes that caught our Joseph with their fluttering lashes. Sent him to his death, they did, along with the whinging and whining.'

'I'm not stopping to listen to this. I did nothing – it wasn't I who killed him; Joseph managed to do that himself. Along with poor Betsy Foster, whom he killed. Are you forgetting her? And are you forgetting that you walked out on him, too? Both you and I know that Joseph was bad to the core. Just why you thought we would want his mother's necklace, I don't know; after all, was she not a prostitute?' Charlotte stood her ground and watched as the woman she had hated for years leered at Isabelle. 'Give her the necklace back, Isabelle, and let's go. I can see I've wasted my breath, thinking that time might have changed her.'

Isabelle held out the box containing the necklace, and Dora snatched it from her hand. 'You're the image of your father; you'll remind your mother of him every day. Deep and dark, good at secrets, are you? He always were a real Pandora's box, apart from there was no hope for him, and I bet you are the same.' Dora clung on to Isabelle's arm as she recoiled from the old woman's clutches.

'Isabelle, come with me. Don't listen to her; she was always whispering poison into people's ears. I hoped that she'd changed.' Charlotte grabbed Isabelle's hand and led her to the drawing-room door.

'That's it: run away to the mansion you stole from my brother, and take your bitch of a daughter with you. You'll have enough headaches when Harriet marries your lad – she's a money-grabber. And that 'un, by your side, I'm sure you know by now is her father's daughter. It's as clear as that mop on her head,' Dora shouted from behind her chair.

Isabelle turned and pulled her hand out of her mother's, then strode back to the old woman who was spouting those hurtful words, and stood full-on in front of her.

'I'm not like my father, and never will be. I love my mother and, no matter what you say or do to our family, we will always be strong. You can just leave Harriet alone; she loves Danny, and I hope that they will be happy. Happier than you will ever have been. And as for the necklace, did you think you could buy me? I'm worth a lot more than that. I'm not like my father; money isn't everything, and I care for the ones I love. One of which you will never be.' Isabelle grabbed the necklace case from Dora's knee and threw it against the marble fireplace, spilling the pendant out of the case and watching as the fake precious stones shattered against the marble. 'Fake, just like you; fake like my father,' Isabelle said quietly, staring at the old woman who wanted to control their lives.

'Isabelle, come – leave her be. Now you know why she's been kept distant from you. The past is best buried with your father, and we will not be entering this house again.' Charlotte waited as a tearful Isabelle walked back to her side. 'I'm sorry you've not changed, Dora. At one time, after Joseph's death, I felt sorry for you and wished you well. Now I realize that you are bitter and twisted, and I will make sure Harriet knows what you are really like. You will not spoil my family's happiness, no matter how hard you try.'

'Get back to your posh house and your posh friends, but remember where you came from. If you hadn't married my brother, you'd be worth nowt,' Dora shouted from behind her chair.

'He had nothing, and you knew it. He left me nearly bankrupt and with child. You were quick to leave and worm yourself into someone else's life. Did Ezera ever know the gutter that you crawled out of, or have you kept that as your secret?' Charlotte shouted back, as she ushered Isabelle out of the drawing room and into the hallway.

'Get out of my house – get out now!' Dora ran the hand-bell that was on the table by her side, summoning her butler to help evict Charlotte and Isabelle.

'We are going, don't worry. The air in here is poison, as you are. Good day, Dora. You'll not be seeing either of us again, and I suggest that you advertise for a new shop assistant, because Harriet will be leaving your employment.' Charlotte marched out through the hall-way, past an aghast butler and maid, slamming the front door and shooing Isabelle down the path into the awaiting trap.

'I take it Dora has not changed then, ma'am?' Jethro helped Isabelle and Charlotte up into the trap, before mounting himself.

'She most certainly has not, but she'll not get the better of me, Jethro. I'm one step ahead of her nowadays. On our way back, Jethro, can you stop the trap outside the vacant shop on Duke Street? I just need to have a quick look at it.' Charlotte put her arm around Isabelle and hugged her. 'Are you alright, my love? Now you understand why you don't need to know about your father's family, and I'm sorry that what I said was cutting and hard. But the woman knows no different. I've learned over the years that you can't let someone bully you.'

'I'm a bit shaken, Mother. I lost my temper too, and perhaps I should not have said anything.' Isabelle looked down and felt sad for the words she had said in anger. 'Perhaps I am like my father; perhaps Dora is right.'

'That's what she wants you to think. True, you have some of his looks, but that is not a bad thing. Your father was a handsome man and a real charmer. Those are the qualities of his that you have, but there is not a bad bone in your body, my love. I know because you are my most precious daughter, whom I love dearly. Now, when Jethro pulls up the gig, we will have a quick look at the shop that is up for rent. I'm thinking that I should diversify and perhaps make Harriet's dreams come true. After all, I can see that Danny loves her deeply, but we have to get her out of the clutches of Dora Bloomenber. I was thinking of perhaps a little dress shop, with you and Harriet putting your heads together: you design the dresses and Harriet can make them. It would be the perfect combination, and it would keep you from becoming as bored as I know you are some days.'

'Mother, that would be perfect, and it would make Danny so happy. So, you like Harriet? I haven't dared ask, since she came to tea.' Isabelle's eyes lit up at the thought of sketching dress designs with Harriet, and then seeing them come to life.

'She is, as you said, a little common and a bit forward. But we will soon make her into a lady, once she is under our wing. And I can see that happening soon, for your brother is infatuated with her. At least she speaks her mind, which is better than keeping things hidden.' Charlotte held her hand out for Jethro to take, as the gig and horse stopped outside the empty shop.

'I'll never keep a secret from you again, Mother. I'm not like my father. And if Harriet agrees to your idea, I know it will work.' Isabelle grinned as she nearly jumped down from the gig, at the thought of her having her own business.

'Right, we will ask her this weekend; we'll bring her to look around the shop, if I find it suitable. Time to add another string to the Atkinson bow, and an upper-class dress shop would be a nice asset to add to our investments, I think.'

Charlotte smiled as she peered in through the shop's empty windows. You could advertise Atkinson's finest cottons and calicos there, she thought, for those who would prefer to make their own dresses rather than buy them ready-made. Every time she had got knocked back, she picked herself up. And damn Dora, because she would never be hurt by her again.

5

'I think you are mad, lass. What do you want with a dress shop? Do you not think you've enough on, with running the mill and doing the books for Crummock?' Archie leaned back in his chair and sighed, as he tried to read the local paper in the morning room of Windfell and listened as Charlotte told him of her plan.

'The mill gives me a few worries, I must admit, but it doesn't take as much of my time, now Bert Bannister is manager, and he's got a good overseer in Edwin Mellin. And Crummock's bookkeeping doesn't take me long; plus, you forget that I've been doing that since I was sixteen and was keeping my father straight with his money. Besides, I have that money that the Midland Railway paid to me for their buying part of the manor's land for the new line to run through. I couldn't invest it better than by setting my daughter, and hopefully my daughter-in-law, up in business, in goods that the mill can partly supply them with and in which I have contacts, for the rest of their supplies. It makes perfect sense to me.'

'And what if our lad decides Harriet's not the one? Have you thought of that? What if her father says our Danny isn't good enough for her? And you heard her say what her parents thought of running a dress shop.' Archie shook his head as he listened to Charlotte's scheming; she was always one jump ahead of everyone else, but sometimes she took things for granted. It had been the same when the Midland Railway had wanted to plough a railway line through the valley: she'd been first in the queue to see how they would benefit and to get the highest price for the small amount of the manor's parkland that the line crossed. Now she was complaining that the smoke from the steam engines drifted up towards the manor most days, hence the invitation for one of the directors to Isabelle's party. As if the manager could do anything about the massive engines emitting the steam that drove them! When was Charlotte going to realize that on some days things would not always go her way.

'Don't be daft, Archie, you know your lad is a good catch and that he's smitten with Harriet. She'd be an absolute idiot to turn him down, and the chance for her to run her own business alongside Isabelle.' Charlotte picked up the embroidery she had been doing for at least six months from the sewing basket next to her chair and looked at it. She tried to be the lady she was supposed to be, but sewing pretty patterns onto a piece of linen had nothing against doing a business deal. It was her father's fault, she thought to herself; he'd brought her up to stand her ground, and not let man or woman get the better of her.

'It'll be *your* business, and you know it. If – and at this moment it is "if" – Harriet agrees to your scheme, you must leave Isabelle and Harriet to run it, and you must keep your views to yourself if they have any disagreements. You promise me, Charlotte, because I know you: sometimes you are like a bull in a china shop with your cutting comments and you are quick to judge.' Archie stood up, walked to the window and looked out down the valley.

'I don't know what you mean. Of course I'll leave them to it, but I'll keep an eye on the profits. It'll do Isabelle good, as she should contribute to society. Besides, I'm fed up of hearing her telling Ralph's how she wants her dresses to look; she can design her own now. It gets quite embarrassing, when she knows more about fashion than they do. The other day she told them that their mantles were too plain. Well, she can design her own from now on.' Charlotte pricked her finger on her needle and swore under her breath as she licked the blood off.

'Well, I wouldn't know what a mantle was, so she's one up on me.' Archie turned and looked at his disdainful wife.

'Yes, you do: it's the little cape-like top that's all the fashion at the moment. Isabelle's got a bright red one with black lace on it, which she wears all the time. I hope Harriet knows that bustles are in fashion.

Crinolines have definitely had their day.' Charlotte screwed up her embroidery, pushing it back into her sewing box; she'd no patience with needlework.

'Listen to you, woman, you can't even do a bit of embroidery.' Archie laughed loudly at his wife's hypocrisy as she sucked her pricked finger.

'But I do know what will sell, Archie Atkinson, and how to sell it, so stop your scoffing. Just you keep your eye on your farming and leave the rest to me.'

Harriet sat in the drawing room of Windfell, across from Isabelle, and sipped her tea nervously. Jethro, the manor's footman and groom, had called into the jewellery shop while she had been working, to ask if she could attend for afternoon tea the following day. She had of course agreed, hoping that she would see Danny there, but there was no sight of him as she sat wondering what the meeting was all about, while her teacup rattled with nerves on its saucer. Did his stepmother want to discourage her from seeing Danny, because of the bad feeling with her employer? If she did, then Charlotte was going to be in for a shock, for nothing would come between her and her Danny. She loved him with all her heart, and nothing would part them. She smiled across at Isabelle, who had greeted her warmly as soon as she had entered the manor, but was now making polite conversation about the weather and how many trains ran on the newly opened railway line, as they awaited the arrival of her mother, who had been held up at the mill.

Isabelle stood up, relieved, when she heard the front door of the manor slam, as her mother rushed into the hallway. She'd promised not to say anything to Harriet before her mother had a chance to. Charlotte entered the room, still with her cape and hat on, and quickly gave her apologies as she untied the ribbons on her hat, passing it and the cape to the butler, Stephen Thomson, who followed hot-foot on her heels, worried that he'd missed opening the door for his mistress.

'Thank you, Thomson. Could you ask Mrs Pratt for a fresh pot of tea, please. And a sandwich of some sort would be most welcome, as I didn't get the chance for lunch today.'

'Yes, ma'am.' Thomson took her apparel and went quickly down to the kitchen.

'I'm sorry, Harriet. I did want to be here on your arrival, but Sally Oversby made me aware of a problem on one of the carding machines, and then I had to discuss it with Mr Bannister. I'm afraid one thing just led to another, leaving me late to meet you.' Charlotte smiled at the nervous-looking girl who was sitting on her sofa and at her daughter, who by the look on her face could not contain her news any longer. 'Well, I'd better tell you why I've asked you here today, before Isabelle bursts. Also, I wanted to apologize for being rather sharp with you last time you were here. I realize that you are an innocent party who is unfortunately caught up in the middle of a family feud.'

Harriet smiled, wondering what was going to be

said next, and not even having a chance to greet her host.

'Isabelle and I visited Dora Bloomenber on Monday, and it was as I feared – Dora not having changed one bit since she left here as housekeeper, apart from ageing significantly. I fear she will use you, Harriet, to cause bother in our family. After you had left on Sunday I started thinking about what we could do, if she did interfere, as I realize you think a great deal of Danny. And his happiness is his father's, and my own, greatest concern, along with that of Isabelle. As it happened, the answer lay in what you said regarding your dressmaking skills and in Isabelle's non-stop sketching of dresses and accessories. To cut a long story short, Harriet, Isabelle and I viewed the shop that is vacant on Duke Street and we wondered if you might be interested in opening a draper's shop, along with Isabelle – on the understanding that you leave Bloomenber's. It would solve the problem of Dora interfering in our lives, and would give you something that you have always dreamed of.' Charlotte hesitated, as Thomson brought in a new pot of tea and a round of cucumber sandwiches, placing them on the table in front of her. She looked at the young woman who had caused her so many sleepless nights, but who had now started to win her over and make her realize that she had her own mind, and that her love for Danny was true.

'Mrs Atkinson, I don't know what to say.' Harriet looked over at Isabelle. 'I'd have to discuss it with my parents. Would I be able to manage? Would we make enough money? And how do I tell Mrs Bloomenber? She's always been reasonable with me.'

'I'm prepared to back you both for a year. By then you should be able to stand on your own two feet. And I would prefer it if you could cut all ties with Dora Bloomenber; once she knows our plan, she will not be amused.' Charlotte bit into her sandwich and sipped her tea, watching the realization of young Harriet's dream dawning on her.

'Does Danny know anything about this? He hasn't said a word,' Harriet asked as Charlotte ate another sandwich.

'No, he knows nothing. We'll tell him once we know that you are interested.' Charlotte smiled.

Isabelle rushed over to sit next to Harriet and grabbed her hand. So much had happened in the short time since Harriet had entered their lives, and Isabelle was beginning to realize that she, too, had misjudged the young woman in front of her. Now, like her mother, she wanted to make things right and welcome the girl properly into the family. 'Please, Harriet, say "yes" – it will be so much fun. I know all the latest trends, Mother can get all the materials we need, and you are a superb seamstress. Just think: our own business. And you'll see Danny every day.'

'I expect you to work, Isabelle, so not too much fun. You would have to work together on not too-complicated designs, and you'll have to undercut Ralph's, when you first start out.' Charlotte sat back and looked at the two young women. They complemented one another – one dark and the other blonde – they were young and eager, and they reminded her a lot of herself when she was younger. 'Isabelle, show Harriet some of your designs, and have a talk together while I go down to the kitchen with this tray. I want to see if Mrs Batty got moved into the cottage down at the locks. It will do you good to get to know one another, without me here to distract you.'

'Thank you, ma'am, I am grateful. I just can't believe what's been offered to me, and of course I will discuss it with Isabelle. I'm sure we can work together.'

Harriet's face was aglow with excitement as Charlotte left the room with her laden tray, and Charlotte smiled to herself as she heard designs and material being discussed while making her way down the steps to the kitchen. Interesting times lay ahead: a new business and, she hoped, a new member of the family, if Danny decided to marry the girl of his dreams, and she realized now that he could certainly do a lot worse than Harriet.

Danny rode up the drive to Ragged Hall, as his father had told him to go and speak to Bill Brown, who farmed there, and ask him if they could borrow his prize-winning Swaledale tup later in the autumn, to service some of his flock. He rode into the yard and dismounted, tethering his horse next to the mounting blocks against the barn. No sooner had he climbed down than a voice called out as he patted the horse's neck.

'Can I help you, sir?'

Danny turned and saw a young woman standing in front of him. Her hair shone like burnished copper in the summer sunshine and her skin was a pure milky-white, like the jug of milk that she was carrying out of the dairy.

'Aye, is your master in? I'm here on a bit of business.' Danny walked over to her, unable to ignore the beauty who stood in front of him. She was a bonny dairy lass, there was no denying that.

'I've no master, sir. I presume you mean to speak to my father, Mr Brown? I'm his daughter, Amy.' She smiled slightly, noticing the embarrassment of the young man who stood in front of her.

'My apologies, Miss Brown. I saw you carrying the milk jug and automatically presumed you were in service here. I do beg your forgiveness.' Daniel apologized and held out his hand to be shaken as he introduced himself. 'I'm Daniel Atkinson; my father farms at Crummock above Austwick, and my mother runs Ferndale Mill. My father has sent me to see about borrowing your prize tup. Is your father at home?' Daniel looked at the attractive young woman with the emerald-green eyes and couldn't stop gazing at her, she was that bewitching.

'He's gone to see my uncle, but he told me to expect you. Moses, our tup, is in the paddock awaiting your inspection, but perhaps you would like to join me in a cup of tea? I was just about to make one, hence the jug of milk.' Amy smiled at the attractive young man in front of her. Her father had told her that she had to entertain him, informing her that Daniel was the best catch in the district, but not telling her how handsome he was, with his blond hair and blue eyes.

'Moses, eh! Was he found in the bullrushes?' Danny laughed.

'He was actually; well, found in the reeds at the top of our main pasture. His mother had died giving birth to a second twin and I reared him as a pet, and that's why he's so soft.' Amy stood next to Danny and watched as he smiled at the thought of a prize Swaledale tup being reared as a pet. 'I hope you'll look after him, if you borrow him. I'm still very fond of him.'

'I'll guard Moses with my life, but he'll have his work cut out, for we've over two hundred ladies awaiting his services this autumn, if I'm not speaking out of turn, Miss Brown.' Daniel blushed.

'I'm a farmer's daughter, so I know exactly how he has to perform. I've no brothers, and my mother died when I was born, so I've been brought up by my father, who believed I should know everything about the farm. I am not a shrinking violet, Mr Atkinson.' Amy pulled her skirt up as she climbed the sandstone steps into the farmhouse. Its name sounded grander than the abode looked. 'Ragged Hall' had conjured up an image of a grand house, in Danny's mind, but instead it was a long, rambling farmhouse that had been built centuries before, by local labourers. The lead-paned mullion windows were framed by rambling roses, which hid the masonry and the fact that the stonework underneath needed some repair. And Danny couldn't help but notice that a slate had slipped from the roof, probably in the late spring storms, and had not been replaced. It was a pity, he thought, that Bill Brown had no son to help with the repairs.

'Please call me Danny. I'm sorry. I didn't mean to insult you, or Moses. A cup of tea would be most welcome. I lost my mother too when I was a baby, and my father's wife is my stepmother, although she treats me like her own and I love her dearly. Your father never married again, I take it?' Danny followed the straight-talking beauty into the low-set kitchen, where he blinked to adjust his eyes to the darkness as he entered from the bright sunshine outside. He looked around the kitchen, at the ancient oak beams with summer herbs drying from them and at the oak dresser adorned with willow-pattern porcelain. The kitchen was homely, with a fire in the hearth on which Amy placed the kettle, before reaching for some of the blue-and-white china, which she placed on the table, urging him to take a seat.

'No, my father never remarried. There's just me and him here, and a farm lad that comes two days a week to help out. We are quite content by ourselves and can manage at the moment, although I do find that my father is struggling sometimes with the amount of work, as he's not getting any younger. Have you had anything to eat? I was just going to have some cheese and bread, perhaps you would like to join me?' Amy hesitated as she placed two plates on the table and pulled open a drawer to take two knives out of it.

'That would be grand – it seems to have been an age since my breakfast this morning.' If she had told him to walk on red-hot coals, Danny would have agreed, for she'd captivated him so much. He laughed and joked with her as they discussed local farmers, their lives and their love of the countryside, as if they had been friends forever. Amy was so easy to talk to, and all thoughts of Harriet and her love for him disappeared as Danny became entranced by Amy's smile, her openness and her infectious laugh. It wasn't until the grandfather clock in the corner of the kitchen struck three that Danny realized he had not done the job he had been sent to do. 'Aye, heavens, Amy, I've never even looked at Moses yet, or asked if your father will agree to lend him to us this October.'

'It's not my father you've to ask over Moses; it's me. If you like the look of him and still want to borrow him, there will be just one condition.' Amy hesitated.

'What's that then? We are willing to pay a fair price for his loan. After all, he should father some good lambs.' Danny waited.

'It's nothing to do with Moses. I'd just like you to come back and visit me. I've enjoyed your company so much, and I know you'll look after him fine; he'll love it up at Crummock.' Amy waited. This was a new lad in her life, one who had made her laugh. He'd never

70

mentioned having a girl in his life, and if there was, it didn't matter. All was fair in love and war.

'If that's what you call a condition, then I'm happy to fulfil your wishes. Now, we had better go and look at the big man.' Danny pushed back his chair and smiled at Amy.

'Yes, he's in the paddock behind the house. I'll take you there.' Amy reached for Danny's hand, touching it gently before going to the kitchen door and out into the sunshine, then leading him to the ram, which was grazing contentedly in the daisy-filled paddock behind the farmhouse.

'By, he's a fair beast. He'll father some good lambs for us next spring.' Danny climbed over the gate and cornered the prize ram next to the gate that Amy stood behind.

'There's no need to be rough with him, he's used to being handled.' She stood on the bars of the gate and watched as Danny checked his teeth, feet and testicles, finally running his hand along the ram's back before letting the poor animal loose.

'Aye, he'll do. He's the fittest beast I've seen for a long time, and his owner's not too bad, either.' Danny cheekily passed Amy a daisy that he'd picked out of the paddock and grinned.

'Why, thank you, Mr Atkinson. I could say the same thing about you. My father, I am sure, will come to an agreement with your father regarding payment. And I hope you will keep your part of the bargain, or Moses and I will never forgive you.' Amy smelled the daisy and twirled it in her fingers as she pretended to be coy with her visitor.

'You just try to keep me away, Amy Brown. Now I know what you have here, I'll never be away.' Danny stroked her cheek, not daring a kiss quite yet. But there would be a time when he would.

'What's up, lad? You look as if you've lost a sixpence and found a penny. Aren't you glad your mother's sorted out your Harriet and our Isabelle with a shop?' Archie looked at his son, who had appeared crestfallen since Charlotte and Isabelle had been full of the new venture at dinner time.

'I just wish she'd asked me. Now I'm committed to Harriet, else my mother will never forgive me.' Danny sighed, remembering the auburn-haired Amy he'd met earlier in the day.

'Well, you've got yourself to blame there. You were full of Harriet the other day: going to leave house and home, if we weren't right with her. Your mother's only trying to help and get her out of Dora Bloomenber's grips. Besides, I think the lass thinks she's going to marry you, like we all did – you were that infatuated with her at Isabelle's birthday. We couldn't do right for doing wrong, and still can't seemingly, by the look on that face. You haven't been leading her on, and I hope you haven't asked to marry her if you don't mean it?' Archie leaned over the limestone wall that ran behind the manor's kitchen garden and waited for Danny to reply. Something was bothering his lad, and he'd a good idea what. 'How did you go on at Ragged Hall – did you see old Brown about borrowing his tup?'

'No, he wasn't in, it was his lass that I talked to.' Danny couldn't look at his father, for he knew him too well; he'd know what he was thinking.

'That'd be Amy, she's a good-looking lass. Bill Brown worships her, but he wouldn't do if he knew how wild she is; she's broken many a lad's heart, with her easy ways. Tha wants nowt looking at that 'un, lad, if that's what you are thinking.' Archie watched his son's cheeks fill with colour. He was right: Amy had turned Danny's head; how he wished he'd not sent him on business there. 'She loves and leaves 'em, lad; just a tease, she must have gone with every lad over at Rathmell. She's going to be a lonely old maid one day, for no decent man would touch her, if he had sense.'

'She seemed alright. She offered me my dinner and was pleasant enough.' Danny stuck up for Amy. How did his father know anything?

'Aye, well, you are a bit like her tup: got an eye for the best ewe in the field. But this beauty's not everything she seems. If you've whispered and promised Harriet the earth, you stick by it. She loves you – any fool can see that. That 'un at Ragged Hall will only look after herself, so get a ring on your lass's finger and get her wed. Your mother's set her up in business and we'll find you somewhere to live. It's not like we are short of a bob or two.'

Danny fell silent, then spat a mouthful of saliva out

73

over the wall into the pastureland and waited for his father to walk away.

'You wed Harriet and stop your gallivanting. You are twenty-three next month – time you settled down. I was only nineteen when I married your mother, and a father by the time I was twenty. That stopped me from roving.' Archie stood and watched as Danny turned to face him.

'Aye, and you regretted every day you were married to my mother, and couldn't wait to get back into my stepmother's arms. So don't you preach to me.' Danny spat the words out and stared at his father.

'Watch your words, young man. And you are wrong there, lad. I loved your mother, and my Rosie will always be with me. I'll never ever forget her; she was more precious to me than life itself, and that nobody can deny. But Charlotte's the woman I love now, and always will until the day I die. She's a good woman: faithful and true, just like your Harriet. So don't let a bit of flighty stuff come between you both. You shouldn't make promises you can't keep, lad. And I know that happen Charlotte's forced you into a corner, by setting Harriet up in business, but she thought you loved her, and she was just protecting us all.' Archie saw the anger in his son's eyes and was hurt; he'd never had a bad word before with his Danny. Women, they ruled your life with their ways and trickery, but you couldn't live without them, and Danny still had a lot to learn. 'Think on, lad. Use your head and don't let Harriet down, she's a good lass.'

*

74

Danny lay back in the fresh-smelling hay. The summer's sun shone down in a sharp shaft of warmth through the forking hole of the barn at Ragged Hall. He turned and leaned on his elbow and smiled as he looked on in awe at the sleeping Amy. She was beautiful and wild, with no airs and graces like other girls. He looked at her skirts, still up above her knees from their hour of pleasure, which had left them both happy and content. Too content, he thought; he would have to be making tracks home, else his father would be questioning his whereabouts. He picked up a piece of sweet-smelling hay and trickled it down Amy's nose as she snoozed, grinning as she twitched her nose in annoyance. A more beautiful nose he had never seen, he thought, as he repeated his torment.

She opened one of her eyes and then stretched and yawned.

'Stop teasing me, Danny Atkinson, else it will be the worse for you.' Amy put her hands behind her head, then smiled at her lover.

'I'm going to have to go, Amy, they'll be wondering where I've got to.' Danny knelt down in the hay and pulled up his braces, tucking his shirt into his trousers as he looked down on his love.

'Don't go, Danny, stay here with me. My father won't be back until supper time, as he's walling up in the top pasture.' She ran her hand over Danny's stomach and urged him down upon her.

'No, I'll have to go, Amy. We shouldn't have done what we've done, as it is.' Danny kissed her and so wanted to stay in her arms until the sun went down. 'I'll be back, I don't know when – it'll be whenever I can sneak away.' He stood up and looked down upon the lass he truly loved, the one who was sheer temptation, nearly losing his balance on the unevenness of the hay stack.

'Well, you know where I'm at, my lover. Don't be too long.' Amy closed her eyes and curled up in the sun's rays and the warmth of the hay.

'I won't. You take care of yourself, Amy.'

Danny climbed down out of the hay and untethered his horse from outside the barn. How he wished he could stay, but he was as good as married, and his father would disown him if he so much as got an inkling that he'd lain with Amy Brown that afternoon. There would be other days for that, he was sure, but now he had to get home.

6

John Sidgwick looked around at his crumbling empire and sighed. High Mill, everyone knew, was on the edge of bankruptcy and there was nothing he could do. The death of his wife had not helped, for her side of the family had withdrawn all support, and now he was counting on old friends and favours, of which he had few. He ran his hand through his thin greying hair and looked out of the office window down onto the busy Skipton street. The cobbled road was busy with shoppers and market traders, and he could just hear the church clock at the top of the high street chime twelve, over the noise of the busy weaving machines on the floors below. That, and his stomach rumbling, reminded him that he had not eaten since early that morning.

He placed his fingers in his waistcoat pocket and felt for the few pence that he allowed himself for his dinner. Damn it, there was not enough there to buy a pie, let alone a gill from the Red Lion, his usual dinner-time tipple. He went and opened the petty-cash box from his desk drawer and took out the last guinea from the almost empty container and pushed it into his breeches pocket, thinking: what the hell, he might be dead tomorrow. Making his way downstairs, past the noise of the weaving machines, he opened the side door into the street, bursting out of it like a bullet from a gun, to escape the hell he had made for himself.

'I'm so sorry – I didn't see you there,' John blustered, as he nearly knocked over one of the prettiest young women he had ever set eyes on in his life.

'No problem, sir. I was unaware there was a door there. I should have seen it and realized it might be used, especially at this time of day.' Isabelle blushed as she regained her composure. 'At dinner time everyone is in a rush to get as much done as possible in the time allowed. I should know, as my mother's mill is just the same.'

'Your mother's mill, my dear? Who is your mother?' John looked at the blushing young thing, who was obviously linked with either the cotton or the woollen industry.

'Yes, my mother is Charlotte Atkinson. She owns Ferndale Mill at Langcliffe. Perhaps you have heard of it, and of her?' Isabelle gazed at the well-dressed gent, who was ageing, but obviously had good manners.

'Indeed I have, and I used to know your mother well. Is she in good health? It is some time since I have seen her.' John cast his mind back to his long-dead friend and his pretty wife. She had always been too much for Joseph Dawson to control, a feisty filly; and he had proved himself right when she had fought tooth and nail to keep Ferndale Mill after her husband's demise. He still kept in touch with Joseph's sister, Dora, and she hated her ex-sister-in-law, with all her charm and brains.

'She's very well, thank you, sir. I will tell her I've had the privilege of meeting you. May I ask your name, sir?' Isabelle waited for his reply.

'I tell you what: I was just going for a spot of dinner. Why don't you join me at the Red Lion? We could catch up on old times. You can tell me how well Ferndale is doing, and make an old man happy by having a young woman on his arm. As for my name, I'm John Sidgwick, and I used to know both your parents well. I own High Mill.' He held out his arm for Isabelle to join him. 'Come on now: I don't bite, and I'm sure your father would have liked us to become acquainted. We were very close, you know?'

'I don't know. And I shouldn't really, as we have had no formal introduction. Although I am catching the coach and horses back to Settle at the Red Lion.' Isabelle hesitated, curiosity getting the better of her. Perhaps this John Sidgwick could tell her something about her father – something that nobody else had told her.

'Dinner is on me, and I can assure you my attentions are quite honourable. I'd just appreciate a pretty face to look at, as I've just lost my wife, and my sons are at university. We don't even have to tell your mother, if that's what is worrying you.' John smiled at the answer to all his prayers. He couldn't believe his luck, in nearly falling over Dawson's only heir: she would be worth a fortune one day.

'Alright, sir, I've just time for some dinner. My name is Isabelle, if you didn't know. I was named after my grandmother.' She linked her arm through his.

'Isabelle, with a voice as clear as a bell. I can see, my dear Isabelle, that we could make this a regular thing. It would make an old man very happy.' John smiled at his conquest. Fate had made him bump into her, and he'd no intention of letting Miss Isabelle Atkinson slip through his fingers.

'That would be very agreeable, sir.' She looked up at the onetime handsome man. What harm could there be, in dining with a fellow mill owner? Her mother would be proud of her. She strolled down the high street of Skipton, glowing with pride as John showered her with compliments. Perhaps an older man would be the answer to her prayers, for young men were so shallow. John Sidgwick was a man whose company she enjoyed more with every step they took. But perhaps he was right; she'd not tell her mother. If John had been a friend of her father, there had been enough upset with the arrival of Harriet in the family and the raising of Dora's ghost.

After their meal, John sat back and patted his mouth with his napkin and watched the pretty little thing trying delicately to finish her plate of cooked ham and pickle. The venue was a bit rough, for one so refined, but it had been the first place that had come into his head when she announced her parentage. Besides, it was all his purse allowed. He looked around the smoke-filled coaching inn with its tobacco-stained walls and low oak beams from which tankards hung, and thought that he could have done so much better, if he meant to impress his guest.

'So, your mother's mill is doing well?' He watched as Isabelle finished her mouthful before speaking.

'Yes, very well, thank you. My mother spends most of her time there – she loves Ferndale.' Isabelle looked across at her dinner companion and imagined him when he was a younger man.

'Aye, your father loved the place as well; built it up from nothing, and bought the grand house you live in. He was a man of vision. If it hadn't been for the Yankees and their war, he would have been alright.' John took a long sip from his glass of wine and smiled across at his young guest.

'We don't talk about him at home. My mother never mentions his name, although everyone tells me I have his looks.' Isabelle looked down at her plate and pushed it away, having had enough of the roughly carved ham and of the boisterous company that surrounded her.

'That you do, lass. He was a handsome man, your father, a real charmer. It was unfortunate he ended up as he did.' John didn't know how much Isabelle knew about her father's dark side and decided not to say any more about him. 'It's getting a bit boisterous in here, let us go outside and wait for your coach. I'm afraid this was not the best of venues to take a young lady to. I never thought, at the time. Next time we will go to the little tea-room across the way.' He drew his chair back and offered Isabelle his arm, pushing back a man who had started to sing as he waved his gill about.

'Next time, sir?' Isabelle looked up and smiled at her protector.

'Aye, if you wish. Next week at the same time? And please, it's John. None of this "sir" business. After all, our families were good friends.'

'I'll look forward to that.' Isabelle smiled, but secretly worried how she was going to explain another trip to Skipton, without her mother becoming suspicious.

John, sensing there was something troubling her, added quickly, not wanting to lose his catch, 'I can come to Settle, if you prefer. The tea-shop on Cheap Street, I seem to recall, does an excellent cream tea.'

Isabelle sighed with relief. 'That would be better, sir.'

'John – it's John. And we will keep our meetings secret. Perhaps it would be better that way.' He escorted Isabelle out into the bright sunlight of the high street and stood with her as she waited for the daily coach between Settle and Skipton.

'I will look forward to our next meeting, John. And

perhaps it is best if we keep this to ourselves, for the time being.' Isabelle blushed.

The coach and horse pulled onto the cobbles in front of the Red Lion and people dismounted from the carriage, while the coachmen unloaded and loaded various cases and packages, as the horses snorted and appreciated the few minutes' rest between destinations.

'Next week it is, my dear. Now you get into the carriage, and safe journey back to Windfell. And don't you worry: discretion is my middle name.' John gave Isabelle his hand as she climbed up the steps into the carriage.

She sat back in the corner of the coach, trying not to show to her fellow passengers the excitement she felt, over having had dinner with John Sidgwick. The next meeting could not come soon enough. He was a gentleman and, what's more, a gentleman of stature. And he was interested in her.

7

Betty Armstrong's short, round body was nearly fit to burst as she told her husband Ted the wonderful news, for the second time that morning.

'So, Mother, them at Windfell have bought our lass a dress shop in Settle to run with their daughter. Is that what our Harriet is saying?' Ted Armstrong looked at his excited wife over the breakfast table and waited for her to reply a little more calmly than the first time she had told him. He stretched his long, lean legs out under the table and wiped a drip of egg yolk from his stubbled chin, watching the late summer sun's rays fill the farmhouse kitchen and wishing that he could escape the relentless banter that his wife was coming out with.

'Aye, Charlotte Atkinson has asked Harriet to go into business with her daughter, Isabelle, and she'll finance them both for a year. It's what our Harriet has always wanted, but you know what this means, don't you, Father? Our Harriet's going to be married to that lad of theirs – she must be, else his mother wouldn't have gone to the bother of renting the shop. You know Danny Atkinson will inherit the lot, after their day. Our lass will want for nowt.' Betty could hardly draw breath as she threw herself into the chair across from her steady husband.

'Now, I wouldn't go so fast, Betty. He hasn't been here to ask for her hand yet, and I'm a stickler for tradition. Don't you go counting your chickens before they've hatched.' Ted looked at the flushed cheeks of his wife and remembered the same look when she had realized that their oldest daughter was to marry one of the Warburton lads from Clitheroe.

'Our Harriet to live at Windfell – now that would be something. I'll have to get a new dress. Oh, and a new hat; a green one, I think, this time with a feather, just like Mrs Dowbiggin had on the other day. It was so bonny, she looked ten years younger and . . .' Betty could hardly draw breath for thinking of her family being upwardly mobile in society.

'Steady now. Mrs Atkinson's only giving Harriet a fresh job, when you think about it. The lad hasn't asked for her hand, and I can understand his mother not wanting our Harriet to work for Dora Bloomenber, if he is serious, given the history between her first husband and her. But we will have to be patient.' Ted chewed his bacon and looked at his wife, who was glowing red with the heat from the kitchen fire and the thought of all the planning in the coming weeks.

'There, you've said it yourself: "serious". He is

85

serious, else she wouldn't have bought the shop. Do you think they'll expect a dowry, because let's face it, the Atkinsons have more brass than we will ever have. I wouldn't want to insult them.' Her face dropped, thinking of their meagre savings and how much the previous year's wedding had cost, just to keep up appearances.

'I tell you what, lass. I'm going down to Settle this afternoon. Why don't we call in and visit the Atkinsons at Windfell? Then you can thank Charlotte Atkinson for helping our lass, and perhaps find out how serious their lad is about her. Then we all know where we stand.' Ted leaned back and listened to his wife reach laying point, like one of his best hens, as she got herself in a fluster about meeting Charlotte and visiting Windfell.

'I couldn't – what would I go in? Would she accept me as a guest? Oh, I've always wanted to have a look around Windfell. Do you think we dare?' Betty tittered and grinned at Ted as he walked towards the door, finishing his breakfast quickly and making good his escape from the madhouse that the kitchen was turning into.

'I'm off to view my sheep. Have yourself ready by twelve. You never know, they might offer you a spot of lunch, if we call at the right time.' Ted quickly closed the door behind him, thankful to be out in the clear air and away from the noise of his panicking wife. He'd never hear the last of the Atkinsons, the new shop and what to wear, if there was to be a wedding. The fellside and his sheep that were suddenly demanding his attention were looking more attractive by the minute. He walked down the garden path that led directly onto the open fell land where High Winskill Farm stood and breathed in the peat-filled moorland air. Glancing back at the small, squat farmhouse tucked under the fellside, he sighed. Why couldn't life be simple, he thought to himself? He'd be happy to the end of his days with his li'l farmhouse and his few sheep; but not Betty, she was always chasing grander things, especially for her girls. One day he hoped she'd realize just how lucky she was and be satisfied with her lot in life.

'How pleasant of you to call on us, Mrs Armstrong.' Charlotte ushered her flush-faced guest into the morning room and bade her sit next to the fire. 'I had Eve light a fire this morning; although it's only late August, I thought it was a little chilly today. I don't quite know how I'll cope, once autumn and winter are upon us. I've got used to the warmer climate down here in the valley and have grown soft in my old age. When I think back to the winters at Crummock, I shudder.' Charlotte smiled at the nervous woman who sat across from her and waited for a reply.

Betty looked around the elegantly decorated room, noting the long green velvet curtains at the window and the ticking clock on the mantelpiece, which had a partly dressed Roman goddess holding a dove adorning the marble escapement.

'Yes, winters are hard up at Winskill, especially

when the yard pump freezes up and we have to break the ice before we have water for the house.' Betty fiddled with her gloves.

'You don't have water piped into your kitchen? That must be really hard. That's another thing I take for granted, although we even had piped water in Crummock, as my father laid pipes down from a water-holding tank when I was young. I remember all the upset, and my grandfather moaning at my father about his new idea, which helped Mrs Cranston so much in the kitchen. It made all the difference to the running of the house, and my grandfather had to eat his words.' Charlotte smiled and remembered her childhood, as she watched the woman in front of her panicking.

'Ted says he'll probably do the same, perhaps next summer if he's got time. In the meantime, I'll just have to grin and bear it. Comes of having two girls, and no lads to help him with those jobs that they could have done together. He's always wanted a son, but it wasn't to be, so I suppose it's all my fault.' Betty blushed even more and decided to change the direction of the conversation. 'You've a beautiful house, Mrs Atkinson. I don't think I've ever been in such a grand house.'

'Yes, I'm lucky, I count my blessings every day and try to make sure my family is happy and content. I presume that is why you are here, Mrs Armstrong – your Harriet has informed you of my offer of employment in a dress shop on Duke Street? I thought seeing that our Daniel is sweet on her, she would be better employed by me, rather than Bloomenber's. I'm sure you know the family history between us, and that it does not need explaining. I assured Harriet that she'd be earning just as much from working for me and would have more freedom in what she did. I aim for her and Isabelle to be their own masters, and I will simply keep an eye on their inputs and outgoings; after all, I can't run it as a charity.' Charlotte waited and watched as Betty grappled with how to ask the question that was preying on her mind.

'Yes, we are grateful that you have made her the offer. Although the break from Dora Bloomenber will be hard for her, because Ezera, when he was alive, was exceptionally kind to her. Mrs Atkinson . . .' Betty paused. 'Just how serious are your son's intentions towards our daughter? He's been walking out with her for some time, and now you ask this of her.'

'Mrs Armstrong, if my son had not shown and laid bare his devotions to your daughter, I would not have given this venture the time of day. Now, Mr Atkinson and I will urge Danny to make his intentions known to you and your good husband. Harriet is a lovely young lady and would be an asset to our family. However, we should not rush these two love-birds, for fear they take flight from being under pressure.'

Betty breathed out deeply. 'I know, I just worried that Harriet is perhaps giving up a good position on a whim. And you know what these young men are like. No disrespect to your Daniel, Mrs Atkinson. He's always a perfect gentleman, and if he was to marry our Harriet we would be overjoyed.'

89

'Well, hopefully, Mrs Armstrong, we can look forward to some good news. And for the time being, we will have our daughters in business together and that is to be celebrated, if nothing else.' Charlotte smiled. 'Tell me, how's your other daughter? Did she not marry one of the Warburton boys?'

'Indeed she did, and our Agnes is as happy as a pig in muck. I don't think it will be long before we hear the sound of tiny feet. Or so I hope, for I long to be a grandmother.' Betty smiled, thinking of her eldest daughter.

'I don't think she will be in muck, married to one of the Warburtons; she truly is fortunate, and I'm sure you will be blessed with grandchildren when they are good and ready.' Charlotte smiled at the eager grandmother-to-be; if Betty was to be an in-law, she would keep her at arm's length. The woman was never satisfied with what she had and lived her life through her children. Harriet, she hoped, would break free of her mother's apron strings and make her own life. 'Can I offer you some lunch perhaps? There is only me here today. Isabelle is visiting her friend William Christie, who's home from Oxford at the moment, and Daniel is over at his grandfather's at Eldroth. As for my husband, he will be making himself busy up at Crummock, where he will probably be getting under the feet of poor Arthur, the farm man. I feel so sorry for Arthur. Archie doesn't realize that he's supposed to take a back seat and leave him to run the farm, but he's never happy when he's sitting here in comfort taking it easy;

he is always itching to be on the farm with his stock. You know what these farmers are like, always looking for the next job.'

Charlotte smiled and walked to the bell pull, which she rang, giving Betty no time to reply before the butler answered the call.

'Can you tell Cook that there will now be two for lunch? Mrs Armstrong will be joining me, Thomson.' Charlotte sat back down in her chair as Thomson nodded in acknowledgment. 'Thomson's new to our family; he's a man of few words, unlike Yates, his predecessor. I grew quite fond of Yates, he taught me a lot when I first came to Windfell.'

'Thank you for offering me lunch. It will be a delight to eat with you.' Betty's face lit up; she was having lunch with Charlotte Atkinson in Windfell Manor, and she never thought the day would dawn when she was lunching with someone of such wealth.

'We will eat in the dining room then. I don't usually bother, when I'm on my own. In fact I must confess I sometimes even go down to the kitchen and eat with the staff. I enjoy catching up with their lives. I always think you should be aware of your staff's problems and lives, for after all they are part of the household.' Charlotte rose and waited for Betty to join her as she walked across the hallway. Her way was interrupted as the main door flew open and Danny entered the hall in a state of panic.

'Where's my father? He's got to come quickly – it's Grandfather, he's ill!' Danny bent double and caught his breath, before gasping out the next few words. 'I've left Mrs Cowperthwaite with him. We think he's had a stroke; he can't talk or walk, or use his left arm.' He nodded his head in recognition of Mrs Armstrong and waited while Charlotte answered.

'He's at Crummock. I'll get Jethro to go for him, he'll get there the fastest.' Charlotte turned to Betty and quickly apologized. 'I'm sorry, Mrs Armstrong, luncheon will have to wait, as you can see we have a crisis on our hands. Please excuse me while I go for our groom and join my husband. Danny, you go back to your grandfather, and I'll come with your father as soon as we can. Call for Dr Burrows on your way back through Settle.' Charlotte picked up her skirts and ran across the hallway, leaving Danny and Betty alone together.

'My pardon, Mrs Armstrong, but I've got to get back to my grandfather.' Danny turned and opened the front door, waiting for a second while Betty spoke.

'I understand, but perhaps we will see you up at Winskill this weekend?' she asked quickly.

'Aye, perhaps.' Danny slammed the door and quickly mounted his sweating horse and galloped off down the driveway, thankful that he had not had to make polite conversation with Harriet's mother. Amy was still on his mind, and he feared that his sudden lack of interest in the fair Harriet was obvious to everyone. He knew his father was probably right: Harriet was more of a lady and had a good heart. But Amy was such a sweet temptation. However, right now it looked like his grandfather was dying and he needed to get back to his bedside, and neither woman should rightfully be on his mind at the moment.

Betty stood in the hallway of Windfell on her own. There was obviously trouble and heartbreak at Windfell, so she'd better go home.

'Are you on your own, ma'am? Can I help you?' Lily, Charlotte's lady's maid, came down the stairs and noticed Betty standing by herself.

'Yes, I was to have lunch with Mrs Atkinson, but I'm afraid she's had to go for the groom. I believe there's a crisis in the family and that she won't be returning. Can you give her my apologies, and I will see myself out. Do tell her I hope Mr Atkinson will be alright, and that I will catch up with her another day.' Betty pulled on her gloves from the hall table and reached for the door handle.

'Please, let me.' Lily reached out and opened the door. 'And I'll pass on your apologies.' She hesitated for a moment. 'Did you say Mr Atkinson was ill?'

'Yes, Mr Atkinson the elder, at Eldroth. Daniel has just come and gone – it sounds like Mr Atkinson has had a stroke – and he was looking for his father.' Through the open door Lily and Betty watched as Jethro, driving the gig with Charlotte alongside him, went past them at breakneck speed.

'Oh dear, poor Mr Atkinson.' Lily watched as the dust rose from behind the gig.

'Yes, truly unfortunate.' Unfortunate indeed, Betty thought, as she had been looking forward to having lunch in the dining room with Charlotte. There would be other days, hopefully, as it seemed that the Atkinsons thought there was a wedding in the air. But now was perhaps not the right time to push for answers.

Archie and Danny stood around the bed of Charlie Atkinson, while Charlotte held his hand tightly as he breathed in slowly and shallowly, faltering occasionally. The family were holding their breath with him, as they waited for the inevitable to happen.

'He's in no pain, I can assure you.' Dr Burrows closed his Gladstone bag and patted Archie on the shoulder, before stepping out into the cool evening's air. He'd been with the old man since just after lunchtime, taking over from Charlie's next-door neighbour, Mrs Cowperthwaite, and watching him slowly drifting off earth's mortal coil with every breath he took. Dr Burrows breathed in deeply and looked at the fields lying in front of him. Across the dale, set between a wooded area, he could just make out the white farmhouse of Crummock, from where Archie had ridden at breakneck speed to be with his dying father. The old man had tried so hard to ask for his beloved son, his words being hardly audible, and only young Danny knowing what his grandfather had wanted. It had been heartbreaking to be witnessing such a sad end to a proud man, but everyone knew Charlie had never been the same since his wife died. The light had gone from within his eyes and his lust for life had slowly dwindled, and now he was about to meet her in the next world, God willing.

Across the farmyard, swallows chattered and swooped, preparing their young for the long flight to warmer climes, and Dr Burrows watched them, feeling the last weakening rays of the summer sun on his face. Charlie Atkinson would no longer feel the sun on his back or the wind on his face, for his days were nearly over.

'Doctor, I think he's gone.' Danny came out and ushered the doctor back into the dark, low-set farmhouse, following him quickly up the stairs. He quietly stood back as Charlotte made way for the doctor to take his grandfather's pulse.

Charlotte looked down on the man who had been her father-in-law, a stubborn old codger, who had thought little of a woman being in business and of the fancy house that his son had lived in. But a Dales man whose love of his family was true, and who had always been right with her, no matter what he truly thought. She squeezed Archie's arm and brushed back a tear from her eye as the doctor confirmed that Charlie had passed into the next world.

'So, that's that then. The old bugger's gone and left me.' Archie breathed in deeply. 'I'll bloody miss the old devil.' He hung his head and thought of all the things he'd done with his father, and of all the times he'd had opportunities to say how much he loved him, but had never got around to doing so. It was too late now.

'We'll all miss him. Won't we, Danny?' Charlotte sniffed.

'Aye, if only for telling me I haven't done that right

95

or this right.' Danny stood at the end of the bed and looked at his grandfather. He'd never seen a dead person before, and he found it strangely fascinating.

'He loved you, lad, and our Isabelle. It's a pity she wasn't here to see him pass.' Archie put his arm around Charlotte. 'He always said I was aiming too high when I married you, but then he grew to love you, along with my mother; they both knew I'd got a good one in you.'

'Yes, he wasn't a bad old stick, I grew really fond of him. I just wish he'd have come and lived with us after your mother died.' Charlotte breathed in deeply, trying to control her grief.

'He'd never have done that, he'd never leave Butterfield Gap. He said the only way he'd leave was to be carried out in a box. Well, he's got his wish. Dr Burrows, I want to thank you for being with him all this time. He always held you in high esteem.'

'It was a privilege to have known him, Archie. Now I'm going to have to be on my way. I presume you'll arrange the undertakers and the funeral, and there's not a lot more we can do this evening.' Dr Burrows put on his top hat, picked up his bag and made for the door of the cottage.

'Yes, I'll see to all that. We'll let him have one more night in the old home. He'd have wanted it that way. I'll sit with him tonight – can't let him be on his own. I owe him that. Good evening, Doctor, and thank you once again.' Archie quietly closed the bedroom door behind the doctor and stood with Danny and Charlotte. 'Danny, you call in at Jackson's in Settle, either tonight or first thing in the morning. Tell them that my father's died and he needs laying out, and a coffin. But take your mother home first. And I'll stay here until they come, and then I know I've done right by my old man.'

'You are stopping here with a dead body!' Danny looked at his father, not wanting to be in his shoes.

'It's only your grandfather – he isn't going to hurt me. He never did when he was alive, so he isn't going to now.' Archie smiled at his son. 'It's the ones that are wick that you've to worry about, not them that are dead. It's the wick ones that'll hurt you.'

'Archie, are you sure?' Charlotte took his hand.

'I'm sure. You go back to Windfell, tell them all that's happened, and I'll be back with you by midday. I'll sleep in the chair next to the fire, and there's food in the pantry, so I'll not go hungry. Besides, his milk cow will want milking in the morning; it'll save one of us riding over first thing. I'll bring it back with me on my return, it can graze on Windfell's land until one of us has time to take it up to Crummock. The rest of the stock will be fine; they'll look after themselves for a day or two. Now, what to do with this old place, I do not know. I presume it is now mine, seeing I'm the only heir.' Archie rubbed his head and looked through the dimming light of Butterfield Gap's kitchen.

'We'll go then, if you are sure. Danny will do as you say.' Charlotte smiled at poor Danny, who looked shattered. He'd done nothing but chase after people all day, and it was beginning to catch up with him. She leaned over and kissed Archie on the cheek, before following Danny out of the door.

Once Charlotte and Danny had left, Archie looked around the house of his birth. He lit the cranberry-coloured oil lamp to fight the incoming dark, and climbed back up the stairs to where his father lay. He stood over the old man, whom he had loved all his life. 'I'll miss you, Father. What do I do now, without you?' He looked around the room, at everything untouched since his mother died, as his father hadn't wanted to throw out anything of hers, he had loved her so much. The washstand with the jug and bowl delicately decorated with violets, and next to them his mother's hair-brush, still with her golden hairs between the bristles. The love between his parents had been so strong and unfaltering, and he'd never heard them say a bad word between them. At least they would be together again now. 'Aye, Father, what a day. I knew you were struggling, but I didn't think I were going to lose you so soon.'

He looked out of the small bedroom window and watched as bats escaped on their nightly venture from under the eaves and, looking out across the valley, he saw a dim glimmer of light at Crummock, as Arthur and Mary lighted their oil lamps and placed them in the windows. He remembered when he had come back home to tell his parents that he was to marry Charlotte and farm Crummock, and live at Windfell. And he started to talk to his dead father again.

'You always said I was mad to want Lottie Booth,

Father. But I'd always secretly loved her since I was sixteen, and I still love her now. Rosie was a good wife and mother, and I'd have made the best of it when she got pregnant by me; and I did love her, once we were married, and I was true to her. I remember you playing hell with me and telling me to do the right thing by her. It broke my mother's heart, I know. I'll always remember her crying as we read our vows, and it broke her heart again when Rosie died, leaving me with our Danny. Aye, our Danny, he nearly cursed me the other day when I pulled him up over the lass at Ragged Hall. He's no idea about life yet. Trouble is, he's a lot like me, Father; likes to have his cake and eat it, always got a smile on his face, especially for the ladies. I must have caused many a sleepless night for my mother. I'm sorry I've been far from the perfect son. I hope you and my mother forgive me, for not being here as often as I should have been, and for not listening to you both. I know now how much you worry over your own children.'

Archie lifted the oil lamp up near his father's face and whispered, 'God bless you, Father, give my love to mother when you see her.' And then he slowly made his way down to the kitchen, where he decided he'd sleep in the Windsor chair until Jackson's, the undertakers, came to prepare his father and best friend, ready to be put to rest.

8

'Well, he had a good turnout. There were a lot of faces there that I hadn't seen for a long time. He'd have been happy, if he'd have been able to see how many were there to pay their respects.' Archie took off his mourning jacket and stood in front of the Adam fireplace in his shirt and waistcoat, undoing his cravat, before helping himself to a glass of whisky. 'That cravat has been driving me mad all day.'

'Yes, he's had a good send-off, he couldn't have wished for more. And the Jacksons had done him proud with the coffin.' Charlotte sighed and then sat down next to Isabelle. 'Are you alright, Isabelle? I couldn't help but notice you were crying.' She patted her daughter's hand and smiled at Isabelle's tear-stained face.

'I'll just miss him. I didn't see him much, but he was always very kind to me.'

'Aye, he never had a bad word for anyone; always

said you should live and let live. Although, if you stepped out of line, you'd know about it. You think I'm an old devil, our Danny, but you should have been brought up by my father. You'd not have got away with half that you do with me.' Archie grinned at his son.

'Didn't think that was possible. I don't seem to get away with nowt.' Danny poured a small whisky and looked out of the parlour's window, wanting to escape from the feeling of gloom that had been surrounding them since his grandfather's death.

'I spoke to Walker, the solicitor, at the funeral. You all know that I couldn't find my father's will when we looked through his house. In fact I don't think he made one, as he never spoke of it to me. However, Walker says there shouldn't be a problem. I'm his only son, so Butterfield Gap automatically comes to me. Which leaves me wondering what to do with it, as it's hardly big enough to make a decent living on. Isabelle, it's no good for you; you're no farmer, and you've no suitor as of yet. Which makes me look at you, Danny: do you fancy taking it on? It might give you an incentive to get proposing to that lass of yours.'

All eyes turned to look at Danny, who seemed shocked.

'No, Father, not Butterfield Gap, it's only thirty acres. Thirty acres of the roughest moorland you could wish on me. I couldn't make a living there. I do appreciate your offer, but it's not for me.' Danny didn't want the smallholding, or the ties it brought with it, but at the same time he knew he appeared ungrateful.

'It would be a roof over your heads for you and Harriet, until you get started, and we'd give you an allowance to help – you'd not be penniless.' Archie stood with his hands behind his back and scowled at his son. If he'd have been offered that, when he was with Rosie, he'd have been down on his knees thanking his father.

'I might not want to marry Harriet just yet, have you thought of that? And I want to make my own money, not be reliant on an allowance and be forever in your pocket,' Danny spouted out to a surprised family.

'Danny, what's got into you? Show your father some respect.' Charlotte looked at her ungrateful stepson.

'I don't mean to be disrespectful, but you are all pushing me into marriage, and I don't know if I want that just yet. I'm sorry, Mother, but I won't have my life planned for me.' Danny looked at his family, put his glass down and stormed out of the room.

Charlotte looked at Archie. 'Well, we all know where we stand now. I can't understand it; a few weeks ago he would have lain down his life for Harriet. Now, when we mention her name, he flies up at us. I wish I'd never looked at that shop, if that's what is upsetting him. I've a good mind to change my mind, as I haven't signed the lease yet. I thought I was doing right, when I made Harriet welcome in the family. I thought he loved her.'

'Please, don't change your mind, Mother. Harriet and I have so many good ideas and all of my friends are going to support us. I'll talk to Danny and see what's wrong with him. I know Harriet loves him dearly – she never stops talking about him,' Isabelle pleaded.

'I tell you what's wrong with him. He's had his head turned by that flibbertigibbet at Ragged Hall. I sent him over there the other month, and he's never been the same since. He talked to Amy, old Bill Brown's lass. All the farm lads in the district are sweet on her, for she's got a way with the men, not to put too fine a point on it. As long as he only *talked* to her, if you know what I mean.' Archie's temper with his son was getting the better of him.

'Father, remember we have Isabelle present,' Charlotte reminded her ruddy-faced husband, before saying exactly how she felt about Archie's confession. 'Daniel had better not have been seeing that worthless girl and be cheating on Harriet. I'm disgusted with him – he's certainly no gentleman, if he has.'

'Anyone who has an ounce of respectability doesn't associate with Amy,' Isabelle pointed out. 'She does have a reputation, and none of my circle ever associate themselves with her. Our Danny's a fool if he's got caught up with her. I may not have been keen on Harriet, when she was first with Danny, but I've grown to like her. She will be an asset to the family, and I think both of us will work wonderfully together in the shop. Besides, to hear her talk, Danny has almost promised his hand to her, so he can't possibly go back on his word. It would cause such a scandal.' Isabelle was astonished at her brother's lack of morals and judgement.

'That's why Mrs Armstrong came here. I thought there was something more to it than a social call and enquiring about Harriet's position in the shop. She knows Danny's proposed on the quiet to Harriet. He's going to make our family the talk of the district if he's not careful. Oh, the scandal of it! Going back on a betrothal of marriage, for the sake of the local trollop – and that's what she sounds like to me.' Charlotte stood up and paced the floor.

'Aye, I wish I'd never sent him over there. I thought he had more sense, and even if Amy did give him the eye, I thought he loved Harriet enough to ignore her.' Archie turned and looked at himself in the mantel mirror and saw an older version of his son staring back at him. Who was he to judge Danny? It was history replaying itself, at his expense this time.

Later in the evening Isabelle decided to speak to her brother; after all, her new business life was in jeopardy, as well as the respected name of the family. A decent man did not offer to marry a respectable woman and then change his mind.

'Mother and Father are worried about you, Danny, and so am I, come to that.' She sat in her brother's bedroom on the side of his bed while he looked out of the window, with one of his arms resting on the wooden panel of the frame. 'We all love you and want the best for you.' She looked at herself in the large oval mirror of the mahogany wardrobe and waited for a reply.

'Worried about me, are you? Worried what I might do next, you mean. Worried that I won't do what's best for the family.' Danny turned and looked at his sister.

'Father says it's Amy Brown that's turned your head. Is he right? She's not a patch on Harriet, you do know that, don't you?' Isabelle looked at her disgruntled brother as he sat next to her on the bed.

'So that's what he thinks, is it? Well, he's right: she has, or not so much turned my head as opened my eyes. I thought that I loved Harriet, and I do. But there's so much more out there – Amy's shown me that; she laughs when she wants to laugh, she doesn't care about formalities and what people think of her. All I hear at home is what is expected from me: to act the perfect gentleman, to run a farm, get married and step into my father's shoes when the time comes. I'm twenty-three, not two hundred and three.' Danny ran his hands through his long blond hair and looked at his sister.

'Oh, Danny, have you been seeing Amy on the quiet? You'll break Harriet's heart, you know. She loves you dearly.' Isabelle reached for her brother's hand and squeezed it. 'Everyone knows what Amy's like; she's friends with all the men of the district, and that's why she's not the marrying kind, and one day she'll be a lonely old lady. Unless she gets caught out with a child.' Isabelle blushed, for such things were never talked about between her and her brother.

'Well, at least she's happy and has plenty of male company. Unlike you; hardly any male suitors knock on our door for you. What happened to Robert Knowles? Left you with a mucky kitten and never came back again.' Danny smiled at his sister.

'Robert's as daft as a brush, just like his kitten. Anyway, you might be surprised: there might be someone calling on me shortly, you'll have to wait and see. But seriously, Danny, don't go back to Amy, she's just playing with you. I hope you haven't got too friendly with her and done something you might regret. Harriet does love you, and our parents just want the best for you, no matter how much they moan.' Isabelle hugged her brother and kissed him on the cheek. 'We all do.'

'Sometimes I wonder.' Danny kissed her back; he knew Isabelle was trying her best to keep the family strong. God help him if there was a hint of scandal in the Atkinson family: that would never do. After all, there was no skeletons in their cupboard; they'd only been the talk of the district a few years back. Danny couldn't help but think there was a hint of hypocrisy in the family's reaction to his actions. 'I'll see. Amy is, as you say, perhaps not the right choice for a gentleman, but she's such fun and I can talk to her so easily.

I feel content when I'm in her arms. And, Isabelle, please don't tell our parents, but I lay with her the last time I was there. I know I shouldn't have done, but it just happened. She made it all seem so easy and natural. Sex is untalked-about in this household, and Harriet won't even show me her ankle.' Danny blushed at a worried Isabelle; this wasn't something you confessed to your sister.

'Oh, Danny, how could you? Harriet's a lady, unlike Amy. You'll just have to hope nothing comes from this dalliance. Father would kill you, if he knew.' Isabelle scowled; she hated Amy Brown for leading her brother astray.

But never mind me. Who's this Romeo who's going to be calling on my little sister?' Danny felt awkward about his admission and changed the subject quickly.

'Not telling, you'll have to wait and see.' Isabelle's mood lightened. 'Anyway, you don't know him – he's not one of your smelly friends, all cow dung and sheep.' She laughed and got up from the bed.

'I'll make you tell me.' Danny jumped up and threatened to tickle his sister.

'You'll have to catch me first,' Isabelle screamed and started running.

Downstairs Charlotte and Archie listened to the screams and giggles from above.

'Sounds like Isabelle has brought him round. I knew Danny couldn't sulk about things forever.' Archie looked across at Charlotte.

'We'll see. They are as thick as thieves, them two.

Secrets are their strong point, if you remember.' Charlotte sighed.

Danny decided to walk up to Ragged Hall from the road that led up along Eldroth. It was a warm, hazy September day and the bees and hornets buzzed around him and his horse as he walked with a joyful heart into the farmyard of Ragged Hall. He tethered his horse to the iron ring that was attached to the side of the barn and walked to knock on the open farmhouse door. He felt that he was betraying his family, as his heart beat faster at the thought of seeing Amy and hearing her voice; he was captivated by her, and although he knew Isabelle and his family were right, he didn't want to believe them.

He lifted his hand to make his presence known, but before he could do so, he heard laughter coming from within the barn. He turned and almost ran across the yard to see his beloved Amy, stopping short as he reached the barn doors. There he stood still for what seemed an age, but was in reality only a few seconds. Right in the middle of the newly mown hay, frollicking with her skirts above her knees, was Amy with another man. Danny stood and stared at them. It was true that Amy was nothing but a trollop; she didn't love him. He cursed as he dropped his crop and reached for it quickly, hoping no one had heard him, then he swiftly untied his horse and walked it out of the yard.

'Danny, Danny, come back. He means nothing to

me – we were just having fun,' Amy yelled at him as he walked past the hedgerow of late-summer flowers.

He carried on walking, without turning for the lass who had nearly ruined his life. His father had been right: she'd have broken his heart, if he'd thrown everything away for her. Come to think of it, she'd broken it already, if he was truthful. Now he had to pick up where he'd left off, and do right by Harriet and take on Butterfield Gap.

Arthur leaned over the gate, watching the herd of belted Galloways graze on the new pasture they had just been turned into, with Archie by his side.

'I might introduce a few Herefords into the herd next year, Arthur. They are good beef cattle. But I like my little Galloways; they are hardy little beasts, just right for up here, with the winters like they are.'

'Aye, they seem to be happy enough and don't take a lot of looking after,' Arthur agreed.

'It might be an idea to graze Butterfield Gap with Galloways; they wouldn't take any looking after, seeing as my lad doesn't want to farm it. I could always rent the house, I suppose. I don't know what to do with it. The trouble is, I've enough on with here and Windfell. Someone has to keep an eye on the grounds and outbuildings, because Lottie's enough on with the house and Ferndale, and now she's involving herself with this new dress shop that she's opening with Isabelle and Harriet. The Gap is home, you know, always will be. Lottie loves Crummock as her true home, and I've always loved the Gap and will class it as my home.' Archie turned and looked over at the long, whitewashed farmhouse of Charlotte's; this was his home now, along with Windfell, and he'd no real need for Butterfield Gap. It was just the sentiment that made him want to keep it.

'If I'm talking out of turn, Mr Atkinson, do tell me.' Arthur paused. 'I just wondered if you'd happen to consider selling it to me and Mary. It doesn't look like we are going to be blessed with children, so it would keep us two quite comfortably, and I've enough savings to make you a decent offer. I know it's a bit soon to ask, seeing as your father isn't yet cold in his grave, but I wouldn't want to miss out on it.' Arthur felt awkward, for not only was he turning his back on a good job at Crummock, but he was perhaps being too forward for his position, with the man who had helped him throughout his life.

'Well, blow me, Arthur, I didn't expect that. You'd leave Crummock to farm the Gap? It'll need a lot of care. Nothing's been done properly for the last few years, and my father had lost heart in it, without my mother.' Archie looked at his farm man and saw the determination in his eyes.

'I know, but the land would be mine, and that makes all the difference. I want to be my own man and Mary deserves her own house. Besides, we rattle around Crummock like two peas in a pod. We only live in the two main rooms downstairs, so we don't do justice to the old house. We are grateful for our positions with you, Mr Atkinson, but I'm sure you understand.' Arthur was quick not to offend his master, for he'd no urge to upset his good relations with Archie.

'Aye, I can understand. There's nothing like picking up a piece of soil and letting it run through your fingers and thinking: this is all mine. I spend many an hour just standing looking around at my lot, thanking the Lord for what I've got; and you are right: you can't beat it. Let me have a think about it. Once the Gap is signed over to me we'll take it from there. I promise you I will give you first refusal.' Archie patted the worried-looking man on his back. He didn't think any worse of Arthur; it was good that he wanted to improve his life, and his own family farm and Arthur were a match made in heaven.

'Thank you, sir, I appreciate it. It'd mean a lot to my Mary to have her own kitchen.' Arthur breathed a sigh of relief.

'Of course it would. We've got to keep our womenfolk happy, else it's the worse for us. Eh, Arthur?'

'Aye, too true.' Arthur grinned and prayed that he could afford the farm he'd had his eye on for a good few years.

Danny looked at himself in the mirror of his wardrobe and combed back his hair. He picked up the posy of flowers that the young girl in the shop down in Settle had put together for him. He remembered her giggling as he asked for flowers that showed true love. She had assured him that a bunch of red and white chrysanthemums portrayed love and truth, with an added sprig of ivy for fidelity.

He opened his bedroom door and listened for any sound coming from the manor and leaned over the bannister, watching Thomson rub his finger along the hallway table for signs of dust before disappearing into the drawing room, then Danny made good his escape. Closing the front door quietly behind him, he thanked Jethro for preparing the horse and gig and drove quietly down the path from Windfell. He'd told nobody of his decision to propose in earnest for the hand of Harriet and now, with the rest of the family at church on the last Sunday of September, he was going formally to ask permission from her father and put the engagement ring that he carried in his waistcoat pocket on Harriet's finger. He calmly drove the horse and trap up the high, winding road to Winskill and looked around him at the limestone escarpment that made up the backbone of the Pennines. Looking down towards nearly as far as the Lancashire coastline at Heysham, he breathed in deeply. This was the day when things changed: he was to be a married man and hope-fully, in the future, a father. He only hoped he was doing the right thing.

'Good morning, Mrs Armstrong. Is Mr Armstrong in?'

Danny stood outside the porch of High Winskill and waited as a flustered Betty Armstrong left him waiting on the doorstep, as she announced to her husband

Danny's need to see him and yelled to her daughter to stay upstairs, out of the way of men's business.

'Danny, what are you doing here?' Harriet leaned out of her bedroom window and whispered down to her beau, only for her mother to grab her back into her room and close the window firmly.

'Now then, lad. What can I do for you?' Ted stood in the doorway in his shirt sleeves, with his braces hanging around his waist. 'I was just having forty winks, with it being Sunday. You've not caught me at my best.' He pulled the braces back onto his shoulders and looked at the nervous young man holding a bunch of flowers in his hand. 'Them for me, I take it?' Ted smiled.

'No, no – they are for Harriet, but you can have them if you want.' Danny's face fell.

'Nay, lad, you'd better give them to the women. They aren't quite my colour. Now, is it some business you are wanting to talk to me about or have you woken me up for the hell of it?' Ted played with the young man; he knew damn well what Danny had come for; he himself had had the same look on his own face when he'd asked for Betty's hand from her father.

'It's business, Mr Armstrong,' Danny said solemnly.

'Well, you'd better come in then. Sit yourself down over there in Betty's chair and tell me what I can do for you.' Ted urged Danny to sit in the rocking chair next to the blackened Yorkshire range, in which a joint of beef was roasting, by the aroma that filled the small homely kitchen. 'Well now, what is it?' Ted sat across from him and waited as Danny fumbled with his flowers and his words.

'I'd be grateful if you would give your permission for me to marry Harriet and make her my wife. We've been walking out now for some months, and I realize that she is the one I want to spend my life with.' Danny had rehearsed the words over and over in his head and waited now for Ted Armstrong's reply.

'Well now, is that how it lies? Do you love our Harriet, and can you afford to look after her in the way she needs?' Ted kept a stern face; he knew well enough that she'd made a good catch.

'I can, Mr Armstrong. My father's already offered us Butterfield Gap, once we are married, along with an allowance. And of course my mother is to sign for the lease of the shop that Isabelle and Harriet are to make their own next week. Once we are married, it would be up to Harriet if she still wished to work there.'

'Well, it sounds as if you have it all worked out. You look after her, mind; once you are married she is yours, but I'll not see either of my girls go without anything. And I'll not be afeared of speaking my mind, if I think anything's amiss. Right, lad, I hope you are both going to be happy, and you have my blessing. And for heaven's sake give our lass them flowers before they lose any more petals. And you two can stop giggling at the top of the stairs and come down here,' Ted shouted up the stairs. 'I heard you listening in, and the poor lad

114

had enough to say, without hearing you two.' He patted Danny on the back. 'Well done, lad, welcome to the family.'

Danny looked up at Harriet as she made her way down the stairs with her mother behind her. 'Harriet, as you've heard, I've asked for your hand in marriage.' He fumbled in his waistcoat pocket and pulled out the box that contained the engagement ring. He held out the bunch of flowers, thrusting them into her hands as he dropped down onto one knee to propose. 'Harriet, I would be very proud if you would become my wife.' He looked up into her blue eyes and waited for her reply, as she picked the diamond solitaire out of the box. Her eyes filled with tears as he rose to both knees and helped her place it on her finger.

'I thought you were never going to ask. Of course I'll be happy to marry you.' Harriet smiled, her hand trembling as he held it tenderly.

'For heaven's sake, kiss her, lad, or have I to do it for you?' Ted stood back and watched the loving couple, as his wife sobbed at the bottom of the stairs, hardly able to speak between sobs. 'I think you've wasted money on them flowers, lad, they look a bit the worse for wear.' He grinned as more petals fell on the ground, the flowers crushed in the pair's passionate clinch.

Danny looked at the fallen petals: love, truth and fidelity, the florist had said, and he only hoped he could keep to all three. He held Harriet tightly and whispered, 'I love you, too, forever and a day.'

*

115

The drawing room at Windfell was buzzing with the news of the engagement of Danny to Harriet, and the Atkinson family welcomed their new member with open arms.

'Congratulations and welcome to our family, Harriet. I can't say it comes as a surprise. I knew Danny was smitten, else I wouldn't have offered you the position in the new shop.' Charlotte kissed her future daughter-in-law on her cheeks and then reached for the bell-pull to summon Thomson. 'What do your parents say? Are they pleased?'

'My mother couldn't stop crying. She barely touched her roast-beef dinner, and Father had to tell her to stop snivelling. But both are happy for us, thank you, Mrs Atkinson,' Harriet gasped, as Charlotte ordered Thomson to bring a chilled bottle of champagne from the cellar.

'I think we should all celebrate in style. It's not every day your son gets engaged.' Charlotte looked at Archie, who was strangely quiet. 'We've just to find a match for Isabelle now, haven't we, Archie? Else she's going to be an old maid.'

'Someone will turn up, no doubt. There's no need to rush, is there, lass?' Archie smiled. 'Better to be sure that he's the right one and take your time.' He looked at Danny and then reached for a glass of champagne from the silver tray with which Thomson had walked into the drawing room.

'Well, Harriet is the right one for me, Father, of that

I'm sure.' Danny looked across at his father, knowing there was an underlying question.

'I'm sure she is, lad. Now let's raise our glasses to you both.' Archie stood up and put his arm around Harriet.

'Yes, cheers, everyone! And don't worry about me. I'll surprise you all one day.' Isabelle winked at her brother; she was glad he'd done right by Harriet.

'Cheers! Now when are you thinking of setting the wedding? I could have had a word with the vicar this morning.' Charlotte sat down and beckoned Harriet next to her on the sofa.

'Can I be a bridesmaid?' Isabelle pulled up a chair next to Harriet. 'Can I design your wedding dress? It will do the new business so much good, if we make your wedding dress really beautiful. And you have such a good figure that we can't go wrong.'

'Isabelle, you must take after me, by putting the business before Harriet's needs. It is up to Harriet to say what she wants. Now, the date?' Charlotte held Harriet's hand and looked into her eyes.

'We thought perhaps March or April; it would be spring then and getting a little warmer. I would love you to design my dress, Isabelle. I only hope that I will do justice to it. And, as you say, it would promote our new business together.' Harriet felt aglow with all the love she was being shown. It was a day she'd never forget.

'Perfect, an Easter wedding perhaps, at Langcliffe?'

Charlotte smiled to herself, thinking of where the reception was to be held and what flowers to arrange.

'Yes, perhaps. I'll have to speak to my mother and father, and see what they wish. My mother was so dizzy with excitement that we never got around to that subject this morning.' Harriet could see that Charlotte would take over her wedding day, if given the chance, when it really was her parents' duty to do so.

'Yes, of course, I was forgetting myself. But we will support and finance any decisions you make.' Charlotte smiled at the tactful young woman, whose cheeks were flushed after sipping her champagne.

'Father, do you think I could talk to you in private in the morning room, please? There's something I need to discuss.' Danny placed his glass down and looked across at Archie.

'Aye, lad, we'll leave the women to it. Let them discuss lace and flowers, which they seem to be obsessed with.' Archie was thankful to have the opportunity to talk to his son alone, and wasted no time in closing the morning-room door to discuss Danny's engagement announcement.

'Well, you took us by surprise there, Danny. I thought you were having doubts about Harriet, and that you wanted to sow a few wild oats before you settled down.' Archie stood in front of Danny, his hands behind his back, and looked at his son, for whom he would lay his life down.

'I was wrong, Father. Amy Brown was all you said she was. Whereas Harriet is all you could wish for in a wife. It's time I sorted out my life, and the offer you made of Butterfield Gap to start our married lives in was very generous, and I must have sounded like a petulant child when I lost my temper. I apologize for my headstrong actions and would like to take you up on your offer of farming Grandfather's place.'

'Oh, Danny, if only you had talked to me yesterday, before I went to see Arthur up at Crummock. He made me an offer for Butterfield Gap and, seeing you were so against getting wed and living there, I accepted it. I cannot go back on my word.' Archie looked at his crestfallen son.

'I see. It's my own fault; you should never look a gift-horse in the mouth. Good for Arthur: he and Mary will be well suited there.' Danny felt his world falling apart.

'But that leaves Crummock empty. Now I'll have to talk to Charlotte, because Crummock is hers and I can't promise anything! But why don't you take it on? It's a grand farm to raise a family in, and you can always get a farm lad to help, and a cook and maid if Harriet still wants to play dressmaker with Isabelle. If she's to be mistress of Crummock, she might think differently.' Archie put his arm around Danny's shoulders. 'You are sure about this wedding, lad? It's no good going through with it if you don't love her.'

'I'm sure, Father; Harriet's the one for me. I'd be grateful if you could talk to Mother regarding Crummock. It's belonged in her family for generations and perhaps she'd prefer Isabelle to live there, if she gets married.' Danny knew his father's concerns and wanted to assure him that he was doing the right thing.

'It's done then, lad, I'll ask her tonight. Now, about that tup at Ragged Hall. I'll go and pick it up next week, saves you a job.' Archie waited for a response from his blushing son.

'Aye, you go and collect it, because I'll not be going there again. I never want to see Amy Brown again, so you needn't worry about that.'

9

The narrow cobbled streets of Settle were thronged with busy shoppers as Charlotte, Isabelle and Harriet made their way down the road. Passing Bloomenber's jewellers, Charlotte turned and looked at Harriet.

'Are you regretting giving in your notice, Harriet? Did Dora treat you alright, once she knew you were leaving?' Charlotte glanced anxiously at Harriet.

'I am, slightly. Mrs Bloomenber changed, once she realized I was leaving. She really does have a cruel tongue on her. Anyway, I have a new life now, with my lovely soon-to-be sister-in-law. The whole of Settle will soon be coming to us for fittings, won't they, Isabelle?'

'Indeed they will. We'll keep up with the finest of Paris's fashions and have the finest linens and silks, because of dear Mama and her contacts.' Isabelle reached for Harriet's hand and held it tightly.

'Right, well, here we are, ladies. Here is the future Atkinson's: Milliner & Ladies' Outfitters, of Duke

Street, Settle. I hope you don't mind, Harriet, but I thought that now you and Danny are to wed, we might as well call it "Atkinson's". I'll get a painter and signwriter to give the shop a fresh new look, as it looks a bit neglected at the moment.'

The three women stood back and looked at the outside of the shop; its brown varnished windowpanes and door were peeling, and there was an unpainted piece of wood where the previous owner's plaque had hung.

'I know it looks a bit tired on the outside, but it's a different matter inside, isn't it, Isabelle? We both had a look inside it the other month and were quite impressed.' Charlotte noticed Harriet's face, as she glanced at the shop's frontage.

'I rather hoped that my name would be over the door, as I will be making the dresses,' Harriet said quietly, not wanting to sound too precious.

'It is your name, dear, for you will soon be an Atkinson. Besides, it is Atkinson money that is enabling you to do this. My money, made possible by working long, hard hours at Ferndale Mill. I didn't have it all on a plate, just for the taking. Besides, Archie asked me last night if I would agree to Danny and you living at Crummock, which I of course do. We couldn't see you destitute, and my grandchildren will want a stable home when they appear on the scene, now won't they? So I think I have every right to have the family name over the door.' Charlotte turned the key in the peeling door and threw it open, letting the morning sunshine flood onto the shop floor, oblivious to Harriet's startled expression.

'Danny's to farm Crummock . . .' Harriet echoed Charlotte.

'Yes, I agreed to it last night, with his father. After your wedding you can move straight into the farm. Arthur, who farms there, is to buy Butterfield Gap, and then you and Danny are free to live in Crummock. It gives us six months to see if we can make a success of this shop, and for both you and Isabelle to decide if this is where your hearts truly lie. I thought if you both decided you did not want to continue with the venture, at least it has my name over the door and I'll just employ a new seamstress.' Charlotte looked at the delight upon Harriet's face and then at Isabelle. 'Don't worry; we won't forget you, when you find your ideal man. We'll find you a property as well. But Danny is the farmer in the family, and it follows that he should have Crummock.'

'I'm delighted for Danny and Harriet – of course he should have it. I wouldn't want to live there anywhere, it is too far out in the wilds for me. But Harriet may find it hard to get into Settle every day, if our business is successful.' Charlotte looked at Harriet with a worried expression.

'We'll cross that bridge when we come to it. Archie was talking about employing a farm lad to help Danny out, and he could always bring Harriet down to work, if she wishes. A lot can happen in six months. Now, what do you think of the shop? I've ordered three dressmaker's dummies, and they should be getting delivered by wagon tomorrow. I thought you could dress three of them and place them in both windows, to show people what you can both do. And an order of silks, satins and some Irish linen, along with lace, cotton, bobbins, buttons, and all the things I thought that you would need to start your business, is on its way from Liverpool. Of course you have an ample supply of cotton from Ferndale; you just need to order direct from Bert Bannister once a week, and I've arranged for him to give you a good discount. The rest, ladies, is up to you. You've got to stun the good ladies of Settle and district with your designs.'

Charlotte watched the two girls as they looked around the bare room. It was going to take a lot of work to knock the old shop into shape, but if they were determined enough, they'd do it. It could be the making of them both.

'We could put the material on these shelves, for people to choose from; and these drawers are ideal for all the haberdashery pieces.' Isabelle ran her hand along the dusty counter and screwed up her face. 'Can we borrow Nancy for a day or two, just to clean the place?'

'You certainly cannot. This is your business, and you can do the work. It will not kill you.' Charlotte looked sternly at her daughter.

'I don't mind doing the cleaning, for it will mean that the business is truly ours. You draw some styles, while I spruce up the place. I see we have a back room, where I can do the sewing and the fitting, if customers prefer to have a personal fitting.' Harriet's mind was racing with the potential of the property.

Isabelle gave a sigh of relief. She was above doing the cleaning. Besides, she had an important meeting at lunchtime.

'Harriet, I wondered if I should look at one of those new sewing machines – the one that the sales-man was showing me in a leaflet, when he came to the mill,' said Charlotte. 'Do you think you could use one? He said it saves hours of hand-sewing, but I don't know how the stitching would compare.' Charlotte admired Harriet's sense of industry; she was the one with her heart in the business.

'I could try one, but I must warn you: I'm not good with contraptions.'

'Right, well, I'll ask him for a demonstration and we will see if you like it. Also, Sally Oversby – a woman who works in the mill, and whom I have great admiration for – makes absolutely beautiful little posy bags in her spare time. Perhaps it might be an idea to come to an agreement with her, to display some of her work in your window. It would be extra income for her, and it would make a good complement to your clothes.'

'If her work is to be trusted, Mother.' Isabelle only wanted the best-quality goods in the shop. 'And of course we will have to get a ready supply of black crêpes and silks for mourning dress, and be able to supply at quite short notice; and perhaps some furs, as they are so in fashion at the moment.'

'Right then, ladies, here is the key. Have another one cut and then you have one each. And now the business is all yours. You'll have to work hard, but that should be the making of you both. I'll inspect the books on a weekly basis, to make sure you are heading in the right direction. And, Harriet, I will let you know about a sewing machine as soon as I see my salesman.' Charlotte left the two young women looking around them, partly in awe about what they were about to take on, and partly excited at the prospect of having their own business.

'It's no good standing around, feeling sorry for ourselves. Let's go and get a brush, some polish and some cleaning cloths and get ready for all the stock arriving tomorrow.' Harriet picked up a bristleless broom from the corner of the room that was gathering dust. 'I think this one's had its day.'

'Can I leave you to it, Harriet? I wouldn't know where to start with cleaning, and I promised to meet up with a friend for lunch. I'll take the key to be copied and cut, while you have a tidy up. I promise I'll pull my weight, once the shop is up and running. Besides, I'm best at home sketching some designs for our portfolio, to show our customers.' Isabelle made a flurry of excuses, not wanting to get her hands dirty.

'I'll clean the shop. Go on and have your lunch with your friend. The shop will be fine left unlocked while I go and get brushes and the rest from the hardware shop, and I'll pick up the key from the locksmith's before I go home.' Harriet pulled her shawl around her and watched as a smile broadened on Isabelle's face.

'Thank you, my dear. I didn't want to miss my lunch date, but please don't mention it to my mother. I'd rather she didn't know about my meeting.' Isabelle checked that her hat was straight, in the long, dusty mirror behind the counter, before kissing Harriet on the cheek. 'You are a true sister-in-law.'

Harriet sighed as she watched Isabelle swan out of the shop. She hoped it wasn't always going to be this way: her doing all the donkey work, and Isabelle doing as little physical work as possible. But Isabelle had the charm of her mother and would probably attract the customers they needed, while she herself lacked vital contacts, so all was fair in love and war. She leaned on the useless brush and looked around her; she'd soon clean it all up, and it probably looked worse than it was. Charlotte was right: it was a good premises, with just a rough exterior. She'd be forever grateful to her future mother-in-law: a business, and now a farm to raise her and Danny's children in. Children: that would be the next step and one she looked forward to; but before then she would have to teach Isabelle to sew. Now, was Isabelle having lunch with someone or was that just a bluff – seeing that her mother was not to be told about it? She was definitely a dark one who liked to keep secrets to herself. She must get that from her real father, Harriet thought, because Charlotte was as open as a book and as honest as the day was long. The Atkinsons were not without their secrets; they were as plentiful as their bank account was bulging, she thought, as she stepped outside onto the street to buy her cleaning materials.

Isabelle quickly made her way through the streets of Settle, turning up Cheapside and reaching the small, homely tea-room, where she had arranged to have luncheon, half an hour later than agreed. She opened the door with zest and quickly looked around the busy room, eager to search out John Sidgwick's face. He was there, looking as dapper as usual, his grey hair and moustache immaculately preened, and he rose as he saw Isabelle enter the room. How she loved the man she had been meeting secretly at this intimate tea-room for the last few weeks.

'I thought you weren't going to show.' John pulled back a chair for Isabelle to join him at the table, then reached out his hand for hers, as she smiled at him with all the love he had hardly dared to dream about.

'Don't be silly. You know I would never let you down. I just got held up with my mother and Harriet, and the new venture with the shop. I've left Harriet cleaning, all by herself. I don't think she was happy with me worming out of the cleaning, but I couldn't say I was meeting you – not yet, not until my parents know about you.' She looked into the hazel eyes of her secret lover and withdrew her hand quickly as the waitress came to take their order.

'Your mother will not be happy, for she will remember me drinking with your father and will say that I'm old enough to be your father, which I am, in truth,' John whispered, as the waitress politely took their order and disappeared into the kitchen to prepare the sandwiches they had both agreed on.

'She should be glad that I'm happy. And just because you used to be friends with my father doesn't mean you are like him. Besides, I don't care what they say. I love you dearly, and nothing will ever change that. I am so glad we met that day when you nearly bowled me over on Skipton high street.'

'In truth, I wouldn't say I was friends with your father. I was taken in by him; he saw a future for cotton that none of the rest of us did. He was so enigmatic – you just believed anything he told you, and wanted everything he said to be true. I can understand your mother's adoration of him. Alas, I've never been to university myself, although – as you know – my two sons are there, James at Oxford and Rob at Cambridge. I have great expectations of both of my boys and hope they prove to be worthy gentlemen, and make their way in society in a respectful and prosperous way. A way that would make their late mother proud of them.' John hesitated and thanked the waitress as she placed their lunch in front of them, along with a teapot and cups of tea.

'If they are anything like their kind father, you need not worry, sir. Because he is one of the kindest people I know.' Isabelle squeezed her lover's hand.

'My dear Isabelle, you are like a breath of fresh air to me. You are beautiful, elegant and a joy to be with. I am simply afraid you will soon become bored with this old man who is in front of you.' John smiled at the young woman whom he had led to believe had captured his heart, and held his breath, wondering if he dared ask the next question.

'I will never get bored with you, John. You are everything I could wish for. As for age, what does that matter, as long as we are happy?' Isabelle squeezed his hand. She loved John Sidgwick; young men were such fools, they had no common sense and did not know how to treat her. Whereas John had been the utter gentleman since the day they met.

'Isabelle . . .' He hesitated, not knowing if he was being a fool, as his close friends had told him he was. 'Isabelle, would you do me an honour and make this foolish old man very happy, by marrying me?'

Isabelle couldn't believe her ears and was speechless as she looked across at John, who was waiting for her answer with bated breath. 'Oh, I don't know – I mean, you've taken me by surprise.'

The bell rang on the door, interrupting Isabelle's answer as she looked up at Lily, her mother's lady's maid, entering the shop.

'Miss Isabelle, I didn't expect to see you in here. Are you alright?' Lily looked across at the mill owner from Skipton that she knew to be John Sidgwick; his reputation, known to all, was that of a hard man, with an eye for the ladies.

'I'm fine, thank you, Lily. I was just keeping Mr Sidgwick company over lunch.' Isabelle smiled at her mother's maid, knowing that her secret was now out in the open.

John rose from his chair. 'Please join us, Miss, we have room for one more.'

'No, thank you. I've just come to see if I can buy some ground coffee. My mother says the best comes from here, so I treat her once in a while, when I have the money. Are you sure you are alright, Miss Isabelle, you look quite flushed?'

'I'm fine, thank you,' Isabelle snapped. She was annoyed to have been found out and just wanted to give John her response.

Lily looked at the couple. He was up to something, and Isabelle was definitely not herself. 'I'll see you this evening, Miss.'

'Yes, Lily.' Isabelle watched as Lily waited for her coffee to be ground and placed into a brown bag, for her to take home. She smiled at Lily, when she turned to look at them both as she closed the shop door behind her. 'I'm sorry, John. That was my mama's lady's maid, and she is bound to tell my mother that she saw me with you, for they are quite close. All the more reason for my answer to you.' Isabelle breathed in deeply. 'The answer is yes, John, I will marry you – it will be an honour.'

'Isabelle, I can't believe it! You have made me the happiest man in the world. Now when are we to tell your parents? They must know of our plans. You must

131

have no regrets, my dear. I will always be there for you and I will ever be the faithful husband. You will want for nothing.' John beamed across at his dark-haired rose; not only had he got a young filly to keep his bed warm, but she was the heir to Ferndale Mill – a rival to his High Mill, which was doomed if he did not have an influx of cash.

'Tonight – we will tell my mother tonight!' Isabelle was adamant that the sooner her mother was told, the better, because she was sure Lily would have tittle-tattled to Charlotte. Besides, her father stopped over at Crummock on a Tuesday night, to play dominoes at The Gamecock with Arthur, and she would handle her parents one at a time.

'Tonight it is, my dear. I will come to the manor around eight o'clock and, if she doesn't agree, then we will elope, because you are to be mine.'

'Elope – how romantic! But I hope Mother agrees to our plans.' Isabelle's face clouded over; she knew her mother and her family would not be happy with her decision, but how could it be so wrong? John was a respectful businessman with his own mill and home, and her mother should be proud that she had landed herself such a good catch, despite John's age. 'Until then, my love,' Isabelle whispered as she left the tea-room, her heart racing at the thought of marriage, but her head aching with the knowledge that she needed to confront her mother with her news. Perhaps it would be better if they eloped.

10

Lily hung her shawl up behind the kitchen door and looked around the room, before sitting down at the table, sighing heavily.

'What's up, Lily? You look worried.' Mazy sat down beside her, noticing that her work colleague and friend seemed perplexed.

'Well, I don't know what to do. I don't like telling tales, and it might all have been quite innocent, but I've heard bad things about John Sidgwick.' Lily rubbed her hands over her eyes and then looked at her friend. 'Young Nancy isn't in hearing distance, is she, if I tell you what I've seen – or think I've seen? She's such a gossip, and Mrs Atkinson will not want this being made public.'

'No, Nancy's out in the kitchen garden, getting a cabbage for tonight's dinner. What's worrying you about John Sidgwick, and who is he?' Mazy sat back

133

in her chair and waited to hear what was on her friend's mind.

'I took advantage of being in Settle, while doing a few jobs for my mistress, and decided to pop into that little tea-shop on Cheapside, for some coffee for my mother. Anyway, as soon as I opened the door I spotted them: Miss Isabelle and John Sidgwick. They were like two love-birds sat in a quiet corner, holding hands. I couldn't believe it; he's just an old lecher and he's such a nasty man. I hope I'm wrong, but I think Miss Isabelle and him might be courting. She was so abrupt with me, and obviously annoyed that I'd found them there.' Lily looked at her friend and waited for her to say something.

'Is he that bad, this John Sidgwick? And are you sure you might not have read it wrong?' Mazy knew her friend was worried, and wondered what she was going to do next.

'I wasn't wrong, Mazy. He was making eyes at her, and she looked besotted. John Sidgwick was a friend of her father's and he is an older man, in his fifties. He owns High Mill at Skipton. Other mill owners are not enamoured with him, and he gives mill owners in general a bad name. He treats his workers with no kindness whatsoever. Isabelle's mother would be heartbroken, if she was to find out and if it was true. Now, am I to tell her what I suspect, or do I keep my mouth shut and see if it develops or dwindles out?' Lily didn't know what to do for the best.

'Well, I think I'd want to know. Miss Isabelle is a bit

vulnerable, when it comes to men's ways, as her mother has protected her so much. How can she prefer an old man to all the young men who are available to her? And if this man is as bad as you say he is, then Miss Isabelle wants nothing to do with him – he'll just be using her. Go and tell Mrs Atkinson; if you are wrong, you can always apologize. She'll understand that you are only looking out for Miss Isabelle's future.' Mazy thought of all the young men who had been at Isabelle's twenty-first birthday party and remembered that Isabelle had not really given any of them encouragement. 'You know, I bet you are right. She showed no real interest in any of the young men that came to her party, except perhaps Robert Knowles, and that was just because of that dratted kitten.'

'I'll have a word with her mother then, although I don't want to. It's only bringing bad news to her door.' Lily stood up and felt her legs shaking at the thought of having to tell tales about Isabelle.

'Mrs Atkinson is in the morning room – she's going through some letters. I've just come back from showing her tonight's dinner menu. Don't worry, you won't regret it; you are not doing anything wrong, just looking after Isabelle,' Mazy reassured her.

'I don't want to say anything, but I feel I have to, although Isabelle is not going to love me for it.' Lily smiled weakly at Mazy and went to do the dirty deed.

'Thomson, could you get Miss Isabelle, please. I presume she is back from Settle?' Charlotte felt sick with

135

worry and anger at the news Lily had given her. Still, she had to keep calm. Lily might have read the situation wrongly. She looked out of the window and tried to calm her fears as she heard her daughter enter the room.

'You wanted to see me, Mama?' Isabelle stood in front of her mother, hoping Lily had not said anything about her secret rendezvous, but knowing that she would not have been summoned to see her mother, if that was the case.

'Is it true that you had luncheon with John Sidgwick this afternoon, at that dreadful tea-shop down Cheapside?' Charlotte stared at her daughter, knowing instantly that Lily had been telling her the truth.

'I suppose Lily has told you. I knew she would, as soon as she came into the shop. You know she was buying coffee for her own use, in your time?' Isabelle wanted to deflect the attention onto Lily instead of her, and wished to cause the maid as much upset as she could, seeing that she had told tales to her mother.

'That's irrelevant. What *is* my concern is that she said you looked more than comfortable with that wretch John Sidgwick. What do you think you are doing, seeing him? He is a nasty piece of work, and old enough to be your father.' Charlotte waited; she remembered Sidgwick when he used to drink with Joseph and recalled how even then, with a young wife and two children, he always had an eye for young girls and women.

'He loves me, Mother, and has asked me to marry

136

him, just this afternoon. Lily came in and spoiled his proposal. He is the man I love, and I object to you calling him a "nasty piece of work", for he's a gentleman. I was happy to accept his proposal of marriage.' Isabelle looked like a dark cloud; her face was sullen and set, and she would defend the man she loved. Who was her mother, to tell her what to do?

'Isabelle, you didn't – you stupid child! He's only after you for the mill, your money and the fact that he wants to bed you. He's a man of few morals, my dear, and I will not have you marrying him.' Charlotte stood next to Isabelle and looked into her eyes. Joseph Dawson had a lot to answer for; his daughter was as secretive and as dark as him, no matter how hard she had tried to bring her up correctly.

'He's no need for my money, and the mill is not mine to have. As for bedding me, well, at least he's marrying me, so it's his right. You know nothing about him anyway. He said you'd not want me to marry him, and that you'd say all these things about him. But I'm twenty-one, Mother. I can marry who I want, and you can't prevent me.' Isabelle stopped in her tracks, as someone knocked on the morning-room door.

'Enter,' Charlotte shouted, knowing who was about to interrupt a most private discussion. 'Ah, Hector, you got my message – thank you for coming. I'm so grateful. I hope I haven't dragged you from something more important.'

Hector Christie walked slowly into the room. The

highly respected mill owner, who was Isabelle's god-father, came and stood next to a raging Isabelle.

'Nothing's more important than my favourite godchild, Isabelle. Now, come and sit down beside me, Isabelle. Your mother asked me to come because Archie is at Crummock, and she knew that when it comes to John Sidgwick, I know all about him. Now, tell me: is it true, have you been seeing him?' Hector ushered Isabelle to sit down by his side and held her hand, as she trembled with temper and fear at telling her much-loved godfather.

'He's asked me to marry him, sir. And I've accepted. My mother is trying to convince me that John is no good for me, and that he is only using me, but I know he loves me and it isn't simply that I am heir to Wind-fell and Ferndale.' Isabelle was nearly in tears.

'Tell me, Isabelle, does he show you off on his arm around Skipton? Does he ask to come and see your parents, and does he take you to see his mill?' Hector held Isabelle's hand tightly and patted it gently, as she wiped tears away with her other hand.

'No, sir, but we have been keeping our love a secret because we knew nobody would understand.'

'And does he spend money on you as if you were a princess, just like your mother and Archie do?' Hector quizzed again.

'No, sir, but he has no need to. And I know he has as much money as I'm accustomed to, and that I'd want for nothing.' Isabelle looked into her godfather's eyes and felt the love that Hector had always shown her.

'Well, let me tell you something, child. John Sidgwick came to my home the other week to ask me for a loan. His mill is failing and he is desperate, Isabelle. I turned him down, because his mill is no good to anyone – it is crumbling into the river upon which it stands. It serves John right, because he is one of the cruellest mill owners in the district. He is a wicked man, Isabelle, with a fetish for young women, and he will bring you nothing but pain.' Hector looked up at Charlotte.

'But I love him,' Isabelle wept.

Charlotte rushed to her daughter's side.

'No, you don't, my love. You just think you do, because he's the first man to come along in your life and you thought he met all your needs. John Sidgwick has cunning ways, and I don't want you hurt and unhappy, the way I was when I wed your father. They are very much alike.' Charlotte knelt down and hugged her sobbing daughter.

'Everyone is always compared to my father. He is like a ghost that continuously haunts every day of my life. John cannot be that bad. He's coming tonight to ask you for my hand in marriage, and he means to get your permission or we are going to elope,' Isabelle sobbed.

'Isabelle, child, unfortunately your father's ghost is something we all have to live with, but we needn't court the ghouls he was friends with. Now, let your mother turn him away from the manor this evening, and promise me never to give him any of your time ever again. John is a desperate man and a selfish man, and he would have made your life hell.' Hector stood up from his seat and patted Charlotte on her shoulder. 'You know, I remember when your mother first entered my father's office, she was nearly the same age as you. She'd just learned that your father had gone, leaving her in debt, and she was desperate to get herself out of the life he had left her in. She clawed and fought her way every day, until that mill at Ferndale was paid for, and she made herself the true mistress of Windfell. You've got a good mother, Isabelle, who deserves a lot of respect. Now don't you let her down by allowing this man – if you can call him a man – to turn your head. Your mother loves you, and it would break her heart.' Hector looked at mother and daughter as they embraced. 'Promise me, Isabelle, that you won't have anything more to do with him?'

'But I love him. I can't give him up!' She held her head up and wiped the tears from her face.

'You must, my child, or live a life of destitution and poverty, when your friends and family turn their backs on you. Because when it comes to John Sidgwick, he knows exactly how to hurt and divide people. And mark my words, that is what he will do, once he has bled you dry and got his hands on Ferndale. He's rubbish, girl. Both your mother and I are begging you not to have anything more to do with him, from this day forward.' Hector looked sternly at the defiant young woman, and sent Charlotte a comforting glance as she reached for her handkerchief.

'How can he show me so much care and attention and not mean it? He must be truly cunning and ruthless, to make me feel so betrayed. And all for money!' Isabelle spat.

'Everyone makes mistakes – it's how we learn. Now, you just find yourself a nice steady man. Our William doesn't know what he's missing out on, but Oxford and his studies are all he thinks about at the moment.' Hector smiled.

Charlotte stood up and touched Hector on the shoulder, as Isabelle broke into sobs, urging him to walk to the hallway while her daughter came to grips with the knowledge that her true love was nothing but a cad.

'Thank you, Hector. I knew she wouldn't believe me, if I was to tell her the truth about John Sidgwick. What I didn't realize, when I sent for you, was that he'd asked her to marry him. I feel quite sick at the thought of him nearly becoming my son-in-law, because I could never turn my back on Isabelle. Although she has, unfortunately, inherited her father's trait of secrecy, which gives me a few headaches.' Charlotte opened the front door and smiled at one of her closest friends.

'Aye, well, she had to have a bit of Joseph in her, and it could be worse. Will you be alright, seeing Sidgwick off your place tonight, or do you want to borrow my groom? He's a big man who'll take no nonsense.'

'I'll be fine, thank you, Hector. Thomson will see him off the place, along with Jethro. I aim not even to let him into the manor. He must have a good idea that he will not meet with a joyous reception, but what he won't have counted upon is your intervention, revealing the truth about him. I can't thank you enough.'

'Well, you know where I'm at. Send Jethro for me if you need me again, Charlotte. Now, good evening, and God bless you both.'

Charlotte watched as Hector climbed into his carriage. Thank God he'd been at home and responded to her letter, asking for his help. Isabelle was fortunate to have such a good, caring godfather, and thank heavens she'd come to her senses. Charlotte leaned against the closed front door of the manor and breathed in deeply. Now to tackle a broken-hearted daughter, whose illusion of a perfect married life had just been broken. Thomson would give Sidgwick short shrift, with Jethro standing behind him for good measure. The man would not even be welcomed over the threshold, so hopefully she would never set eyes on him again.

'I'm sorry, sir. Mrs Atkinson says you are not welcome in the manor, and that neither she nor Isabelle is available to see you now, nor ever again. Now, please go, before I have to forcibly escort you from off the manor's property.' Thomson stood his ground, as Sidgwick swore at him and demanded that he talk to his mistress.

'You let me see Isabelle and her mother. I have important business.'

'Are you having problems, Mr Thomson? Is this man harassing you?' Jethro came out of the darkness with a pitchfork in his hand.

'I am indeed, Jethro. This man seems unable to understand that he is not welcome on our premises and that he is not wanted here.' Stephen Thomson puffed out his chest and stepped out of the manor, closing the door behind him. 'Would you mind helping me to escort him off the premises?'

'Not at all, Mr Thomson. I've just been killing some rats, so throwing one more off the premises is nothing to me; no matter how well-bred they are, a rat is still a rat.' Jethro pointed his pitchfork at Sidgwick.

'Alright, I'm going, but you'll all regret the day you did this to me. John Sidgwick will not forget being treated like this, believe me. She gave me a promise of marriage, so she is beholden to me.' He turned and shouted loudly up at the bedroom windows.

'Off – get off the property, else I'll use this.' Jethro pointed the pitchfork gently into Sidgwick's posterior, as he climbed into his gig.

'This is not the last that you'll hear of me,' he yelled as he whipped his horse into action, noticing the middle bedroom's curtains move.

'I think it will be, Mister, as there's nothing here for you any more,' Jethro shouted as the gig raced out of the gateway.

Charlotte lay in her bed and listened to Isabelle

143

sobbing in the next room. She remembered the nights she had sobbed over Joseph, and the hurt and pain he had caused her. Isabelle might not thank her now for saving her from a marriage of hell with John Sidgwick, but in time she would realize how close she had come to ruining her life. She was, however, right: Joseph would always be a ghost that haunted them all. They would never be free of him and his associates.

11

'Heavens, Harriet, just look at the difference to this place!' Charlotte cautiously opened the door to Atkinson's, aware of the wet paint and of the painter who was balanced precariously on a ladder, painting the top of the shop's window. She gasped as she was met with clean, swept floors, a polished counter and washed-down walls.

'Mmm . . . looks a bit different, doesn't it? I decided just to get on with it. I was here until dusk last night, and then my father brought me down first thing this morning. I wanted to get it done before any of the materials and haberdashery come this morning.' Harriet beamed. 'I feel quite proud of myself; the place looks so different. And I've tried the gas lights and they do work, so we can open late in this coming winter's evenings.'

'I don't suppose Isabelle helped with any of this yesterday? I'm afraid she is unable to join us this morning, either, for she feels a little under the weather. I fear she is going down with something.' Charlotte made an excuse for her heartbroken daughter, who had struggled to face the world and to come out of her bedroom that morning. She'd sat across from Charlotte and had sobbed between mouthfuls of her breakfast, so much so that Charlotte had instructed Thomson to take Isabelle, and her breakfast, up to her room for her to eat there in private, away from the prying eyes of the servants.

'No, she left me to it. I think she had a luncheon date that she didn't want to miss. It didn't matter, as I just got on with it. I enjoyed cleaning it, if that doesn't sound stupid. I aim to put my all into running this business, and prove to you that I fully appreciate the faith you have in me. I am grateful for all that you are doing for Danny and myself.' Harriet wanted her future mother-in-law to know just how much she appreciated her help, and wished to make up for the way she had acted, in expecting her name to be over the door.

'My children mean everything to me, Harriet, and all I want for them is to be happy. I'm sure your father and mother think the same.' Charlotte smiled at the young woman, whom she had judged completely wrongly on their first meeting.

'Yes, my mother especially. She was overjoyed when my sister married Roger Warburton. I'm sure everyone got absolutely sick of hearing her broadcast the wedding, and I'm afraid she is doing the same again over Danny and me. She's placed an order for a new dress with us already. I'm told it has to be green taffeta with a bustle, not a crinoline, and that it has to make her look younger than the forty-five years she is. At least it is an order for us to get started with.'

'Your poor mother; I asked her for lunch and then left her standing in the hallway. I do hope she forgives me. It was just that, with Archie's father dying, I couldn't spare her the time. Do you think both your father and mother could perhaps make Sunday lunch sometime shortly? We need to discuss your and Danny's wedding plans. The reading of the banns will have to be organized, and a guest list put together. I know it's only early October, but time goes so quickly and, before we know it, Christmas will be upon us.'

'I'm sure they would, and they'd appreciate being able to discuss the arrangements. I know my mother is worrying about what will be expected of them. She's all too aware that she cannot match you in money, if I am not speaking out of turn, ma'am.' Harriet was glad to have this conversation in private with Charlotte, for her mother had done nothing but nag and worry over who was to pay for what, saying that it was really the bride's family that paid for most things.

'Well, tell her to stop worrying. Danny is our only son, and no expense will be spared on your wedding, as it will be our delight to foot the expense. As long as our son is happy, that is all that matters. I only wish I could make Isabelle as happy; she does not seem to be able to find a suitable partner.' Charlotte stopped short when she looked out of the window as the painter hoisted up the new sign over the doorway. 'Look, Harriet, let's go and watch as the sign goes up.' She was as excited as Harriet, in truth; this was her business, not one inherited by default, like the mill. It was her family firm, to provide for her most precious daughter, and she just knew it was going to be a success.

'It looks perfect, ma'am.' Harriet looked up at the sign, and at the clean-looking shop front and the young man who was aligning the sign skilfully. 'We just need everything for the interior now.'

'Please, Harriet, call me "Charlotte" and then, when you are married, "Mama". I can't stand formality. The carter was pulling up at The Naked Man with his wagon full and I noticed under the tarpaulin what looked like our dressmaker's dummies, so he should be with us shortly. And the printer promised to place an ad for me in the Settle directory. I have a copy that I brought for you to look at in my purse, inside. Let me show you.' Charlotte hurried back into the shop and pulled out a piece of paper with the advertisement that she had placed. She handed it to Harriet.

'This makes it real, but I still can't believe it.' Harriet breathed in deeply. 'I hope Isabelle comes up with the patterns and designs. I don't mind sewing and dealing with the customers, but she must make the patterns.'

'Don't worry, she will not let you down. She will be back with you shortly – she's just feeling unwell today, as I said. Now, we just need our stock and some customers. Where can that carter have got to? I bet he's been led astray by the landlord at The Naked Man. Wherever he is, I'm afraid I'm going to have to leave you, Harriet. I need to go to the mill at Ferndale. Bert

Bannister will wonder where I am at. He's already voiced his concerns that I will be torn between the two businesses.'

'Don't worry. I can take care of everything; in fact the carter is here now – look.' Harriet opened the door for Charlotte to leave and the carter to enter. 'Mind the wet paint, please!' Harriet shouted at the grubby old man who was pulling back the tarpaulin on his cart.

'I'll leave you to it, my dear, you are more than capable.' Charlotte kissed her future daughter-in-law

149

tenderly on her cheek, before making her way gingerly past the carter and the freshly painted doorway.

'Three dead bodies for you, Missus,' the carter joked as he offloaded the tailor's dummies and grinned a toothless smile at Charlotte as he passed her.

'It won't be the first time I've been told that,' Charlotte answered back and then went on her way.

'I hope she didn't mean that,' the old man said as he passed the dummies through the doorway to Harriet.

'Let's just say she hasn't had the easiest of lives, and she'll just be thankful that these are only dummies, and not bodies.' Harriet held out her arms for the rest of her delivery and watched as the old man shook his head. All he was doing was delivering his load, and he wished he'd never joked, now that he'd remembered it was Charlotte Atkinson to whom he'd just delivered. He'd forgotten her tragic past. Why couldn't he have kept his big mouth shut?

The mill office was strewn with papers when Charlotte arrived. The files were piled high, in readiness for her visit, and Bert was gazing out of the office window down at the workers below. He was watching as the spinners kept a wary eye on the mules spinning the thread that went back and forward, stopping only when a thread broke, for the piecers to mend the thread quickly, before restarting the huge machine again. Eventually they filled the bobbins with clean white cotton, ready for the doffers to remove and replace with new empty bobbins. The spinners' job was not an easy one, but they were paid well for their skills.

Bert was dressed in his usual pair of dark trousers with matching waistcoat, his white shirt crisp and starched, which made him look quite the gentleman, with his silver pocket watch and fob hanging just below his chest for adornment. He ran his hands through his hair and tackled Charlotte with his thoughts as soon as she closed the door behind her.

'Charlotte, we are going to have to doing something about Walter Gibson. He's forever whinging and whining, and upsetting the workers in the carding room. He just doesn't have a good word for anyone.' Bert sat down in the chair across from Charlotte as she looked through the invoices that she was about to pay.

'Is he a good worker?' She looked up from her pile of paperwork and realized Bert didn't complain about somebody without just cause.

'That's just it: he's one of the best ones we have, but he's a troublemaker, always finding fault with something or other, and whipping the rest of the workers up so that they constantly query our every move. We can do without his sort working under our roof.' Bert sighed. He'd had enough of the cocky carder, who was always demanding a better lifestyle and causing bother.

'If he's a good worker, that's all that counts. He might voice his opinions, but the rest of the workers won't take much notice. They know they are looked after better than most mill workers in the district. Tell

Sally Oversby to keep a close eye on him; she'll take no nonsense from him.'

'Walter's already tackled her this morning, when she brought you in those things she's made for your shop. Sally caught him telling everyone that she's in the boss's pocket, and that you make her inform you about their business, and pay her nothing for the things she makes for you. A "boss's scab", I think he called her.' Bert looked at Charlotte, knowing he'd touched a sore point, bringing Sally into the argument.

'Those accessories are nothing to do with anyone, except Sally and myself. For what it's worth, she will get paid fair and square for them. A "boss's scab", is she? I'll give him "scab". I'll dock his pay by a penny a week, until he learns to toe the line. I don't usually listen to gossip, but I know it's not the first time you've complained about Walter. Bert, can you bring both Sally and Walter to me immediately? I'll sort his mouth out, and if he doesn't like it, he can find employment elsewhere.' Charlotte stood up and glanced out of the large glass windows that looked down upon the busy working mill. She watched as the mules raced back and forward, with cotton dust and fluff filling the air, the noise of the machinery making conversation only possible by lipreading.

Bert stood with the door half-ajar, letting the noise into Charlotte's office. 'I don't like causing bother, you know I don't, but Walter needs pulling up before he goes too far.'

'It's alright, Bert, I'll sort it. I'm not having one of

my overseers and management undermined by a man who knows nothing.' Charlotte smiled, reassuring Bert that her intentions were sound, and then went to sit back down in her chair. She felt her stomach churning. She didn't really enjoy confrontation, but she knew this man had to be reprimanded.

'Mrs Oversby, Mr Bannister informed me that you caught Walter here accusing you of being in cahoots with the management, and said that you were made to inform me about the workers' private lives.' Charlotte sat back in her chair and looked at the twisted little man who liked to cause so much trouble.

'I did. I told him – and those who were listening to the rubbish coming out of his mouth – that he was wrong, and that he was only making trouble. I don't want to know what folk get up to, and I'm sure you've better things to do with your life.' Tall, well-built, blonde-haired Sally looked at Charlotte Atkinson, whom she respected and admired for being such a strong woman and who had always treated her as a near equal.

'And I understand he called you a "boss's scab"?' Charlotte looked at Walter and saw him hang his head, hoping that Sally wouldn't grass on him.

'He did, along with complaining that you weren't going to pay me for the things I make in my spare time. Not that it's any of his business what we do.' Sally looked at the bags and gloves she had brought in that morning, piled up on a table at the back of the office, and waited for Charlotte's next question.

'You, sir, what have you got to say? It seems you are constantly at loggerheads with your betters. Perhaps you do not need your employment with us? Do you think your wife and five children will appreciate you being without employment, for the sake of that loose mouth of yours?' Charlotte looked at the small man in his plush velvet waistcoat, with his grey-white shirt tucked into his corduroy trousers, and waited for his reply.

'It was only a bit of banter, ma'am, I didn't mean it. I need my job, and I'm good at it.' Walter cupped his hands behind his back and knew he was in trouble.

'It's always just a bit of banter, Mr Gibson. Last month Mr Bannister reprimanded you for complaining that you'd been underpaid, when your wage was correct; and for telling everyone they would be better off working for anyone other than myself. How about I make your wish come true and let you go for this better-paid job elsewhere?' Charlotte looked stern.

'Please, ma'am, I didn't mean it. I know there's no better place than Ferndale to work. I just come out with rubbish sometimes. I should know better, with another baby on the way. I can't afford to be out of work.' Walter looked worried.

'Well, perhaps a penny a week docked from your wage will make you think twice about opening your mouth again. I will not have troublemakers in my mill, Mr Gibson. One more bit of slanderous gossip from your mouth and you will find yourself out of a job and out of a home, as you live in one of my cottages at the locks. Do you understand?'

'Yes, ma'am.' Walter Gibson hung his head; he was going to miss a penny a week out of his wage, especially with a baby on the way.

'Go on, get out of my sight. Mrs Oversby – any more negative comments from Mr Gibson, and you let me know.' Charlotte watched as they both walked out of her door. Walter was a snivelling little man and she was sure this would probably not be the last time she would be reprimanding him. But for now he needed his job, and she would hate to see his family have to pay the price for his stupidity.

'Where's everybody at?' Archie pulled up his chair to the dining table and waited until Thomson had placed his napkin on his knee and served him with his dinner.

'Thomson, you may leave us, once you've served Mr Atkinson.' Charlotte looked across at Archie and waited to answer until after Thomson had left the room.

'Yes, ma'am.' Thomson quickly served both his master and mistress and then discreetly left the room.

'That bad, eh?' Archie looked across at Charlotte and waited. He'd not had a chance to talk to her since his arrival back from Crummock.

'Worse.' Charlotte poked at her devilled kidneys, chasing them around her plate with her fork.

'So where are they, and who's causing bother now?' Archie put his knife and fork down and waited.

155

'Don't worry. It isn't your Danny; he's just gone to see Harriet up at High Winskill – her parents have asked him for supper. They are eager to get to know him better. I've told him to ask them here for dinner, a week on Sunday, as we had better get to know them a little better ourselves.' Charlotte hesitated.

'And Isabelle, where is she?' Archie asked, aware that he could see tears welling up in Charlotte's eyes.

'She's up in her room. She asked if she could have dinner there, while I tell you what we underwent yesterday evening. She's frightened you will be angry with her.'

'So, go on: tell me what happened with Isabelle yesterday? Whatever it is, it must be bad, for her not to be able to face me, and for you to look so upset.' Archie left his dinner and came to sit by his wife's side as she told him about Isabelle's promise of marriage to John Sidgwick.

'I'll go and sort the bastard out – he'll regret the day he led our lass on behind our backs. And how could she be so stupid, not to see that it was her status and money he was after, not her?' Archie was angry; he'd never come across John Sidgwick, but he'd heard enough about him for his flesh to crawl, as Charlotte unfolded the story of his offer of betrothal to Isabelle. 'Thank heavens Lily had the sense to tell you she had seen them together, and that Hector was good enough to come and talk some sense into Isabelle. At least you had time to act, before Sidgwick got to worm his way into the house and confront you in person. What on earth did Isabelle see in him? He's old enough to be her father and is nearly penniless, if what you tell me is right.'

'If you knew him, you'd know what a charmer Sidgwick can be. And she knew no different than that she was to marry a rich mill owner. He had warned her there would be no love lost for him here, as he would be known by us for being a past friend with Joseph.' Charlotte looked at Archie as he wrestled with the thought of a man of his age touching Isabelle.

'I'll go and talk to her. It isn't right that she's sitting up in her room, afeared. It isn't her fault – it's Sidgwick's, the dirty, manipulating cad.' Archie moved from the table and made for the door.

'What about your dinner?' Charlotte asked.

'Tell Cook to keep it warm for me. I've lost my appetite for now. Or she can make me a sandwich later.' Archie stomped out of the room, and Charlotte watched as he ran up the sweeping stairs to Isabelle's bedroom.

She put down her napkin and looked at her half-eaten dinner; she had no appetite, either. The thought of John Sidgwick nearly becoming her son-in-law made her stomach churn.

'Isabelle, my love, stop your crying. It won't be the first time a young girl's been fooled by an older man – one who is up to no good. At least you have listened to your elders and have realized what he was about.'

Archie sat beside his stepdaughter and watched as her body shook between sobs.

'I didn't know him. How could I have been so blind? And I loved him so much. My heart's broken because of him. I don't think I'll ever look at another man,' Isabelle sobbed. 'And I could have brought both you and my mother so much worry. How could I have been so stupid?'

'It's over now, Isabelle, and Sidgwick's been sent on his way. Just don't have anything more to do with him. You owe Lily a word of thanks. If it hadn't have been for her, it could have ended in more tears and heart-ache for you, if she had not thought of mentioning to your mother your little rendezvous that she witnessed. Sidgwick would have turned you against your mother, with his sloppy words, if she hadn't thought to get Hector Christie to back her up, before he declared his intentions.' Charlotte had told Archie that Isabelle would not let Lily attend to her needs, because she blamed the maid for her heartache.

'I can't look at Lily. I feel such a fool, and she must think I've no sense whatsoever. And likewise Thomson and Jethro – they must also think I'm an idiot,' Isabelle sobbed.

'They have stood by you, Isabelle, and they all understand that you were being led by that despicable man. I'm afraid he will find another victim. And that's what you were, for he is so desperate to save his mill. Your mother was in a similar situation with your father; she was his victim, and that's why she knows your pain so well and is downstairs fretting over your well-being.' Archie looked at the red-eyed girl seated next to him.

'Mama shouldn't cry over me. It's just the shame – I don't think I'll ever get over that.' Isabelle raised her head.

'How about you come downstairs, go into the kitchen, where the staff will all be having their dinner at the moment, and thank them for their support. Then you can close the door on John Sidgwick and forget him. They will all understand, believe me.' Archie took Isabelle's hand.

'Oh no, I don't think I could.' She shook her head.

'Yes, you can. You can't sit up here, hiding away from the world. Come on: take my hand and let's do it together.' Archie pulled her up from the bed and ush ered her to the door. 'Look at them and thank the staff for their help, then hold your head up and get on with your life, else John Sidgwick's won. Think of what your mother went through; she didn't hide in her bedroom, and things were ten times worse in her case.'

Isabelle followed Archie down the stairs towards the kitchen, where she could hear the laughter and talk as the staff enjoyed their dinner together around the kitchen table. She hesitated for a moment just out of view of the staff. 'I can't; they will all look at me.'

'Yes, you can. Get it over and done with, and then come and join your mother and me in the drawing room.' Archie smiled and waited as Isabelle stepped down the last few steps into the kitchen.

'Miss Isabelle, we didn't expect you down here.' Ruby Baxter, the cook, pulled back her chair and offered it to her, as the staff stood up and stopped their chattering.

'Please don't stand up. And I'm sorry I'm interrupting your dinner. I've just come down to thank you for your help with John Sidgwick. Especially you, Lily – please don't think I will hold any grudge against you, for telling my mama. You did right by telling her your concerns. And thank you, Thomson and Jethro, for seeing him off the property, as he could have turned nasty. I've been a fool, and I feel stupid for being taken in by such a cad.' Isabelle turned and looked at Archie, nearly crying now.

'Oh, Miss, you don't have to thank us and apologize. You are no fool. It was him; he's known as a devious man. And I know you'll be hurting, but you are better off without him.' Lily walked over to Isabelle and touched her arm. 'We'd do anything for you and the family, and I'm sorry that he has caused so much worry.'

'Thank you, Lily. I'm sorry I was sharp with you in the tea-room.' Isabelle smiled.

'You call that sharp – you should hear Ruby here, when she's squaring us all up in her kitchen; now that's sharp!' Lily laughed and looked around at the worried faces of all the staff, especially Ruby Baxter as she scowled across at her.

'Nay, sharp was the end of my pitchfork that nearly caught John Sidgwick on his backside, as he got into his gig. Sorry, Miss, but he deserved all he got from me and Thomson, and we'll do it again if he ever shows his face here once more.' Jethro looked up from his chair.

'Thank you both. I'll be always in your debt.' Isabelle smiled as she wiped away a tear. 'I'm lucky to have such good friends, because that's what you all are.'

Archie put his arm around Isabelle's shoulders and then winked and mouthed 'Thank you' at all his staff as Isabelle made her way back up the stairs and into the drawing room. 'See, they don't think any the worse of you. Now, get on with your life. Tomorrow, go into Settle and help Harriet in the shop, because I have a feeling she's been treated like second best.'

'Poor Harriet. I left her with all the shop to clean, for the sake of him,' Isabelle confessed as she entered the drawing room, sitting down next to her mother.

'Yes, you need to thank her, but perhaps it's best you don't mention John Sidgwick to her. Let's just keep it in the family.' Charlotte looked at her red-faced daughter.

'But she is family, Mother,' Isabelle said.

'Not yet she isn't, dear, not until they are wed. Besides, we can do without the gossip, if she decides to tell her mother. She's such a tittle-tattle.' Charlotte was glad to see her daughter facing her commitments, but didn't want her to become the talk of Settle.

161

'Whatever you say, Mother. At least one of us is happy in love.' Isabelle hoped that her brother *was* happy with Harriet, and that Danny had put any past loves behind him – unlike her.

Archie sat on the bed edge and pulled his nightshirt over his head, before climbing into bed next to Charlotte. 'You know, I thought it got easier once your children grew up, but they seem to be becoming more of a worry at the moment.'

'I know. I don't even dare to think of the consequences, if Isabelle had married Sidgwick. She had the choice of any of the young men who came to her twenty-first, and then she was foolish enough to fall for his charms.' Charlotte sighed.

'Well, there is one bit of good news I can tell you.' Archie turned and smiled at Charlotte. 'I went over to Ragged Hall today, to pick up the tup, and I saw Bill Brown. He told me his lass, Amy, is to be wed, and she's expecting a baby. He's bloody fuming – seemingly it's to a lad over Slaidburn way. So that gets her out of the way of our Danny.'

'Thank heavens for that. At least that removes her from the picture, and keeps him focused on his marriage to Harriet. And at least the baby's not his, which is a blessing.' Charlotte kissed Archie on the cheek, before burrowing down underneath the bedclothes.

'Aye, hopefully it isn't our Danny's. Perhaps she doesn't know who the father is, and the poor lad at Slaidburn is just the one that's been caught.' Archie dimmed the lamp at his side of the bed and joined Charlotte under the covers; he put his arm around her, in the hope of a loving response.

'Don't even think it, Archie Atkinson. I've had enough of men. Now, keep yourself to yourself, and goodnight.' Charlotte pushed his arm off her.

'Tha never used to say that, Lottie. Perhaps thou's got another man in your life.' Archie kissed his wife and cuddled her tightly as she protested, knowing that she would quickly submit to his advances.

'Do you really think I've got time for another man? And why would I want one, when I've got you, Archie Atkinson?' Charlotte felt guilty at her rejection of the man she loved and turned and kissed him tenderly.

'Aye, I might be a bit long in the tooth, but you'll not find a better tup than me.' Archie grinned. 'Now come here: we are not too old for a bit of passion.'

'No, we never will be – me and you. Just hold me, Archie, I need to be loved.' Charlotte looked into the eyes that she had always loved and held him tight. He was her love, her rock when everything around her was wrong, and most of all he was her lover and, as he said, the best tup in the district.

12

Harriet watched the salesman's every move as he demonstrated how to thread the needle and how to alter the tension of the stitches, by adjusting the coiled spring on the metal contraption that he'd delivered to the fitting room of Atkinson's. He then got hold of a scrap of material and flicked a switch at the back of the machine, to pick up what he called 'the foot', and placed the material underneath it.

'Look, you pedal with your feet, back and forward on this iron plate. This in turn makes this leather belt turn round this wheel, which then makes the movements inside this casing move your needle up and down. The faster you pedal, the faster your needle goes up and down. Watch me.' The salesman started to pedal and the needle began to go up and down as he pushed the material under the foot, leaving a beautifully sewn line of stitches. 'What do you think? Good, eh!' He passed Harriet his handwork and watched her face.

'That's fantastic! It would have taken me a good hour to do all those stitches. Can I have a go?' She couldn't wait.

'Yes, here, have a go – that's what I'm here for.' The salesman stood back and watched as Harriet sat down on her stool, putting her feet on the metal plate to be pedalled. 'Be careful of your fingers, and keep your skirts out of the belt.'

Harriet pushed down with her feet, making the machine come to life.

'That's it, back and forward; go with its rhythm, you are doing fine.' The salesman looked at Charlotte, who was watching with interest as Harriet enjoyed getting to grips with her new piece of technology, and smiled as he knew he had a sure sale. The sound of the treadle going back and forth was the only noise, as all eyes were on Harriet.

She beamed as she picked up the foot of the sewing machine, cut the length of cotton thread from the end of her material and looked at her handiwork. 'I could nearly make a dress in a day, if I had one of these. The fittings are going to take longer than the sewing.'

'I take it you would like to keep the machine then?' Charlotte smiled. 'Isabelle, you could learn to use it as well, so that you both can sew, if you are ever in the favourable position of being busy.'

'I would love it. It makes life so much easier, although there will still be a lot of detail that I will need to do by hand.' Harriet's face lit up, thinking of the dresses she could make with such a machine.

'I'd like to learn, too. As you say, Mother, it is best if I also learn how to use it. I'm not the best seam-stress, but this looks faster than sitting hand-sewing, which I don't have any patience for.' Isabelle went and stood by Harriet and investigated the Singer sewing machine's functions.

'Be careful not to leave any pins in your garments, for the needle will break if it hits a pin. Look, this screw here needs to be turned, to enable you to change the needle.' The salesman bent down and pointed to a tiny screw above the needle, which held the needle in place. 'We can supply you with a tin of spare needles, so this will never be a problem. Also, you will notice the drawers on either side of your machine, for storage of any of the things you need to keep in there. It really is a superb machine.'

'I think you've earned your money today. My girls and I will definitely take it, Mr Rogers. I'm sure it will be of benefit to our business. Could you invoice Fern-dale Mill, please, and not my two girls here. This is my treat, my enjoyment, if I'm to tell the truth. However, I have every faith that my new venture is in good hands.'

'Of course, ma'am, and I'm sure the machine will not disappoint you. I can see every good home owning one in the future.' Mr Rogers tipped his hat and smiled at the girls as they laughed, and Isabelle pedalled and started sewing as he made his way to the door.

'I sincerely hope not, Mr Rogers, as there would be no need for our new venture. And that would never do.' Charlotte showed the salesman his way out. 'Good evening, Mr Rogers, thank you for your help.'

She closed the door and watched Isabelle and Harriet laughing at one another's stitching. Thank heavens Isabelle had moved on from the gloom that had surrounded her; or at least she seemed to have done, although she thought she had heard Isabelle sobbing the other night. A broken heart took longer to heal than a few days, as she knew all too well herself. But the shop, and Harriet, would give Isabelle a sense of purpose, and keep her mind off John Sidgwick and the life she nearly had. The sewing machine was a good buy; it would help Isabelle forget everything, albeit just for a few moments as she learned her new skills. Just as she herself had buried her hurt at being used, and had ploughed her energies into running Ferndale.

She'd arranged for Hector Christie to have Isabelle for lunch this coming Sunday, knowing that the last thing Isabelle wanted to hear about were the wedding plans of her brother. Hector's son, William, was up from Oxford, so she would have some company to lighten her visit. It was, as Hector said, a pity that William was so intent on his studies, as they would have made a perfect couple, but Isabelle cherished William as a friend and thought none the worse of him. Sunday was going to be Danny's day, and a chance for both Archie and her to meet the Armstrongs and get a feel for what sort of family their son was to marry into.

Charlotte had hoped Danny would marry somebody with more stature in society, but Archie seemed to be quite happy that Harriet was from a good Dales family, a farmer's daughter, and that was all that mattered. She had agreed to them having Crummock because after all they both needed a home, and Danny loved his life in farming and had not once shown any interest in running the mill. Horses for courses, Charlotte thought, as Harriet beamed at her, showing her the first seam she had just sewn on a lady's petticoat. Whatever life threw at them, they'd manage; Isabelle and Danny were their children and she'd try and protect them from the world's evils.

'I said to my Ted what a beautiful home you had here at Windfell. I told him it was so grand it would take his breath away,' Betty Armstrong chattered, while Thomson lightened her of her mantle and waited for her gloves, as she gazed around the hallway of Windfell.

'Yes, we are lucky to have such a beautiful home. I sometimes wonder what I've done to deserve it.' Charlotte smiled at both of the Armstrongs and watched as Archie came quickly down the stairs, tidying his cravat as he raced into the hallway.

'I'm sorry, I meant to be at the door with Charlotte to meet you, but I got delayed up at Crummock. We had a cow calving, and Danny and I decided we would be better helping Arthur see it into the world.' Archie quickly gave his apologies and looked across at Charlotte's scowling face. She'd let Danny and him know exactly how she felt about putting a calving cow before the wedding plans. 'Danny will be down shortly. He'd have been here by now, but he fell backwards as he pulled the calf free and fell into a pile of shi—'

'Yes, well enough of calving cows. Come through into the drawing room. Once Danny is with us, we'll sit down for lunch.' Charlotte quickly stopped Archie in his tracks, frowning at his lack of decorum. He sometimes reminded her of her father; he'd had a habit of saying it as it was, and it seemed that Archie was starting to do the same.

'Bullock or heifer?' Ted Armstrong said to Archie.

'A bonny little heifer. From a Hereford. I thought I'd try them up at Crummock. I was going to buy them for Butterfield Gap, but now that Danny's going to farm there, I thought we'd try them up on the fell. They are sturdy little beasts.' Archie looked at the tall weather-beaten farmer and knew he'd be alright talking farming with him over dinner.

'Men – it's all they talk about! I swear Ted loves his sheep more than me and our Harriet. Doesn't he, Harriet? I heard him talking to his new Rough Fell sheep that he got from his cousin up Ambleside the other day. He had kinder words for them than I have ever had said to me.' Betty took Harriet's arm and followed Charlotte into the drawing room.

'You've got Rough Fell sheep? Now, I must have a look at them. I was thinking of buying some, but I've kept to my Swaledales, as they are hardy and lamb well.' Archie had had his eye on some Rough Fells for a while, for they were such a bonny breed with their big black-and-white faces and white fleeces, but until now he didn't know anyone who kept them.

'Aye, come up and see them. I've only ten of them, but you can have a look at them. If I have a good spring and they lamb well, I'll sell you some.' Ted looked at Archie; he was a farmer like him, and his lass would be alright. She'd been brought up to live a farm life, and that's what he hoped she'd do, rather than play in a fancy dress shop.

'Gentlemen, Danny's joining us now. No more talk of sheep, cows and farming. Let us go through to the dining room and have dinner, and then discuss the wedding plans.' Charlotte decided to set the agenda and not let farming take over the day.

'I'm sorry I've kept you waiting.' Danny entered the room and took Harriet's hand as he kissed her gently on the cheek.

'Look at the love-birds, don't they make a lovely pair?' Betty smiled and wiped back a tear of joy.

'They do indeed. It will be a joy to see them both walk down the aisle.' Charlotte looked at Danny and held her breath, knowing full well that things might not have been so straightforward.

'I tell you what, lass, after dinner you, Harriet and Mrs Armstrong sort out the wedding, and Ted, Danny and me will have a walk around our grounds while you sort it all out between you. After all, it's women's talk and, no matter what we say, we'll be wrong.' Archie grinned across at his wife as Danny rushed to the side of his betrothed.

'It probably will be better. What do you think, Mrs Armstrong?'

'Please – "Betty" and "Ted"; after all, we are soon to be related. Yes, we are better sorting it. I don't know about your husband, but Ted knows nothing about organizing a wedding. And we have so much to sort out: the dress, the bridesmaids, the church and where to have the marriage and wedding breakfast. We have quite a big family, and you will have so many guests, too.' Betty had been having sleepless nights over the thought of how much this society wedding was going to cost, and who was to do exactly what.

'Well, the dress is no problem. Isabelle has designed it already, and I've put some of the taffeta that came from Liverpool to one side. I will, of course, pay for it,' Harriet added quickly.

'Come, let us have dinner, and then we will talk about it in detail after we've eaten and are free of these three men. Just listen to them; sheep, cows and market prices . . . you'd never tell, from them, that we have a wedding to plan.' Charlotte ushered everybody into the dining room and guided them to their seats.

'My, what a beautiful room.' Betty looked around the lavish dining room and breathed in deeply, then smiled as Thomson served her a steaming bowl of soup.

'Well, Betty, I wondered if we should have the

171

wedding breakfast in this room. I have an excellent cook, plenty of staff, and the room lends itself so nicely to a wedding. I remember my own wedding breakfast here and it was a grand occasion, one I'm sure we could follow – if not exceed.' Charlotte looked across at Betty and waited for her reply.

'That would be perfect. Of course we would pay towards your outgoings.' Betty looked at Harriet. 'Would you be happy with the breakfast here, Harriet?'

'Yes, it would be lovely. And if we have it in spring, our guests can go out onto the lawn and look around the gardens.' Harriet smiled, thinking of her special day.

'I would not hear of you bearing any of the costs. I have all the amenities to hand and it would be no hardship for us to hold the wedding breakfast here. Likewise, my cook will make the cake, and my gardener will make sure you have a bouquet of your choice.' Charlotte looked at Harriet and hoped she wasn't dictating too much.

'This is such a relief, Mrs Atkinson. I must admit, I've had a few sleepless nights, wondering how we were going to organize things.' Betty sighed.

'Call me "Charlotte", please. Now don't you worry, Betty, we will sort it out between us. St John's at Langcliffe for the actual wedding? It should be big enough.'

'Yes, we both thought that.' Betty glanced at Harriet and saw her smiling in recognition of the decision.

'Harriet and Danny will have to go and see the vicar and get the banns read. That just leaves bridesmaids and the guest list. Harriet's sister as maid of honour, and Isabelle as chief bridesmaid, do you think?' Charlotte enquired.

'Yes, perfect.' Betty couldn't believe there was hardly anything else to arrange – it had all been sorted while sipping her soup.

'Then all that's left is the guest list. If I write the invitations for our side of the family, will you do yours? I'm afraid the guest list will be rather large.'

Ted Armstrong pushed his soup dish away from him, empty, and looked up at his wife and daughter. 'You've worried yourself sick, lass, for a week or two, and Charlotte here has organized it before the main course and it's all to everyone's liking. There's only one thing: I think we should pay some of the costs, else I'll be offended.'

'You will do no such thing. It is our privilege to welcome your Harriet into our family.' Charlotte smiled. 'But I would not want to offend you. How about you give my husband two of your Rough Fell lambs in the spring? That would go some way towards part of the costs.'

'Aye, I'll agree to that: a tup lamb and a gimmer, to start your own flock. How about that, Archie? Like these two, who will hopefully soon be starting their own flock.' Ted grinned.

'Father!' Harriet whispered, while blushing and daring to glance at Danny.

'Not before they are wed, please. We don't want the perfect wedding to be spoilt now, not with all these plans to put in place.' Charlotte chastised, and then smiled at, the blushing young couple. 'We want a perfect day – and it will be perfect, believe me.'

'Did you enjoy your day with the Christies?' Charlotte sat across from Isabelle and watched as she sketched patterns for Harriet to give her approval to.

'Yes, thank you, Mother. It was good to catch up with William; he won't be back up in Yorkshire now until Christmas, which I suppose will soon be upon us. The leaves are falling from the trees in profusion now, so autumn is definitely here.' Isabelle looked out of the window at the wild, blustery day and watched as the copper-beech leaves twirled and twisted to the floor.

'Yes, I don't like this time of year, with everything dying. I much prefer spring, which always seems a lifetime away, now it comes in so dark of an evening. We had a pleasant lunch with the Armstrongs. I think I might have judged Betty Armstrong wrongly; she's just an excitable body. She gets giddy and carried away with the situation, but she's not a bad soul.' Charlotte edged her way into talking about Danny's wedding plans. 'Harriet would like you to be chief bridesmaid: would you be in agreement with that? It's only right, as you have been brought up as Danny's sister.'

'That would be fine, Mother. Please don't feel you have to edit your excitement over the wedding, just because I made a fool of myself. It's Danny's and Harriet's big day and I will be happy for them. I know you sent me to dine with the Christies to get me out of the way. After all, you couldn't have my sullen face at the table while all the plans were put in place.' Isabelle lifted her head from her sketching and looked at her mother, whom she knew was worrying about her feelings.

'I just want you to be happy, Isabelle, put that horrible business of John Sidgwick behind you and move on with your life.' Charlotte brooded. 'Are we to have our usual Christmas Ball this year? It lifts spirits at that time of year, although I have taken the decision to pay for Harriet and Danny's wedding, and I might have to cut the guest list slightly. I couldn't have the Armstrongs have the worry of paying for half, for after all most of the guests will be from our side.'

'Mother, do as you wish – you usually do. A Christmas Ball, as you say, would be welcomed by our friends and neighbours, I'm sure. Uncle Hector asked after you and Father yesterday, he hopes you are both well. He had a guest staying with him, an acquaintance of William's: a designer and artist called William Morris. I must confess I'd never heard of him before, but William told me he is in fact one of the most radical artists and painters of our day. He was quite interesting to talk to.' Isabelle did not want to show just how fascinated she was by William Morris, but she was aware that her voice belied that fact. However, she was going to mention her conversation with him, before Hector Christie reported back to her mother.

'An artist? What was he doing staying with the

Christies? Is he young, old, married, single?' Charlotte looked worried.

'I'd say he is in his early fifties and he's married, Mother, so you don't need to worry. He was just interesting to talk to, and his ideas on art are fascinating. I learned so much just by sitting and talking a short while with him. He gave me some new ideas on design – that's what I've been sketching now. We should embrace nature and incorporate it in our designs.' Isabelle lifted up her sketch of Harriet's wedding dress to show her mother and moved next to her. 'Look, I got these ideas from him yesterday. I'm hoping Harriet can embroider them into the taffeta, as they would look so beautiful.'

Charlotte looked at her daughter's sketch of a straight wedding dress with a very small bustle, embroidered with the most beautiful leaves and intertwining curling flowers.

'I thought if we could embroider the flowers with a silver thread, it would catch the light.' Isabelle looked excited and waited for her mother's response.

'Isabelle, it's beautiful. I've never seen you draw anything more exquisite. Indeed, I've never seen anything like these designs before. I'll have to ask Hector just who this William Morris is, if he's had such an influence on you.' Charlotte's eyes filled with tears as she looked at her daughter, who had thought so much about the wedding dress for Harriet while her own heart was still broken.

'You would love his patterns, Mother. He designs

wallpaper, so perhaps we could get rid of that horrible flock wallpaper in the drawing room and replace it with one of his designs, which depict nature. You would love them.' Isabelle smiled; she wanted the best for Harriet and Danny, and had been racking her brains about how to make the wedding dress special.

'We'll see, regarding the wallpaper. And you will have to hope that Harriet likes your design, although I'm sure she will, and that she can embroider them onto the taffeta. It will certainly show everyone what you both can do. I'm so proud of you, my love.' Charlotte reached over and hugged her daughter.

'I love you, Mother, and I'm sorry to give you so much worry.' Isabelle hugged her mother tightly.

'We will pick ourselves up and go forward. The right man for you will turn up when you least expect it, Isabelle, and he will make you so happy.' Charlotte kissed her daughter on the cheek and prayed that her words would come true.

Isabelle picked up the taffeta that was being carefully embroidered, in between customers and dress fittings. The wedding dress should have been hers, she couldn't help but think, as she looked at the curling design of drooping tulip heads, which shimmered in the faint winter's light. She would have been married by now and living in Skipton with John Sidgwick, if she had not been forced never to see him again.

'Oh! It's cold out there, it feels like snow.' The shop bell and Harriet's bustling arrival brought Isabelle out of the dark place that she seemed sometimes to find herself in, when she was left to her own thoughts. 'Here, I got us mutton pies from Mrs Askew's; they are still warm, and I thought that they would keep us warm. We'll have to mind that our fingers are not greasy after we have eaten them, as I've to finish that petticoat for Mrs Bibby, and you've got Mrs Lawson coming for a fitting this afternoon. Let's sit around the fire and have five minutes to ourselves.' Harriet pushed a pie into Isabelle's hand and pulled two chairs up next to the coal fire that was merely a glimmer in the grate. 'You've nearly let the fire out, Isabelle. I'll put some coal on it before I sit down, although I'm loath to go out and wash my hands under the water pump in this bitter weather.'

'I'm sorry, Harriet. I was busy thinking of my design for Mrs Lawson, and I forgot. Thank you for the pie.' Isabelle looked at the mutton pie that had been thrust into her hands, wrapped in brown paper. Was she supposed to eat it without a knife and fork and plate – what would her mama think? She watched as Harriet picked up the coal scuttle and tipped an ample helping of coal on the dimming fire. This was something that Nancy, the maid, would have done at Windfell, and Isabelle would not lower herself to such a degrading task. With her pie still unwrapped, Harriet quickly went out of the shop again and washed her hands under the communal water pump just outside the shop, shaking them free of the freezing-cold water and then wiping them on her skirts.

'Have you not taken a bite yet? Get it eaten before it goes cold, and mind the gravy doesn't run down your chin.' Harriet pulled up a stool as close to the fire as she could and bit into her pie, grinning at Isabelle as she watched her friend take the pie out of the brown paper and bite into it. 'Good, eh! Mrs Askew's pies are the best for miles around.' She demolished her pie in just a few mouthfuls and watched Isabelle pick, lady-like, at hers. 'Go on: get it eaten. There's no easy way, just bite into it.'

Isabelle decided to take her advice, else half of the pie was going to end up down the front of her dress. She had to agree she hadn't tasted anything so good for a long time, and the fact that she was eating it like a savage made it even more so.

'Just look at him – who does he think he is?' Harriet got up from her stool and looked out of the window down Cheapside, at a couple walking arm-in-arm down the street. 'I saw them both coming out of Bloomenber's. Dora was giving him a kiss on the cheek; they always were good friends. I can't stand the man, he's always chatting young women up. I gave them a wide birth,' Harriet growled.

Isabelle wiped her mouth with her handkerchief and threw the brown paper onto the fire, while checking that her hands were free of grease. 'Who are you moaning about?' She walked over to join Harriet at the window and spy on the couple who were upsetting Harriet so much.

'John Sidgwick, that's who. Look at the old fool,

with a young bit of a thing on his arm. She must have been daft enough to fall for his charms; he's an old lecher with no money. He owes Bloomenber's a small fortune for the trinkets he buys for his young fancies.' Harriet watched the couple wandering down the street and making their way closer to the shop, not noticing the colour drain from Isabelle's face. 'I hope he doesn't come in here. I had enough of him when I worked for Ezera.'

'Harriet, I'm just going into the fitting room. Could you serve them, if they come in?' Isabelle was filled with fear at the thought of having to serve John Sidgwick and see his latest victim on his arm.

'Yes, of course, Isabelle. Are you alright? You look quite pale.' Harriet turned and looked at her distraught friend.

'Yes, I think the pie may have been a bit too rich for me.' Isabelle rushed into the fitting room and sat at her desk, looking down at the pattern she had been working on, and wiped it free of the tears that she could not stop. John Sidgwick was nothing but a rogue; he was no gentleman – everyone had been right. How could she have been such a fool? She felt stupid to have been taken in by him, and angry at the same time. Damn John Sidgwick, she hoped he rotted in hell!

'Thank heavens for that, they just looked in the window and then turned around. I heard him say that he would not waste his money on such shoddy work. The cheek of the man! It'll be because your mother is better in business than him, and he's jealous.' Harriet came to check if Isabelle was alright and noticed that she had been crying. 'What's wrong, Isabelle? Have I said something to offend you?' She sat down next to a trembling Isabelle and took her hand.

'Oh, Harriet, I've been such a fool. Up to the other week, I was the young woman on John Sidgwick's arm. I didn't know I was being used. I promised him that I'd marry him, and I would have done, if my mother and Hector Christie had not stopped me.' Isabelle wiped her eyes; she hadn't wanted anyone to know of her stupidity, but she couldn't hide her heartache any longer from Harriet.

'Oh, Isabelle, how could you fall for his charms? He's such a cad and money-grabber. But I can understand how he'd twist you around his finger, for he knows all too well how to manipulate people, he and Dora, who he's close friends with. I wouldn't put it past Dora to put him up to it. I wouldn't have been so cruel with my words if I'd have known the situation. Danny has not said anything.' Harriet hugged her sobbing future sister-in-law.

'Danny knew nothing. I asked Mama and Father to keep it to themselves. I felt such a fool, and I didn't want to spoil your wedding plans.' Isabelle looked into Harriet's eyes and played with her wet handkerchief between her fingers.

'Then I won't say a word to Danny, either, and your secret's safe with me. As for "shoddy" clothes, we'll give that John Sidgwick shoddy; he will regret the day he took on Isabelle and Harriet Atkinson, because we are the greatest dress designers and milliners Yorkshire has ever seen. We may be small at the moment, but as my mother says, great oaks from little acorns grow.'

'Oh, Harriet, if only I had your strengths,' Isabelle sighed.

'You are the strength of this firm – just look at these designs. Have you not looked at how busy our books are? We have orders coming out of our ears! As for John Sidgwick, clear him from your mind, throw him out on the rubbish pile where he belongs; he's a chancer you shouldn't give a second thought to. You are Isabelle Atkinson, the most eligible young woman in the district: beautiful, elegant and extremely clever. You don't need any man. Especially a man who would have bled you dry within a matter of months.' Harriet couldn't believe how vulnerable and insecure Isabelle was.

'You are right, Harriet. I was being used.' Isabelle breathed in deeply. 'Now, let's get our heads down and get on with these orders. As you say, we'll show him. Thank you for keeping my secret and for giving me your support. I owe you.'

'Not another word, especially when it comes to Sidgwick. Anyway, I'm sure there is somebody out there who is just right for you. Why, only this morning I saw the most handsome man. He was walking into the empty shop on New Street across from the new railway station. He was so handsome. I wonder what trade he's going to be setting up there. Perhaps you should go and see?' Harriet smiled. 'You could also ask Robert Knowles around for tea, as Danny says he's sweet on you.'

'Oh, Harriet, give me time to get over my upset. I couldn't look at another man, not just yet.'

'Don't let the grass grow under your feet, Isabelle. Life is for living.' Harriet squeezed her tightly and then went into the shop as she heard the doorbell ring.

Isabelle drew another deep breath. Harriet was right: it was time to stop moping and get on with her life. She had everything she could ever wish for, and she could have lost it all for the sake of John Sidgwick. She would never make the same mistake again. The world was hers to take, and that was exactly what she was going to do.

13

'Looks like winter is upon us.' Archie looked out of the morning-room's window and watched the first snowflakes of winter fall.

Charlotte stood by his side. 'You know, I still feel a tingle down my spine with excitement, just like a small child, when I see the first snows of winter. It reminds me of being up at Crummock, and waking up to fern patterns on the windows made by the frost, and having to dress quickly because the house was so cold. Your aunty used to lay me out all the layers of clothes I had to wear that day, and I used to pull them quickly on, to get down to the warm kitchen and be fed by her. She was more like a mother to me than the family cook. I do miss her.'

'Aye, she was a good woman, was Aunt Lucy. She would do anything for anybody and she never hurt a soul. The world's a worse place without her. I don't like the look of this sky, Lottie, it looks full of snow.

I hope Arthur's got the sheep down off the fell and into the lower pastures at Crummock. It looks as if it could come soon.' Archie scowled and looked hard into the grey, snow-filled skies.

'Surely he will have done. He usually has them down around the house by this time of the year.' Charlotte walked to her writing desk and looked at the wording for the Christmas Ball invitation that she had been toying with, then sighed. 'I don't know whether to hold a Christmas Ball this year or not. After all, we have the wedding to pay for; and then I've invested a bit in Isabelle's and Harriet's shop – not that they are struggling, I'm quite impressed with their takings; they've got a nice little business building there. But the mill isn't making as much profit as it used to, because there's so much competition nowadays. I feel dark days are just around the corner.' She sat back in her chair and looked at Archie, who was obviously worried about the weather.

'Suit yourself, lass. It makes no difference to me – you know I'm not keen on such dos. I hate having to watch what I say to folk, and I'm not exactly light on my toes. If you think we can't afford it, don't bother. It's only keeping up with appearances. Are you struggling at the mill? You've never said anything afore now.' Archie turned and looked at his worried wife. She'd always thrown a ball at Christmas, so something must be wrong.

'Not struggling, but not making as much money as I'd like, Archie. And there's that many mills closing.

Two at Keighley closed last month, and then there's John Sidgwick's High Mill at Skipton; he's going to lose it. He's in hock to the bank, and they'll close on him any day now.' Charlotte looked at her draft invitation again and decided to screw it up and not bother with a ball.

'Don't mention him in this house. He deserves all he gets, after leading our Isabelle on. She still looks like a washed-out sheet. I feel like telling her he's not worth bothering about, but I don't want the tears again,' Archie grumbled.

'She's been a bit better this last week or two. She's enjoying throwing herself into her work, and Harriet is like a tonic for her. To say I doubted that lass when I first saw her would be an understatement, but she's done wonders for our Isabelle, and she is such a worker. I'll not bother holding a ball. Let's just have a quiet family Christmas. We can always invite the Armstrongs to join us, as they don't seem to be a bad family. Betty gets a bit excited, but she's been easy to deal with over the wedding.'

'You mean she didn't question your decisions. The poor woman didn't have a leg to stand on, when you railroaded her with your suggestions over dinner. She couldn't say no, because she knew she couldn't afford anything, poor woman.' Archie grinned. 'A family Christmas would be better. After all, it isn't long since we lost my father and we should show him some respect. I'm going to miss him sitting around our Christmas table saying that the pheasants aren't cooked enough and that he'd have been better at home. Yet he never wanted to go home to be on his own, when the time came for him to do so. I think, in his heart of hearts, he loved it here, just couldn't say it.' Archie walked back to the window and gazed out, thinking of his father.

'I miss him, too. I never took the place of Rosie, in his eyes. I was a bit too forward for him, I think. But he was a good man and we all miss him. It's been a bit of a year, when you think what we've been through: Isabelle's birthday, your father dying, then Danny and his loves, not to mention Isabelle's flirtation with marriage.' Charlotte smiled as Archie sat down in the chair across from her.

'I'll be happier when Arthur moves into Butterfield Gap. I don't like to see the old place empty. Although, looking at the weather, I'm glad I've moved all the stock up to Crummock. At least Danny and I haven't to go back and forward between farms.'

'Just look at the snow now – it's a blizzard out there. I can hardly see the beech trees down the drive,' Charlotte gasped.

'I think, at the first break in this weather, Danny and I had better go up to Crummock. Arthur will need our help, for the water troughs outside will be frozen over and if he hasn't brought the stock down off the fell, we could be looking at a disaster.' Archie stood up again and looked out of the window. 'I don't like the look of this day, but you've no control over the weather and the snow's come a little early this year.'

'If you must go, my love, Isabelle and I will be fine. Jethro will take me to the mill and Isabelle to Settle, so don't worry your head about us.' Charlotte knew that Archie was worried; his sheep were his life, as the mill was hers.

Archie drew back the bedroom curtains and looked out into the darkness of the winter's morning. He'd not slept a wink, and now the mantel clock lit by the dying embers of the fire was telling him it was only five-thirty. Too early to put into practice his decision of having breakfast, stirring Danny and going to Crummock, no matter what the weather was doing. He peered out into the darkness, hoping to be able to see if the snow was still falling.

'It's no good you not sleeping – that will not stop the snow. Come back to bed, just for another hour, until it gets a little lighter, then we can all have breakfast together and leave the house at the same time. You'll not get anything done in the dark.' Charlotte yawned and urged her husband to stop worrying and to climb back into bed with her.

'I tried not to waken you. I haven't had a wink of sleep, because even if Arthur has brought the sheep down from the fell, they've no protection.' Archie lit the oil lamp at his bedside and peered out into the darkness yet again; he sighed as the light illuminated falling snowflakes. 'It's not stopped since yesterday morning. If we have a good covering, Crummock will be feet under. And listen to that wind – it'll be whipping the snow into drifts. I'll be lucky if I can get up to Crummock.'

'More reason for you to wait until light, else you'll not be able to see where you are going. Blow out your light and get back into bed, Archie. Worrying will not save your sheep, nor will losing your way in the dark in a snowdrift.' Charlotte patted the bed as her husband relieved himself in the chamberpot under the bed.

'I suppose you are right. There is nowt I can do until it stops snowing and folk get stirring.' Archie blew out the flame on his lamp and climbed back into bed, lying still beside Charlotte, who had turned her back on him. 'Arthur's lost a bit of interest in farming Crummock, now he's coming out of it. You can't blame him, they are never going to be his stock,' he muttered as he lay looking up at the ceiling.

'For heaven's sake, will you be quiet? You've tossed and turned all night and kept me awake. There is nothing you can do until it's light. Now go to sleep. Eve will be here soon enough to relight the fire, and Lily to dress me. Just try and get forty winks. Arthur will have done all that he can, but like you, he isn't God, and he can't stop the snow.' Charlotte pulled the bedclothes over her, listening for Archie to continue his worrying as her eyes grew heavy with sleep.

'Morning, sir.' Jethro shovelled the snow to clear a path from the back door of the manor to the stable.

'It's put a good bit down, sir, and looks like we are in for more.'

'Aye, there's at least nine inches, and that's just down here. Can you get our horses ready for Danny and me, Jethro? We'll have to get up to Crummock and see what's afoot up there. We will try and get there between showers.' Archie looked up at the heavy grey skies. 'You are right: the clouds are still full of snow, there's a lot more to come. I'll get my breakfast and then we will be away.' He watched as Jethro put down his shovel and walked back into the stable. The sooner he and Danny got to Crummock, the better.

'It's bloody cold, Father.' Danny sat on his horse and looked around him. The journey up to Crummock was taking an age, as the horses picked their way carefully through the snow, struggling with the height of the drifts. The wind bit into every bone and the horses faltered with every step, as they tried to pick the best way through the foot-high snow. The heavy grey clouds folded around them both as they started up the solitary farm track, which was hidden to the eye, with a silence around them that was eerie.

'Look, you can just see Crummock, so we are winning.' A snowflake fluttered down onto Archie's face. 'Here we go again: the weather's closing in once more. I think we'd probably be better getting off our horses now, lad. They are exhausted, and we'll walk the last half-mile. My old Sheba isn't as young as she used to be and I can feel her struggling. The walking should

190

warm us up, if nothing else.' Archie climbed down from his beloved horse and patted her on her neck. 'I'll make your load lighter, old lass. We can manage the last uphill stretch.' Archie dismounted, grabbed the reins and started walking through the snow, slipping and sliding with every step he took as the flakes started falling down, gently at first and then turning into a full-scale blizzard.

'We'll never make it.' Danny pulled on his horse's reins and shouted to his father, as he kept his head down, out of the path of the stinging snow. The drifts were getting deeper with every step they took.

'Yes, we will. Look, we are nearly at the corner of the wood that shelters the house. Another few yards and we turn the bend into the farmyard, and then we will be out of this wind.' Archie looked back at his son. 'Think of the warm fire that awaits us, and of Mary's dinner. We'll soon be in the kitchen and nice and warm.'

Archie had lost all feeling in his hands now, and his face was blue with the biting wind that ripped at his cheeks. He couldn't stop thinking about his sheep out in fields around him, covered in snow. He raised his head and looked around at the limestone walls, which the sheep would have stood against for protection. The snowdrifts were nearly four to five feet high now, whipped up against the walls, which acted as a barrier for the high winds to build the drifts onto. It would be a matter of finding the sheep, once the blizzards had stopped. The air that filtered through the

191

limestone walls would keep them alive for a while, and the grass below their feet would keep them fed, but digging them out would be his own and Danny's priority.

'Come on, lad. We are nearly there, and Arthur will be glad to see us.' Archie turned around and looked at his son, struggling with the ice and snow, as they rounded the corner into the farmyard of Crummock. 'Look: the house is there and they've a good fire going. I can smell the wood smoke in the wind.'

Arthur turned around from his seat in front of the kitchen fire and looked at two snow-clad bodies that had just entered the house.

'You must be frozen! Here, sit up next to the fire. Mary, take their coats and make a brew. Get some warmth back into these bodies.' Arthur made way for his master and son, as Mary quickly put the kettle on the hob and took their snow-laden clothes.

'We've put our horses in the stable. That lad of yours will make sure they are looked after, won't he? Sheba is feeling the toll on her old bones, for she's not as young as she used to be.' Archie shivered and stood up, with Danny, next to the fire and breathed in deeply, grateful they had both made the warmth of the kitchen.

'Aye, he's a good hand with horses. She'll be looked after, don't worry. Whatever possessed you to come up here in weather like this? It's a wonder you've made it. I've never known weather as bad as this, all the time

I've farmed up here.' Arthur sat himself down at the kitchen table, as Mary brought out a newly baked loaf from the pantry and stirred the stew that was simmering on the hearth.

'Sorry, Mary, we are dripping all over your clean floor.' Danny apologized and moved to allow Mary to get to the stew.

'Don't worry, sir. At least you are getting warm, and you are safe now.'

'I was worried about my sheep. I didn't know if you'd brought them down from the fell yet. Not that it's going to matter, as the snow's that deep, but at least we will have some idea where they are at, if they are in the home fields.' Archie lifted his placket and warmed his backside, the steam rising from his damp trousers as he waited for a reply.

'Well, you needn't have worried. They are all down in these front fields, including the tup from Ragged Hall; and your Herefords are in the Knot paddock, with the barn to run into, and everything else is bedded and dry and fed.' Arthur looked at his master and sensed that there had been some doubt about him undertaking his job. 'I'm glad you've come, though, as it will be a devil of a job digging for them under these snowdrifts. The farm dogs, Jip and Floss, have good noses when it comes to finding sheep, so they will soon root them out.'

'Thank the Lord for that. I thought they might still be up on the fell, and I didn't fancy their chances.' Archie relaxed and patted Arthur on the shoulder.

'Nay, just because I'm leaving this place doesn't mean I wouldn't be right with you. I could feel the snow coming in the air, and we had a few flakes before you in the valley, so I gathered the fell sheep a few days ago and brought them all down. You'll be glad to know the tup you borrowed seems to be doing his job and keeping his ladies happy. You should have some good lambs in the spring.' Arthur sat back and knew that he'd done right by his master.

'That's good to know, as long as we can find them. I'm grateful to you, Arthur. I thought—' Archie stopped.

'You thought that I'd lost interest, just because I'm moving out of Crummock. No disrespect, sir, but you should have known I'm not like that. Until April I will do my job here, and then hand it over to Mr Danny.' Arthur smiled at the young lad who sat across the table from him. 'Both Mary and I are grateful for all that you've done for us, and that you gave us first option on Butterfield Gap. It'll be our first real home, and it'll be something grand to look out of my door in a morning and say: This is my land and nobody can take it away from me.' Arthur smiled at Mary as she placed bowls of stew on the table for her guests to eat. 'Now, you enjoy my Mary's stew and warm yourselves up. I take it you'll be staying with us for a few nights? Mary will see to the spare rooms after we've eaten. She'll make sure you've a fire lit and that the beds are aired.' Arthur picked up his spoon and smiled at his wife.

'Anything you need, sir, please ask. I'm afraid I've no maid, but I'll try and do everything you need.' Mary curtsied.

'Thank you both, I appreciate your loyalty. And I hope you are both happy in my old family home. This stew looks delicious, Mary. I hope we haven't caused you too much disruption?' Archie picked up his knife and fork and started to eat the welcome stew.

'Not at all, sir. It will be good to have some extra company, especially if this weather is to be with us for a while.' Mary smiled as she sat down at the table and watched her visitors enjoy her straightforward stew.

'If it carries on like this, we may be with you for some time, as the path up here was barely passable.' Archie enjoyed a mouthful of stew and looked out of the small-paned windows of the kitchen across Crummockdale, which was obliterated by the blizzard's grip.

'It's a bad day for a wedding. I feel sorry for the lass from Ragged Hall.' Mary innocently made conversation as she looked out of the window.

'Amy's getting married today?' Danny pushed his plate away and looked at Mary and then at his father.

'Aye, to a lad from over at Slaidburn. I think her father will have made sure it'll go ahead today, as she's carrying his child. She's broken her father's heart, so I understand. He had high hopes for her, and little knowing that she was a bit wild.' Mary stood up and started to clear the empty plates, not noticing that Danny looked upset.

'If you'll excuse me, I'll just check the horses.' Danny pushed back his chair, giving his father a quick glance before heading for the door.

'They'll be fine, lad. Bob will have seen to them, stop in here,' Archie shouted after him, but got no response as he heard the back door slam.

'I take it that Danny knew Amy Brown, like many of the lads in the district?' Arthur looked across at Archie, who appeared worried.

'Aye, he did. I'm thankful there's a blizzard, else I could see him riding over to stop the wedding, because when it comes to her, he sees no sense,' Archie growled.

'I'm sorry I mentioned her. I was just making conversation.' Mary stopped for a moment from her chores and sat down next to her employer. 'I don't think Amy knows who the real father to her bairn is. The lad from Slaidburn was the one her father caught her with, so he's got the blame.'

'Well, I'm damn sure it's not Danny's, so I'm not even thinking about it. And he's to marry Harriet this Easter, so he needs to forget Amy bloody Brown.' Archie got up from the table and looked out at the snow-filled sky and the white landscape outside, regretting yet again the day he'd sent his lad to Ragged Hall and Danny had set eyes on Amy Brown.

Outside in the stable, Danny stood in the doorway and watched as the snow fell, obscuring his view of the valley below. He knew he was doing the right thing by marrying Harriet, but the shock news that Amy was marrying, and was with child, had hurt him.

196

She still captivated him, tugged on his heartstrings and made him smile, when he thought of her wild ways. 'God bless you, Amy Brown, may you and your child be happy in your new life,' he whispered, as he looked across at the white wilderness of the winter's day. 'You'll always be special to me, and I'll never forget you.'

The three men walked out through the virginal whiteness of the snowy field, armed with long shepherd crooks and shovels, and with the two sheepdogs struggling to follow them. The sun shone in triumph over the battle between the winter's elements in the vividly clear blue sky, catching every crystallized snowflake and making them shine like diamonds across the crisp landscape.

'If we hadn't such a hard task in front of us, I'd say this was a grand day,' Archie said to Arthur as they reached the bottom wall of the first field, looking around at the perfect white of the snow-covered Dales and the trees glistening in the winter's sun. 'There's going to be hardship all round, if we don't find them. No spring lambs for us to sell in the autumn and no wool payment. How would Crummock survive without sheep?'

'Aye, we are going to be sweating a bit by the time we've dug out a few score. But we've got to find those poor creatures,' Arthur agreed. 'I saw some of them making for this bottom corner. Where there's one, there will be a few, as they tend to stand all together.'

Arthur prodded his crook into the snow as far as he could and pulled it out again unsuccessfully, without reaching the hard body of a sheep in his probing.

'Here – there's some here!' Danny pulled out his stick and started shovelling quickly as he found a buried sheep. The snow quickly piled up and the dogs yapped excitedly at the sight of the buried body.

'Here, Jip.' Danny held the dog to smell the sheep and then pulled it out of the dug hole and said, 'Find, Jip. Go. Go find, Jip.' The dog looked confused and then, as if by magic, registered what Danny was asking of it, slowly sniffing its way along the side of the wall until it came across another group of hidden sheep in their snowy enclosure. It pawed and scratched at the frozen snow in excitement, at the thought of the sheep underneath. Danny pulled at the back legs of the emerging sheep, as his father and Arthur went to uncover the other sheep that Jip had found, nearly falling backwards as a disorientated Swaledale ewe saw her first sight of the sun for more than three days. 'There you go, old lass. How many of you are there in here with you?' Danny looked down into the snow cavern made by the sheep's warm breath and quickly uncovered another six. All of them bleated as they were dug from their snowy graves and ran to stand together and watch as the rest of the flock was rescued. 'Seven down – how many more to go?' Danny shouted, as his father and Arthur dug out another grateful victim.

'Just another two hundred or so. But look on the bright side: the sun is helping our job,' Arthur shouted across as a group of five sheep made their way through the gateway and towards the watching flock. 'They've made it on their own.'

'No worries then, hopefully we'll not lose many.' Danny moved on, with Jip barking excitedly around his legs, as Floss pawed frantically further down the field. 'Then it's just a matter of foddering them and keeping the water trough free of ice. Remind me: why did I say I wanted to be a farmer?' he shouted at his father, as he prodded with his stick to find the sheep that both dogs were telling him were buried under his feet.

'Because it's in your blood, lad, and always will be.' Archie pulled at the hardened horns of a tup that he'd just located, and stood back as Moses – the tup from Ragged Hall – was freed. 'Well, that's one less worry. Bill Brown will be getting his tup back.' Archie watched as Moses shook himself free of the clinging snow and then went to stand with his ladies, stamping his foot in defiance as the dogs sniffed around the freed flock.

Danny put his head down and said nothing as his father watched him cursing, as his latest hole bore no fruit. That bloody tup; he wished he'd never set eyes on it – or its owner. Amy had broken his heart, and now he had to live with the consequences.

14

Charlotte was in the kitchen of Windfell Manor, looking at the dinner menus for the week. She sat at the scrubbed-spotless, long pine table and was bathed in the kitchen's warmth, as the Yorkshire range was throwing out heat from the coal that had just been added. The smell of home-made mincemeat pervaded the room, as Nancy filled jam jars to the brim, in preparation for the many pies to be made for Christmas.

'Do you think Mr Atkinson will be back with us shortly?' Ruby asked as she sat across from her mistress, twiddling her thumbs. She hated waiting for her mistress's acceptance of her menu; it was rare that Mrs Atkinson did not like anything on it, but she always felt like a small child, waiting to be told that her work was full of mistakes and she must redo it, as her teacher used to.

'I don't know, Ruby. I've had no word from either

Mr Atkinson or Danny since they went there. I presume they are still busy finding sheep and making sure they are cared for. The road was still blocked yesterday, but I noticed it had started to rain, so that should begin to clear some of the snow. I hope so. Another fortnight and it is nearly Christmas, and I'd like all my family to be with me by then.' Charlotte looked up from her menu and sighed.

'Are we not holding a ball, this year, ma'am? It's just if we are, both Thomson and me are beginning to need to know. There's quite a bit to organize and I'll have to order some provisions in. I asked Mazy, but she seemed to know nothing. And what would you like for Christmas dinner this year – have I to put an order in with the gamekeeper for a few brace of pheasants, or is it to be goose this time?' Ruby hadn't seen her mistress down in the kitchen for a while, for she had seemed to be preoccupied with the mill while the menfolk were up at Crummock, and Miss Isabelle had been similarly occupied with her new dress shop.

'The menu's fine, Ruby. I'm sorry, I can't say how many you are cooking for, as I don't know myself who will be sitting down to dinner with me, so if you can bear with us and play it by ear.' Charlotte brooded. 'Tom Beresford from the Craven Lime Company will be joining us, along with his wife, on Tuesday evening – or should I say joining me, if Archie is not back in time. He's invited me to look around the Hoffmann kiln to see how the lime is made that day, too. It's to be hoped that the snow has cleared by then. I personally think I would be better looking around in spring, but Mr Beresford was quite insistent on me visiting next Tuesday, so the least I could do to thank him for his hospitality was invite him back for dinner. It's best I keep him sweet, as he's on Settle town council and has a lot of sway on planning, and he's such an insistent little man. He's made – or broken – many a firm in the district, but I hear that his own management skills are not to be recommended.'

'Aye, he's not a good man, I don't think. I wouldn't worry about the snow being around the Hoffmann kiln, ma'am. I've heard them say that the ground around the kiln is so warm that it melts any snow or ice for a good distance around it. The fires inside the kiln are never left to go out totally.' Ruby took her menu from Charlotte and put it in her apron pocket for safety.

'You seem very knowledgeable about how it works, Ruby. I must confess I feel guilty because I've turned down Mr Beresford's offer of a guided tour of the kiln ever since it was built, over ten years ago now. It's something that I'm just not interested in, and it has little consequence in my life. But his wife is a good customer of Miss Isabelle, so I feel I should perhaps not ignore his invitation any longer. Answering your question regarding the Christmas Ball, we won't be having one this year, I'm afraid. We have Danny's wedding next spring and, with Mr Atkinson's father dying in the autumn, I didn't think it quite correct to be celebrating the season as much as we usually do.'

Charlotte sipped her cup of tea that Ruby had placed in front of her and looked around the kitchen, while pondering what to have for Christmas dinner.

'It's a shame we won't be hosting the ball, ma'am, as it's part of Christmas here now and all your staff look forward to it. But we will understand, what with Mr Atkinson senior dying and a big wedding to pay for.' Ruby regretted saying her last few words as soon as she had spoken them. It was common knowledge that the mill at Ferndale was not as profitable as it had been a few years ago, after picking itself up following the American civil war, but there was no need for her mistress to know that everyone was talking about the slump in orders that was taking place at the mill.

'Goose, I think, Ruby – we will have goose. I never feel guilty about eating goose, as they are nasty creatures. I always remember one we had when I was a child. It used to chase me around the farmyard. I was petrified of it.' Charlotte smiled at Ruby and remembered the times she hid behind Lucy Cranston's skirts from the fiercest creature in the farmyard. Suddenly she remembered she hadn't been to see Mrs Batty, her faithful cook from Windfell, for a while. There seemed to be no time for pleasant things in life at the moment, especially with Archie being away. 'How's Mrs Batty? I must go down and see her over Christmas and take her a basket full of gifts. She will miss us this Christmas.'

'She's doing well, ma'am. Lily, Mazy and I take turns in going down to see her once a week, and I don't think she's ever been as happy. Gertie Potts and Mrs Batty keep an eye on the comings and goings at the lock's cottages, so if there is ever anything you need to know about what goes on there, just ask them two.' Ruby sipped her tea and watched as Charlotte thought about Mrs Batty and Gertie Potts sharing gossip together.

'Mrs Potts must be a good age now.' Charlotte thought back to the old woman who had been one of her longest-serving residents.

'Yes, I believe she must be in her late eighties, but you wouldn't know it – she's still spritely.' Ruby smiled and cleared away her teacup.

'I hope I am spritely when I'm her age, Ruby.' Charlotte finished the last drop of tea and rose from the table.

'Thank you, ma'am. If you can let me know how many we will be expecting for Christmas as soon as you can, both Mazy and I would appreciate it. We will both have a lot to do, and then we will have to look at how many will be attending the wedding and what menu you will be wanting. Easter will soon follow Christmas; time usually flies, once the cold months of January and February have done their worst.' Ruby was relieved really that there wasn't to be a ball, for she wouldn't have had time, between making wedding cakes, Christmas cakes and all the frills of Christmas.

'I will, Ruby. And if you can put me a basket of baking and cooked meats together, I'll take them down to Mrs Batty towards the end of next week. I'll surprise her.' Charlotte walked up the stairs and out of the kitchen. She'd enjoyed her cup of tea with Ruby, it made a welcome change from keeping her own company. Ten days without Archie had seemed like a lifetime, and she was even missing Danny. It was time they both returned home.

Thomson held the front door of the manor open, as a carriage sent by Tom Beresford pulled up for Charlotte and she climbed hesitantly in. She really didn't want to waste her day looking around a lime kiln, with a man she thought quite obnoxious, if she was truthful. She sat back in the seat and looked out of the window at the frozen, sparkling white countryside passing by. She saw the familiar sight of Ferndale Mill and couldn't help but worry what was taking place there, as she squandered her day with Beresford. The mill's chimney was puffing out thick smoke and it was hanging around the mill in the crisp winter's air. With the River Ribble in full flood, the slowly melting snow made the river swell over its banks. Looking down on her empire, Charlotte realized how tired she was; the running of the mill had sapped all her energy for the last twenty years, and even though she was no longer so involved, she ultimately had responsibility for the running of it and the welfare of all its workers. She was tired; tired of being a strong woman, whom everyone tried to please and who was even afeared, in some cases. How she would like to be a genteel lady, sitting sipping tea with her friends and hopefully, in the future, having time for her grandchildren, if God was willing.

The carriage jolted suddenly, as the horses shied from the noise of a steam train passing over the small bridge they had turned under, to enter the Craven Lime Company's yard. The coachman shouted down his apologies into the carriage, bringing Charlotte back out of her thoughts as they pulled up into the yard.

'Charlotte, how wonderful you could join us. Please take my hand and let me escort you to my office. I have some tea and biscuits waiting, and then I thought I would show you around the kiln before my driver takes you home.' Tom Beresford held his hand out and guided Charlotte down from the carriage. 'I'm sorry the yard is a little dirty underfoot; no matter how hard we try, we cannot keep it clean, so please mind your skirts.'

Charlotte smiled at Tom as she took his hand and then walked carefully across the yard. 'I didn't realize Craven Lime was such a big concern, Mr Beresford.' She looked around her: the yard was a network of rail sidings, water tanks, engine sheds and stables, all surrounding and leading to the kiln itself. A huge kiln made of fireproof bricks dominated the yard, built under the hillside with twenty-two separate entrances to chambers within it and one hollow chamber, where a large chimney drew up the smoke that hung around the yard like a low grey cloud. Charlotte looked around at the wagons used to hold the coal, and at the crushed limestone waiting to be placed in the kiln by the men who were manually filling each individual chamber. She watched as the men, stripped to their waists even though it was midwinter, pushed the carts into each individual doorway, entering the soon-to-be blazing-hot kiln. The smell of burning lime and the noise of stone being crushed filled the air. Charlotte coughed as the lime-filled smoke hit the back of her throat.

'Come, let us go into my office, away from this putrid smoke.' Tom opened his office door and offered Charlotte a seat next to the window. 'I'm glad you have paid me this visit, as I wanted you to see how your support for building the Settle-to-Carlisle railway benefited my business as well as yours. If the line hadn't have been opened, it might have been a little different, for we would still have been transporting our lime by horse and cart. As it is, now we can load the railway wagons on the sidings and get them on their way, and sometimes with our customers by the following day.'

'Yes, we have benefited from the line as well – both by getting our supplies from the docks and dispatching to our customers more quickly – but perhaps not in the same way as you.' Charlotte watched as the yard came alive with men, some on top of the kiln, feeding coal down into whichever of the individual chambers was the next one to be lighted.

'We don't have that problem of receiving raw materials, as we have them on our own doorstep in the nearby quarry. The tubs of stone run by gravity, from the quarry to the weighbridge over there; and then, as you can see, once it is weighed, the ponies pull the stone around to the individual kiln that we are to fire next.' Tom squatted next to Charlotte, as he pointed out various stages of the limestone process and smiled at her after each sentence, making her feel uneasy as he touched her shoulder and breathed heavily next to her ear. He turned, just inches away from her lips, as he quickly rose to his feet once the maid came in with the tea and biscuits. 'We've a tight little firm here, and I don't stand for any nonsense. Profit, at the end of the day, is what we are about. Of course my position on the town council helps. Nobody dares to complain, else it will be the worse for them.' Tom sat on the edge of his desk and watched as Charlotte took in the scene of the busy working yard.

'Do you ever give the men and the ponies a rest period? It seems such a hard manual job to be doing.' Charlotte thanked the maid who passed her the cup of tea and watched some of the men; she noticed a few who were quite elderly struggling with the wagons of coal and stone.

'If they want their pay, they work the hours. Surely you work the same at the mill? Workers will only take advantage of you, if they think you are soft.' Tom laughed a shallow laugh, before picking up his teacup and taking a sip.

Charlotte looked out of the window and watched as a pony was thrashed across its back when it struggled with a load that it could not manage to pull. She decided not to ask to see any more at the yard. 'I believe people should be treated and paid fairly, as I hope we do at the mill, and I have tried to improve the conditions we have there.' She smiled at her host, who was reminding her by each second of her late husband, Joseph. Tom made her skin creep, with his fondness for getting too close to her and his disrespect for human life – or any life at all, if the treatment of the pony outside was common practice.

'Then they'll turn around and bite your hand eventually. Believe me, you should let them know who's boss, Charlotte, else you'll live to regret it,' Tom said quite sharply.

'I think, on that subject, we will agree to differ, Mr Beresford. Now, is your wife joining us tonight? I would dearly love to meet her; she is supporting my girls so well, with her purchase of their dresses.' Charlotte wasn't going to listen to Tom's advice. He was a hard man, a man with no morals, and she knew his sort.

'Please, it's "Tom"; after all, I'd like to think we are friends. Yes, she told me to tell you that she is looking forward to this evening. She is impressed with your daughter's designs. I can't say I'm impressed with her spending so much money on them, but whatever makes her happy. Because I certainly don't make that much money, at the moment.' Tom's face clouded over.

Charlotte sipped her tea and watched and listened to the man who reminded her, with every word he spoke, of her ex-husband. She'd make an excuse and make good her escape. 'Well, it will be wonderful to meet your wife. I hope you don't mind, Tom, but I've just remembered I've got an urgent matter to see to at Ferndale. Would you think it terribly rude of me if I take my leave, until this evening?' Charlotte had heard enough from the ignorant man, who seemed to hold no one in high esteem, and she pitied his poor wife for being in such a loveless marriage.

'No, not at all. As you say, we are seeing each other tonight. I'd hoped to show you around the yard, but I'm sure there will be future opportunities.' Tom opened his office door and shouted for his coachman to bring the coach and horse to the doorway.

'Until tonight. I'll be counting the minutes.' Tom gave Charlotte his hand and helped her up into the carriage.

'Until tonight.' Charlotte sat back in the darkness of the carriage and felt guilty about her lie, but she couldn't have stayed another minute looking out of the window or at Tom. Thank heavens his wife would be with him this evening. Perhaps she would curtail his ways; she certainly hoped so.

Charlotte looked across the table at her guest and sipped her soup slowly, aware that Tom Beresford was watching her every movement. She patted her lips with her napkin and smiled across at him. 'I'm sorry to hear your wife is unwell. I do hope that she recovers quickly. These stomach upsets can be most discomforting, so it's as well she stayed at home.'

'Yes, and that has left us two having dinner together, with your husband stuck up at Crummock. Just the way I like it, because I would like to get to know you better, Charlotte. I hope that you'll forgive me my honesty.' Tom smiled a rat-like grin across at his prey, making Charlotte's stomach churn.

'I'm sorry, Mr Beresford, but I feel that you have got the wrong end of the stick.' She pushed her napkin down onto her knee, accidentally making it fall to the ground.

'Come, Charlotte, you know it's "Tom". And you know exactly how I feel about you, else you wouldn't have visited the yard today – after all, it's no place for a woman. Just like the mill at Ferndale is no place of work for you, for it's a man's world that you are in.' He pushed his chair back and made his way to where Charlotte sat, bending down on one knee and grabbing her hand, before kissing it.

'Mr Beresford, you forget yourself, please resist. I'm a married woman and have no intention to appeal to you in that way. Now, kindly stand up and continue your dinner, else I will have to ask you to leave.' Charlotte pulled her hand away from her would-be suitor and stared at him.

Both heads turned as they heard the dining-room door open. Tom Beresford got quickly to his feet as soon as he realized someone was about to enter the room.

'Hey up – while the cat's away, the rats will play!' Archie entered the room and sat down in his chair at the head of the table. 'What do you think you are doing, having dinner with my wife, Beresford? Are you trying to fill my shoes?' Archie laughed, joking as he watched Tom Beresford pick up Charlotte's napkin and give her it back to her.

'Your wife was gracious enough to ask my wife and me for dinner this evening. Unfortunately, Flora wasn't well enough to join us. So yes, I've been greedy and had her all to myself.' Tom covered his tracks quickly.

'Archie, it's lovely to have you back home.' Charlotte got up from her chair, blushing as she hugged her husband and squeezed him tightly.

'By the left, I should leave home for a day or two more often, if that's the welcome I get.' Archie squeezed Charlotte in return, as she kissed his cheeks and whispered, 'I missed you.'

Tom looked down at his empty soup bowl, embarrassed by the couple's embrace and knowing that his plan of wooing Charlotte had not worked. 'I think I'd better return home now. I'm rather concerned that my wife might need me, for she did look ill. Besides, I'm sure you've news to share between you.'

'But you've not finished your dinner, man!' Archie sat back in his chair and beamed at Charlotte as she went to sit in her chair.

'There will another time, I'm sure. Thank you, Charlotte, for your invite this evening, and I hope you enjoyed your visit to the yard today.' Tom rose from his chair and made his way to the open doorway.

Charlotte followed him out into the hallway, summoning Thomson to get Tom's cloak, before whispering to him, 'I value your wife as a customer of my daughter, so I will not mention your behaviour to my husband or her. But believe me, you will not be welcome again in my home. And if you think you can threaten me in any way, through your position on the town council, think again. I am a woman of influence and strength, and don't you ever forget that. Thomson will see you out.'

Charlotte left Tom standing in the hallway as she walked back into the dining room, closing the doors behind her.

'I take it Beresford has been the lecher that he's known to be. Good job I came home when I did.' Archie laughed at Charlotte's fuming face.

'That man is a disgrace. His poor wife!'

'Come here, Mrs Atkinson. Come and show me just how much you've missed me.' Archie grabbed Charlotte by the waist and kissed her hard on the lips. 'No competition, Beresford, this woman will always be mine, and me hers, as long as we both have breath in our bodies.'

15

Charlotte glanced at the local paper with John Sidg-wick's image on the front page, looking decidedly riled and disgruntled. She shook her head as she read the report on the financial ruin of Sidgwick and the fore-closure of High Mill. Three hundred people to be made out of work because of his mismanagement. It would hit Skipton hard, unless a successor could be found to give the mill a new life. The week before Christmas as well, just the time of year when people relied on every penny.

'Here you are, ma'am, a basket full of things I know Mrs Batty likes. And I've put some slices of ham and a good roll of cooked brisket in there for her, as you suggested. It'll keep her fed for a week or two, never mind over Christmas.' Ruby handed over the brim-full basket to Charlotte and stood back to await her response.

'Thank you, Ruby. At least I take responsibility for

my workers, both young and old. This man doesn't give a damn about anybody but himself.' Charlotte folded the paper and placed it down on the table.

'I take it you mean John Sidgwick of High Mill. He's a wicked man. His poor workers, it's them I feel sorry for – they'll have empty bellies for sure this Christmas.' Ruby sighed.

'What goes around comes around, and he's only himself to blame. He should show respect for his fellow men. I have no sympathy for him, but as for the doffers, spinners and weavers who will have nothing, my heart bleeds. He'll be alright; he'll have siphoned enough off for himself – believe me, he'll have some funds somewhere. It's just his pride that will be hurt.' Charlotte picked up the basket from her side and walked into the hallway with Ruby. 'I'll be back for lunch, or I hope to be, if Mrs Batty doesn't keep me talking too long – you know what she's like. And if Gertie Potts is there, well, I'll be hard pressed to get a word in edgeways.' Charlotte smiled and waited as Thomson handed her cape to her. 'Once Mr Atkinson and Danny return with the Christmas tree, we will decorate the hall and the parlour, although perhaps we should wait for Miss Isabelle, else she will only be disappointed, like a petulant child. Can you tell Mr Atkinson just to leave the tree outside the back door, Thomson. Knowing him, half the needles will have dropped off before the tree has even been placed in the parlour, and he's no patience when it comes to putting up the tree, but he would insist that he went for it instead of Jethro. I dread to think what Mr Atkinson will be like when we are blessed with grandchildren. He will revert to his own childhood, I'm sure.'

'Whatever you wish, ma'am. Jethro has brought a good supply of holly and ivy from out of the wood, and he's already bashed the stems of the holly to make it last longer, once inside the house. And Mazy has taken the candles and their holders out of the cupboard, ready for the erection of the tree. Is Jethro taking you to see Mrs Batty?' Thomson held the door open for his mistress and watched as she stepped out into the icy morning.

'No, I'll walk and take the path down by the river, by cutting down through the park. It's a pleasant morning and the fresh air will do me good.' Charlotte hung the basket on her arm and walked away from the manor, making her way over the icy silver grassland of the surrounding park, until she came to the path that followed the river down to the weir and locks that fed the millpond; this brought her out to the small rows of cottages that had been built years back, for the mill's workforce. She caught her breath; no matter how hard she tried, every time she walked along the cobbles between the rows of workers' cottages she remembered how Joseph did the same walk, visiting his lover, Betsy Foster. Now she was even visiting Betsy's old cottage, to see Mrs Batty. It was unfortunate that hers had been the only cottage available for occupation at the time of her need.

She opened the wicket gate and knocked on the

red-painted door, the same door that she had knocked on the day her husband had been in bed above, while she had sympathetically given Betsy a loaf of bread to make up for lost hours in the mill. He must have heard every word she said and then laughed about her ignorance of the games he was playing, before returning to lie in his lover's arms. She looked up at the bedroom window and fought back the tears as she heard Mrs Batty making her way to the door.

'Give me a minute, I'm coming.' Mrs Batty yelled from behind the closed door before opening it. 'Oh, ma'am, what are you doing down here on this cold morning! Come on in, I've just lit the fire, and you must have known the kettle was nearly on the boil.' Mrs Batty shuffled forward and urged Charlotte to close the door behind her. 'I don't get up that early, these days – I'm making the most of my new life. After all the years of getting up at five to prepare breakfast and get the kitchen up and running for the day, I'm enjoying my leisure. Besides, the days are so long now. I've hardly anybody to talk to.'

'I don't blame you, Mrs Batty. But I thought you had Mrs Potts next door for company, and Ruby tells me she calls in on a regular basis.' Charlotte rested her basket on the kitchen table and quickly looked around the cottage that belonged to her, but which she had never been in before, because of its dark history. The cottage was basic: a two up and two down, with a lavvy outside, down at the bottom of the garden. A picture of Queen Victoria hung on the wall of the

217

small front room and various knick-knacks, collected over the years, made it home for the ageing cook.

'Oh, aye, but it's not the same as all the comings and goings of Windfell's kitchen. You'd always have someone coming or going, and something to do. The days are so long now, especially at this time of the year. There's only me and Gertie down here that doesn't work at your mill, so it is quiet through the day; and then it's dark by four of an evening and everyone's closed their doors to the night.' Mrs Batty placed two cups and saucers onto the table, her hands shaking as she did so.

'Can I help?' Charlotte took the milk jug from her and watched as Mrs Batty shakily filled the teapot from the kettle that had boiled on the fire.

'No, you cannot, ma'am. I might take my time, but I'm capable of making a pot of tea. Now, how are you and the family? I hear there's to be a wedding this coming spring, and that Miss Isabelle and Master Daniel's intended have a success on their hands, with the dress and milliner's shop on Duke Street.' Mrs Batty sat down and stirred the teapot until the tea had brewed, and then poured Charlotte and herself a cup each.

'Yes, it seems all to be happening. Danny is marrying Harriet on Easter Saturday. They've just set the date at St John's at Langcliffe. Isabelle and Harriet are busy sewing the dress, probably as we speak, in between customers, as they do seem to be very busy. Which is good, as I've invested heavily in the shop and need it to do well.' Charlotte watched as the old cook went to her dresser top and carried over a biscuit barrel.

'Have a biscuit. They are your favourite – ginger, the chewy ones made with a lot of syrup.' Mrs Batty pushed the biscuit barrel over the table to her visitor and bit into her baking, before dipping the remaining biscuit into her tea.

'You always did know what I liked. I shouldn't really, for my waist seems to expand at the slightest sight of food at the moment.' Charlotte smiled as she dipped her hand into the barrel and pulled out one of Mrs Batty's famous ginger snaps.

'Contented, that's what you are. Everything's going well in your world, and I couldn't wish it on anyone better. Not like my old employer, John Sidgwick – he's for the paupers' gaol if he's not careful, from what I hear. But knowing him, he'll have some money tucked away to save himself, but not his poor workers. Not that he'll care. He was a terrible man to work for, and I remember when he recommended me to Mr Dawson and how I breathed a sigh of relief when I got the position of cook at Windfell. I'd had enough of being at Sidgwick's beck and call at Skipton; he used to try and take advantage of all the young maids and he knew it was only a matter of time before I told his wife, so he was glad to see the back of me. Then, if you don't mind me saying, I ended up with one worse, with Joseph Dawson and his sister Dora. That was, until you came along.' Mrs Batty looked at Charlotte and held her hand out for her to hold over the table. 'You were like a breath of fresh air. He was such a fool not to realize what he had, but – like all men – he was never satisfied.'

Charlotte turned the conversation back to her present family. 'I don't know about "contented", Mrs Batty. To be honest, nothing seems to be going right at the moment. Danny's got pre-wedding nerves; Isabelle I don't think will ever be content with her lot in life; and we aren't exactly run off our feet at the mill. Testing times, with Archie just returning from Crummock after the recent blizzards; he's had to leave some of his sheep buried in the drifts that are still up there, he just can't find them all. So he's moaning about losing money.' Charlotte sipped her tea. She could have confessed so much more to the homely Mrs Batty, but knew that if she did, it would no longer be a secret. Mrs Batty and Gertie Potts would talk about the goings-on with anyone else who stepped over the threshold, so she had to keep her worries to herself, rather than let half of Settle know her business.

'I heard one of the workers saying things were a bit slack at the mill. You never know: if High Mill's gone to the wall, you might pick up a bit of work from them. They must have had some customers that will miss them.' Mrs Batty offered another biscuit, which Charlotte declined with a shake of her head.

'Something will turn up. And besides, it's Christmas next week. Three days of no worries, with just the family. We are having a quiet family Christmas this year and will probably do more for the New Year. What are you doing for Christmas?'

'I'm going to Gertie's. She's no family here, what with her lad being abroad, so we are keeping one another company. What we will have to eat, I don't know, as meat is that dear. I'm sure that butcher under the Shambles up in Settle thinks of a number and doubles it, just for fun. We'll probably have to make do with bread and dripping.'

'Well, that is the reason for my visit. With the manor having visitors, the kitchen is going to be busy, else you could have come and had dinner with the staff. But I've brought you the next best thing, thanks to Ruby. I think you'll find a Christmas cake and pudding, made from the manor's recipe, and meat for your dinner, along with pickles and whatever else you'll need for the festive period. We thought you would probably be having Christmas with Gertie, so there's enough for the two of you, and more besides.' Charlotte passed the full basket over to her red-faced cook.

'Oh, ma'am! You shouldn't – how can I ever thank you? I don't deserve all this. I'm already lucky enough to have this cottage, which you don't charge me for.' Mrs Batty wiped back a tear and looked quickly into the basket of delights.

'Are you alright living here, Mrs Batty?' Charlotte looked around the sparse but spotless cottage.

'Yes, I'm alright. A drop of gin sees me right before I go to bed, so don't you worry your head. I'm just grateful for a roof over my head.' Mrs Batty smiled.

'I'm glad you are happy. You will always have a home, as long as I'm alive.' Charlotte gave the old cook a hug and smiled.

'You keep your head up. Think of what you've done, and be proud of your family. You are a good woman, ma'am. I've always kept you in high regard, as does everyone that works for you.'

'Thank you, Mrs Batty, that means a great deal to me.'

'No problem, lass. I hope you and yours have a grand Christmas, a good family one with a lot of love – that's all anyone wants. Look forward, not back, and you'll not go far wrong. The past has gone, the future is yet to be written, and I'm sure you have plenty of ink still left in your pen.'

'Thank you, Mrs Batty, you have a good Christmas, too.'

'I will, lass, especially with all this basket of good stuff. Now go on, before this cottage reminds you of bad times and makes you more miserable. Go and tell Ruby that she'll miss me in that kitchen this Christmas. I'm not there to clean the fowl, and she hates taking the innards out of anything.' Mrs Batty laughed.

'I'll tell her. I bet she gives Eve the job,' Charlotte laughed.

'Aye, she will. It will save her retching, because she always does. Happy Christmas, ma'am.'

'Happy Christmas, Mrs Batty.' Charlotte left the cottage with a sense of relief. She loved her old cook, but the cottage stifled her every breath as she thought of the past tenant, God rest her soul.

'No, no – not there, and it isn't straight,' Mazy yelled at Jethro as he fought the branches of the largest fir tree that had ever entered the manor's parlour. 'Turn it that way a bit; just hide those branches at the back, they are a bit sparse. That's it, that's perfect.' Mazy stood back and admired the majestic fir tree, which was freshly cut from Windfell's small copse. The smell of pine filled the room, making her smile, for it was now the familiar smell of Christmas. 'I do love seeing the Christmas tree going up. It was a lovely idea that Prince Albert gave us, when he married our Queen, bless his soul.'

'Aye, bless him. It weighs a ton, does that tree. I'd have liked to have seen Prince Albert turn it this way and that way on a whim.' Jethro stood back and looked at his handiwork and got his breath back. 'I think it's a lump bigger this year, or it seems to be; it certainly weighs more, or I'm losing my strength.'

'It's you – you're just a weed, Jethro Haygarth; there's no strength in those weedy arms of yours,' Mazy joked with the man Windfell depended on, for any job that nobody else wanted to do.

'I'll give you weedy, Mazy Banks – come here!' Jethro chased her around the settee and caught her as she giggled and protested, falling into a heap on the soft cushions. 'Here, put this in your hair: a sprig of fir for a right bonny Christmas rose.' Jethro flumped down beside her and smiled as he placed a piece of fir in her hair. He placed it gently behind her ear and smiled as she looked at him, holding his breath as he decided to do what he'd been meaning to do for a good few months now, and closed his eyes and kissed Mazy on the lips. His life above the stable had been lonely of late and, while horses were his everything, they'd not look after him in years to come. Mazy had always been kind to him and he felt something for her – something he couldn't quite put his finger on, until that moment.

She pushed him back gently, surprised by his spontaneous action. 'Jethro, what did you do that for?' She looked into the green eyes that she'd admired from afar and blushed.

'Because I've wanted to do it for months, and have never dared until now. You didn't seem to mind too much, though, Mazy. Should we do it again – quickly, before they find us?' Jethro held Mazy's hand and looked into her eyes.

'I don't mind if we do.' Mazy looked at the groom that she'd had her eye on for a while, although she had not dared to make her feelings known. She closed her eyes and felt a warmth that she had never before experienced in her life, as Jethro kissed her gently. She had thought she was never going to know a man's touch; and here she was, kissing and carrying on, on the settee in the parlour of Windfell.

'Will you walk out with me, Mazy? I know I'm only a groom and jack-of-all-trades, and a bit below your station, with you being the housekeeper. But I'm not a bad soul and I've saved a bob or two, so I can take you out and treat you like a lady.' He held Mazy's hand and waited for a reply.

'I'd be honoured to, Jethro.' Mazy leaned forward and kissed him back on the lips.

'By, I never thought you would – you've made my day.' Jethro grinned. 'Sunday then, we'll have a look around the Christmas market in Settle?'

'Sunday it is. Now we'd better get a move on, before we are found.' Mazy smiled as she felt her stomach flutter, at the thought of walking around Settle on Jethro's arm, as she rose from the settee.

'That's grand. I can't wait.' Jethro beamed as he walked out of the parlour for the stepladder, nearly bumping into Charlotte as she walked across the hallway.

'Are you alright, Jethro? You look quite flushed.' Charlotte stopped him in his tracks.

'I'm fine, ma'am, just been putting up the tree with Mazy. It took some putting in place, but it looks lovely now.' He gave a quick glance at Mazy as she quickly patted a strand of hair in place, before talking to her mistress.

'The tree looks magnificent, ma'am. We just need Miss Isabelle to say where she would like the candles placing, when she returns from Settle. Jethro's going for the stepladder now.' Mazy gathered her thoughts and watched as Jethro made his escape. She hoped her looks didn't reveal her true feelings, as she resorted to her position of housekeeper.

'Thank you both. It must be Christmas, if the tree is up and about to be decorated. I must say, I don't feel like it this year,' Charlotte admitted.

'You will, I'm sure, once it's here. Ruby's already filling the kitchen with the amazing smells of Christmas. And then, before you know it, we will be into a new year and it will be Master Daniel's wedding.' Mazy tried to cheer up her mistress. Her spirits had been down since reading about the closure of High Mill and visiting the Langcliffe Lock cottages.

'You are right. I've a lot to be thankful for, and a lot to look forward to. Now, let's have a look at this tree. Archie tells me that he's done us proud.' Charlotte smiled and walked into the parlour. 'Heavens, no wonder Jethro looked red in the face!' Charlotte stood back and looked at the tree that dominated the parlour and reached just shy of six inches from the ceiling.

'Yes, it took some putting up this year. I think it's the tallest we have had so far. Poor Jethro struggled a bit.' Mazy laughed.

'Well, it should definitely be the centre of our Christmas. Also we have a musician, in Harriet, this year. I believe she can play the piano quite well, so we can have a singalong. I've been waiting for someone to play it as it should be played, ever since I bought it. I can play, but only a little, and Isabelle has never shown any interest.' Charlotte looked around her parlour. This year it was going to be a family Christmas, just

Archie and her and the children, including Harriet. It was to be spent with people whom she loved. She'd survived yet another year, with her close family intact and the mill still working, and for that she was thankful. She should be more positive, and not dwell on the negatives, for life was good really.

16

John Sidgwick sat in the corner of the King Billy inn and listened to the incessant talking of the little mill worker, who obviously had a gripe with his employer.

'Bloody woman – she looks after her own, that's what she does. Doesn't care the amount of hours we put in, or that we have mouths to feed.' Walter Gibson looked into the bottom of his gill and wiped the dribble off his chin.

'I think it's time you went home, Walter,' said the landlord. 'As you say, you've plenty of mouths to feed. All the better fed if you don't waste your money here. Your Martha will be wondering where you've got to. Be thankful Mrs Atkinson has given you Boxing Day off, as some other mills are back open and working.' The landlord had heard enough from the loquacious troublemaker who liked the sound of his own voice. 'Mrs Atkinson is a good soul; she does right by them that do right by her. Now, get yourself back up to your cottage at the locks.'

'Bugger you, you bloody hypocrite! You were keen to take my money off me when I first come in, but now I've nowt left, you don't want me here.' Walter stood up from his seat and wobbled unsteadily, before making for the door. He glanced around the rundown, mucky pub and at the equally grubby landlord.

'Night, Walter, you take care,' the landlord yelled after him, as he watched Walter nearly bump into a customer who was entering the King Billy.

'He looks a bit worse for wear.' Sidgwick placed his tankard on the bar and ordered another, as he talked to the landlord.

'Oh, aye, he likes his gill, does Walter. Trouble is, he doesn't keep his thoughts to himself. He doesn't realize when he's well off. I think if I was Charlotte Atkinson, I'd be getting rid of him, as he never has a good word for her. You don't bite the hand that feeds you, I was always told.' The landlord passed the gent in front of him his drink and pocketed the payment.

'He works up at Ferndale then?' Sidgwick quizzed.

'Aye, he does at the moment, in the carding room. I wouldn't have him working for me, for he'll never be satisfied with what he's got. He's just one of those that thinks he knows better than anyone else. Yet he knows nowt.'

'Lot of them about.' Sidgwick smiled and then went back into his corner and savoured his pint, before going to see his close friend Dora Bloomenber.

*

229

'So, John, as you suspected, the year's not been good to you. I read all about High Mill being closed, in the local rag. They like to kick a man when he's down, don't they?' Dora sat back in her chair and sipped her brandy, looking slowly across at her brother's onetime best friend.

'Aye, well, you know all about that. They are like a dog with a bone – they never let anything drop.' John Sidgwick leaned forward in his chair and warmed his hands in the baking heat from the grand fire that warmed the luxurious drawing room of Ingfield House. 'You've done well for yourself, Dora. Old Ezera must have been worth a bob or two.' He leaned back and took a sip of brandy as he looked around the extravagant furnishings.

'True, there's not a lot I want for. But I earned it, mind you. Married to an old man, and all he thought about was his shop; never showed me an inch of affection or gratitude. He lasted a lot longer than I thought he would, with only dying last year. Ninety-bloody-two he was, would you believe it? When I married him, I thought he only had a few years left. I thought of knocking him off a time or two, but I'd never have got away with it; folk have long memories, when it comes to being Joseph Dawson's sister. And once Ezera found out the truth about me, he was never the same, never trusted me.'

'I think I should have gone for an older woman – not a young bit of a thing.' John sighed. 'My courting and sweeping your niece off her feet came to nowt, once her mother got to know. The bloody bitch! She didn't even let me across the threshold of Windfell. She had her butler and groom throw me off the premises. I had her darling Isabelle in the palm of my hand, because she was so gullible. There would have been no scandal over High Mill, because she'd have had to back me, to keep her pretty daughter away from bankruptcy, if I'd wed her.'

'You moved too fast, John. You should have listened to my advice and played it slower. I did try and help you as much as I could, warning you that Charlotte Atkinson is a bitch – a strong bitch who will protect her family, no matter what. She came from next to nothing, and now she thinks of herself as God's gift. Ferndale Mill and Windfell should be mine, for they were my brother's – nothing to do with a poor little farm girl. Have you seen the fancy dress shop she's set up her precious daughter in, and the dumb bitch that worked for me? From what I hear, it's a success, because all the leading local ladies are supporting her. Sheep, that's all they are!'

'She's not as popular as you think. I've heard one of Mrs Atkinson's workers cursing her, in the King Billy. I don't know who the drunk fool was, but he hated her.' John laughed and swigged back the last drops of his brandy. 'I thought: here is a man to be admired, for he obviously sees through the all-caring Mrs Atkinson.'

'You may joke, John, but perhaps this man could be of use to us. An insider who hates Charlotte: we could use him for our purposes. Perhaps we should start to think about bringing Charlotte Atkinson back down to earth.' Dora sniggered.

'Dora Dodgson, your brother had nothing on you. He had the charm, but you have the brains and, looking around here, the money. We'd make an interesting couple, Dora.' John smiled and thought about the bank account of the rich widow sitting across from him.

'I think not, John. As you've already said, I have brains, and I don't wish to share my life with anyone other than myself.' Dora knew John Sidgwick well and only endured his company because he might be useful to her at some point in her life. But as a husband – never!

'Get yourself back home, Gibson, and consider your wages this week docked by a day. We can't have you coming into work as you are. Go home and sober up.' Charlotte watched as Bert Bannister gave Walter Gibson his marching orders for the day, after a near-accident at the carding machine.

'But my wife: she'll play hell with me. We need the money.' Walter stood in the doorway.

'You should have thought about that last night, when you were swigging gills back in the King Billy. You are neither use nor ornament to us, in the state you are in. Nelly Hodgson nearly lost her hand because of your neglect. Think yourself lucky Mrs Atkinson isn't giving you the sack. Many a boss would.'

Walter walked down the stairs, moaning about his lot for the whole world to hear.

'You need to get rid of him, he's trouble. He was bad enough when he just moaned, but now he drinks and moans.' Bert sat in the chair across from Charlotte, picked up a pencil on the desk and played with it, to control his frustration over the mouthy worker.

'But he's got a large family, and Martha is such a good wife. She doesn't deserve any more worry in her life. Besides, Walter's only celebrated Christmas a little too much – we can overlook it this time.' Charlotte looked across at her right-hand man and smiled. 'This will make you happier.' She passed the order that Smedhurst Textiles had just placed with her and waited for Bert's reaction.

'This can't be right. Surely they've placed the nought in the wrong place!' he gasped.

'No, it's right. I've just seen their main buyer out of the building. It will clear the warehouse of all back-stock and keep us in production well into spring. When we finished at Christmas, I wondered whether to sell the mill and call it a day, and then he walked in and made me realize that I'd be a fool to do so – or not just yet anyway.' Charlotte grinned.

'Who has he been dealing with up to now? Because I bet they will miss his order.' Bert sat back and looked at the order that secured work for one and all.

'Sidgwick at Skipton. Smedhurst was ashamed to tell me. They had been trying to leave High Mill for some time, but his late wife, Mrs Sidgwick, and Mrs

Smedhurst were sisters, so they kept it in the family.' Charlotte smiled at Bert and then stood up and looked out through the glass window across the mill. 'I love a good order; keeps your mind sharp and makes the workers happy and secure.'

'You'll have all on to make Walter Gibson ever happy, Charlotte. He's a whingeing, ungrateful sod who doesn't do right by anybody. But the rest of the workers will appreciate the news; perhaps not so much the hard work they've to put into it, but they will appreciate keeping their jobs. Everyone was a bit nervous this Christmas, with Sidgwick's going to the wall.' Bert stood next to her and looked down at the mill floor. Everyone was working flat out, all doing their part to keep Ferndale Mill going.

'Walter Gibson is on his own. Look at them all, Bert, all these people depend on us. When I first stood here, I thought I would fail within the first month, but I was determined not to, as much for the families working down on the mill floors as for me. I must never forget that it isn't just about me and my family, but my extended family who work for me. No matter how much they whinge, I am responsible for them, whether they like it or not. Besides, the New Year will get off to a good start, and most of them will be happy with a few more bob in their pockets. I have a feeling this year is going to be a good one.' Charlotte leaned back and looked again at the order that was going to secure the next twelve months. It had filled her with new determination and hope.

*

The Atkinson family stood around the grand fireplace of Windfell's parlour and made their guests welcome.

'Come, sit a bit closer to the fire and get warm. We've a good blaze going, and there's a bowl full of punch that will warm the cockles of your heart,' Charlotte urged Betty Armstrong, who still looked cold after her ride down from the frozen moors above Winskill.

'Never mind punch – I've a good malt, Ted, that'll be more up our street.' Archie made his way to the sideboard and poured himself and Ted a tumbler each.

'Erm . . . what happened to "ladies first"?' Charlotte commented.

'You're alright. Thomson's coming to serve you, ladies. Danny, do you want a malt, or is that a daft question?' Archie poured another and passed it to his son, then winked at him as he went to be with Harriet. 'Did you lose many sheep in that blizzard, Ted? We've still some missing, but the drifts are shrinking now; they should be making their selves free, if they've survived. I always remember when I was a lad, an old lass of a sheep was found late spring in one of the last drifts to melt. She was still alive, but she'd eaten her own wool and was bare as could be. Now, that's survival for you.'

'No, I've been lucky. I can account for nearly all my flock, but I haven't a quarter of what you have.' Ted sipped his malt and warmed himself against the fire.

'What a beautiful tree! We don't bother with one,

235

now the children are older. But next year we will have to.' Betty smiled and couldn't control any longer the secret that she was keeping. 'We are going to be grandparents. Our Agnes is expecting her first; it's due in June, they think, so I'm excited.'

'Congratulations to you both. We must raise our glasses to that news.' Charlotte thanked Thomson as he filled everybody's hands with a glass of punch. 'To the new baby!' Charlotte toasted.

'To the new baby!' Everyone cheered.

'Yes, Agnes is sorry, but she has declined the invitation to be maid of honour at our wedding. She said she would feel uncomfortable.' Harriet looked at Isabelle. 'It's a good job we hadn't started on her dress, Izzy.'

'Not to worry. That gives us more time to concentrate on your dress, and mine. We have been so busy in the run-up to Christmas and the ball season that we haven't really been giving the wedding our full attention.' Isabelle shrugged.

'I never realized we were going to be so busy. It is a good job you bought the sewing machine, ma'am. We would never have coped without it, and Isabelle is getting to be as good a seamstress as myself.' Harriet looked at her family gathered around her and smiled.

'We are really proud of both of you,' said Archie. 'And this time next year, you and Danny will be ensconced in Crummock, enjoying your first Christmas and New Year together, and perhaps announcing the same news as your sister.' Archie grinned as Harriet blushed at the thought of producing a child.

'A toast to our families: may we always be happy and successful, and blessed with money, but most of all let us keep our health, because without that we are nothing.' Archie raised his glass and beamed at the faces made rosy with drink, and at his children both looking up at him with adoration. He was a lucky man.

'Good health!' Everyone cheered, stopped short by Thomson's entrance.

'Dinner is served.' Thomson stood in the doorway and held the parlour door open for the family to go through to the dining room, then patiently waited as each one went through and he heard the excited exclamations of the guests as they looked at the extravagantly laden table.

'Oh, Charlotte – this is too much, really!' Betty Armstrong caught her breath. 'Pineapple: where did you get that from? I have never tasted it, and never thought I ever would.' She gasped at the fresh pineapple in the display in the centre of the table. 'And just look at that side of beef on the sideboard.'

'Nothing is too much for my family. They mean everything to me. Now please, everyone, enjoy your meal. And afterwards, Harriet, if you are prepared to play, we can have a singalong around the piano. Although I wouldn't advise you to stand next to Archie – he's tone-deaf.'

'Don't worry, my dear, I will just sit next to the fire

and listen. I aim to fill my stomach and then have a snooze.' Archie grinned as Thomson helped him into his seat at the table and then served him his soup. 'It's nice to have a day with no worries, and with my family around me. Now, please, enjoy all this and let us welcome in the New Year in style.'

'Just listen to Miss Isabelle singing, hasn't she got the most beautiful voice?' Ruby stopped for a moment from serving the servants' dinner at the kitchen table down in the basement of Windfell.

'She certainly has. I think Miss Harriet plays the piano beautifully, too. The family seem really happy.' Thomson waited as Ruby placed a dish of leeks in white sauce next to him, to help himself from.

'I wish Miss Isabelle would find herself a young man, and then the family is complete. A decent young man – not like the old fox Sidgwick that nearly broke her mother's heart.' Ruby sat down and watched her colleagues help themselves to the results of her hard work.

'She will, there's always someone for everyone.' Mazy smiled across at Jethro. 'It's never too late to find true love.'

Jethro smiled at the young woman he'd enjoyed escorting around Settle's Christmas market and knew that in the coming year they would grow closer.

'Listen, Mr Atkinson is reciting "The Mistletoe Bough".' Thomson paused and looked around at the faces as they heard their master's voice shouting out

the much-loved lines of the Thomas Haynes Bayly
verse from above stairs:

> *The mistletoe hung in the castle hall*
> *The holly branch shone on the old oak wall*
> *The Baron's retainers were blithe and gay,*
> *Keeping the Christmas holiday.*

> *The Baron beheld with a father's pride,*
> *His beautiful child, Lord Lovell's bride.*
> *And she, with her bright eyes seemed to be*
> *The star of that goodly company.*
> *Oh, the mistletoe bough.*
> *Oh, the mistletoe bough.*

The servants listened as the drawing room erupted
with applause at the end of the verse.

'Aye, I hope he's not brought bad luck on this
house tonight. I always think it's a dark poem, especially when they get to the bit where they find his
bride's skeleton in that chest after all those years. I
don't think he's given much thought to the fact that
his Danny is about to get married. Let's just hope he's
not cursed it.' Ruby Pratt got up from the table and
walked over to the pan that was steaming a spotted
dick in it for pudding.

She pulled the steamed dessert out of the pan
of boiling water and started to unfold it from the
muslin that surrounded it, before taking it to the table,

239

looking around at expectant faces as she served it up, before adding the thick custard around it.

'This'll be better than any fancy pineapple, and a lot more filling.' She grinned as she watched the dishes empty.

The mill was working full out as the winter's night closed around it. The gas lights were burning brightly, to enable work to be carried on later into the hours leading up to New Year's Eve.

'You'd think they'd let us go a bit earlier tonight. It's New Year's Eve, and I'd like to have a gill to see the new year in,' Walter moaned, as he picked up a basket of full spindles from the carding room to be taken downstairs and spun on the busy mules.

'I'm just glad of the hours. My Gladys needs new shoes, and the rent is to go up, so I'm not moaning. Besides, it's only another day – it's nothing to celebrate, is New Year.' Walter's co-worker, Josie, wished he'd shut his mouth for once and get on with his job.

'Aye, but them in the big house will be toasting it in, you can be sure of that. I bet if I go downstairs with this lot and I look up into the office, Charlotte bloody Atkinson won't be there looking down on us. She'll not want to work on New Year's Eve,' Walter growled.

'Trouble with you, Walter, is you don't know your place in life. There's them, and there's us. And we are just thankful we've got a job and a family to go home to. Besides, Mrs Atkinson's been here most of the day.

She walked around and said hello to everyone this afternoon with Bert Bannister.' Josie had no time for the moaning that her work colleague indulged in nearly every day. It was beginning to wear on her.

'Hmm . . . they only came around to make sure we were ahead with this big order. They don't care.' Walter lifted the basket of spools and walked away from Josie, who was shaking her head and pretending not to hear above the noise of the carding machine.

Opening the double doors into the spinning room, he carried his basket along the pathway with laboured breath, to the first mule that looked in need of replenishing. The noise from the busy mules was deafening, as he indicated to the worker that she had a new delivery. He stood back and caught his breath, then watched the spinning mules going back and forth, quicker and quicker, as their handlers watched for any irregularities in the process. Dust and cotton fluff filled the air, and Walter coughed as he found it hard to breathe. An exceptionally large piece of fluff floated over his head in the upward draught caused by the mules and landed on the unguarded gas light next to him. It caught light instantly, and Walter's immediate reaction was to pull it away from the flame and stamp it out on the wooden floor below. He raised his hand and wafted the burning fibres down to the floor, but a downward draught caught it and blew it into the nearby working mule. Immediately the lit fluff spread within the workings of the mule. The dry cotton fibres caught ablaze and spread within the working machine. Walter watched

241

on in horror as the mule-minder shouted, 'Fire!' and the young lad who had been working as the piecer screamed and yelled, as the fluff from underneath the mule caught light and travelled to him, setting his trousers ablaze.

Walter watched in disbelief as the boy ran, alight, down the length of the mules, screaming as he made for the double doors and escape. In the blink of an eye the whole floor descended into chaos, as the fire spread along the floor from mule to mule, with the dry cotton fluff feeding it. The fire spread like lightning, up the pulley belts and into the room above. The women and children screamed and made for the doors, piling on top of one another in a bid to escape. Some of the men grabbed fire buckets filled with sand from the walls, in a desperate attempt to extinguish the strengthening furnace. Flames licked the walls, and the smoke crept upwards and down to the rooms below. The workers in the carding room above were caught in the fire and smoke, and the women screamed in desperation as they tried to flee the licking flames. The sound of clogs clattering down the stone stairs filled the air as the fire cracked and burned.

Walter followed the wall out of the spinning room and pushed and shoved his fellow workers down the stairs, hoping and praying that he could save his own life as well as that of his co-workers. All the time he was worrying that he was responsible for the raging fire that was engulfing the mill. Had anyone seen him accidentally feed the fire? He hadn't meant to cause this damage, and he had intended to put out the piece of fired cotton fibre. His mind raced back to the previous evening's conversation with John Sidgwick, who had asked Walter if he could cause as much disruption to the mill as he could, if he were to offer him a small payment. Walter had dismissed John instantly; he might not like Charlotte Atkinson, but he knew better than to jeopardize people's jobs and safety. Now he felt responsible for this – the burning down of Ferndale Mill. If anyone had heard John Sidgwick and his conversation, the blame would lie on him.

Workers jostled and pushed Walter as he tried to keep his footing on the steep stone steps. One more flight to go and he'd be out through the warehouse doors. Women screamed and there was a bang, as a loom was heard crashing down through the floorboards from above, as the floor gave way. Then suddenly the smell of fresh air hit his nostrils as he approached the warehouse doors, where everyone rushed to get out into the night air, away from the burning mill. He'd never been so grateful in his life to smell the frosty, cold air of New Year's Eve.

Out in the yard, women and children wailed as the men ran back and forth with buckets full of water, dousing whatever flames they could get at and dampening the attached weaving shed, which the flames had not yet reached. Coughing and bent double, Walter looked up at the four storeys of Ferndale Mill: flames were licking out of every window, and the breaking of glass made standing anywhere near the mill impossible.

He watched as Sally Oversby gathered the carding-room women and children together, and Bert Bannister did the same with the spinning-room and warehouse staff out on the open roadside, which was lit up by the orange-and-yellow dancing flames, making a note of who was missing and who had escaped the devastation. Walter put his head in his hands and sobbed. He was responsible for this night's work. Why had he not let the cotton-fluff dust just burn on the gas light – it would have done no harm there. A momentary lapse of his senses had led to this. Lives were sure to have been lost and it was all his fault.

'Shift your arse, Walter. Grab this bucket and join the chain. Let's at least try and save the weaving shed, or are you too lazy to help with this an' all?' One of the overseers thrust a bucket into his hands and pushed him into the chain of men who were battling to save the shed. Walter grabbed the bucket and passed it from right to left down the line to the millpond, his face covered with smoke and tracks of tears visible to all as the fire raged on. In the distance the sound of the horse-drawn fire-cart could be heard coming from Settle, the bell only distant at first, then becoming clearer as it came down the lane and drew up alongside the millpond. Quickly the double-serving police-fire-officers unharnessed the team of frightened horses and led them into the safety of a nearby field, before manning the pumps and setting about saving the mill. The officers ran hoses along the sides of the millpond and aimed them at the high windows, while two officers pumped fervently on the wagon to transfer the water and give the men holding the hoses good pressure. The workers watched as the race to save Ferndale Mill started. They'd lost their jobs and some of their possessions, with coats and whatever had been in their pockets left behind, but at least they had all escaped with their lives. A count had assured the workers that everyone was accounted for, and the injured were quickly taken in a horse and cart into Settle to be attended to by Dr Burrows. All they could do now was watch and pray that the damage was not too substantial, and that the great mill could be saved.

'Ma'am, ma'am, you'd better come and have a look. I was just adjusting the curtains in the drawing room and I noticed a flickering of flames down by the mill, and I think I can hear the sound of the fire-engine!' A flustered Thomson took hold of his mistress's arm and pulled back the curtains for her to see.

'Oh my God – Ferndale, it's Ferndale on fire!' Charlotte caught her breath and watched for a second. 'I've got to get down there. People might be in there!' She turned to Archie.

The whole family caught their breath as they watched the flames climbing high into the winter's sky, lighting up the darkness with the cracking of sparks, like a spectacular bonfire, with flames licking around the outlines of the black trees and branches.

'Come on, I'll take you down in the trap. It will be faster than walking.' Archie looked at his worried wife as she waited for Thomson to get her cape. 'It'll be alright, don't worry – just as long as nobody's lost their life.'

'I'll get the trap, you look after Mother.' Danny walked quickly to the back door of the manor while Archie put his arm around Charlotte.

'Is there anything we can do?' Betty and Ted echoed together.

'No, stay here. Isabelle, you look after our guests. It may not be as bad as it looks. Oh, my Ferndale . . . how can this have happened?' Charlotte was shaking as Archie took her arm to the front door to await the trap.

'Please, all of you, stay here. It'll be no place for party dresses this evening. Ted, I'll send for you if we need you.' Archie looked at the women dressed in their finery; a few seconds ago they had been laughing and joking, enjoying the evening. Now all were in tears. 'Where is that lad? How long does it take him to get Jethro to put the pony into the trap?' Archie swore as what seemed an age passed, while they waited for the pony and trap to arrive at the front door.

'Sorry. I was asleep in my bunk, else I'd have been here a long time before now. I can't believe I hadn't noticed, or smelled, the burning on the wind, but as I say, ma'am, I've been asleep. Are you alright, ma'am? It might not be as bad as it looks from up here.' Jethro watched as Charlotte pulled up her skirts and Archie joined her in the trap. 'Mr Danny is saddling his horse – he's following us down.' Jethro cracked his whip, feeling guilty at not noticing that something was wrong at the mill, and set the pony off at breakneck speed.

Charlotte held back the tears as the smell of burning filled the air and sparks lit the dark skies overhead. As they turned down the lane to the mill, they could see the outline of figures fighting the fire, and the women workers standing high on the grass banking, watching in disbelief as their livelihoods disappeared in front of their eyes. An almighty crash filled the air as the roof of the mill collapsed in on itself, and the watching crowd gasped and moved further back from the flames.

'Bloody hell, Charlotte, it's gone – you've no mill left!' Archie helped her down from the trap and stood looking at the burning carcass of the once-proud mill.

'Ma'am, I'm so sorry, ma'am. Your beloved mill, gone in a matter of minutes!' Sally Oversby ran to her employer's side. 'It happened so quickly, we were lucky to escape with our lives.' Smoke-tracked tears ran down her face, and her clothes reeked with the smell of the fire that had raged around her.

'I'm sorry, Sally – are you alright? Does anyone know yet how it happened?' Charlotte put her arm around the shaking woman who, up to the moment of seeing her mistress, had acted so strongly, protecting and accounting for everyone else.

'I'm fine, but like most of us, a bit shaken. And heartbroken at the loss of Ferndale. I don't know how the fire began, but it moved quickly. There was nothing more the fire service could have done, ma'am.' Both women watched as the fire and bright-red sparks floated up into the sky, outlining the distraught figure of Archie.

'What am I going to do now, Archie? Look at it, my beloved Ferndale.' Charlotte gazed around her at the desolation, and at the sobbing women and children. 'My world of cotton has ended this night.'

17

Bert Bannister stood in the cobbled mill yard and watched as Charlotte walked around the ruins of Ferndale. 'At least we saved the weaving shed, and we'd supplied Smedhurst's with part of their order.' He tried to cheer up his employer.

'But look at it, Bert. I can never build it up again. And the workers, what are they going to do?' Charlotte walked over to where Bert stood, picking her way through the rubble and past the singed bales of cotton that had been flung out of the warehouse in a vain attempt at salvage.

'At least you were insured. Surely it's just a matter of waiting for the insurance company to pay out to you and then setting about putting it all back together?' Bert looked up at the burnt-out shell and knew he was being optimistic.

'I don't know if I want to do that. I became the owner of Ferndale by misfortune, and happen this is

249

where it and I part ways. Perhaps it is time for me to sit back and wait for my grandchildren, and be a lady of leisure.' Charlotte sighed.

'If you don't mind me saying: that you could never do. You'd be bored within the first week.' Bert knew his mistress well and couldn't believe that she was admitting defeat.

'I don't know, Bert. Lately life has thrown a lot at us, and this just tops it. But there's all the workers – I've to do right by them. I just don't know what to do any more.' Charlotte looked around at her destroyed empire and breathed in deeply. 'I've paid everybody's wages up to the end of the month and told them to try and find work elsewhere, because let's face it: it will be months, if not years, before this place is up and running again – if ever.'

'Mrs Bannister and I appreciate the money; it gives us a little breathing space until we both know what to do next. If you decide to rebuild and need a labourer, I can turn my hand to almost anything.' Bert looked worried. Unlike his employer, he hadn't many savings to fall back upon and, no matter how much he revered Charlotte Atkinson, he needed work to keep his world as he knew it.

'Bless you, Bert, you have always been there for me, and I don't think I've ever told you how much I have appreciated your support over the years. You would be the first I offered employment to.' Charlotte patted his shoulder.

'Just don't take on Walter Gibson again, if you

250

decide to rebuild. He might be good at his work, but he's easily swayed by circumstances and gossip. Even on the night of the fire, he just stood and watched like a gormless idiot until he was made to help.' Bert shook his head.

'I won't, and at least he's got a roof over his head, living in the lock cottages. I can't turf him out, not with all those children around his feet, and no work now. It's his wife I feel sorry for, with another baby on the way and Walter with such a bad reputation. No one will want to employ him.' Charlotte scowled.

'You are too good to him – he doesn't deserve your sympathy. Did the insurers have any idea how the fire started?' Bert enquired.

'No, not really, but the women in the spinning room said there was a lot of dust and fluff in the air, so they are blaming a lamp igniting a piece and it floating into the mule that Margaret Alderson was at. She said that was where the fire started, and the blaze came from nowhere. Her son got badly burned, as the fire caught hold of the fluff on his trousers and the lad was that frightened he ran out of the building, alight, instead of staying still and someone dampening him down. It's frightening to think of everyone who was in there, and I'm thankful we have only her son and a few others with burns. It could have been so much worse.'

'Aye, well, there's nothing that can be done, for now. You'll just have to wait and see what comes out of it all. And don't blame yourself; it was an accident, there was nothing you could have done about it.' Bert kicked a loose stone across the cobbled yard and felt like swearing. Of all the mill owners in the district, Charlotte Atkinson was the most honourable and she didn't deserve the trouble she was in.

'I'll try not to. It's just that I can't bear to think of so many lives being affected by the blaze. I lie in bed of a night and think of the families that the mill supported, and I worry how they are going to exist.' Charlotte turned her head from Bert and wiped a tear away from her cheek.

'Folk around here are as hard as nails, Charlotte. They'll make a do, don't you worry. If they want work, they'll find it.' Bert felt like putting his arm around her, but knew that was not the done thing. 'Now come on. I'll walk up to the lane end with you. I don't like the look of this sky; it's threatening rain. And it's no good moping down here, for there's nothing either of us can do.'

'Alright, Bert. Once I've decided what to do, I'll let you know. Poor Archie watched me leave home this morning and just didn't know what to do to help me. I should get back to him and put on a brave face, for the sake of him and my family. After all, it's not the first cotton mill that's been razed to the ground – it's a hazard of the trade.' Charlotte picked up her skirts and walked along the furrowed track back up the road to Langcliffe.

*

'You've visitors awaiting you, ma'am, in the library. I've made them comfortable and served them tea.' Thomson took Charlotte's mantle, hat and gloves.

'Who awaits me, Thomson? Did you not tell them I was out?' She was in no mood for visitors and just wanted some peace and quiet while the manor was empty.

'It is Lorenzo and Hector Christie. They insisted that they would wait until you returned.'

'I suppose I will have to talk to them. Hector's a close friend, and he will have come to give me his sympathies.' Charlotte smoothed her skirts and checked herself in the hallway mirror.

Thomson opened the library door for Charlotte and watched as she walked over to the Christies, revered cotton manufacturers in the area. Both men rose from their seats to greet Charlotte.

Hector, Lorenzo's son, held out his hand for Charlotte to take and smiled. 'You look pale, Charlotte. You must be going through hell. We can't begin to know what it feels like, and the burning of the mill must be a huge loss to you.'

'Thank you, Hector. I feel like my whole world has fallen apart. But not as much as my workers, who are left with nothing.' Charlotte urged both men to sit and make themselves comfortable, and watched as Lorenzo struggled to sit down with a stick supporting him, to help with the pain in his knees. 'Has Thomson made you comfortable? Would you like the teapot

253

refilling?' She smiled at the elder Christie, the founder of the Christie cotton empire.

'We have been made most welcome in your absence, so don't you worry, my dear.' Lorenzo leaned back in his chair. 'Have you just returned from Ferndale? I hope you don't hold this against us, or find us presumptuous, but we had a stroll down to look at the site yesterday. You have quite a problem on your hands, my dear. There's not much left of the main building.' He smiled at the worried-looking woman, whom his son respected greatly and was close to.

'Yes, I've just been down there again. I still can't believe that the mill is no longer there. It breaks my heart to see the devastation. I don't quite know what to do. The mill will take a lot of rebuilding, and at the moment my heart isn't in it.'

'Well, we will be honest and tell you the reason – or should I say reasons – for our visit, besides giving you our support after losing the mill to fire.' Hector moved his chair and sat closer to Charlotte. 'Smedhurst's have been to see us and have asked if we can supply the rest of the consignment that you are unable to.'

'They've not wasted much time, have they?' Charlotte looked down at her hands, hurt by the disloyalty of her customer.

'They don't have much choice really. They need the supply badly, and it is the second time they've been let down, through no fault of your own. I just wanted you to know that we have taken over the order. I didn't want it to look as if we had stabbed you in the back.' Hector looked worried; he hadn't liked accepting the order, but at the same time business was business and he'd have been a fool to say no to the money.

'I understand. After all, I did the same to Sidgwick's after their demise. I'm glad that it is you supplying them, and I don't bear you any hard feelings.' Charlotte lifted her head up and looked at her close friend and his father.

'Then, my dear, perhaps you might be interested in my suggestion.' Lorenzo Christie leaned forward in his chair and looked hard at the woman who was down on her uppers. 'Would you sell what remains of Fern dale Mill to Hector and me? It would make sense as we could still use the weaving shed, for the fire did not reach that, and you clearly have no use for it at the moment; nor, I suspect, in the coming months – that is, if you decide to rebuild the mill. Let's face it, trade in cotton can be a bit unpredictable.' Lorenzo sat back again in his chair and rested his hands on his walking stick while he watched the hard-headed businesswoman, which he knew Charlotte to be, thinking.

'It would mean some of your workers would be back in employment straight away, and we could promise places to your old staff. At least it might save some families from the workhouse.' Hector knew how much her workers mattered to Charlotte, and he also knew how for years his father had wanted Charlotte and Ferndale Mill to fail, as a competitor. Hector thought a great deal of Charlotte, but blood was thicker than water and this was the chance he and his father had been waiting for, ever since Charlotte had taken over the mill, following Joseph's disappearance and death.

'I don't know. I haven't thought what to do with it yet. Could you really take the weaving staff back on – there's over forty of them?' Charlotte thought of all the staff who had greeted her most mornings and she felt beholden to them.

'Aye, I give you my word. And I'll find a position for that manager of yours, Bert Bannister. I always have admired him, he's a good worker.' Hector stood up and looked at Charlotte, hoping that he could sway her.

'If it's the money you are thinking about, Mrs Atkinson, I'll pay you a fair price; and I can give you the cheque today, if you want. That, along with the payout from the insurance, which I presume you had in place, will make you a wealthy woman.' Lorenzo smiled at Charlotte and patted his inside pocket, where he had placed the already written cheque.

Charlotte looked at both the Christies. She knew they were taking advantage of her being down on her luck, but their offer was tempting. If it hadn't have been for the Smedhurst order that had been placed directly after Christmas, she might have been thinking of putting Ferndale up for sale anyway. It would also secure some of her workers' lives and that meant a great deal to her. 'Gentlemen, can you give me some time to sleep on it? I can't deny I'm tempted by your offer, but Ferndale has been my life for over twenty years, as you well know. Selling it isn't something I'm going to do lightly.'

'Of course, Charlotte, I understand.' Hector smiled at her and then looked at his father.

'Perhaps if I leave this for you to look at, it might make your decision easier.' Lorenzo took the cheque out of his inside pocket and placed it on the tea tray. 'Now we will give you time to think. Should we say we'll meet again on Monday?'

Charlotte glanced across at the cheque on the tray and decided to look at it after both men had left the room, as she didn't want to show either disgust or satisfaction with the amount. 'Yes, Monday, and I promise I will have an answer for you by then.' She smiled and shook Lorenzo Christie's hand, while his dark-brown eyes tried to read her mind, and Hector gave her a reserved hug and whispered, 'Take care, I'm thinking of you' as he left the room.

Charlotte picked up the cheque and looked at the amount written on it. She supposed it was a fair price for a burnt-out shell and a weaving shed with no mill attached. But who was Lorenzo Christie really thinking of: himself, or did he genuinely care about her welfare? She walked through to the drawing room and looked out of the small-paned windows, down through the bare winter trees, to where once she could just have made out the shape of the mill. She thought back to her first meeting with Lorenzo, when he had tried to take advantage of her bad luck once before. This time

257

it was different; there was nothing left to fight for, and her life and that of her family were comfortable. Why did she need the burnt-out shell of a mill and all the worries that went with it? She knew why: because, unlike a lot of women, she liked her independence, the feeling of power that she got when entering her mill. And, no doubt about it, Ferndale had been her mill for the last twenty years, and no one could take that away from her, no matter how they tried.

The small church at Langcliffe was full of Sunday worshippers as Charlotte sat by herself towards the end of the long-drawn-out service. She'd heard a wave of whispers as she walked down the aisle and took her usual pew. Bowing her head, she had fought back the tears as she thought of the families praying together, and hoping for a resolution to their problems, as they recited the Lord's Prayer.

'God bless you, ma'am. Walter and I are ever so grateful that you are letting us stay in our cottage at the locks until he finds something.' Martha Gibson stopped to thank Charlotte as she came down the steps that led from the small church.

'It's no problem, Mrs Gibson. I wouldn't want to see you and your family out on the streets, especially with you in your condition. Are you keeping well? When is the baby due?' Charlotte pulled on her gloves and glanced at the tired-looking woman, with children who had been scrubbed to within an inch of their lives and made to put on their Sunday best, in order to attend church and Sunday school.

'The baby's due anytime now and, aye, we are all well – worried, but well. My Walter is taking it really hard, because he knows that at the moment we are all reliant on him. I just wish our Lizzie was a bit older; she could go into service then and bring a bit of something in.' Martha put her arm around her daughter, who stood next to her and looked no more than ten years old, with the biggest ribbon in her hair that Charlotte had ever seen. 'It's alright the vicar saying as God will provide, but I think he's going to have all on to provide for all those that worked at Ferndale. And then there's yourselves: you must be devastated – a good business gone up in smoke.'

'Yes, it's a blow to all of us. I wish I could do more for everyone, but at this moment I can't. Is Walter not with you today? Unlike my husband, he always attends church with you. I'm afraid Mr Atkinson has never attended since he lost his first wife, and he lost his faith.' Charlotte had noticed Walter's absence as he had one of the finest tenor voices when it came to the singing of hymns, and the lack of it had been noted by one and all.

'No, he said he wanted some time to think, and a bit of time to himself. I left him looking after the youngest; she usually bawls through the service anyway.' Martha ushered her children through the church gates, chastising her youngest son as he pulled his sister's pigtails.

'Take care, Mrs Gibson, and try not to worry.' Charlotte watched as the family made their way past the village green and couldn't help but wonder just how they were going to survive. She'd wondered the same as she sat in her pew and looked around at all the familiar faces. Faces of people who were nearly all now out of work. The weight of responsibility towards them was consuming her and she'd prayed hard to be shown an answer – an answer that she knew would not come from on high.

'Charlotte, are you alright?' The vicar put his hand on her shoulder.

She turned around and looked up at the grey-haired clergyman. 'Yes, I'm coping. Which is more than can be said for all my workers. I feel so guilty. They all look so worried and I don't know which way to turn to help them.'

'God will help you in your decisions, so put your trust in Him,' the vicar assured her.

'Thank you, I will.' She climbed into the waiting trap and pulled her rug over her knees. It was alright the vicar having faith in God above, but she herself was a bit of a hypocrite, paying for a family pew and showing her face at church on a Sunday just because she thought it the proper thing for one of her standing to do. She doubted that God would have any time for her.

'Jethro, let's go home.' Charlotte sat back in the trap and tried not to look at her ex-employees as she passed the steady stream of worshippers. She was going home to a roast-beef dinner and all the trimmings, while the best they could probably hope for would be bread and dripping.

Walter looked down on his sleeping daughter and kissed her gently on the brow. She should sleep until her mother and the rest of the children came home from church, with the amount of laudanum that he had laced her dummy with. He looked around the room that had been home to him and his family since he got married more than eleven years ago, and placed the small handwritten note by the fireplace. He hoped Martha would forgive him when she read it.

He walked down the back-garden path to the privy and opened the door, then looked up at the noose that he had attached earlier to the solid beam that ran the full length of the attached buildings. Best way out, he thought, as he balanced on the wooden seat of the privy and pulled the rough rope around his head. He'd burned down Ferndale Mill and ruined the lives of everyone around him, as well as that of his own family, so he deserved no less. The rope and beam creaked as he stood out into nothingness. His legs fought for the security of support, until the life that had once been so precious to him gradually ebbed away.

There was one less worker to worry about in Charlotte's life.

18

Charlotte lay in bed and pondered her worries once again, the early hours of the morning magnifying her situation.

'You don't need the mill any more, Charlotte. If the Christies are offering some of your workers positions, let it go.' Archie pounded his pillow as she asked him for the hundredth time what to do with Ferndale.

'But it's my mill – I love it.' She sighed and looked up at the ceiling.

'There is no bloody mill any more. It's gone and if you were to build it back up again, you'd have no money left, and half of your workers would have starved or buggered off elsewhere. Take the money and enjoy it; find something else to put your time into, if that's what's worrying you.' Archie looked at his wife and wished he could get her to see sense.

'But I'd lose my status in the district. I am the owner of Ferndale Mill, a force to be reckoned with.

Everyone in textiles knows my name.' Charlotte stared at Archie. 'And then there's the workers – what are they going to do without me?'

'Christie will take some of them on, and the others will find work. You are not responsible for everyone's life. Folk aren't as loyal as you think, lass. If Christie is offering some of them work now, they'll go. They'll not wait for you and your bloody mill. If it's lack of status you are worried about, then you are talking out of your arse. You own Crummock, Windfell and, if what you keep telling me is right, a profitable business in that shop that our lass and Harriet are running for you. I think you've enough status without Ferndale. You've proved your point over the years, and perhaps it's time to take a back seat.' He turned over and waited for the next outburst from his wife.

'But I won't have Ferndale. You just don't understand.' Charlotte pulled the covers up to her chin and tugged her share of the blankets off Archie.

'No, I bloody don't. And I tell you, what I have never understood is you wanting more all the time. Be content with what you've been offered. If you are so worried about the welfare of your workers, snap the Christies' hands off, because they can do more for your workers than you can. Workers can't wait months until you rebuild your empire; they need work now, not in twelve months' time. You'll no doubt take no notice of whatever I say – you never have done yet. But, just for now, let me go to sleep. It's been a long night and I'm over at Butterfield Gap first thing, just to make sure all's in place and to clear out the last of the furniture, before Arthur and Mary move in before Easter. You aren't the only one with ties to the past disappearing. I'll miss my old home, but you have to move on.' Archie turned over and left Charlotte thinking; she could be a selfish madam, when she wanted to be.

Charlotte snuggled down into the bed. 'Sorry, Archie, I forgot that you were clearing out Butterfield. It's just I don't know what to do.' She waited for a reply, but none came. 'I do love you.'

Archie growled, 'And I you, but go to sleep; things will sort themselves out. They always look bad in the middle of the night.'

'Are you helping your father today at Butterfield Gap?' Charlotte buttered her toast and looked across at Danny. The breakfast table was quiet, as Isabelle and Danny sensed tension between their parents.

'Yes, along with Jethro, we are clearing out the bigger furniture and putting it into the carthouse, until Father thinks what to do with it.' Danny bit into his toast and looked across at his father.

'I thought we could put the grandfather clock in the hallway, if you are in agreement, Charlotte. The rest Danny and Harriet can have, to help furnish Crummock; it isn't as if we need it.' Archie looked across at his wife. She looked pale and tired. The sooner the Christies came and backed up their offer, the better.

'Yes, the clock will suit the hallway. I've always

admired it, and it belongs in your home. And of course Danny is to have what you don't wish to keep – your father would have wanted that.' Charlotte sipped her tea and looked nervously at her husband, who was tucking into his bacon and eggs. 'What are you doing today, Isabelle? There still look to be plenty of orders on the shop's books. I thought, after Christmas and New Year, the women of Settle would not give us as much trade, but it seems I was wrong.'

'Er . . . yes, we are quite busy, Mother. January seems to be a time for funerals, and the amount of black crêpe that I have used is nobody's business. And I'm about to start on my bridesmaid's dress, because Danny and Harriet's wedding will soon be upon us.' Isabelle smiled across at her brother. Her mother had, in truth, caught her deep in thought about the young man who had bumped into her the previous day. She kept thinking about his enticing smile as he apologized for his haste; and of the blush in his cheeks, as he hurriedly picked up the hatbox that he had knocked out of her hands. She had recognized him instantly as the new man to Settle that Harriet had been so keen for her to meet, but she had decided to keep their brief encounter to herself. He seemed such a flutterbrain, and not at all what she had expected, after talking briefly to him.

'I know. Something to look forward to, so let's hope the weather is kind to us. Not like today – just look at it, the rain is pouring down.' Charlotte glanced out of the dining room's window at the grey skies that surrounded Windfell and was glad she had nowhere to go for once. 'You'll have to cover the cart well, my dear, else everything will spoil on the trip over from Butterfield.'

'Aye, we'll sheet it over, things will not take any harm.' Archie was in no mood for the move, but it had to be done and today was as good as any other. It got him and Danny out of the house while Charlotte entertained her guests, who were causing her so much anguish. 'Who the blazes is that?' He looked up from his breakfast as he heard the door knocker reverberate around the hallway. 'I hope it's not them Christies – they are bloody early, if it is.'

The eating of breakfast stopped until Thomson entered the room, followed closely by Sergeant Capstick, looking decidedly uneasy.

'I'm sorry to bother you all, but could I have a word in private with you, Mrs Atkinson and Mr Atkinson? I think it would be best if you joined us.' Sergeant Capstick removed his helmet and waited; he'd known the Atkinson family for more than twenty years and had never forgotten the time when he and the now-retired Inspector Proctor had dealt with the murder of Betsy Foster.

'Certainly, Sergeant. Is something wrong? Whatever it is, you can tell it to us all, for our family are not children any more. It must be something serious, if you have come out this early and in weather like this,' Archie answered. Charlotte pushed her chair a little away from the table and wished he had not given the sergeant permission to tell his news to one and all.

'It isn't good news, so perhaps it is best I just tell you and your wife.' Sergeant Capstick paused and looked at Charlotte.

'Tell us, man, what is it?' Archie was sharp and threw his napkin on to the table. He was fed up of not being respected as head of his own household, and the sergeant would tell everyone the news that he had seen fit to bring to their door.

'Walter Gibson was found hanging by the neck in his outside privy by his wife yesterday afternoon. It sounds as if he blamed himself for the burning down of Ferndale and was worrying how he and his family were going to survive.' Sergeant Capstick paused and looked at the faces of the two women sitting around the table. 'He left a note for his wife to find on the mantelpiece on her return from the church, so there's no suspicious circumstances to his death.'

'Oh no, poor Martha. He's left her with all those children, and another on the way.' Charlotte hung her head and thought about the man she had chastised so many times for lacking any work ethics. She looked across at Isabelle, who was in tears, and urged Danny to take her out of the dining room and give her some comfort.

'Why did Walter think he burned down Ferndale? The inspectors thought it was a pure accident?' Archie queried the sergeant, once Isabelle and Danny were out of the room.

'We don't know, and he didn't make that clear in his letter. His wife said he had taken it badly, but she thought he'd just been worrying about no money coming in, like everyone else. He'd never said anything to her to make her think that he was at fault, or that the fire might have been caused by arson. It's strange what stress can do to your mind, and I believe Walter liked a drink – he's had a few near run-ins with my constables.' Sergeant Capstick looked across at Charlotte. 'Do you think he caused the fire, Mrs Atkinson? You'd know him better than most.'

'I can't say he was my most popular employee, although I don't like speaking ill of the dead. I had to pull him into line more times than I care to admit. But Walter would not set fire to Ferndale, for he depended on his wage, as most did who worked there. He was just keen on the sound of his own voice and liked to cause a bit of trouble when he got the opportunity, but he would not maliciously set light to the mill. The poor man, to take his own life, he must have been weighed down with burden.' She recalled Martha Gibson telling her how hard Walter had taken the mill fire, and then remembered Bert Bannister moaning that Walter had to be forced to help put out the flames. Perhaps he had started it, for he had hated his job. Charlotte decided to keep her thoughts to herself. If the insurers sensed any hint of arson, they would withhold their payment and she needed that money, whatever she was going to do

'Aye, well, there's nowt anybody can do for him

now,' said Sergeant Capstick. 'He didn't think about his family, selfish bugger. I feel sorry for his wife with all her bairns around her – how's she going to cope? I expect it'll be the workhouse for them all. Unless you are kind enough to let her stay where she's at, like you have Mrs Batty and Mrs Potts. But that's nowt to do with me. I've just come to inform you of the death and to tell you that, as far as I am concerned, there's nothing to link him to the fire, now I've spoken to you.'

'My wife would tell you, Officer, if she thought there was anything untoward about the man. It must have been the burden of having no income, and so many mouths to feed, that sent him to his death.' Archie walked over to Sergeant Capstick and looked across at a white-faced Charlotte. 'Thank you for informing us of his death. We will of course think of his family, in such terrible circumstances, and may the Lord have mercy upon his soul.' Archie shook the officer's hand and walked him out into the hallway and to the front door.

When he returned, Archie said to his wife, 'You think Walter did have something to do with the fire at the mill, don't you, Charlotte? I could tell by your face. Just be thankful Sergeant Capstick believes everything you say, else you could be in bother. He never has been the brightest button in the box, thankfully.' Archie sat down in his chair and looked at his half-eaten breakfast, before looking across at Charlotte.

'I don't know. Walter was always causing bother, like I said. But I don't think he hated me that much that he'd burn my mill down.' Charlotte looked across at her husband, who was still in a mood.

'Well, this afternoon when the Christies come, you smile, thank them very much for the cheque and you get rid of the damned place. It has brought you nothing but hard work and bad luck. You don't need it. And don't get it into your head that you are responsible for Walter Gibson's family, because you aren't. The workhouse at Castlebergh will take them, or someone else will come to their rescue. Just for once let someone else take responsibility.' Archie stood up and looked out of the window at the wild day blowing outside. 'I'll not bother going to Butterfield Gap today. It's too bloody wet; we'd all be sodden by the time we'd stepped outside the house.'

'I thought you were being a bit rash. After all there's no need for you to go today, as the wedding and Arthur moving out of Crummock are months off yet.' Charlotte got up from the table and touched Archie on the shoulder. 'I know you are right; my time with Ferndale has probably run its course, and I'd be a fool not to accept the amount that the Christies have offered me. We will be quite wealthy, with the insurance money and their payment for the mill. You might even be lucky enough to have a wife who is content with running the family home and tending to your every need.' Charlotte kissed him on his cheek and smiled as she pushed her hand into his.

'You content, staying at home, behaving yourself – it will never happen. You'll always do as you like, but this time, Charlotte, do as I say: sell the mill and be free of its worry. For once think of us.' Archie turned and looked into the eyes of the woman he loved. She pushed him to the edge of despair, if she did but know it.

'Alright, the mill belongs to the Christies as from this afternoon, and once Charles Walker signs and gives the paperwork his blessing. But, Archie, I'd like to keep the lock cottages. That lets Mrs Batty and poor Mrs Gibson and her family keep a roof over their heads. The mill workers who wish to stay in them will have to pay me direct. Jethro can collect rent from them once a month, instead of it coming out of their pay, like it does now.' Charlotte had been thinking about keeping the cottages, but selling the mill. It would give her an income, without any worries; and seeing that one of the tenanted cottages only paid a peppercorn rent, because of her soft heart, she couldn't have seen the inhabitants struggle to pay the Christies when they raised it, as they certainly would.

'I know what you are doing: you are meeting me halfway, and you are still too soft for your own good. I can talk till I'm blue in the face about not looking after other folk than your own, but you'd not listen. Keep your cottages, sell the mill, and poor Jethro will have to become a rent collector. He might be wanting one of those cottages himself yet anyway, from what I've seen.'

'I knew you'd understand.' Charlotte kissed him on the cheek and then quickly realized what Archie had said. 'Why will Jethro want one of the cottages? He's happy in his two rooms above the stables, isn't he? Else he'd have said.'

'Just for once you've missed something going on right under your nose.' Archie laughed. 'Have you not noticed the flush in Mazy's cheeks, and the way she is always willing to run errands to the stables? You'd think she was sixteen, not nearly forty.'

Charlotte paused for a moment. 'Jethro and Mazy – never! She can't be courting Jethro.'

'Believe me, they are as thick as thieves. I caught them walking hand-in-hand up in the copse last Sunday. They both coloured up like your best red dress. I don't think they wanted anyone to know their little secret.' Archie grinned.

'Well, I'm glad for both of them. Jethro is a good-looking man, although Mazy could have done better for herself, if she'd set out her stall correctly. He's only a stable lad really.' Charlotte said the words without thinking.

'A bit like your husband was only a "poor little farm boy" – that's what you once chastised me with, that morning you lost your grandfather. I'll never forget you saying those words. I was only a poor little farm boy, but you were forgetting that you were only a poor little farm lass.'

'I'm sorry I was so shallow back then. Money turned my head. Oh, Archie, where have the years gone? Our children are both grown-up, and we have the worries of the world on our shoulders.' Charlotte put her head on Archie's chest and held him close; she loved him to the last inch of her life. He was the man who kept her steady and was always there for her, no matter what her mood.

'We'll have one less worry, when you sell that mill. And we haven't the worries that Mrs Gibson has, poor soul. Walter will have left her in a right state. You keep the cottages, Charlotte, keep your widows warm and dry. They are the deserving poor. Someone should help them with their lives, and we are in a position to help those less fortunate than ourselves.' He kissed Charlotte on her brow and held her tight.

'I will, and then I'll have a think about what I can do next.' She leaned up and kissed Archie on the lips. 'I can't sit at home and do knitting and tapestry. I'll find something.'

'Charlotte, you are impossible, and I give up,' he sighed; she'd not be content until she was running something somewhere.

'I know, but you love me.' She squeezed him – he would always be her Archie.

Lorenzo and Hector Christie sat across from Charlotte and noted how calm she was. She'd obviously been thinking about the situation and had come to a decision.

'It's bad news about one of your workers – terrible for the wife and family he's left behind. I suppose he never thought about them. I heard he was a bit of a drinker, not a deserving soul. His family will be bound for the workhouse, from what I hear. They can't expect to stay where they are.' Lorenzo Christie sipped his tea and watched as Charlotte poured herself a top-up in her crisp bone-china cup.

'Walter Gibson, I'll be honest, was not the most dependable of workers, but he was reliant upon his job, with having such a big family. And it is such a sin that he took his own life. I aim to go and see his widow and family later this afternoon.' Charlotte sipped her tea and looked across at Hector, who was fidgeting, wanting to get on with the main business of the day. 'Let's not beat about the bush: you both need to know what I've decided, and I don't mean to keep you hanging on.' Charlotte put down her cup and saucer and from the side of her chair pulled out the written cheque. 'As you can see, I haven't cashed this. I'm not that reliant upon it, or foolish enough, to go into a sale without a lot of thought.'

'We never thought for one moment that you were, my dear. The sale will have to go through the proper channels. My solicitor will need to be informed, and no doubt yours, too.' Lorenzo leaned back in his chair and gave Hector a quick glance.

'Have you decided what to do, Charlotte? We all want the best for everyone involved.' Hector looked across at her with an earnest look upon his face.

'I have and, as you say, we all want the best for everyone.' Charlotte paused. 'I will sell you the mill and weaving shed for the price of this cheque, which you so kindly wrote the other day. However, I want to keep the street of lock cottages. Some of the tenants are in need of the housing there, and you will only fill them with workers for the mill. I promised at least two of the tenants a home for life, and I'd like to do the same for Mrs Gibson. After all, she and her family are more in need of it than ever.' Charlotte watched the two men as they glanced at one another, unable to talk in private. 'The weaving shed and the mill – what's left of it – are worth every penny of that cheque to you both. And with Ferndale no longer operating, you are the main cotton suppliers for Craven, which is a long-awaited gift for you. I'm sure, gentlemen, that is what you wanted all those years back, when my first husband left me in such a state. Well, now it can all be yours, providing I can keep the cottages.' Charlotte sat back in her chair and waited for their reaction.

'I don't know, Charlotte. Those cottages belong with the mill. Where would our workers live, if you fill them with every unworthy cause and hard-luck case?' Hector looked across at his father.

'You are too soft for your own good, Mrs Atkinson. Why do you want to keep penniless people under good roofs? They will never be able to pay you, and they will never have gratitude enough to thank you. And why do you think I should pay you the same amount as written on my cheque originally?' Lorenzo Christie leaned on his walking stick and waited for her reply.

'I remember when I hadn't a penny to my name. I was pregnant, with nobody to turn to, but you both helped me. Initially, I know, you helped me because you thought I'd fail and that you'd be able to buy Ferndale at a rock-bottom price.' Charlotte bowed her head, remembering the early years as mistress of Ferndale Mill. 'Since then, we have worked quite well together, but I've always known that secretly you still coveted Ferndale. This is a small price to pay for a monopoly on Craven's cotton supply.' She lifted her head and watched as the Christies exchanged glances with one another. 'Plus, you can be seen to be doing good for the local poor, if I keep the cottages, and we can all be seen as pillars of society. Especially at this moment in time, with poor Mrs Gibson and her children about to turn to the workhouse for succour.' Charlotte watched Lorenzo's face, and smiled at Hector. Poor Hector, he was a good man; one day he would have his own way, but at present it would be his father's decision.

'Mrs Atkinson, you are a force to be reckoned with. Hector told me you were a hard woman with a soft heart, and he was right. Just you be careful that soft heart doesn't get you hurt.' Lorenzo shrugged. 'You have a deal: you keep the cottages, do your good deeds and end up with a row of houses and no rents being paid, when your tenants have spent their wages over the bar at the King Billy or the Talbot Arms. Go and see your solicitor and have him draw up the papers and deeds; that's the least you can do, with your hard bargaining – cover his fees – and then we will call the deal done.' Lorenzo looked across at his son and pulled himself up by his walking stick. 'Come,

276

shake my hand and then the deal is firm.' Lorenzo held out his hand to Charlotte and smiled.

Charlotte held his hand, and held it firmly.

'It's a pity my son was married when he first met you. What a union that would have been! No one would have stood in our way.' Lorenzo shook her hand and looked into her eyes.

Charlotte blushed. 'I wish you well with Ferndale. I'll give you a list of my workers, if you need one, and I'll get Charles Walker to draw up the papers.'

'I'll rewrite the cheque, my dear – tear up the one you hold. I no longer hold an account with that bank; it was just for effect, a trick I learned from my father.' Lorenzo laughed. 'But it did not sway you as much as I'd have liked.'

'My father is a cunning old devil.' Hector took Lorenzo's arm and helped him across the room.

'I know he is, but he's a good man at heart and that's what matters.' Charlotte held the drawing-room door open for her guests. Her legs felt like jelly, and tears were close to spilling down her cheeks. She'd just sold her mill, the place she had loved and had found her niche in running.

'We'll look after your beloved Ferndale, don't you worry,' Hector shouted to her as he accompanied his father out of Windfell.

'I hope you do, because I love every charred and burnt stone of it,' Charlotte whispered under her breath as she brushed back the tears.

19

Charlotte stood on the stone step of Number 4 Lock Cottages and listened as someone pulled back the bolt on the front door. She was taken aback as a sweating, red-faced woman with blood on her apron answered the door.

'What do you want? Now is not the time for visitors,' the stout woman said and rubbed her bloodied hands on her apron.

'I've come to give my condolences to Mrs Gibson, and to assure her that her home is safe. Is she alright?' Charlotte looked at the hard-faced woman and peered behind her into the dark interior of the cottage, where she spied four of Martha's children huddled around the fire.

'She's not good; she's just lost the baby I've been delivering – stillborn, it was. Which comes as no surprise, with the shock that she's had this last weekend, poor woman. There was nowt I could do about it.' She shook her head and looked at Charlotte.

'Oh, I didn't know. I'm so sorry to hear that. I'm Mrs Atkinson. I own these cottages, and Walter worked for me. I just wanted to assure Martha not to worry that she will be losing her home, and to bring her this basket of groceries, to help her out. I hadn't realized she had gone into labour, the poor woman – as if she hasn't lost enough.' Charlotte bowed her head and looked down at her basket of things, which she hoped would be of comfort to Martha and her family. But how could a few items of food console someone who had just lost their husband and child?

'Would you like to come in? I've just made her comfortable and wrapped the baby up, ready for it to be buried. She wants it to be buried with Walter, so I'll pop it in beside him, once she's said her final farewells to the li'l thing. He's laid out in the back room, ready for his funeral on Friday. If you ask me, losing the baby was a blessing. It would only have been another mouth to feed, and she has enough to look after, as it is.' The hard-hearted midwife held the door open and waited for Charlotte to enter the cramped front room of the cottage.

Charlotte smiled at the children, who looked frightened and worried as they watched her walk past them. 'There's some toffee that my cook made for you in the bottom of the basket. You help yourselves, while I go and see your mama.' She placed her basket on the scrubbed-clean kitchen table, glancing quickly at the youngest, asleep in her crib, before following the midwife up the stairs to where Martha lay in her birthing bed.

'Oh, ma'am, you shouldn't have come. I'm in a terrible state.' Martha was holding a wrapped, sheeted bundle close to her, and ushered Lizzie, her oldest, to clear the basin of bloodied water in which the midwife had washed the baby.

'Nonsense, you are in need of help. I'm so sorry for your loss, Martha, you don't deserve all this heartache. Walter must not have been thinking straight. The mill fire was not his fault, and now you've lost this poor little soul.' Charlotte sat down in a chair and pulled it next to the heartbroken mother of five.

'I don't know what had got into his head. I knew he was down, but I didn't ever think he'd take his own life. And now we've lost this one. God has a funny way of showing His love,' Martha sobbed as the tears began to fall.

'Pass me the li'l soul, and I'll place him in with his father before I go.' The midwife leaned over and tried to take hold of the bundle Martha was holding so tightly.

'His name's David. Tell the undertaker his name is David, after Walter's father – that's what we agreed before he killed himself.' Martha bent down and kissed the small, wizened face within the wraps. 'God bless you, my little son. None of this was your fault, and you just came at the wrong time.' She held her breath and wiped away a tear as the midwife took

280

her precious son away from her, then she looked across at Charlotte.

'I'll get away now, Martha. You should be alright. Just don't overdo it.' The midwife said her farewells, and both Martha and Charlotte listened as she banged the front door behind her, leaving a home full of sorrow.

'You'll be wanting your cottage back, ma'am. If you can give me to the end of the month, I'd appreciate it. I don't just know what I'm to do, but there is always the workhouse, although I don't want my family splitting up, if I can help it.' Martha wept, as she tried to make herself comfortable in bed.

'Don't worry about the workhouse. The cottage is yours to stay in as long as you want. That is what I've come to tell you, as well as paying my respects. We will come to an arrangement about a payment for rent – perhaps just until Lizzie gets to an age when she can go into service, and then she can help. We will think of some way around it, I'm sure. The main thing is that you get your strength back and get well enough to look after the worried little faces downstairs.'

'You can't afford to do that, ma'am, you've just lost the mill. You've no money coming in, either, and I don't like accepting charity at the best of times.' Martha shook her head and scowled at Charlotte.

'I'm selling the mill to the Christies, so I'm not about to be penniless, but I'm keeping the cottages, to rent to whomever I like. Some, of course, I will rent to mill workers; it makes sense, once the mill is rebuilt.

But if I can't help the likes of you and Mrs Batty, then I don't deserve to live such a privileged life. Let's say it eases my conscience. Why should I have everything, while others go without the basics of human life.' Charlotte reached for Martha's hand and patted it.

'I don't know, ma'am, I don't like charity. I can understand you giving Mrs Batty her cottage, because she was your cook at Windfell, but let's face it: Walter was not your most dependable worker, both you and I know that.' Martha lay back on her pillow and winced as a pain gripped her.

'Do you take in washing sometimes? I'm sure I have heard Walter talking about it.' Charlotte looked at the proud woman as she moved slowly to the edge of the bed.

'I do, just to help out a bit. Five mouths take some feeding.' Martha lowered her feet to the floor and groaned.

'Then perhaps I could send some washing down for you to do sometimes, as way of payment. Don't you get out of bed; stay where you are, just for today?' Charlotte looked worried as Martha reached for her shawl from the chair next to her.

'Aye, I'd feel better if we came to that arrangement. But right now my family will need feeding, and the little ones will wonder what's wrong with me.' Martha looked stressed as she tried to rise from her bed.

'I've brought a stew with me. Lizzie just needs to heat it up, and at the moment they are all quite content, I think, chewing the toffee that Ruby, my cook,

282

made for them. Your youngest was asleep in the crib next to the fire, so stay where you are – all's in hand. It will not harm Lizzie to take the reins, just for one day.'

'I don't think I can stand anyway. The birth has knocked the stuffing out of me.' Martha slumped back into bed. 'How can I ever thank you. I will always be grateful for the kindness you have shown me this day.' She lay in her bed and wiped her brow, as she looked at the mistress of the manor that her late husband had always cursed.

'You can thank me by staying in your bed, at least today, and taking care of yourself just for once. Now try and have a sleep, and I'll make sure your family is alright as I leave. I'll ask Gertie Potts to keep her ears and eyes open for your children, this next day or two. But I'm sure I will not even have to mention it, as she will have seen the midwife come and go and will already know about Walter's death.' Charlotte stood up and pulled the bedroom door to, as she left Martha to sleep for a while.

Closing the door, she walked across the landing to the small room where she could see Walter's coffin lay. She peered into the room and stood against the unclosed coffin and looked down on Walter, dressed in his Sunday best and with two pennies on his closed eyes, to pay for his safe passage to the next world. Next to his arm lay the swathed body of baby David. 'Your secret goes with you, Walter. Whatever you did, or knew, is buried along with you,' Charlotte whispered. 'God have mercy on your soul.'

The mood in the kitchen of Windfell was subdued. Since New Year's Eve, the night of the fire at Ferndale, there had been an air of uncertainty among the staff.

'Well, that was a strange funeral. I've never been to one like that before.' Jethro sat down at the kitchen table and took a long, deep sup of his tea.

'Aye, I'm glad that none of us women from here went. It wouldn't be pleasant.' Mazy sat down next to Jethro and felt sympathy for the fact that he had had to wait outside the church for the master and mistress, in the misting rain that had fallen all day.

'He's buried just under the northern wall, along with the baby. Seemingly it's the done thing for suicides and unchristened babies to be buried in the north of the graveyard, in the shadow of the church. Old Fraser, the gravedigger, told me that, while I was waiting for the Atkinsons.'

'A few years ago he wouldn't even have been allowed to be buried in consecrated ground, and would have been buried at night until last year – and before that you used to be buried face-down at a crossroads if you'd committed suicide. I remember my mother telling me, when I was small.' Ruby chirped in.

'You had a lovey childhood, by the sound of it, Ruby. Why on earth would your mother tell you that?' Jethro asked and looked at her in surprise.

'I don't know. She was always dark, my mother,

and fascinated with death and suchlike. It was because she'd lost my father early on. Where do we go when we die, anyway? That's what I'd like to know.' Ruby gazed out of the window. 'There must be something after this life, else it doesn't make sense.'

'We could always have a seance, get in touch with the other side. I'm sure there must be one or two ghosts around this place,' Jethro joked.

'We will do no such thing, Jethro Haygarth! We don't want to bring the monster that was Joseph Dawson back and, knowing our luck, that would be just who we'd get. We've had enough bad luck this year already, we don't want any more.' Mazy quickly stopped him in his tracks.

'Oh, I don't know. Some of us have fallen lucky.' Jethro looked at his Mazy and smiled as she blushed.

'Anyway, what do you think's going to happen next, to them upstairs, and do you think all our jobs are safe? Now the mill's gone, what do you think Mrs Atkinson's going to do? Will she rebuild it, or what?' Ruby sat back and waited, for she'd been quietly worried that, with the mill gone, the family might decide to leave Windfell.

'Well, I can tell you some news now, because she'll be telling you herself shortly.' Stephen Thomson leaned on the sink and looked at the gossiping bunch.

All heads turned and waited for the news that the butler had been keeping to himself. He was known by the staff as an eavesdropper and, as such, they never quite trusted him.

'She's sold Ferndale. She sold it on Monday to the Christies. I heard everything, as I waited to see them both out after their visit.' Thomson sat down amongst the staff and looked like the cat that had got the cream, as he dropped his bombshell.

'She's sold Ferndale – she can't have,' Jethro gasped. 'She loves the place.'

'Well, she's sold it, but she's keeping the lock cottages, so she can't be going that far. I'll tell you something else I heard as well: Walter Gibson blamed himself for the fire, that's why he committed suicide. You keep that to yourselves, though. I only heard that when I was picking the master's shoes up from next to their bedroom door, and I just happened to overhear their conversation.'

Ruby poured Thomson a cup of tea, something she rarely did. She was not a fan of the quiet, skulking man who had replaced Yates, the original butler at Windfell. She watched as he supped it.

'Well, Walter didn't like Mrs Atkinson. He made no bones about that and, as they say, there's no smoke without fire, if you forgive the pun.' Mazy looked around at the astonished faces. 'But we keep that to ourselves. It would only cause problems for Mrs Atkinson and poor Mrs Gibson, and both have got enough on their hands. Best let sleeping dogs lie.'

'Aye, she wouldn't get paid out by the insurance company, if they thought foul play had been involved. Then we might not be kept on in our places. We all say nowt, because we know nowt.' Jethro looked around the table and breathed a sigh of relief at all the heads nodding in agreement. 'We know where our first loyalties belong, and it's to them upstairs. If we look after them, they look after us. Right, Thomson?'

'I thoroughly agree. What I heard was indeed interesting, but I need my job as much as you all do.' Thomson smiled.

Jethro looked across at the butler. He'd never taken to the man. He always felt belittled by him and only hoped he would keep his mouth shut.

'So, what are you going to do with your time, now that you are a lady of leisure?' Archie looked across at Charlotte, who was clearing out her desk in the morning room.

'I'll find plenty to do, I'm sure. Besides, once the insurance company has paid out and Charles Walker makes sure completion for Ferndale goes through on Friday, I can start to look for something that I can turn into a profitable business. Not a mill, though. I think the days of cotton mills being profitable are nearly over. Cheap imports are spoiling the cotton trade.' Charlotte scrunched up an old bill for Ferndale and threw it onto the blazing fire.

'Be careful what you are throwing out. Just because the mill's no longer yours doesn't mean to say you might not need some of the paperwork that belongs to it.' Archie was always cautious when it came to paperwork; even if the mill was no more, it might be something that was needed.

'It was a bill from five years ago that had been paid. So stop twittering like an old woman,' Charlotte snapped as another handful of bills and receipts were thrown onto the fire, making the flames jump up and lick up the chimney in an alarming manner.

'You are going to have the chimney on fire, if you are not careful. What's up with you today? The wind will change and your face will stay like that, if you don't start to smile.' Archie looked up at a scowling Charlotte.

She sat down heavily in her chair and rubbed her hands over her face, trying hard to hold back the tears as she looked across at Archie. 'I've no mill, my family have all grown up and you are always at Crummock. I'm going to be left here twiddling my thumbs. At this moment all I can see is a miserable future, pounding the floors of this house.'

'Aye, Charlotte, by the end of the week you'll be one of the richest women in the district and no worries attached, with a family that loves you and the world at your feet. Forget the mill; stop feeling sorry for yourself, and get on with life. We've a wedding this spring, and Isabelle and Harriet are going from strength to strength. Enjoy the time you've never had before: go for a ride on the train up to Carlisle or Leeds for a change, and get yourself out of the house. I can understand you feeling a bit down, because January's been a bad month, but believe me, both you and I know there are people a lot worse off than us.'

Archie walked over to his spoilt wife and put his arm around her, then lifted her chin up, kissing her tenderly on the lips. He wiped a tear away from her cheek and looked into the blue eyes he loved so much.

'Things will take a turn, lass. Something will come out of the blue, and you'll forget bloody Ferndale. I'm glad it burned down; it always reminded me of Joseph Dawson, and it's gone to the right folk, the Christies. They'll rebuild it, and all them who depended on you will be in his employ – and his worries. Happen I'll get a bit more time with you, because I still love you, lass.' Archie bent down and kissed her again.

'What are you doing, you idiot – let me down!' Charlotte squealed as Archie picked her up off her feet, carrying her struggling body across the morning room and hallway to the bottom of the stairs.

Archie could hardly catch his breath and halfway up the stairs he stopped, as Charlotte giggled and fought against her determined husband, who was heading for a heart attack if he didn't put her down. 'Well, you were bored, and I know how to pass an hour on a wet January day. Now get up those stairs.' He put her down on the stairs and slapped her bottom.

'Archie Atkinson, I'm a lady of power and position – you just stop that,' Charlotte yelled.

'I'll stop when you stop feeling sorry for yourself. Besides, a slapped arse is what you were always short of.' Archie grinned when she laughed in delight as he chased her up the stairs.

The bedroom door closed loudly behind the flirting couple, making Thomson stop in his tracks as he cleared the breakfast table.

'Sounds like fun and games!' Mazy grinned at the po-faced butler. 'Good for them, they deserve a laugh. Especially the mistress, for she's had the troubles of the world on her shoulders. You just remember to keep the secret to yourself, else your life will not be worth living,' she whispered into Thomson's ear as she helped clear the table. She, like Jethro, did not trust him. He was sneaky, always somewhere he shouldn't be, and he rarely joined in with the others' conversation. Perhaps he was just quiet; time would tell, no doubt.

20

The shop had been busy all morning as Sally Oversby walked in with her latest creations.

'Sally, these are lovely. How did you make them?' Isabelle picked up a pair of fine crocheted gloves and examined them.

'My gran was always good with her hands and I must take after her. I spent time with her while my ma was out working at the mill, and she learned me all that she knew. I find sewing and suchlike so pacifying – it's not hard work at all.' Sally's face lit up as Harriet and Isabelle examined her handiwork.

'You can knit as well. I'm sure these gloves, socks and scarves will sell well. I'd be only too happy to place them in our shop. Your pretty little bags are a steady seller; we sell at least one a week.' Isabelle smiled at Sally, who was so embarrassed by the fuss her goods were getting.

'I'd have gone to your mother with them, but I

know she will be busy sorting things out after the fire. I'm hoping she will soon have Ferndale up and running, and then I can hopefully get my job back. In the meantime, if you can sell these for me, it would bring in a little income.' Sally unwrapped more of her work and laid the items on the shop counter.

'The word must not be out yet, but I might as well tell you.' Isabelle looked at a worried Sally. 'My mother has sold Ferndale to the Christies. They hope to rebuild the mill, and of course the weaving shed was untouched by the fire, so it should not be long before it is back in operation.'

'I hadn't heard. I'm sorry for your mother; she was one of the best bosses I have ever had. She was always fair. She must be heartbroken at losing Ferndale.' Sally's face belied her thoughts, as she pondered losing the main way she knew to make money.

'I think the Christies will be taking on workers as soon as they get things up and going, and I know my mother has passed on a list of her staff to them. She was up all night making sure she didn't forget anyone who she knew was worthy of employment, which of course was all of Ferndale's staff. She's like a bear with a sore head, without something to do, and we are all keeping out of her way.' Isabelle picked up two pairs of crocheted gloves and draped them over an evening bag of Sally's that had already been displayed in the window.

'I don't think I want to work for the Christies, good folk that they are. I prefer your mother. You look as if you are both doing well. Do you not need another assistant? You know I can sew.' Sally looked around the busy shop at the boards of cloth and the drawers full of ribbons, cottons and trimmings, which she would love to sit and work with.

'Sorry, Sally, we are quite busy, but there's only room for Harriet and me at the moment. But we will sell anything you can bring in to us, if we think it suitable.' Isabelle knew Sally was desperate for money, but could do no more to help.

'Aye, well, you know where I'm at, if you want anything. And don't think I'm not grateful for all that you do for me. Selling a few of my things just keeps the wolf from the door. Tell your mother she'll be missed, and give her my best wishes.' Sally made for the door and walked out into the busy street.

'Poor Sally. Did you see her face drop when you said your mother had sold the mill? She was visibly upset.' Harriet leaned over the shop's counter and gazed out of the window down the street. 'Isabelle, quickly, look out of the window: the man walking towards us past the doctor's is the man who's bought the shop down New Street. He's a photographer!'

Isabelle turned quickly from putting Sally's things away and went to look out of the window at the man who was causing such a stir in Settle. She recognized him instantly as the man who had literally bumped into her on her way to deliver a hat to a customer. Now she pretended to be adjusting the dress on one of the dummies in the window, as she glanced at him.

293

'He's coming this way – he's heading straight for us, and he's coming to look in our window! If he comes in, you serve him. I feel such a fool, because he will remember me from when he bumped into me and sent the hat and its box sprawling.' Isabelle looked up through the window and caught the eye of the young blond-haired man with the immaculately kept moustache. He smiled at her and she smiled back, before hurrying to the safety of the counter. 'He's coming in!' she whispered as she tried to hide her flushed cheeks from Harriet.

'Good afternoon, ladies. It's a little on the parky side, but not too cold for a late January day,' the young dashing man said as he entered the shop.

'Good afternoon. It is indeed not a bad day, for the time of year,' Harriet smiled and replied to him.

Isabelle looked at the man who stood in front of the counter and noted again his every feature: his high cheeks, blue eyes and just how dandy he appeared, in his sharp grey suit with a gold watchchain hanging from his waistcoat pocket.

'I wondered, might I take a closer look at the black gloves and bag that you have displayed in the window? They just took my eye.' He pointed with his swagger stick at the window bottom.

'Certainly, I'll get them for you.' Isabelle quickly usurped Harriet in gaining his attention and left the safety of the counter to help their customer, retracting her original instructions to Harriet as she realized how handsome he was. She handed them over to him and watched as he looked at how fine the stitching was and tried the drawstring on the posy bag that Sally had just left with them.

'They look perfect. How much are they?' He passed them over to Isabelle, his hand touching hers as she took them from him.

'The gloves are a florin, and the bag three shillings, so five shillings altogether, sir.'

'Then I'll take them both.' The young man smiled. 'I'm sorry, I am sure we have met before, but I can't think where.'

'You accidentally bumped into me and knocked the hatbox out of my hand!' Isabelle smiled, before walking away from him to wrap up the goods, and glancing quickly back at the dashing gent.

'That's it – I knew I'd seen you before. I never forget a pretty face. My sincere apologies again. Please, let me introduce myself. I'm James Fox. I've bought a shop down New Street, and I'm in the process of turning it into a photographic studio.' He pulled out his wallet to pay for the goods and watched as Isabelle wrapped the gloves and bag.

'It's nice to meet you, Mr Fox. I'm sure your wife will love her gloves and bag, won't she?' Harriet smiled and plied him with the question that both of them wanted an answer to.

'Oh! Dear no, I'm not married. Nobody could put up with me. These are for use in my studio. I'll use them as extras – they are ideal. They just caught my eye.' James smiled as Isabelle handed his parcel across to him. 'I can't help but notice the wedding dress hanging up by your back-room door. May I say it is exquisite. Did one of you design it?'

'Thank you. Yes, Isabelle, designed it, and I'm to be married in it, in another few months.' Harriet smiled.

'Congratulations, Miss . . . er – I don't think I caught your names?'

'I'm Harriet Armstrong, soon to be Atkinson; and this is soon to be my sister-in-law, Isabelle Atkinson.' Harriet glanced at Isabelle. She'd been sly about not mentioning her meeting, no matter how brief, with the dashing Mr Fox.

'Well, it is the most beautiful wedding dress I think I've ever seen. You are both to be congratulated. You, Miss Harriet, upon your wedding; and you, Miss Isabelle, on having such marvellous skills. I do believe it has a look of a William Morris design about it. Were you influenced by his work?' James looked at Isabelle and noted her dark good looks.

'You know about William Morris? I was beginning to think I was the only one. Yes, you are quite right, he has influenced the design of the dress. And, thankfully, Harriet loves it. I was quite worried that she wouldn't, because I'm afraid I did get carried away with my thoughts and forgot that not everyone is a fan of such things.' Isabelle was delighted that somebody had recognized her influence, and all shyness disappeared.

'It's Morris's feel for nature that I have high regard for; the patterns and designs are taken straight from his garden and surroundings, but they are made to look so beautiful. I wish I could get the same feel in my photography.' James looked at Isabelle, whose eyes sparkled with excitement at the thought that she had come across a like-minded individual.

'Morris is quite a man, and he's not afraid of saying what he thinks. He thinks art should be for everyone, not just the privileged few.' She tried not to show her fascination with the striking photographer.

'You've met him?' James asked, surprised.

'Yes, it's how I became aware of his work. He was most entertaining, and I enjoyed every minute spent with him at my godfather's house. Morris gave me the confidence to join Harriet here, in my mother's new venture.

'You are so lucky. He has so many connections within the art world.' James sighed.

Harriet watched as the couple compared their love of the art world, and felt happy for Isabelle that she had found a like-minded person in Settle. The conversation only came to an end when the shop bell rang.

'Oh, I've had such a morning. Mrs Pratt would not shut up, and there was a queue at the bank.' Charlotte entered the shop with her hands full of various packages, barely noticing the young man now standing at the end of the counter, engrossed in conversation with her daughter. 'I hope you girls can put the kettle on. I'm parched—' She stopped in her tracks as she looked across at Isabelle and her new-found friend, who were lost in conversation. 'Oh, I'm sorry. I didn't realize you had a customer. I do apologize.'

'Mama, let me introduce you to Mr Fox. He owns the photography studio along New Street.' Isabelle quickly walked over to her mother and turned to James. 'He approves of my Mr Morris and is a fan, too.'

'A pleasure to meet you, Mrs Atkinson. I've heard quite a bit about you, but until this moment had not linked you with this lovely dress shop. I have just been getting acquainted with your daughter. She's got a good knowledge of the art world and a head for design, by the look of the exquisite dresses that she designs. You must be very proud of her.' James reached out his hand and shook Charlotte's firmly, as she dropped her parcels around her feet.

'A pleasure to meet you too, Mr Fox. Yes, I'm proud of my Isabelle and, of course, of Harriet – one complements the other. One has the design skills and the other the practical skills to bring it all together; both equally as important as one another, would you not say?' Charlotte watched as James and Isabelle sneaked a quick glance at one another. 'You are a photographer, did I hear Isabelle say? Perhaps we should employ you for some photographs of our impending wedding. Would you be interested?'

'Indeed I would, Mrs Atkinson. It would give me – if I am not being too open – a break into the social circles that I require, if you were to recommend my work.' James spoke forthrightly, for he didn't believe in beating around the bush.

'Right, so we will initially book you for Danny and

Harriet's wedding, on Easter Saturday. But at this moment in time, are you joining us for a cup of tea? I can hear Harriet is laying out the crockery in the back room.' Charlotte looked the young man up and down and watched as Isabelle never took her eyes off him.

'I'm afraid I'll have to decline the tea. I have a sitting at two, and it's already one o'clock. However, I will put Harriet's wedding in my diary and will contact you the week before, to see what you would like.' James looked at the two women who were gazing at him and smiled. 'Or perhaps you would like to come to the studio and visit me.'

'Oh yes.' Isabelle exclaimed.

'Isabelle, as you are the arty one amongst us, you must go and visit Mr Fox in his studio. And perhaps, in return, you would like to come and have dinner at Windfell? Would that be to your satisfaction, Mr Fox?' Charlotte smiled across at the young photographer who couldn't take his eyes off her daughter.

'That would be most satisfactory, Mrs Atkinson. I can't thank you enough. Isabelle, any time next week will be fine. I'm not exactly run off my feet as yet, and next week I'm having a skylight added to my studio to give me better light, so I'm there all week. Miss Harriet, if you would like to accompany her, you are most welcome.' James bade farewell to the three women who had made him so welcome.

'Well, what a pleasant young man, with good prospects, too. I do believe photography is going to be all the rage. You seem to have taken his eye, Isabelle.' Charlotte smiled as Harriet placed the tea tray in front of them.

'Mother! He's just a customer.' Isabelle blushed.

'A customer that you've talked to for the last half-hour, and you were so similar in ideas, you'd think you were peas in a pod.' Harriet laughed.

'Just drink your tea. I was only being polite.' Isabelle grinned. She thought of the blond-haired man who had known exactly what she was talking about, and who was actually interested in listening to her. Her visit to the studio could not come too soon, just to get another glance at him.

The following week Isabelle found herself in a tizzy as she made herself ready for her meeting with the handsome photographer.

'Enjoy your visit to Mr Fox's. I will just have to keep our customers satisfied all by myself,' Harriet joked, as Isabelle looked at herself yet again in the full-length mirror of the shop and pinched her cheeks to add some colour.

'I've never known a photographer before, and you must admit he was dashing.' Isabelle giggled.

'Well, he's a lot better than the last man you set your cap at.' Harriet smiled and gave her a hug. 'Go on, go and have a look around his studio. You are as interested in that as you are in him.'

'I am, I have to admit. I find it fascinating that you can capture an exact image of yourself and put it on paper.' Isabelle quickly opened the shop door and walked out down Duke Street, turning on the corner of New Street and nearly making the same mistake again, by almost bumping into a customer as he made his exit from Mrs Garnett's tea-rooms. She arrived outside the new studio flustered and excited, not quite knowing what to expect inside. She calmed herself down and walked in through the glass-fronted door.

'Will be with you in a moment,' James's voice called from behind the draped curtain that led through to the actual studio.

Isabelle stood in the reception room and looked around the photographs that adorned the wall. There were pictures of local scenes on one wall, and on another photographs of well-to-do families, all standing and sitting in beautiful surroundings, their stance perfect, with their eyes focused on the camera. Isabelle was fascinated. The only distraction came from the builders that she could hear, hammering and sawing as they replaced some of the building's roof with glass for James's new studio. The green chenille curtain moved and James came out from behind it, his face beaming as he realized it was Isabelle waiting for him.

'Isabelle, how lovely to see you! I'm so glad to see you again. I do apologize for the noise and racket. I thought the builders would have finished with the roof by now, but it seems to be taking longer than I expected.' He took her hand. 'Please come with me and we will go through into my temporary studio for a while. And then I thought, if you wish, we could go to Mrs Garnett's on the corner for tea?'

'That would be wonderful, James. But please, if you are busy, I do understand.' Isabelle followed him into his makeshift studio and gazed around her at the room that was filled with all the equipment needed in a photographer's life.

'Please, take a seat. The chaise longue is quite comfortable, or would you like to look around?' James realized that while he was busy having his roof repaired, and developing the photographs in his darkroom, his temporary studio had got into a bit of a mess. 'I do apologize. I'm usually tidier than this – it's the upset from having the roof adjusted. Plus, I went to take a photograph of the Proctors' little girl, at Bridge End, who died last week. Her parents wanted a photograph to remind them of her, after she was buried. I was just developing the plates as you entered the shop.'

'Don't worry. It is always an upset when you are having building work done. Did I hear correctly when you said you took a photograph of a dead child this morning?' Isabelle was shocked.

'Yes, it is the latest thing people are requesting. It is a way of remembering the ones they have lost. I must say, I do feel a little uncomfortable with it, but you can't upset the grieving family. The Proctors sat their little Beth up between her three sisters on their sofa and then I took their photographs. She looked so lovely, as if she were a sleeping angel. They bury her

302

tomorrow.' James looked wistfully out of the window and then at Isabelle.

'I find that rather unsavoury, although I can understand the parents wanting something to remember her by. But why not a lock of her hair in a locket, like most people do?' Isabelle looked around her at the contraption that she knew to be a camera and at the tripods stacked in a corner, and her eye was caught by the backdrop to the room: a beautifully painted scene of a wooded garden. 'You have a garden in your back room?' Isabelle laughed.

'Yes, I have many scenes that you can choose from. A friend of mine paints them for me to use as backdrops to my photograph. They make them look more real. Have a look through this camera lens and you will see they look quite genuine, with someone standing or sitting in front of them. Do you know how a camera works?' James looked at Isabelle as she tried to focus through the small lens of the concertinaed wooden box of the camera.

'No, I've no idea.' She shook her head and watched as James bent down next to her and showed her how it worked.

'Well, let me explain. This is called a "bellows camera", which is obvious because, as you can see, the concertina piece made of leather, in the centre of the two wooden boxes at either end, is flexible – like bellows – and allows me to position the lens to change focus on the picture. The lens focuses the picture onto the glass plate at the back of the camera.'

James looked at Isabelle, who was enthralled by his explanation.

'The wooden box at the back of the camera is called the plate-holder. I put a glass plate that I have coated with light-sensitive chemicals into this slot, then attach this black hood to the back of the camera, so that no light – except the light from the lens – is let into the camera while I take the photograph. It's then a matter of the sitter staying still while the plate develops the image, hence that gadget over there, which sometimes helps my sitter to stay still. I know it looks like a thing of torture,' he grinned as he picked up the metal frame that held a person's waist and head steady, as they posed for their photograph to be taken, 'but I couldn't work without it. Then, once the photograph is on the glass plate, I take it into my darkroom to develop into the photographs that you see on the surrounding walls. I'd take you in there, but it has to be kept dark, and the smell of chemicals can make you cough. And, as I say, I am in the process of developing the death-shots of Beth Proctor.' James smiled at an inquisitive Isabelle, who was looking through the lens and then at the groove into which the plate slotted.

'It's fascinating. So, will Harriet and Danny have to come to your studio for their photographs?' Isabelle stepped back and looked at James.

'No, I'll use my field camera, if they wish to have them taken outside. It's lighter and takes landscape photographs easier than this studio camera. Although

I thought they would be better taken at the manor – not that I'm wishing bad weather on their special day, but it can be unpredictable at Easter.'

'May I help you? I'd like to see how it works,' Isabelle asked.

'You'll be busy being a bridesmaid. I tell you what: let's go and have tea, get away from the deafening din of the builders and then, if you've time, I'll take your photograph to keep, if you wish. A present from me – your first venture into photography.' He smiled as Isabelle blushed with excitement.

'But I'm not dressed for the occasion,' she whispered.

'You look perfect to me, and I'm sure there will be many more occasions. This is just the beginning of a very special friendship.' James squeezed her hand. 'Come, let's go. Mrs Garnett at the tea-rooms in Duke Street makes a very lovely Bakewell tart, and my stomach is complaining that it has not been fed enough today.'

Isabelle looked around the studio. She would like to spend many an hour understanding how everything worked, and perhaps paint some backdrops for the sitters. And just be in the same room as James, with whom she felt a strange affinity. She would feel special, and proud, to be walking down New Street with him next to her. Not skulking in the shadows, as she did when meeting John Sidgwick.

'Miss Atkinson, would you do me the pleasure of

taking my arm?' James asked as he opened the studio doorway.

'I will indeed, Mr Fox.' Isabelle beamed. 'And the pleasure is all mine.'

21

'You know, this will always be home. I know Crummock was a good farm, and I know I should be so grateful that I live in a place like the manor. But Butterfield Gap will always be home.' Archie leaned over the yard gate and looked towards Austwick and Crummock.

'You didn't have to sell it. You could just have rented it to Arthur and Mary.' Charlotte ran her hand down Archie's back and leaned over the gate next to him.

'Nay, he wanted a place to call his own and I can understand that. And who am I to begrudge him a farm of his own. Although he'll struggle to make a living on this 'un. It's a good job he's not got any family; it doesn't yield enough to fill many bellies.' Archie sighed.

'I'll miss it and all. I'll never forget getting up in a morning and looking out of my bedroom window,

307

straight across here. Little did I know that I'd end up wedded to the lad who lived here. And then your mother made me so welcome when you said we were to be married, even though the scandal was rife, after Joseph left me. I always remember my father saying that you couldn't keep me in shoes, and back then he was right. But look at us now: we both want for nothing.' Charlotte smiled, remembering old times.

'That's more of your doing than mine. I came to you with nothing. Nothing, that is, except big ideas and a lot of bluster. You looked so broken-hearted that first Christmas you came to stay at Crummock, and I watched you as you wandered from room to room, just glad to be back in the old place. I knew then how much you loved your old home, and that I had to make sure you kept it.' Archie put his arm around Charlotte's waist. 'Do you think our Danny will feel the same way about Crummock, when he's our age, and that Isabelle will love Windfell as much as we do?'

'I'd hope so. If they are sensible, after our lifetime both should always be their homes. We've set up them and future generations well, and really they should never want for much. I just wish I could have kept the mill, not that either of them was interested in the cotton industry, but it would have brought them some income in.' Charlotte pulled her shawl around her, as the February wind showed its strength on the bare moorland side.

'Never mind, lass. At least you've a healthy bank balance, now the Christies and the insurance have paid up, and your life's your own for once. And this wedding will keep you out of mischief for a while. I didn't realize that Easter is early this year and that we only have just over six weeks before it is here. No wonder Arthur and Mary were pushing me to clear out my old home. I meant to do it last month, but never got on with it.' Archie rubbed his head and looked at Danny, as he threw a rope over the furniture and belongings that he had just finished loading onto the flat cart, to take back to Windfell.

'Not a lot to show for a lifetime, is there?' Charlotte looked at the cart and then at Archie.

'No, and some of that was my grandparents' before us, and is not worth a lot. We can make room for the old grandfather clock, can't we? It was always prized by my father as it was made by Weatherheads of Kirkby Lonsdale. He was very proud of it.'

'Of course we can, my love – and anything else that you wish to keep. Danny won't say no to the rest; he's plenty of rooms to fill up at Crummock. Those two end bedrooms have never had any furniture in, except a bed, for as long as I remember. And you never know, he might have more children than we can count, as I'm sure Harriet will want a family.' Charlotte looked at Archie; he didn't show his feelings very often, but today he looked really sad at the thought of selling and leaving his old home. 'It is a pity we have no children that are both ours, but that is what nature has decided our fate to be. Isabelle thinks of you as her true father, and I hope Danny loves me as his mother, although I know I will never replace Rosie – and have never tried to. But a child to us both would have been a blessing, and he or she could have had Butterfield Gap to farm, and then you wouldn't have dreamed of selling it.'

'Nay, that wouldn't have been right fair. Poor devil would have had next to nowt, compared to the other two. I'm content with having just Isabelle and Danny. Besides, we've another good one in our future daughter-in-law, Harriet. The farm will be in good hands with Arthur and Mary, so don't worry about me. I'll be alright. It's just a sad day, and the place holds so many memories, and always will.' Archie held his hand out, for Charlotte to join him and Danny on the seat of the cart.

She held it tight as she climbed up next to Danny, pulling her long skirts around her and wrapping herself in her shawl.

'Aye, how the mighty have fallen! Look at your mother, lad, sitting on the seat of an old flat wagon full of junk, in a dress that's seen better days with a shawl around her shoulders.' Archie laughed.

'Should we go around by Lawkland Hall, just to show her off? You know what the Moore family who live there are like. They'd never want to speak to her again,' Danny joked.

'Don't you dare, Danny Atkinson. I don't want to see anybody, dressed like this. I feel a right scruff. But it was no good emptying Butterfield dressed in my

Sunday best.' Charlotte walloped her son hard and grinned.

'It doesn't matter what you look like, Charlotte Atkinson. Fine clothes do not maketh the person, and you should know that. And we love you, no matter what you are dressed in.' Archie grinned. 'Now let's go home, lad, before anybody thinks we are homeless beggars.'

'That looks just grand there.' Archie stood back and admired the grandfather clock, standing in its new position in the great hallway of Windfell.

'It's a country clock really, a bit plain. It's a pity it doesn't have fluted columns and a bit more brass decorating it.' Charlotte looked at the squat, dark-oak clock and thought it to be completely out of place in such a fine hall, but she knew Archie loved it dearly, so that was where it was to stay.

'I'll ask Colin Ward to come and mend those back legs, and then it won't look as bad. I think they must have gone rotten, with folk mopping the floor around them. My mother used to scrub and mop our flagged floor to within an inch of its life, as did my grandmother.'

'You've not forgotten we have a visitor tonight for dinner? In fact I should say two, as Harriet is coming back with Isabelle as well. But the main visitor is the young gentleman who seems to have caught our Isabelle's eye, James Fox. He has the photography studio up New Street. I've provisionally booked him for the wedding, I thought it would set a trend if we had a photographer recording the event.' Charlotte walked into the morning room, with Archie not far behind her. 'Have you see the wedding invitations? I finished writing them yesterday, I think I've covered all on our side of the family. I hope Harriet's parents have finished writing theirs.' Charlotte handed the huge bundle of invitations to Archie and waited for his comments.

'Do we need to ask as many folk as this? This wedding is going to cost a fortune. It's only my lad that's getting wed.' Archie looked at the pile of lovingly written invitations and sighed.

'He's your only son, and we both love him – surely he's worth spending a bit of money on. And Harriet has settled so well within the family already. Anyway, the invitations are written now and are about to be sent out. I can't believe the wedding is nearly upon us. It seems like only a few weeks ago that we were worrying about Danny's head being turned by that wretched girl at Ragged Hall, and that perhaps there was never going to be a wedding. I understand her baby is due in early May. Thank heavens she married that lad from Slaidburn, else Danny's head might still be turned.'

'Amy Brown would have made a good farmer's wife, I'll give her her due, but our lad would never have been able to trust her. She would always have had an eye for the men.' Archie sat down in the chair across from Charlotte and looked out of the window. 'I hate February; it's cold, miserable, and if it wasn't for the first sign of snowdrops, you'd think spring was

312

miles away. I'm glad our lad is getting married before lambing time at Crummock At least he'll be there, and able to keep an eye on the flock. I've told Danny to go to the spring hiring fare and take a man on to help him this year, because I'm not getting any younger.' Archie rubbed his knee; it had ached all winter and the damp, cold month of January had taken its toll on him.

'Get Dr Burrows to have a look at your knee. He'll give you something to stop it aching.' Charlotte looked across at him.

'Nay, it's only rheumatics, and it's to be expected. I'm taking after my father, I suppose. Time for the new generation to do a bit more.' Archie closed his eyes and sat back in the chair.

'You have a sleep. I'll come and I'll wake you when our visitors arrive.' Charlotte rose from her chair and kissed him on his brow, before closing the morning-room doors behind her. She loved her Archie with every inch of her. He was hurting at saying goodbye to his old home. He'd have to learn to look forward, and relish the coming years of grandchildren and the growing family. Besides, she'd done her duty as a mother and owner of the mill. Now she was going to find something to occupy her hours – something to leave to the grandchildren, hopefully.

Isabelle looked at the photograph that James passed her as he entered Windfell.

'I hope you like it. I think you look very beautiful,

if you don't mind me saying so.' He waited for Isabelle's reaction.

'I can't believe it's me – it is just like my reflection. Mother, look what James has given me.' She raced to show her mother her image. 'Isn't he clever?'

Charlotte picked up the photograph of her daughter and smiled, before looking over at James. 'Very talented indeed. You have captured our Isabelle just perfectly, Mr Fox. I'm impressed.'

Danny leaned over Charlotte's shoulder and looked at the image of his sister.

'That's better than a kitten, our Isabelle.' And then whispered in her ear, 'I'd keep this one if you can, he's alright.'

Isabelle scowled at her brother. 'Look, Harriet, your wedding pictures will be wonderful. If you have them taken here, you can have the manor in the background.'

Harriet took the photograph from Charlotte and admired the likeness.

'It will be a pleasure to take the wedding photograph at the manor. It is so beautiful, it will make the perfect background.' James looked around him.

'Then please do, Mr Fox, and speaking of which I have your invitation. I have just finished writing them. I'll go and get it now and wake up Archie. He'll have to hurry and change for dinner, as he's been asleep in the morning room since our return from Butterfield. Do please excuse me.' Charlotte looked around her at her happy family, talking and laughing with one another in the comfort of the warm drawing room, before making her way across the hallway to the morning room. She opened the door quietly and looked across at her snoring husband, who was still fast asleep.

'Archie, Archie, come on, love, wake up. Our visitors are here, and dinner is about to be served.' Charlotte shook him gently and smiled as a bleary-eyed Archie woke up.

'How long have I been asleep? Why didn't you wake me up?' Archie yawned and looked around him. The morning-room curtains were pulled and the fire was burning brightly, after being replenished with fresh coal.

'I told everybody to leave you to sleep, as you looked so tired. Eve was as quiet as a mouse when she tended the fire. But now, my love, it's dinner. And come and meet Mr Fox. He's brought a photograph of Isabelle and it is such a true likeness. Do get changed and then come and join us.' Charlotte urged her husband to be quick.

'I'm coming.' Archie stood up and yawned widely. 'So what's this Fox fellow like? You've not said that much about him.' He followed his wife out of the room and started to make his way up the stairs.

'He's just perfect for our Isabelle, but I'm not tempting fate. I remember your Aunt Lucy trying to matchmake – and look where that got her!' She patted Archie on his arm and smiled.

'She was right, though. So let's hope you are, with these two.' Archie made his way steadily up the stairs and listened to the excitement and laughter coming from the drawing room, before entering his bedroom. He looked at himself in the wardrobe mirror as he put on his starched collar, fastening the ruby stud securely, before pulling on his evening jacket, which Thomson had previously set out for him. He sighed, looking at himself; he wished he was as young as Danny again, with the world at his feet. He'd have played it differently. He ran his fingers through his blond hair, which was now beginning to turn grey. 'Aye, Rosie, I sometimes wish you were still with me. I do love Charlotte with all my heart, but life would have been so much easier, farming steadily away at Butterfield by now. No fancy dinner jackets or having to keep up appearances – just you, me and the bairns.' He checked himself once more in the mirror, pulling his stomach in to make himself look thinner, then made his way down the stairs, to do what he'd always done: smile and be there for the family, something everyone took for granted, and always would.

22

Charlotte sat in her favourite chair in the morning room, reading the latest edition of the *Craven Herald & Pioneer*. She came to the property page and stopped in her tracks as she read the notice declaring that High Mill at Skipton was up for sale. She read the auction notice, outlying all the details and giving the date of the auction as Monday 26th February at 2.30 p.m.

She folded the paper after reading the details and looked out of the window. The mill would go cheaply, as the bank was after the money it had invested in the mill. Should she go and have a look around, perhaps even bid for it? She had the money sitting in the bank, and there would be no trouble finding staff. Depending on the state of the actual mill, it would take no time at all to get it up and running again. Hector Christie was probably embroidering the truth when he said the mill was sliding into the river; he would have said anything, to help her protect Isabelle from John

317

Sidgwick's clutches. She breathed in deeply and read the details again. Viewing of the property was to take place, on request, in the run-up to the auction. She'd go and view the mill, and take Bert Bannister with her for his advice. Archie had said she should take a trip out; well, she'd take his advice and have a ride on the train, but not let anyone know the true reason for her trip. After all, they'd only try to talk her out of it. Charlotte felt a tingle of excitement as she thought about a fresh venture: a new mill in a new place, and hopefully bought at a reasonable price. What an idea! Something to get her teeth into, instead of moping around like a lost soul.

'I don't know why you are even thinking of buying this place.' Bert Bannister sat down next to Charlotte as they climbed into a horse-drawn cab that was waiting for passengers just outside the railway station.

'Because it could be a good investment, and because I miss my mill and being in charge of something other than Windfell. But I don't expect you to understand that. I know I'm being a bit rash, with cotton not being that profitable at the moment, but we could always spin wool – that would be a challenge for both of us.' Charlotte looked out of the window and listened to the familiar sound of bobbins flying back and forth on the looms of Belmont Mill, as they passed the towering building that was known for producing silk yarn.

Once over Belmont bridge, the horse and cab pulled into Caroline Square and then along the high street, with the parish church dominating the top of the street majestically. 'Just look at the folk here, Bert. It's a lot busier than Settle.' Charlotte kept looking out of the cab until the horses stopped, just a few yards down from the church. Skipton thronged with people, with shops and market traders on either side of the busy high street. A gaggle of geese were making themselves known to everyone, as their owner tried to guide them into a pen, ready for sale; and a tinker shouted out his trade, while sharpening knives on a wetted sandstone. 'This isn't your quiet Settle, Bert. Surely, with the right product, we could make money here.'

'Here you are, ma'am. High Mill, as you requested.' The cab driver got down from his seat and opened the cab door, then offered his hand for Charlotte to take.

'Thank you. How much do I owe you?' She opened her small bag and reached in for her coin purse.

'Tuppence, ma'am.' He held out his hand to be paid and closed it quickly as Charlotte pressed the coins into it. He climbed back into his seat as soon as Bert had got out, then urged the horses on, mixing back in with the busy street traffic.

'Well, he was a man of few words.' Bert leaned over the canal bridge that stood to the side of the dark and forbidding High Mill. 'I don't think your Hector Christie was embroidering his words, when he said that High Mill was in a bad way. I can tell you now that his loading bay to the canal side needs replacing. Just take a look at that bulkhead – a good push and it would be in the canal. That side wall has a crack in it, the size of my back lane at home, and I'd say there's subsidence going on somewhere under the building. Just look at the water wheel; it looks as if it's held on by God's good grace. Your mill fire was pure bad luck, but this building is simply waiting for an accident to happen.' Bert sighed heavily and waited for Charlotte to say something as she leaned over the bridge.

'It does look bad. I didn't realize the mill was in such a poor state, and it's not as big as I imagined. But I can see the agent down by the main door, waiting for us. I don't want to waste his time – we'll just go and look around the first floor. That will give us a good idea if it's worth anything.' Charlotte looked up at Bert, who shook his head in disbelief at the stubbornness of the woman. Ferndale had been like a palace compared to what lay in front of them. She stepped out, following the well-worn steps to take her down to the mill entrance.

The smartly dressed agent stepped forward and held out his hand for Bert Bannister to shake. 'Delighted to meet you, Mr Atkinson. And this must be your lovely wife. Perhaps she would rather sit and wait in the tea-shop across the road while we discuss business.'

'No, no, no. It is Mrs Atkinson you need to be dealing with. I'm just here to give her some advice. Mrs Atkinson will be discussing the business, while I have a look around.' Bert looked at Charlotte's face. She was obviously offended, but was doing her best not to show it.

'Mr Rogers, I presume? Now we have established who's who and, as Mr Bannister says, I'm the would-be purchaser. Although I must admit, from the view outside, I don't know why I have wasted my time.' Charlotte put the bigoted little man in his place and decided not to shake his hand, when he offered it grudgingly.

'Looks can be deceiving. Come – I'll show you around. I'm sure you will be impressed. The mill, if you don't already know, was working up to Christmas and then unfortunately had to stop production, because of lack of orders. It is hard, as I'm sure you know, running a business in this economic climate.' Mr Rogers checked through the bunch of keys and eventually found the right one to open the huge doors of the warehouse.

'I don't think Mr Sidgwick had a lack of orders. I think it was a lack of money to pay his bills,' Charlotte replied, as she stood and looked around the empty warehouse space, not impressed by the state it had been left in. She went over and read the mill's rules for the workers to abide by – rules made for the advantage of John Sidgwick, although he had shown no care for his workers, looking at the state of his building.

'So you know Mr Sidgwick?' Mr Rogers stood in the middle of the warehouse and watched as Bert

Bannister pushed his finger through the rotten window-frame and turned in disgust to shake his head at Charlotte.

'Yes, I know him. To be honest, Mr Rogers, I think we are wasting your time. This mill is too far gone to warrant any of my time and money. We will bid you farewell.' Charlotte nodded to Bert and stepped back into the daylight.

'We are open to offers. The bank will listen to any decent proposal.' Mr Rogers fumbled with the keys as he locked up quickly.

'I've just sold a mill that was in a better state than that, even though it was simply a burnt-out shell. I don't think you will get one decent bid for that pile of rubbish.' Charlotte stopped in her tracks and looked back at the decrepit mill.

'Then I'm afraid it will be the debtors' prison for Mr Sidgwick – which would be a great shame for a man of his stature – if we don't recoup some of the money owing.' Mr Rogers looked at Charlotte and her accomplice.

'No shame at all, Mr Rogers. It's a shame for the people he will be sharing a cell with, because he will be the biggest rogue they have ever met. Good day, Mr Rogers, thank you again for giving us your time.' Charlotte and Bert walked out down the high street, Charlotte's skirts swishing around her as she stepped out in a temper.

'I take it you didn't like our Mr Rogers, and didn't

think much of the mill.' Bert could hardly keep up with her as she walked quickly down the street.

'Ignorant little man! He knew it was me he was meeting. And then to show his allegiance with John Sidgwick! I hope Sidgwick does get locked up in the debtors' gaol – it's what he deserves.' Charlotte stopped and looked at Bert, her face clouding over with temper.

'You should have known the mill wouldn't be in that good a shape. And that little man has to stand by him; he's after Sidgwick's money.' Bert grinned at the hard-headed businesswoman who stood in front of him. 'You should be looking at something like that,' and he pointed across at a newly built shop frontage that had a 'For Sale' sign on the front of it. 'Get your girls set up properly in business, along with Sally Oversby's bits and pieces that she does for you.' The three-storey property stood proudly on the high street, with market traders all around it.

'I'm not a shopkeeper, I'm a mill owner.' Charlotte looked across at the clean new sandstone building and noticed the number of people coming in and out of the adjoining shops' doorways.

'You *were* a mill owner, Charlotte. Perhaps it's time to move on. Your girls are doing well in Settle, according to your accounts, but they could do better in Skipton.' Bert watched as she looked across at the shop.

'Have we to cross the road?' Charlotte took Bert's arm and stepped out onto the dusty high street, negotiating a path between the horses and their cabs.

Bert smiled. He could almost hear the cogs in Charlotte's brain working, as she gazed into the shop window. Perhaps their trip to Skipton had not been wasted after all.

23

Charlotte leaned over the lichen-covered packhorse bridge and looked down at the swirling brown waters of the River Ribble. In the distance she could hear the noise of the gushing Stainforth Foss. She watched as a dipper dived into the swirling waters, only to re-appear a few yards further downstream, gleaming as if bedecked by the most precious jewels, and with some aquatic grubs in its mouth. The sun shone and played on the reflection of the water, and Charlotte smiled as she noticed the cream-and-brown speckled froth that the force of water had created around nearby tree roots. It swirled round and round, unable to escape the capture of the roots and the current of flowing water. 'Ale water', her father would have called it. Charlotte heard his voice as clearly as if he stood next to her, and remembered his loving smile. She missed him so much.

It was the first day in March, St David's Day, and

the sun was trying its best to prepare for spring, by sneaking a little warmth from behind the clouds. And the river bank foretold the coming of spring, as the dainty wood sorrel and dog's mercury were starting to show. Another week or two and there would be wood anemones, primroses and the pungent smell of wild garlic, which the locals would gather to cook with, making a delicious soup, when added to potatoes.

Charlotte sighed. She'd tossed and turned all night and had taken this walk to clear her head of worries. The wedding was getting nearer and nearer, but her main concern was the decision she had taken, after her visit to Skipton. It was going to affect all aspects of her family's life. After returning on the train with Bert, she had decided to go back to Skipton on her own and, as Bert had suggested, look around the newly built retail property. It was, as he said, not carved in stone that she must remain a mill owner. The more she had thought about it, the more running a haberdashery and milliner's shop appealed to her. In fact, when she had looked around the space, she had realized that the shop could sell all manner of things. Plus, she could employ some of the young mill girls who had lost their jobs and offer them positions as shop girls. Unfortunately, she had not yet plucked up courage to tell Archie her new plans, and she was now feeling guilty. She knew straight away what he'd say: that she was mad in the head, as Skipton was more than ten miles away; and even more than that for Harriet, once she had settled into Crummock.

However, Charlotte did not regret signing for the deposit on the shop without Archie's or the rest of the family's knowledge. She'd decided to keep it to herself, just until the wedding was over; she didn't want to spoil the run-up to the happiest day of Danny and Harriet's life, by perhaps making Archie cross with her, for going back into business without his knowledge. Her news would keep. The lease on the shop at Settle ran for quite a few months yet, so at least Isabelle and Harriet were secure.

With this all settled in her mind, she opened the wooden gate and stepped onto the foot-worn grassy path that led the length of the river; if she followed it, she could walk back to her home along the river bank. She picked up her skirts and walked down by the side of the flooded river, stopping at the Foss as she gazed into the swirling whirlpool that frothed and bubbled at the foot of the falls. In summer it was a favourite place for couples to stroll and enjoy the scenery, and in the coming months salmon would be seen leaping up the falls, in an urgent attempt to return to the place of their birth further upriver, to spawn; and their skins would shine like rainbows as they fervently made attempt after attempt to jump the falls.

Today, the Foss was dark and forbidding, and Charlotte did not lurk for long on the slippery limestone rocks that overhung the falls. Making her way down the river bank, she climbed the stile that led into the parkland of Windfell and the path that, if it was followed, went to Ferndale Mill. She stopped as she drew

327

level with the railway line that ploughed through the bottom of her park, and wondered whether to walk further and see the progress being made in rebuilding Ferndale, which the Christies were rumoured to have started. She thought better of it, as the weather had turned into a fine drizzle, so she pulled her shawl around her and headed out of the river bottom, up the hillside that led back to Windfell. She stopped once on top of the hill and looked down amongst the trees, hearing the sound of pickaxes at work, confirming that the Christies had indeed started work on Ferndale. She watched as a plume of smoke rose from further down the dale, signifying an approaching steam train and its coaches, with the steady shunt of the engine building up, louder and louder, as it climbed to the next station at Horton-in-Ribblesdale. Charlotte looked on as the train and carriages passed her, filled with passengers going who knew where. Perhaps she was like those passengers: following a track that she knew not where it ended. But if it was up to her, it would end in success; and she would not regret selling Ferndale, if her plans for her new venture came to fruition.

'Have you had a good walk, ma'am?' Lily took her mistress's shawl and gloves.

'Yes, thank you, Lily. Although it's a little nippy out there and it is just starting to drizzle.'

'I think Ruby's been waiting for your return. She's eager for you to see the wedding-breakfast menu. She says she's to order quite a bit of it in and doesn't want to disappoint, if she can't get anything from either the butcher or the fruitier, ma'am.' Ruby waited, with her hands full of Charlotte's shawl and gloves.

'I suppose I will have to look at it – she's quite right. To be honest, I've been putting it off until everyone responded to the invitations, which they now have. I think we will be looking at around eighty-five for lunch. I hope Cook and the kitchen staff will be able to cope.' Charlotte sat down in her chair and warmed her hands in front of the fire. 'Ask Ruby to bring me her menus and we will work through them. Could you ask her to bring me a cup of tea as well, Lily, please. I need to warm up.'

Charlotte leaned back. She was beginning to regret being fully in charge of the upcoming wedding. She couldn't help but think that Betty Armstrong was getting off lightly with her daughter's marriage. But it had been all her own doing; she had, after all, set out her plans, without giving the Armstrongs a chance to add their four penn'orth. A decision that she was now regretting, with her new business plans looming.

'Ma'am, Lily said it was a good time to sit down with you now.' A flustered Ruby pushed the tea-tray onto the small side table next to Charlotte and waited with her notepad in hand. 'I wouldn't have been so forward, but it's only a good three weeks away. I've almonded the wedding cake and it is in hand, but all the rest is a bit undecided, as you've been out of the house a lot lately and I haven't had time to catch you.'

'I'm sorry, Ruby. Sorting out the sale of Ferndale

has led me not to concentrate on this wedding, and I must admit time is taking me by surprise. I don't know where the months since Christmas have gone. Thank goodness Isabelle and Harriet have sorted their dresses, and that the menfolk have already got suitable attire. So that just leaves the wedding breakfast to be sorted, and I'm sure you will have that in hand, if I know you.' Charlotte poured the milk in her tea and smiled at a frustrated-looking Ruby. 'Are you not joining me with a cup of tea?'

'Oh no, ma'am, it wouldn't be right.' Ruby sat patiently as her mistress took a long sip.

'Right, you tell me what you've planned for our eighty-five guests.' Charlotte sat back and waited.

'Eighty-five, ma'am – that's going to stretch us all. Can Thomson hire some serving staff from the Craven Heifer at Stainforth, perhaps? Because otherwise I don't know how we will cope. Getting the food to everyone warm is going to be an art in itself.' Ruby looked horrified at the number of bodies she was going to have to feed; she only wished she'd been told beforehand, before she had put the menu together.

'Yes, tell Thomson to get whoever he needs, and to let me know how many extra staff I need to pay for the day. Tell him to vet those he gets. I don't want any empty-headed young girls who are worth nothing.' Charlotte could really have done without employing more staff.

'Yes, ma'am. He'll be careful, and we will make sure the day goes well, with no upsets. Now I know we are in Lent at the moment, so we have been eating very little meat, but with the wedding being on Easter Saturday, I hope I've put together a set menu that you agree with. All the produce is in plentiful supply, which is a good job, now that I know I've got to cook for eighty-five. I thought I'd make Apple Charlotte – after yourself, ma'am, and of course the old Queen Charlotte.' Ruby passed over her menu and watched as Charlotte cast her eyes across it:

Ox-Tail Soup, or Grilled Fresh Herrings
with Mustard Sauce

*

Crépinettes of Chicken

*

Roast Loin of Mutton

*

Brussels Sprouts Dressed in Butter

*

Boiled Potatoes

*

Apple Charlotte Pudding with Custard

*

Cheese

'I couldn't have done better myself, Ruby. Mr Atkinson can supply you with the mutton, I'm sure, and the vegetable garden is still full of sprouts. I noticed them this morning as I passed it on my walk. You are to be applauded for your use of seasonal produce and for keeping to a sensible budget, no matter how many guests we have attending. It may not be as fancy as my wedding breakfast, when I first got married to Joseph Dawson, but it is filling and satisfying. We will decorate the tables with fruit and flowers, and it will be a wedding that they will remember.' Charlotte smiled at Ruby. She was good with the kitchen purse strings, and she should have had more faith in the prudent cook.

'Thank you, ma'am. We will decorate the dining hall and make it a day to remember, as you say. Young Master Danny is a lucky man to be marrying Miss Harriet – she will make him a good wife.'

'Yes, I should be thankful. I've got a loving family and, as you say, Harriet will fit into the family well. How's things downstairs, Ruby? I hear we have another blossoming romance, between Jethro and Mazy. I couldn't quite believe it, when Mr Atkinson told me.' Charlotte smiled.

'Yes, we are all happy for them. They tried to keep it a secret for a while, but I think they gave that up as a bad job, especially when young Eve found them kissing in the coal shed. It's good to think they have one another. At one time I thought Jethro would always live with his horses, but he's even taken to having a

332

bath twice a week. Eve takes buckets of hot water across to the stable, for him to wash in the tin bath. I've never known him do that before.' Ruby laughed.

'I'm glad he's taken to washing more frequently. As you say, he was beginning to love his horses a bit too much, and smell like them as well.' Charlotte smiled; she had a soft spot for Jethro, for he had always said things as they were, and had always supported her since her arrival at Windfell.

'Mazy will sort him out. He'll be turned into a gentleman before you know it.' Ruby stood up from her seat and looked across at Charlotte. 'Are you alright, ma'am? You look a little pale, if you don't mind me saying.'

'I'm fine, thank you, Ruby. Just a little tired, and wondering where all the years have gone. What with our Danny getting married, and Isabelle being infatuated with her charming Mr James, I'm beginning to realize that I'm not as young as I feel. That I've got to make my mark on the world before it's too late.'

'It's losing Ferndale – that's taken the wind out of your sails, ma'am. But knowing you, you'll bounce back with something bigger and better. And a wedding in the family will make everyone feel better. It's been a hard winter, but a lot of folks have had it harder than us at Windfell. We should count our blessings, ma'am, that's what I always say.' Ruby looked down at her list and thought of the families that had no bread on the table, and there she was, planning an extravagant five-course meal.

'You are right, Ruby. I will give myself a good talking to. Stop myself floundering in the doldrums, which I seem to be in at the moment. I took a walk down by the river this morning, and I think I heard the sound of picks and shovels being used on Ferndale, so I presume work has begun to repair it. I can't bear to go and actually look at the place, for it holds so many memories for me.'

'Yes, ma'am. Lily walked up that way from her home at Stackhouse, and she said it was thronged with workmen. So it won't be long before the mill is back up and running, thank the Lord. It hit everyone badly. You'll know that some families have actually left the district – they've had to, as without work they'd starve.' Ruby shook her head.

'Yes, it was a tragedy, not just for me, but for everyone. Three families have moved out of the lock cottages, leaving them empty. I'll be glad myself when the mill is rebuilt and working, as at least I'll be able to get tenants for my cottages.' Charlotte picked up her embroidery from her sewing box next to her and looked at it, uninterested.

'If that's all, ma'am, I'll go and prepare dinner for tonight.' Ruby curtsied and wished herself a penny behind her mistress in savings, as she left Charlotte looking at the embroidery that she had struggled with for the last countless months.

'Ruby says there's three cottages at the locks empty. They are bonny little cottages with a good lump of garden. I've always fancied living there, but they've always gone to mill workers in the past.' Mazy lay back in Jethro's arms and tested the waters with her idea. Although she had only been walking out with him for three months, Mazy knew that she had found the man she wanted to live with all her life; and she had imagined doing so, since knowing there were empty cottages just waiting to make them both a perfect life there. Happy and content in one another's company.

'Aye, it's a sad do. But you can't expect folk to stop, if there's no work. Have you really fancied living down there, even after Walter Gibson hanged himself and Betsy Foster was murdered down there? I don't know if I'd fancy them. And you've Mrs Batty living down there – she'd never be away.' Jethro yawned and placed his hands behind his head as he looked up at the rafters of his home above the stables, spotting a bit of daylight from where the rain had been dripping regularly.

Mazy turned and leaned on her elbow and looked at Jethro. She ran her finger over his striped collarless shirt and then kissed him sweetly on the lips, as his iron bedstead creaked with the weight of two people on it. 'It would be alright if I'd somebody to live with down there. It would make the perfect first home, and Mrs Atkinson wouldn't charge a lot.'

'Get her asked then. Eve might share with you, then the rent wouldn't be as much.' Jethro concentrated on the hole in the roof, only half-listening to the suggestion that had been put in front of him.

Mazy sat up on the bed edge. 'I wasn't thinking of sharing with Eve,' she snapped.

'Then who were you thinking of sharing with, and what's up with you?' Jethro realized suddenly that his momentary lack of interest had caused Mazy to become upset.

'I thought we could live there, me and you. It would be better than this frozen room over the stable.' She reached for her shawl.

'What: live over the brush? I could never do that, Mazy. I was brought up right.' Jethro was disgusted at her suggestion; they might be lying in one another's arms in his bunk, but that was different from living together out of wedlock.

'I'm going to have to spell it out, aren't I? I thought we could get married – you and me – and rent one of the cottages from the mistress.' Mazy held her breath. It should have been Jethro who asked her. And if he said no, she wouldn't know what to do.

'You and me get married? You mean you want to marry me?' Jethro beamed.

'Well, I thought that was what we were leading up to. And I don't really want to share our sleeping arrangements with Sheba, even though she is a thoroughbred.' Mazy looked at the dumbstruck groom.

'Bloody hell, lass. Yes, let's do it! Let's get married and, aye, let's get one of those lock cottages. It'll be

336

better than having rain peeing down on me.' Jethro looked up at the roof again and grinned.

'You are so romantic, Jethro Haygarth. I don't know what I see in you.' Mazy shook her head in dismay.

'I'll show you what you see in me, Mazy Banks.' Jethro grinned and pulled her down to him, making the bedstead creak even more. 'We can do this every night and every day, if we've a mind, when we are wed.' He rolled on top of her as she screamed. 'Of course I'll bloody marry you.'

24

'Where does time go, Arthur? It doesn't seem five minutes since it were me moving in there.' Archie stood by the side of the cart that was loaded with the belongings of Arthur and Mary, and patted the patient nag waiting to be driven off.

'Aye, we've had some fair times at Crummock, but it's being left in good hands, with your lad Danny and his wife-to-be. They'll farm it well.' Arthur looked around the farmstead that had been his home for more than twenty years and had given him some of his best years, along with his wife Mary.

'Well, I want to wish you and Mary all the best for the future, and I hope you will both be happy over at the Gap. I know you'll look after it well, just like you looked after Crummock well. Both Charlotte and I owe you a lot.' Archie shook Arthur's hand as he climbed up on the cart next to Mary.

'And I owe you a lot. You're a good man, Mr

Atkinson. If your lad turns out to be as big a gentle-man as you, he'll not go far wrong.' Arthur tipped his cap at Danny, who stood in the doorway of Crum-mock, watching the couple departing. 'Tell him to get himself down to Settle market place next week and hire the usual two Irishmen for lambing, because he'll need them. But I don't need to tell *you* that. It'll be strange, just having my own spot to worry about, but my old lass here can't wait to have a place to call her own.' He turned and smiled at Mary.

'Aye, get yourself gone, before dusk is upon us. Get your fires and lamps lit, ready for the night.' Archie looked up at Arthur, before hitting his nag on its flanks, stirring the horse into motion. He watched as the cart and its occupants made its way down the farm path and around the wood end, until it was out of sight.

'Well, lad, Crummock is all yours now.' Archie put his arm around his son's shoulders and walked into the kitchen. 'Your mother loves this house and land, so you make sure you farm it right. It's as good a place as you could hope for, and I'll always be here to help you, while I'm still alive.' He looked out of the kitchen window and across towards Eldroth and Butterfield Gap, his first home.

'I'll do my best, Father.' Danny stood beside him.

'Then your best is all I can ask, lad, and it's good enough for me.'

Danny and his father wandered around the market place of Settle, past the three-storey building known as the Shambles. It dominated the market place, with cottages on the top floor, followed by a myriad of small businesess behind a row of arches on the second floor, and an array of merchants just below ground level. It was busy with traders, butchers, bakers and chandlers all selling their wares, as the crowds gathered for the spring hiring fare, their voices shouting out above the crowds, tempting people to try and buy their goods. They were making the most of one of the busiest days of the year, and hoping to have a healthy bank balance at the end of the day. Farm lads and Irishmen, looking for employment with those farmers who could afford to pay them over the spring and summer months, mingled in the crowd, waiting to be taken on by a good and honourable farmer. They hoped their billet for the coming months until late autumn would be a good one, but were just glad if they had work.

A gaggle of geese squawked and protested as their drover shooed them through the crowd, to be penned and auctioned after being walked from Skipton. Their feet were covered in tar to keep them from becoming sore on their ten-mile walk. Pens of sheep bleated as their owners haggled the best price for them, and then exchanged coinage for them. The market square was alive with the noise, smells and colours of the spring fair.

'Bloody hell, it's busy, lad.' Archie walked through the crowd next to his son, ignoring the gypsy who was trying to sell him some lucky heather.

'Aye, just a bit. I think it gets busier every year.'

Danny pushed his way past the crowd that was gathering, watching a dancing bear that was being made to stand on one foot. Its owner was prodding it with a stick and pulling on the chain threaded through its nose. 'Look at them! Folk are just like ghouls, watching that poor creature being tortured for their enjoyment.' Danny spat as the crowd cheered in delight while the bear achieved the impossible.

'Aye, poor thing. It would be better to set it free, but then again it wouldn't last long before somebody shot it. Arthur and I usually meet our two Irishmen outside The Naked Man. They've never let us down yet, so they should be there waiting. At least you can trust them; they've always been good workers and have family back in Ireland, so they don't drink all they earn.' Archie bobbed and weaved through the gaps in the crowd and then shouted at the two men who were standing with packs of belongings underneath the sign of The Naked Man inn. 'So, you've made it back to us again?' He shook the hands of each man and patted them on the back.

'Aye, we're here again, and we are both glad to see that you are, likewise.' Declan, the weathered Irishman, smiled. 'Is Arthur not with you? Have you left him behind with his good wife, Mary?'

'Nay, he's left Crummock, only last week. He's bought my old home and struck out on his own. I've Danny with me – he'll be your new master at Crummock. He's to be wed in a fortnight, to a right grand lass called Harriet.'

'Well, would you believe it? Things move on so fast while we are away. Good luck to you, Mr Danny, and may all your problems be little ones.' Declan smiled at Danny; and Pat, the quiet one, shook his hand. 'Are you wanting to be away? 'Cause that would suit us fine.' Declan and Pat both picked up their few belongings and waited for Archie to reply.

'Well, I've done, but perhaps my lad wants to stop a bit longer. Danny, we'll take the horse and cart, and you can ride Sheba back home. It'll do you good to have a wander and catch up with folk.' Archie looked at his son; he'd not get the chance much longer to spend his time as it suited him, not with a farm to run and men to see to.

Danny watched as the three men walked away through the throng, his father talking to the two hired men as if they were his best friends. That was just like his father, he thought; no matter what anyone's background was, he treated them with the same respect and concern. He was a good man, a father to be proud of.

Danny walked out through the crowd, trying his hand at a game of quoits with some of the local farm lads, then deciding to go for a gill at the Talbot Arms before he made his way home. He walked up Cheapside, past the doctor's and dentist's and the many shops that lined the street, and just before he reached the doors of the Talbot Arms, he noticed the unmistakable flash of auburn hair that could only belong to Amy Brown, bobbing above the crowd. He pushed his

342

way past the hawkers and street sellers, towards where she stood. His heart raced, remembering the times he had with Amy, and the love that might have been.

'Amy!' He jostled his way to where she was standing and reached for her elbow as he came up behind her, smiling from ear to ear as she turned around. Her face was pale and drawn, and she looked worried as she looked at him.

'Danny, it's good to see you.' She smiled as she realized who it was shouting her name.

'It's good to see you, too. How are you keeping?' Danny looked at her extended stomach underneath her skirts and regarded the woman who could have had his heart, if only she had been faithful.

'I'm fine, waiting for this one to make himself known. I've a few more weeks yet.' Amy looked down at her stomach and then started to walk away from him. 'I hear you are to wed shortly.'

'Aye, next weekend, Easter Saturday.' Danny pushed his way against the crowd, trying to keep up with Amy as she made her way to the horse and cart that stood waiting for her, tethered outside the Talbot. 'Wait, Amy, stay and talk. I need to ask you something.'

Amy walked on, not daring to reply.

'Amy, who are you talking to? My father and I have been waiting for over half an hour for you. We were starting to get worried.' The dark-haired young man held out his hand to help Amy mount onto the seat next to him.

'Aye, get your trailing arse back up here with us.' The wizened-faced old man spat out a mouthful of tobacco and scowled at his daughter-in-law. 'You shouldn't be talking to any men, in your state. You should have stopped at home,' he growled.

'I've only been talking to Mr Atkinson here. His father farms at Austwick.' Amy pulled her shawl around her and sat quietly between both men.

Her husband looked Danny up and down. 'This is my wife, sir, and I'll remind you to bear that in mind, next time you see her. She is no longer available for anybody's affections other than my own. I ask you to ignore any conversations that she wishes to have with you in the future. Now, I bid you good day.' Amy's husband flicked his whip across his team's flanks and set off down the cobbled street, without even giving a backward glance at Danny, as he watched the three bodies disappearing into the crowds. Amy was now wedged between the two men who meant to control her life, looking fragile, drawn and lacking the spirit that once Danny had loved her for so much.

'What time did Danny get in this morning? I say "this morning" because I heard the grandfather clock strike twelve, long before I heard his bedroom door go.' Charlotte buttered her toast and looked across at Archie.

'Late, that's all I know. By the sound of him, he was worse for drink. I heard him curse when he lost his boots down the stairs. I suppose he was making the

344

best of his last few days of freedom.' Archie folded the paper and then placed it down beside him. 'Has Isabelle gone to Settle already?'

'Yes, she's got to put the finishing touches to Harriet's veil and dress, and to hem her own. I can't believe the day is nearly upon us.' Charlotte looked across at Archie and smiled.

'I'll just finish this, and then I'll go and rouse our wayward son. What are you doing today? You never seem to be at home lately.' Archie knew Charlotte was up to something, but hadn't quite worked out what. He knew that she had visited High Mill at Skipton and had been disgusted at how dilapidated it had become, but it wasn't that, as she'd told him she wouldn't have anything to do with the mill. But something had been keeping her occupied, and she was definitely scheming.

'I'm going to Skipton – there's things I need to do.' She sipped her tea and looked across at Archie and hoped he'd ask no more. She wanted to put things in place a bit more, before announcing her new venture to the family after the wedding.

'I'll come with you. I haven't been into Skipton for a while. I'll get our lad up, send him to Crummock, and then we can have a day together for once.' Archie pushed back his chair and watched as Charlotte's face told him what he wanted to know: she was up to something!

'You'll be bored. I'm only having tea with Mrs Rogerson, and you know how she talks.' Charlotte waffled and blustered, trying to keep Archie at home.

'Mrs Atkinson, I know you too well. What are you really up to? If I didn't know you better, I'd think you had another man in your life.' Archie sat back down quickly.

'Oh no, Archie, there's no man involved. You know there's only ever going to be you in my life. I didn't want to tell anyone until after the wedding, and not until I had everything in place.' Charlotte hesitated.

'Go on, what have you done? I've known for weeks you've been up to something.' He grinned.

'I've bought a shop, on the high street in Skipton. It's newly built and has room for Isabelle and Harriet's dressmaking, and I'm filling each room with fancy goods and things that every lady wants. Perfume, furs, gloves, hats and shoes. I'll even rent the upstairs room to James Fox, seeing as Isabelle and he are getting very friendly. My customers can have their photographs taken while they shop. The top room has a large sky-light, so it is ideal for him.' Charlotte sat back in her chair and waited for Archie's reaction.

'I knew you were bloody well up to something. Another shop never entered my head. So does anyone else know, or is this just your secret? And I suppose you are funding your venture from the Ferndale Mill money? By, there's a lot to be said for a man having control of his wife's money. Bring back the good old days – you'd have had to tell me all this, a few years back, and I'd have said you were bloody mad.' Archie looked across at the wife he knew he'd never be able to control.

'Oh, Archie, don't be mad with me. I couldn't have sat here doing nothing, you know that. Bert Bannister has been helping me. I've taken him on as my warehouse man, and he's been making sure that the stock I've ordered has been taken in; he's also been busy putting everything together for me. I'm still going to keep on the shop at Settle, until the lease runs out. So I've not cut off my nose to spite my face. And, Archie, I really can't go wrong. The high street at Skipton is so busy. I've already got ladies peering through the window, wanting to see what we sell.'

'Bert bloody Bannister . . . you and he are as thick as thieves. I suppose Sally Oversby is part of the scheme as well. I saw her the other day, knitting like mad next to her cottage window.' Archie rubbed his head and looked across at the excitement in his wife's eyes. 'What if Harriet and Danny decide to have children? She'll not want to trail to Skipton.'

'Isabelle is not far behind, in becoming a good seamstress, and anyway I've sourced some ready-made dresses. I couldn't believe it when I came across a firm in Bradford – their dresses are perfectly practical for everyday use. Isabelle and Harriet's are more special, and I'm thinking of asking them to teach Sally how to use the sewing machine – or should I say machines, because I bought another last week.'

Archie shook his head as he watched his wife planning the new life ahead of her. 'You've already done everything, haven't you? No matter what the rest of us think.'

'I've done it for all of us. It's a family business, just like Crummock is. I'm sorry I've kept it quiet, but Isabelle and Harriet and Danny have enough on their plates at the moment, without wondering what I was up to.' Charlotte reached over the table and patted her husband's hand.

'Well, I think it's time I had a look at this new family business, as I've lost my wife to it already,' Archie growled. 'One day, Charlotte, your pig-headedness will be the undoing of you. You can't just not tell me things.'

'You'd only worry, Archie. As it is, most of the work is done now. You can glory in the opening of Atkinson's of Skipton, once we've got over the wedding.' Charlotte grinned as she kissed him on the cheek. 'You'd only be bored if you had a sensible, dull wife.'

'That'll be the day! I've never had a dull day since the day we were married.' He raised his head and looked across at Danny as he entered the dining room. 'Bad head?'

Danny nodded and slumped down in his chair, unshaven and with a face like thunder.

'Aye, I have and all', Archie agreed. 'It's called your mother.'

'We aren't open yet for business, unless you are making a delivery.' Bert Bannister turned the key in the lock and tried to pull back the bolt of the wide doors leading from his new place of employment, wondering who the man outside was who had no patience; he was rattling the shop's doors violently.

'Open the bloody doors, Bert. Charlotte here has forgotten her keys.' Archie stood outside the double-fronted shop, rattling the door handle, with Charlotte by his side.

'He's opening up, Archie, calm down.' Charlotte tried to defuse the situation.

'About bloody time, man.' Archie pushed his way past a worried Bert and gazed around the shop floor, stopping quickly in his tracks at the sight that confronted him. 'Lord above, what have you done? I've never seen a shop like it. There's anything you women could possibly think of needing. And the smell of the perfumes is overwhelming.'

'This is just the first floor; second floor is haberdashery, Isabelle and Harriet's millinery, Sally's bags and gloves; and then on the third floor there is a fitting room and, hopefully, a photograph studio – if Mr Fox is as keen on our Isabelle as he seems, and if he wants to become part of the Atkinson empire.' Charlotte turned around to reassure a worried Bert, as Archie passed from counter to counter, looking at the shining glass perfume bottles, ladies' toiletries and beauty aids.

'I've never seen owt like it. You've everything that you need under one roof.' Archie stood back and looked around the long shop floor, then gazed at himself in the full-length mirror, positioned to emphasize the shopper's finer points.

'That's exactly what every woman wants: not to

have to wander the high street, in search of two or three different shops. I'm not even concerned if Mr Fox doesn't show interest in a studio, as I might even try serving tea and coffee, so that women can come and shop and chat with their friends.' Charlotte winked at Bert. She knew that Archie had seen what she saw in the shop, and that his anger was subsiding.

'Would you like a drink of tea, Mr Atkinson? I was just making myself a cup when you landed.' Bert walked past the couple, trying to make his escape.

'Nay, I'll just have a look around, see what you've both been up to.'

Charlotte watched as Archie walked from counter to counter, looking at all the products she had been busy buying over the last few weeks. Then she followed him up the main stairs to the second floor. He stopped and looked out of one of the big open windows and watched the busy high street, full of people going about their jobs.

'You've taken on something now, lass. "Atkinson's of Skipton." If this is a success, it could lead to Atkinson's of Leeds, or Bradford. I think the world is your oyster.'

'Now who's excited? I was so worried you wouldn't understand, and I didn't want to spoil Danny and Harriet's big day.' Charlotte linked her arm into his.

'We'll keep it quiet until they are wed. One thing at a time. It'll be the making of this family.' Archie patted her hand. 'I should have known you'd not have done things by halves, Mrs Atkinson. This beats sitting at

350

home with that bit of embroidery you've struggled with for years – and your cotton mill. Let the Christies make their money at Ferndale. We own Atkinson's of Skipton. And if first impressions mean owt, it's going to be one hell of a success.'

25

Betty Armstrong was in a fluster, for her new corset was nipping her too tightly, and she just knew her dress would not meet the expectations of the Atkinsons – let alone her hat, which, now that she had it on her head, looked ridiculous.

'Mother, you look wonderful – stop flapping.' Harriet stepped into her underskirts as Isabelle helped her dress for her big day.

'Yes, you look wonderful, Mrs Armstrong, a real lady. My mother will be so jealous of that fabulous hat. It is so striking, with the peacock feathers adorning it; and Sally Oversby's little blue-and-green bag finishes your attire just right.' Isabelle smiled at the nervous woman, trying to reassure her that all was fine, and that she should be worrying about what Harriet looked like, for after all it was her wedding.

'Well, thank you both. Isabelle, your mother always

looks so sophisticated and I never seem to look quite as good. Oh, my heavens, Harriet: just look at you!'

Isabelle pulled on the laces of the wedding dress, tying them tightly, then stood back to admire the sight that had taken Betty's breath away. 'You look beautiful, Harriet. Our Danny is the luckiest person I've ever known. You look perfect.'

Harriet looked in her wardrobe mirror and smiled at herself, blushing at the sight of herself in her wedding dress. 'It's you I've to thank for this stunning dress, Isabelle. Anyone could look beautiful in this dress.'

'Oh, my baby girl, I'm losing you today. What am I going to do? This old house is going to be so quiet without you. Your father prefers his sheep to me. I'll have no one to talk to.' Betty wiped a tear away from her eye and sniffed into her handkerchief.

'Oh, Mother, you will be fine. You'll have grandchildren – more than you can cope with, between my sister and me, or at least I hope so.' Harriet hugged her mother as she kept sobbing.

'Our Danny, a father – it doesn't bear thinking about. He can't even look after himself.' Isabelle stepped into her dress and pulled the bodice up onto her shoulders. 'Can you help me fasten this, please, Mrs Armstrong?' She turned her back to Betty, who dropped her hanky as she struggled with the laces.

'Oh my Lord, I don't think I can pick up my hanky, my corsets are so tight,' she gasped, as she tried to bend down to retrieve it. 'Pride is a terrible sin, especially when it doesn't let you bend.' Betty sat down in a chair and laughed at herself for being such a proud and stupid old woman. 'I should leave the high fashion to you two – you've the figures to get away with it. I just don't know if I'm coming or going: tears one minute and laughing the next. I'm just a silly old fool.'

Isabelle looked at Harriet and herself in the mirror. 'I hope, Harriet, this is the happiest day of your life, and I hope our Danny makes you happy.' She turned and hugged her sister-in-law, whom she had come to love.

'Thank you, Isabelle, you have been so kind and you deserve a good man of your own. I hope your Mr Fox is the man for you. He certainly seems more than interested, seeing how many times he visits the shop and invites you for tea every week.' Harriet squeezed her back.

'Oh, you girls, stop it or you'll make me cry again. I really don't know whether I'm coming or going,' Betty sighed.

The sweat was running down Ruby's brow as she brushed the endless slices of bread with melted butter and patted them into the sides of eighty-five individual pudding moulds for her Apple Charlotte pudding. 'Eve, have you not finished those potatoes yet? You are going to be late with putting them on. Thank heavens we peeled the Brussels last night.'

The whole kitchen smelled of roasting mutton and was like a hive of busy bees, with all the manor staff occupied with extra jobs, and the additional maids from the Craven Heifer going back and forth.

'Chop it finer, lass, then add a cupful more of sugar to it. The last thing you want is a big leaf of unchewable mint in your sauce.' Ruby watched as one of the helpers from the Craven Heifer followed her instructions. The lass had no idea how to use a knife, and Ruby realized she'd have been better doing the job herself.

'The dining room's set. The main table looks lovely; the little bunches of primroses and violets that Jethro picked look perfect on the smaller tables. I don't know where he managed to find that many, at this time of year.' Mazy smiled. 'What do you want me to do next?'

'He's half-gypsy, is that Jethro of yours. He knows the countryside and its ways. I hope you know what you are taking on, when you wed him, for he'll take some taming. Just take over from this lass and finish off the mint sauce, else I'll still be waiting for it when the day's done.' Ruby ordered the lass who was making the mint sauce over to the sink, to deal with the washing up, which was growing by the minute.

'Back to where you started: making mint sauce. I always remember Mrs Batty watching you when you first came.' Mazy laughed while remembering a timid Ruby making perfect mint sauce; and now she was running the kitchen.

'Aye, at this moment in time I wish I was back

there, and not in charge of the whole kitchen. Be careful what you wish for – that's my advice.'

'Oh, I got my wish when Jethro asked me to marry him. I can't wait for our wedding. Although it will be nowhere as grand as this. Just a few friends. You'll be invited, Ruby.'

'That's what I mean: be careful what you wish for. One morning you'll wake up and find yourself sharing your bed with a horse, knowing Jethro – you'll never tame him. He's a grand lad, but he's a law unto himself.'

Mazy poured her stewed apples and lemon zest into her bread moulds, then leaned back for a second, before placing the circles of buttered bread on top, to seal the puddings ready for baking.

'I don't want to tame him. I like him just as he is. And now we've got a cottage to rent down at the locks, we'll both have a home.' Mazy cleaned her knife with her fingers and placed a portion of the chopped mint and sugar in each waiting silver sauce-boat, before adding the vinegar. 'There, that's done. I'll make sure all's going as it should upstairs.' She hadn't realized Ruby felt that way about Jethro, and the cook's words had cut more sharply than the knife had cut through the mint. Perhaps she would never change her stable boy, but that was Jethro's charm. He cared so much for Mrs and Mrs Atkinson that he'd got up straight after dawn to pick the bunches of primroses and violets, knowing that Mrs Atkinson loved them so much. He might be wild, but his heart was true; and that was all that mattered.

'Oh, ma'am, you look absolutely beautiful.' Lily stood back and admired her mistress. She looked stunning. Her pale-blue, tight-bodiced dress swept down to the floor, shimmering slightly in the sharp light. Pearls adorned her shoulders and neckline, telling of the richness and cost of the bespoke dress.

'Thank you, Lily, that's just what the mother of the groom wants to hear. You know you are not getting any younger, when your son gets married. Or should I say when Danny gets married, for I sometimes forget that he is not, technically, my son. Some days I forget I did not give birth to him, for I've always regarded him as mine.'

'That's just how it should be, my love.' Archie put his hands on Charlotte's pearl-covered shoulders and looked at his beautiful wife's reflection in the dressing-table mirror as she threaded her drop earrings into her ears. 'You look wonderful.' He kissed her hand as she reached for his.

'You don't look too bad yourself, Mr Atkinson. Is Danny dressed and ready? I can hear that terrible Robert Knowles in the entrance hall. I presume Thomson will have served him with a drink. Why Danny had to choose him to be his best man, I don't know. I've never quite forgiven him for giving Isabelle that kitten. I'm quite thankful Jethro has adopted it, and it seems to be more contented sleeping with him in the

357

stables than in our Isabelle's room. I knew it would soon be forgotten by our Isabelle.'

'The Knowles are a good family. I once hoped that Robert would marry our Isabelle. It would have been convenient, when it came to the farms. I'll go and see if Danny's ready; he came up some time ago and insisted he'd get dressed himself, as Thomson is run off his feet preparing the wedding breakfast.' Archie walked over to the bedroom door.

'I keep telling you, we need a valet.' Charlotte turned and looked at Archie, who appeared just as handsome as he did when she first met him, in his best suit.

'Nonsense; if I can't dress myself, I want shooting. Eh, Lily?' Archie winked at Lily, who was busy putting her mistress's belongings in order, ready for her return from the church.

'I couldn't possibly say, sir.' Lily smiled.

'Always the diplomat, Lily. No wonder you've lasted this long with my wife. Right, I'll see Danny and go downstairs with him. You do look beautiful, my dear. I could marry you all over again.' He looked at his wife and grinned.

'Go on, you soft old fool, go and check on Danny – do your fatherly duties.' Charlotte turned and looked at herself in the mirror again. She did look good for her age, there was no denying it.

'Danny, it's only me.' Archie knocked on the door and then walked into his son's bedroom. 'What's up, why

358

are you only half-dressed? Here, let me fasten your necktie and help with your cufflinks. Your mother's just played hell with me for not having a valet. Now, we don't want her to win the argument.' Archie picked up the necktie, stood in front of Danny and attempted to lift his starched collar for the necktie to be added.

'Stop it, Father. I can't do this. I can't go through with this marriage.' Danny stared at his father, eye-to-eye. 'I'm sorry; everyone is waiting for me, the manor's staff are run off their feet because of me, and Harriet will be nearly setting off from High Winskill by now, but I just can't do it. I really can't marry her. I'm not ready.'

'Not ready, lad! It's only wedding-day nerves. I was the same. But I'd a shotgun aimed at my head by your grandfather, so that was a bit different.' Archie sat down on Danny's bed and looked up at his son. 'Here – sit here. Folk can wait a while. Tell me what's really worrying you?' Archie looked at his lad. There was something more than wedding-day nerves going on in that blond head.

Danny put his head down and nearly sobbed as he confessed, 'I think I'm the father of Amy Brown's baby. I saw her in Settle at the hiring fair, and I'm sure it's my bairn.'

'Did she say you were?' Archie scowled.

'No, she never got the chance. Her husband yelled at her.' Danny wiped his face and looked at his father, expecting him to lose his temper at his confession.

'Well, you forget her, lad. You get your suit on, you

359

put a smile on that miserable face of yours, and you go and marry that bonny lass who loves you. Amy Brown has made her bed, and now she must lie on it.' Archie could have cursed his son, but that would have got him nowhere.

'I can't forget her. I've wronged her, Father,' Danny sobbed.

'Aye, and you are going to break another heart, if you are not careful. Not to mention your mother's. Proud as punch she is – she's so happy for you. Like I am. You are going to be good for Crummock and that bonny li'l lass who, as you say, will be making her way to the church now. Life's all spread out in front of you, lad. Don't throw it away because of nerves and Amy Brown.' Archie patted his son on the back.

'But the baby, Father!' Danny dropped his head and rubbed his hands over it.

'It might not be yours, lad. And Harriet need never know. It won't be the first child that doesn't know its true father.' He hugged his son tightly. 'I love you, lad. Life's hard, but you've got a good one in Harriet; she will always be there for you, and you need love like that to walk through life together. Not the fleeting kind that burns too brightly and breaks your heart.'

Danny looked at his father and knew he was right. Harriet would always be there for him, and Amy was like the early-morning dew: beautiful and captivating for the fleeting moments she had loved him.

'Now then, I'm going to leave you to get dressed, and I'll wait for you downstairs with your mother. I know you'll not let all those folk that love you down today. Else you wouldn't be my lad.' Archie stood up and listened intently to a sound that was drifting across from the village at Langcliffe. 'Listen, they are your wedding bells – they are ringing for you and Harriet. Jethro's all done up like a dog's dinner, with the best team awaiting all of us. Now get a move on, and stop dwelling on things too much.'

Archie closed his son's bedroom door behind him and said a silent prayer that Danny would see sense. He swore quietly to himself and wondered if he'd advised him correctly.

'Is he ready? Has he not heard the bells have started ringing already? If Harriet's on time, he's going to be late,' Charlotte called up from the hallway.

'He just needed a hand with his necktie and cuffs – he'll be down in a second,' Archie bluffed, hoping that his words would be half-true.

'Nice to see you, sir. It's a grand day for Danny and Harriet's wedding.' Robert Knowles shook Archie's hand as he balanced a drink of claret in the other.

'Aye, the sun's shining at least. I'm glad Thomson's got you a drink, lad. You've been looked after, haven't you?' Archie stood in line with Robert and Charlotte and watched as his wife mouthed her concerns silently.

'Yes, thank you, sir. I've just been telling Mrs Atkinson that I hope Danny will be my best man this autumn. He doesn't know it yet, but I'm to marry Anne Whitfield from Austwick.' Robert grinned.

'One of the Whitfields that farm as you drive out to Wharfe? She'll be a good match for you – your land will join up with theirs, like ours does.' Archie smiled and sighed in relief as he heard the bedroom door close behind Danny, and his son appeared fully dressed on the stairs.

'That's right, sir. My father can't believe his luck.' Robert blushed.

'No, neither can I, lad. We are both blessed with good sons, ones that do right by their family. Isn't that right, Danny?'

'If you say so, Father.' Danny stood at the bottom of the stairs.

Charlotte walked over and kissed him on the cheek. 'You look exceedingly handsome, Danny. You do know that you have all our love on this day, and that you will always have our support.'

'Yes, Mother. I know that no matter what life throws at Harriet and me, we will always have you both there for us.' He hugged Charlotte and held back his true feelings.

'Danny, I need you as best man this autumn. Anne and I are to be married. It's time to settle down and become a father. None of us are getting any younger, and you've set the trend, by marrying Harriet.' Robert slapped Danny across the back as he felt for the wedding ring in his pocket.

'Congratulations! I'm sure you'll be the perfect couple, and it would be an honour to be your best man. Anne and Harriet will be neighbours, and that will be good, especially over the winter months when the days drag.' Danny looked around him at his concerned parents and at the slightly drunk Robert. 'I think we'd better get a move on. It would never do if I'm late and make poor Harriet worried.'

'That's it, lad, let's go and get you wed. The church will be packed by now. And look, the sun is doing its best to fight the clouds away.' Archie put his hand up to his face and looked at the spring sunshine that had been playing hide-and-seek with the clouds all morning. 'It's a day for celebration, and the sun is joining in. Besides, the smell coming from the kitchen is making me hungry, so the sooner we are back and sat around that dining table, the better.'

'Archie, you are unbelievable! Come on, give me your hand up into the carriage. I want to look my best, and this dress creases easily.' Charlotte stopped at the carriage and took Archie's hand as Jethro opened the door.

'You will always look perfect to me, my love.' Archie winked and turned to Danny and Robert. 'Remember: flattery will get you a long way with your women.'

'All of you get in, and don't listen to your father – he hasn't got a clue about what a woman wants to hear. He just makes it up as he goes along,' Charlotte laughed. 'To the church, Jethro, and thank you for making the team look so grand.'

'The church it is, ma'am.' Jethro closed the carriage door and whipped his team into motion. It was a day of celebration, for Master Danny was getting married and had become a man.

Harriet, Isabelle and her father stood outside Langcliffe village church and listened to the organ music coming from within. Children gathered around the gate, waiting for guests to throw coppers to them after the wedding; and local women stood and nattered, gasping in awe as Harriet took her father's arm to walk along the pathway up to the church's doorway. They walked slowly and steadily up the hill and to the waiting vicar, who smiled at the bride and her attendants. As he did so, the sun broke out from behind a cloud, the rays falling on Harriet's shimmering gown and making the crowd gasp at the beauty of it.

'My veil's alright, isn't it?' Harriet whispered as she felt it slightly with her hand, making sure the wreath of delicate flowers was still holding the fine embroidered lace in place.

'You look perfect. Danny is so lucky,' Isabelle whispered.

'That he is. I just hope he realizes how much,' Ted Armstrong whispered, as he watched the vicar walk down the aisle and signal to the organ player to start playing the wedding march. 'Here we go, my lass. You are no longer mine from this day onwards.'

The group walked slowly and steadily down the church aisle, smiling at the guests, who caught their breath at the beauty of the bride and her maid walking behind her.

Danny turned and looked at his bride-to-be. She was beautiful. How could he have doubted his marriage to her? It was the fleeting conversation when he met Amy Brown that had started his mind racing again. How miserable she had looked. He took Harriet's hand and felt the love that flowed through her. A love that would always be there for him, as his father had said.

The vicar looked around his congregation and started the ceremony.

Harriet turned round and gave Isabelle her bouquet of lily-of-the-valley, which Jethro had force-grown for her wedding day. She smiled as she noticed James Fox in a pew towards the back of the church. It was a romance that was blossoming with every day. Isabelle had found her perfect man, just as she had.

'Daniel Arthur Atkinson, do you take this woman to be your lawful wedded wife . . .' The vicar's words were like mystic muttering, as she heard Danny respond with an 'I do.'

'Harriet Margaret Armstrong, do you take this man . . .' She could barely wait for the sentence to end, as she looked lovingly into Danny's eyes, before answering, 'I do.' She was married to her Danny, for now and always.

'Well, that's them married.' Archie stood on the church steps as he watched children scattering for the pennies that had been thrown, and the new couple kiss one another as people wished them well. 'I almost thought he wasn't going to go through with it.' He put his arm through Charlotte's. 'We may have another wedding beckoning, by the looks of them two.' He nodded towards James Fox and Isabelle, walking hand-in-hand through the budding spring churchyard.

'I knew, as soon as I saw him in the shop, that he was right for Isabelle. I do hope Harriet and Danny will be happy together. I misjudged Harriet at first. I shouldn't have been so hasty; she'll be good for the family.' Charlotte held Archie's arm tightly. 'Rosie would have been proud of Danny today – she'll be looking down and watching us all.'

'Aye, she will. She loved her lad. He was everything to her, in the short time she was with him. I often see Rosie in Danny. She was such a kind soul, and she didn't deserve me. I think she always knew I loved you.' Archie looked at the love of his life, the woman who often drove him mad, but was the passion of his life. Rosie had been kind and caring, and would always have been the perfect mother and wife. Charlotte was that, and more – she kept him on his toes, kept him excited, with her lust for life.

'We've both been true to her memory, and we've brought Danny up well. I shouldn't have listened to my father back then. I should have listened to my heart and married you.' Charlotte kissed Archie, her eyes nearly filling with tears.

'We all make mistakes, but as long as we try to rectify them, we'll be forgiven. Look at them two: the crowds have let them through the church gate and they are walking back home. Danny's intent on showing off his new bride to the world.' Archie grinned.

'It's been a perfect day, but it's not over yet. Mazy will be getting in a tizzy with the wedding breakfast, and then we are all to have our photographs taken by the dashing Mr Fox.' Charlotte walked down the path with Archie. 'A "family portrait", I think he called it. I hope he can get Betty Armstrong's hat into the picture – have you ever seen such a creation? The feathers looked far better on the peacock.' Charlotte giggled as she watched the huge blue-and-green feathers disappear out of sight, as Betty followed the newly-weds down the road.

'Charlotte Atkinson, behave! If it was in your new shop, you'd be trying to sell it to the first customer that came in. Come on, let's walk home. Time for dinner, and for us to be content with our lot. There's a lot worse off than us.'

'I know. I love you, Archie Atkinson, and always will, and we are indeed lucky. Time to go home and celebrate with friends and family at our good fortune. We all deserve this day.'

The wedding breakfast went without a hitch, with the hired servants following Mazy and Ruby's instructions to the letter. And Thomson served, along with help, like a professional top waiter. Ruby had excelled herself and everyone appreciated the food, as they listened to Ted Armstrong, Robert Knowles and Danny give their speeches, sitting down afterwards to a good glass of port. Archie looked around at the empty dishes and happy faces, and knew it was his turn to say the few words he'd been practising in his head all day. He stood up and banged the spoon on the table for attention.

'Now, that was a wedding breakfast! I think the staff of Windfell deserve a hand.' Archie stood and clapped in appreciation of the hard work put in by one and all, and everyone else joined in, embarrassing the staff in the room and making Ruby cry with pride and exhaustion as she heard the ripple of applause. 'Now, when Harriet first started seeing our Danny, we didn't know if she'd fit into our family or not. You know how it is; you watch them together and think: Is he good for her, and is she good for him? But even if I was blind, I'd know that these two were made for one another. Not only is Harriet good for our Danny, but she's good for the whole family, showing a lot of love and devotion, both to Isabelle here and to the shop they run in Settle. Charlotte and I will always love Harriet as the daughter she now is. You can be proud of yourselves, Ted and Betty, for having such a wonderful daughter, and you can be assured that she's in good hands with our Danny. Now we've just to wait for some grandchildren, so that we can spoil them in our dotage – not that I'm rushing you two.'

Harriet blushed. She'd kept herself pure for her wedding night, as she was sure Danny had.

'Can you raise your glasses to Danny and Harriet?' Archie bellowed.

'To Danny and Harriet!' the guests cheered.

'And to their future children!' Archie shouted, as Charlotte glowered at him. Her father had done the same thing at her wedding, and that had been the downfall of her marriage. God willing, history would not repeat itself. No matter, he'd said it now.

High on the windswept fell between Clitheroe and Slaidburn, in a long, low farmhouse, the first cries of Amy Brown's newborn were heard.

'You've got a boy, Amy. He's only small, with being born early, but he's a bonny baby – a blond, blue-eyed boy. What are you going to call him?' The old woman passed Amy her baby, wrapped in a warm blanket.

'I'm calling him Daniel. Danny for short.' Amy kissed her new bundle on his cheek as a tear fell down her cheek.

'Daniel in the Lion's Den,' the midwife joked.

'Aye, he's that alright, but he'll be loved – just as I love his father.' Amy looked down at her newborn and held him tightly. A baby created from true innocent love, a love she would never forget.

RULES TO BE OBSERVED
BY THE HANDS EMPLOYED IN THIS MILL

Rule

1. All the Overlookers shall be on the premises first and last.
2. Any Person coming too late shall be fined as follows: for 5 minutes 2d, 10 minutes 4d, and 15 minutes 6d, &c.
3. For any Bobbins found on the floor, 1d for each Bobbin.
4. For single Drawing, Slubbing or Roving, 2d for each single end.
5. For waste on the floor, 2d.
6. For any Oil wasted or spilled on the floor, 2d, each offence besides paying for the value of the Oil.
7. For any broken Bobbins, they shall be paid for according to their value, and if there is any difficulty in ascertaining the guilty party, the same shall be paid for by the whole using such Bobbins.
8. Any person neglecting to Oil at the proper times shall be fined 2d.
9. Any person leaving their Work and found Talking with any other workpeople shall be fined 2d for each offence.
10. For every Oath or insolent language, 3d for the first offence, and if repeated they shall be dismissed.
11. The Machinery shall be swept and cleaned every meal time.
12. All persons in our employ shall serve Four Weeks' Notice before leaving their employ; but J. Sidgwick shall and will turn any person off without notice given.
13. If two persons are known to be in one Necessary together they shall be fined 3d each; and if any Man or Boy go into the Women's Necessary he shall be instantly dismissed.
14. Any person wilfully or negligently breaking the Machinery, damaging the Brushes, making too much Waste, &c.,

they shall pay for the same to its full value.

15. Any person hanging anything on the Gas Pendants will be fined 2d.

16. The Masters would recommend that all their workpeople Wash themselves every morning, but they shall Wash themselves at least twice every week, Monday Morning and Thursday morning; and will be fined 3d for each offence.

17. The Grinders, Drawers, Slubbers and Rovers shall sweep at least eight times in the day as follows, in the Morning at 7, 9, 11 and 12; and in the Afternoon at 1, 2, 3, 4, 5 o'clock; and to notice the board hung up, when the black side is turned that is the time to sweep, and only quarter of an hour will be allowed for sweeping. The Spinners shall sweep as follows, in the Morning at 7, 10 and 12; in the Afternoon at 3 and at 5 o'clock. Any neglecting to sweep at the time will be fined 2d for each offence.

18. Any persons found Smoking on the premises will be instantly dismissed.

19. Any person found away from their usual place of work, except for necessary purposes, or Talking with any one out of their Alley will be fined 2d for each offence.

20. Any person bringing dirty Bobbins will be fined 1d for each Bobbin.

21. Any person wilfully damaging this Notice will be dismissed.

The Overlookers are strictly enjoined to attend these Rules, and they will be responsible to the Masters for the Workplace observing them.

REPRODUCTION FROM AN ORIGINAL MILL NOTICE
FROM WATER-FOOT MILL, NEAR HASLINGDEN,
SEPTEMBER 1851.

371

For the Sake of Her Family

DIANE ALLEN

It's 1912 in the Yorkshire Dales, and Alice Bentham and her brother Will have lost their mother to cancer. Money is scarce and pride doesn't pay the doctor or put food on the table.

Alice gets work at Whernside Manor, looking after Lord Frankland's fragile sister Miss Nancy. Meanwhile Will and his best friend Jack begin working for the Lord of the Manor at the marble mill. But their purpose there is not an entirely honest one.

For a while everything runs smoothly, but corruption, attempted murder and misplaced love are just waiting in the wings. Nothing is as it seems and before they know it, Alice and Will's lives are entwined with those of the Franklands' – and nothing will ever be the same again.

OUT NOW

For a Mother's Sins

DIANE ALLEN

It is 1870 and railway workers and their families have flocked to the wild and inhospitable moorland known as Batty Green. Here they are building a viaduct on the Midland Railway Company's ambitious new Leeds to Carlisle line.

Among them are three very different women – tough widow Molly Mason, honest and God-fearing Rose Pratt, and Helen Parker, downtrodden by her husband and seeking a better life.

When tragedy strikes, the lives of the three women are bound together, and each is forced to confront the secrets and calamities that threaten to tear their families apart.

OUT NOW

For a Father's Pride

DIANE ALLEN

In 1871, young Daisy Fraser is living in the Yorkshire Dales with her beloved family. Her sister Kitty is set to marry the handsome and wealthy Clifford Middleton. But on the eve of the wedding, Clifford commits a terrible act that shatters Daisy's happy life. She carries her secret for the next nine months, but is left devastated when she gives birth and the baby is pronounced dead. Soon she is cast out by her family and has no choice but to make her own way in the world.

When further tragedy strikes, Daisy sets out for the bustling streets of Leeds. There, she encounters poverty and hardship, but also friendship. What she really longs for is a love of her own. Yet Daisy doesn't realize that the key to her happiness may not be as far away as she thinks . . .

OUT NOW

Like Father, Like Son

DIANE ALLEN

From birth, Polly Harper seems destined for tragedy. Raised by her loving grandparents on Paradise Farm, she is unknowingly tangled in a web of secrecy regarding her parentage.

When she falls in love with Tobias, the wealthy son of a local landowner of disrepute, her anxious grandparents send her to work in a dairy. There she becomes instantly drawn to the handsome Matt Dinsdale, propelling her further into the depths of forbidden romance and dark family secrets.

But when tragedy strikes, Polly is forced to confront her past and decide the fate of her future. Will she lose everything, or will she finally realize that her roots and love lie in Paradise?

OUT NOW

The Mistress of Windfell Manor

DIANE ALLEN

Charlotte Booth loves her father and the home they share, which is set high up in the limestone escarpments of Crummockdale. But when a new businessman in the form of Joseph Dawson enters their lives, both Charlotte and her father decide he's the man for her and, within six months, Charlotte marries the dashing mill owner from Accrington.

Then a young mill worker is found dead in the swollen River Ribble. With Joseph's business nearly bankrupt, it becomes apparent that all is not as it seems and Joseph is not the man he pretends to be. Heavily pregnant, penniless and heartbroken, Charlotte is forced to face the reality that life may never be the same again . . .

OUT NOW

FOR MORE ON

DIANE ALLEN

sign up to receive our

SAGA NEWSLETTER

Packed with features, competitions, authors'
and readers' letters and news of exclusive events,
it's a must-read for every Diane Allen fan!

Simply fill in your details below and tick to confirm that you would
like to receive saga related news and promotions and return to us at
Pan Macmillan, Saga Newsletter, 20 New Wharf Road, London N1 9RR.

NAME

ADDRESS

POSTCODE

EMAIL

☐ *I would like to receive saga-related news and promotions (please tick)*

*You can unsubscribe at any time in writing or through our website where you can also
see our privacy policy which explains how we will store and use your data.*